Love, Chai, and Other Four-Letter Words

Annika Sharma

sourcebooks
casablanca

Published by Sourcebooks Casablanca, an imprint of Sourcebooks
P.O. Box 4410, Naperville, Illinois 60567-4410
(630) 961-3900
sourcebooks.com

Library of Congress Cataloging-in-Publication Data

Names: Sharma, Annika, author.
Title: Love, chai, and other four-letter words / Annika Sharma.
Description: Naperville, Illinois: Sourcebooks Casablanca, [2021] |
Series: Chai Masala Club; 1
Identifiers: LCCN 2021016350
Subjects: LCSH: East Indian Americans--Fiction. | GSAFD: Love stories.
Classification: LCC PS3619.H35663 L38 2021 | DDC 813/.6--dc23
LC record available at https://lccn.loc.gov/2021016350

Printed and bound in the United States of America.
VP 10 9 8 7 6 5 4 3 2 1

To my parents and Sri...the air in my lungs. The sun on my skin. The beat in my heart. The wind underneath the wings you created. I will love you until the end of time.

And to Sanjeev...my happily ever after.

Chapter One

KIRAN

For an Indian like Kiran Mathur, spicy-sweet chai might as well have run through her veins, fueling her existence in New York City like the diesel powering her uncle's auto rickshaw back home.

Her stomach leapt pleasantly as she opened the door to the Upper East Side café where she and her besties—Payal, Akash, and Sonam—met every other week. They had dubbed themselves the Chai Masala Club or, affectionately, the CMC. And just as New York City was her home away from home, the CMC was her family away from family.

Always first to arrive, Kiran settled at their usual table, facing the door. Payal had discovered the tiny café, Chaiwala, six months ago. Of all the places in the city they had hopped around to, this one served the chai that most reminded them of the special vanilla, cardamom, and nut-filled goodness Kiran concocted during the nights when they discussed every heartbreak, triumph, and obstacle in their path to adulthood.

The café was a hole-in-the-wall place with gray hardwood floors, navy walls, and pops of color in the form of artistic photographs of their motherlands by South Asian artists. Tiny lanterns sat in the middle of each table, LED candles glowing inside. Market lights dangled on the walls. It was one part metropolitan hideaway, one part Eastern dream.

At five on the dot, Akash Rao strolled up to the glass door and politely pulled it open for Sonam, arriving from the opposite direction. Sonam offered a grin of thanks as she strode into the café. She raked her fingers through her cropped black hair, the waves bouncing back into place. Akash followed, confident and collected in his black power suit, which highlighted his slim waist and ramrod-straight posture. Their brown eyes scanned the room— Akash's starting at the left and Sonam's from the right—before settling on Kiran at the same time.

As they approached the table, Kiran noticed that Sonam walked with even more confidence than Akash did, chin up against the world and upturned eyes that perpetually gave off the impression of determined ferocity. Kiran felt a little envious, filled with pride at her friend's accomplishment while wishing she could measure up to the same greatness.

Akash casually pulled a chair out for Sonam. It might seem a couple-y gesture, but he had always been gentlemanly, the first to open doors, pull out chairs, cover a tab, or order a round.

In the months when they'd either been holed away in their own apartments or seen each other on rare, socially distanced picnics in Central Park, Kiran had forgotten the tiny details about her friends that filled her with warmth, like a hearth inside her chest. Watching Akash, she was reminded how his height, at five ten, made her feel safe when he was next to her five-four body…and that he spiked his hair in the front with enough gel to spackle a building together. She noticed again, like a long-misplaced fact, how Sonam's short hair, wavy and bobbed, gave her an edge and amplified her loud personality, which many people made the mistake of underestimating when they encountered the curvy firecracker.

"Kiran's lost in thought," Sonam teased.

"I am not!" But her smile gave her away.

"You were frowning," Akash noted, settling into his chair. "You're engineering something."

This was his favorite euphemism for her rigid type-A sensibility. She supposed he was right. Just a little. Kiran handwrote notes in a planner. She was the fixer of off-center pictures hanging on the wall, even when it wasn't her place. She was level-ten flustered when a presentation was interrupted by a question before its designated Q-and-A time.

"I wasn't 'engineering' anything, yaar. I was zoning out and people watching. It's what I do when you guys leave me in peace!"

"Like you'd know what to do with any kind of peace," he replied.

Kiran laughed. "You know me well, Obi-Wan."

"I think I died and went to heaven." Akash clutched his heart. "You've finally made a *Star Wars* reference."

Kiran and Akash slapped a high five as Sonam chuckled.

"Should we order?" asked Sonam.

"Payal isn't here yet," Akash and Kiran reminded her in unison.

"We get the same thing every time. It's not like we have to wait for her approval," Sonam grumbled.

On cue, the waitress arrived—one Kiran recognized from the group's countless outings to this café.

"Four chais?" She didn't bother to note anything on her pad.

All three affirmed their orders, and she went on her way.

Minutes later, the door opened with a gust of wind. Payal followed close behind. Her long hair remained immaculately curled around her heart-shaped face despite the breeze, and her dark eyes, which always made Kiran think of Princess Jasmine, were lined with kohl so pristine, one would think she was born with doe eyes. A pop of red lipstick to her thin lips was the only color in an otherwise neutral outfit—a cream blazer over a black sheath dress, without a trace of lint to be seen.

"Hello there!" she cheerfully chirped in her British accent, then set her bag on the chair Akash pulled out for her, unwrapped the expensive-looking cream scarf from around her neck—Hermès, Kiran noted—and took her seat, crossing her legs underneath the table.

"Are you ever on time?" Sonam asked.

"Well, you know what they say…fashionably late." Payal dismissed the age-old complaint with a casual wave of her hand. "I had a client."

Akash thanked the waitress as she placed their drinks in front of them, then turned to his friends. "Okay, Sonam, go first."

"Can I order some food before we start?" she asked. "I could eat the butt off a skunk right now."

Akash snorted with laughter while Payal crinkled her delicately pointed nose.

Kiran giggled. "Where do you even come up with expressions like that?"

"Ahh, Miss India," Sonam said with an overdone stereotypical Indian accent. "If you'd grown up here, perhaps you would have heard it."

"I never would have *said* it… That's gross." Kiran matched Payal's disgusted expression.

Sonam smiled, clearly proud she had elicited the reaction she'd hoped for.

As the others stirred their chai, adding enough sugar to put someone into a diabetic coma (Payal) or letting it cool off until it reached—by straight-up Indian standards, anyway—an unacceptable level of lukewarm rather than burning hot (Akash), Kiran gazed at the three of them. She was truly home. No burden. No worry.

"Okay, can I say how nice it is to meet in person again instead of on Zoom?" Kiran said.

"You've said it every time we've met, but to be fair, seeing all of your normal and unfiltered faces in person is a treat...or maybe the fresh air is getting to me," Akash said.

"It's really nice to see the city come alive again," Sonam said. "I yelled at an asshole who catcalled me on the subway today, and it felt like we were back to normal."

They laughed.

"And now that we're all here—" Payal started.

"You mean now that you're finally here?" Sonam asked.

"Yes." Payal reached into the Chanel bag next to her feet. "I was cleaning out last season's clothes to donate to Goodwill, and I discovered my box of college memories—you know, all those photos that are never allowed to see the light of day from our dorm-room days. And look what else I found!"

She produced a few battered sheets of paper, folded into quarters, and put them at the center of the table.

"Is that your diary?" Akash asked.

"Oh, shut it. It's our lists!" Payal said.

"I don't think I've been with that many people," Akash said.

She shot him a glare. "We made these lists the summer we graduated, remember? All the things we wanted to do in New York."

Payal unfolded each sheet of paper, examined the name at the top, and handed it out to the appropriate friend. They spent a few moments in silence examining their lists before looking up.

"Well?" Akash asked. "Did we do everything we expected?"

"Yes." Sonam turned her list around. On it was written: BUCKET LISTS ARE STUPID.

They all laughed.

"I did them all," Akash said, a hint of pride in his voice. "Visit the Empire State Building. Road trip across the country. Have a threesome. Eat at Eleven Madison Park—"

"You ate there? Really? It's, like, $300 a meal," Sonam interrupted.

"When I got my last promotion at work, I may or may not have splurged."

"I've done almost everything too." Payal skimmed her paper. "I went to all the major landmarks. I worked at New York Fashion Week twice. I've eaten at five restaurants owned by celebrity chefs… Except for falling in love, which, let's be real, might not exist, I've done it all."

"Gosh, I've only done a few of these," Kiran said, glancing at her list again and feeling a stab of disappointment.

She'd done a few classic New York tourist things when she'd moved to the city, excited to be in a new place, and often with someone from the CMC with her—*Empire State Building, a boat ride on the Hudson, a Broadway play*. But the other ones…not so much. *Ride a horse*—not yet. *Dance under the stars*—not done yet. *Do a macaroni and cheese tour. Go to Smorgasburg every summer. Play in an arcade*—nope. *Find a way to reunite Kirti with Ma and Baba*—her heart fell.

"Which ones?" Payal tried to peer at her paper.

"I went to Smorgasburg the first summer we moved here, but haven't been since."

"You order mac and cheese everywhere, so you've essentially managed a tour," Akash said, spying that item on her list.

"Kiran, you're the only one who hasn't come close to finishing hers. Get on it. We're turning thirty soon. We should be able to say we lived our twenties to the fullest," Payal said.

Thirty. The number felt daunting all of a sudden, like Kiran had to speed through all her goals before she crossed some proverbial threshold where she couldn't anymore.

"I agree," she said. "Maybe these should be the before-thirty list since it's been so long since we moved here…and we can add a few things and try to do them all."

"Okay, let's do it," said Sonam.

The other three looked at her in surprise.

"You literally just showed us a list that said lists are stupid," Akash said.

"Well…things change. It could be fun."

"What would be the first thing on your new before-thirty lists?" Payal asked.

Sonam leaned back, seeming to consider her answer. Kiran frowned, thinking of her family. Akash spoke first.

"I'd like to fall in love and get married."

"Really?" Payal asked. "The serial dater wants to settle down?"

"It's kind of nice to think about coming home to someone and knowing they're yours to share a life with," Akash replied.

Payal gave a soft smile. "I'd start a fashion line and have a runway show."

"I'd start a charity," Sonam said. "I'd do something that protected women and girls across the world. Maybe even go to India and do reproductive health work there."

Kiran grinned, knowing Sonam would fulfill her wish someday. It was a matter of *when*, not *if*. She thought about her own list—what would she do?

"I'd follow my heart," she said suddenly. "I've done everything expected of me, you know? But I don't know how to trust myself and just *be*. I guess I'd do that."

"There's time," Payal said with a conspiratorial wink. "Okay, so everyone bring a new, revised list to the next CMC date, all right? Kiran, you can add a few things to yours or just bring it as is since you still have stuff to do."

They all nodded or murmured their assent.

"So, speaking of following hearts, guess who did something stupid with the opposite sex?" Akash asked.

"You," Kiran answered. "That question was an opening for you to tell us."

The rest laughed.

"I met a girl, actually. But let's see where it goes."

"You met a girl, did you?" Payal's eyes sparkled. "Do we get to meet her?"

"Not yet."

"Come on, Akash!" Sonam protested. "Quit being a dick and tell us some details so we can judge her."

"She's cool. You know the New York dating scene, though. We may find new people in the next couple of days." He shrugged.

"This is true," Payal conceded as she added yet another packet of sugar to her chai. "It's all so fleeting."

"Well, forever *is* fleeting nowadays, isn't it?" Kiran asked. "It's not like it used to be with our parents meeting and getting married a month after maybe seeing each other once. The entire game has changed."

"It's pretty much all over in a swipe," Akash agreed.

"But it hasn't actually gotten any easier, has it?" Payal spoke. "I mean, you'd think with all these options to meet people, we'd all be in relationships, but if anything, the choices have made us less decisive and more fearful of commitment."

"Unless we choose our parents' route, I guess it has become harder," Kiran considered.

"But you've already decided to go their route, so it's a moot point for you, isn't it?" Sonam pointed out.

"I went on a date the other day—friend-of-a-friend situation," Kiran said, proving Sonam's point.

"Do tell!" Payal encouraged.

"It tanked. No personality. Believed in a dowry. Had the balls to say that men could sleep around but that they should only marry virgins. You know how it can be."

Sonam looked outraged, and even her hair seemed to stand on edge.

Payal shook her head, taking a sip of tea. When she put her cup down, there was no ring of red lipstick around the white rim.

"Well, that's outdated. Sounds like a douche," Akash said, raising his cup as a toast. "You dodged a bullet."

"That's okay. There's plenty of fish in the sea." Sonam shrugged.

"You have to kiss plenty of frogs," Payal said.

"You'd know. You've probably made out with most of them," Kiran retorted.

"Whatever. We're young. Successful. Awesome. Why not take advantage of it and have some fun?" Payal dismissed all notion of the conservative propriety Kiran had grown up with. "And did you just make a joke?"

"I did." Kiran flipped her hair over her shoulder. "I thought it was pretty good."

"Yeah, yeah," Payal grumbled. "Like I said...we're young and we should enjoy life."

None of them asked why Kiran couldn't have a love marriage. They all knew about her family and their traditional view of how marriage was supposed to be: parents talk, parents introduce their respective boy and girl to each other, boy and girl speak for long enough to cover education, income, values, and children, and then *poof!* Marriage arranged. *We didn't have chemistry* was not a reason that made any sense for turning down a proposition, at least in her community's eyes.

Falling in love was nothing like a formulaic equation of course. Anyone in the current generation knew that, but Kiran wasn't about to fight that battle with her parents, who had barely left their village, let alone India, and who had grown up in a strict atmosphere where boys and girls didn't mingle more than necessary.

But marriage…the word alone prompted gray hairs to pop up on Kiran's head.

The swirling thoughts must have shown on her face, because Sonam picked up on it immediately.

"Payal is right, Kiran. We're young. Stop thinking about it," she said.

"I agree with her!" Kiran protested. "But it's hard to remember that when my parents are getting older and I get phone calls every other day about how thirty is two years away."

"Actually, my parents have said the same," Payal said. "As if thirty is a line you cross, and our eggs will shrivel up and disintegrate at 12:01 a.m. on our thirtieth birthdays."

Akash laughed. "Benefit of being a guy. I get to milk this I-need-to-settle-down-and-make-money argument for a few years longer."

"You don't get to gloat!" Sonam smacked Akash's arm. "Or I will tell your mom that you mentioned to us that you're ready for a wife and kids."

Akash chuckled in response, shaking his head. "Thirty, though. What comes after that?"

"Thirty-one," Kiran said. "I know you went to a chilled-out American school, but I would hope they taught you to count."

He shot her a look. "I mean...thirty kind of *is* a line to cross in life. You're expected to have your shit together after thirty."

"Don't you guys feel like we're in between milestones?" Sonam asked. "I mean, eighteen was the military, graduating from high school, starting college, cigarettes... Twenty-one was getting plastered. And if thirty is the end, the mark of us having it together...then twenty-five was, like—"

"It was the age we always looked forward to when we were little, so it's hard to look past that to thirty and beyond," Kiran finished for her.

Sonam nodded with enthusiasm. Being understood always brought a glow to her eyes.

"Marriage, a house, kids, a car, and being a doctor," Sonam reminisced.

"One out of five isn't bad," Kiran teased.

"Wow, you all were pretty advanced," Akash said. "At age five, I wanted to live in a tree."

The entire group burst out laughing.

"I wanted to be rich, live in a city, and wear pretty dresses," Payal said.

"Achievement unlocked, then?"

"Shut up, Akash."

"What did you want, Kiran? I mean, now that you're in between the age that we all thought we'd have everything we dreamed of and the age everyone says is the end of immaturity... what did you think would happen?" Sonam leaned toward her on her elbows.

"Do you know that in the United States, universities have lots of

buildings and lots of students? They are some of the best univer-sities in the world," Kirti said to Kiran as she set her back on the ground after giving her a rib-crushing hug in a way that only big sisters could.

"Isn't that far away?" Kiran asked. *"Ma and Baba said Am-reeka was across an ocean."*

"It is. But sometimes if you want good things, you have to go on a journey to find them."

"I don't ever want to leave!" Kiran proclaimed. *"I'm never leaving you, or Ma, or Baba!"*

Kirti laughed. *"You will have to someday when you get married, Chottu. But I hope that you go to school first. You can do anything with your parents' blessings and love."*

"Even fly across an ocean!"

"Yes, you can even fly across the whole world! But you have to work hard, take care of your parents, and keep your family happy so they will bless you and you succeed."

"I always want to keep you happy."

"Good. Then go to college in America someday!" Kirti tickled Kiran's belly.

"I wanted to leave India and support my parents," Kiran said now.

The three others smiled.

Payal set her napkin on the table with finality.

"Looks like you're living your dream."

Chapter Two

KIRAN

One of Kiran's favorite things about the United States, to this day, was grocery shopping.

She knew it was weird, but it was so easy here.

When she was growing up in her residential colony in India, it took four trips: to a milk vendor, a vegetable market, a grains shop, and stores that had odds and ends to gather all one's food together, but here it was all in one place. She could take her time. There were no aunties pushing behind her or stressing her vocal cords to be heard by the subziwala as he measured out orders of vegetables with rusted weights older than her.

Kiran hauled a basket on wheels behind her, like a child with a wagon, strutting her way through the aisles.

She squeezed a Roma tomato, turning it in her hand, uncaring about any looks she might get for playing with a vegetable. This was how Ma had taught her to gauge a vegetable's freshness and flavor. Just as her fingers left slight imprints on the tomato, deeming it worthy of the tanginess she so loved when she cooked, her phone rang.

It was as if Ma had heard her thoughts from across the world.

"Hullo, Ma."

"Kiran, beta, kaise ho?"

"I'm fine, Ma," Kiran responded back in Hindi.

"What are you doing? I hear people in the background."

"I'm grocery shopping. How are you? Why are you up at"—Kiran checked her phone and calculated ten hours ahead—"4:00 a.m.? Is everything okay?"

"Yes, yes, everything is fine. I couldn't sleep."

"Why not?"

"I'm a mother, Kiran. We worry all day and all night. It's what we do."

"What are you worried about?" Kiran pulled her basket to the checkout. "Is Baba okay? Is it his heart again?"

"He's snoring like a lion right now."

Kiran exhaled a sigh of relief and placed her vegetables and a half gallon of milk on the belt. "Aren't you going to wake him up, Ma? You're shouting at me like I'm supposed to hear you from India."

"Arrey, your father could sleep through an earthquake. Don't you worry about him. It's you we worry about more."

"Why me?" *Here goes.*

"You're nearly thirty, Kiran. At some point, we have to do our duty and get you married. We supported you through your school and college and while you needed to get settled with your career. Now you need to get married."

"I'm not against getting married. It hasn't clicked yet."

"What *clicking*? You speak to a boy—look at his education, how much money he makes, if he comes from a good family—and bas, you're married."

Kiran swiped her credit card, gave the tired cashier a smile in gratitude, collected her bags, and took a deep breath before walking toward the exit. "It's not that easy."

"You keep saying it's not easy, but you're making it complicated."

Kiran breathed into the phone but said nothing.

"Beta, you are already older than most of the girls back home and unmarried. Many of them are on their third child already. We want to be grandparents too. It's our last duty before we die."

"You're not going to die."

"Baba almost did, remember?"

Kiran felt a guilty jab. "I don't ever forget. I worry about it every day."

"We would like to give our daughter away proudly. We haven't had that chance before."

There it was. The elephant in the room raised its colossal pink trunk and sounded a trumpet that would rattle the very sidewalks Kiran walked on...and she was supposed to ignore it. The references to her sister were a combination of family baggage and guilt trips, packaged as a reasonable argument.

"I'll keep talking to people, Ma," Kiran said, resigned.

"Good. That's all I ask. What parent doesn't want to be proud of their daughter as they marry her off?" Ma's very tone shifted to a bubblier one, and Kiran could tell her mother was imagining her dressed like a dulhan on her wedding day. Only that level of positive visualization could make her mother so happy so quickly.

"No one I know."

"Ah, your baba has woken up. Here he is."

There was a shuffle on the other end and an irritated grumble from her dad at Ma's very noisy sleep interruption. But his voice was upbeat and full of love when he spoke to Kiran.

"Hello, Kiran, beta. How are you?"

"Baba, hi. Did we wake you?"

"Ahh, your ma never lets anyone rest peacefully. If she's up, the whole neighborhood must wake up too. I can practically hear Chadda Bhai down the road, shining his auto already."

"I wonder if he already has paan in his mouth."

"It's four thirty in the morning. He's probably on his third one." Baba chuckled.

Kiran smiled softly, remembering the uncle down the street who always slipped her a hard candy from his pocket and whose affectionate smile was tinged with red from his habit of chewing betel nuts. It was he who had suggested Baba and Ma move to Delhi permanently and had even referred them to the apartment her parents now occupied.

"How is the shop?"

"You know how it is. Your chacha says it's good. But even small towns like Ramnagar are growing fancy."

Kiran thought back to the village. She'd moved her parents to Delhi, two hours away from Ramnagar and closer to medical attention and better doctors, after Baba's heart attack two years ago. He'd given his small shop to his younger brother to take care of, and her parents received a monthly deposit from the profits.

"Baba, are you taking your medication?"

"I try, beta. These medications are hard to remember."

"Baba! You can't forget." Kiran stopped in the middle of the sidewalk. "These pills save your life."

"Kiran, your mother already chews my brain about these things. Must you do it too?"

"Who else will? You only have us."

"At least a man feels loved."

"I'm not there to look out for you. Only Ma can. And she's busy enough with taking care of the house. Make sure you take those pills."

"When did my daughter become such an adult, huh? Telling her father what to do," he teased.

"That's life, no? Parents become children and children become parents."

"Ever the philosopher, my Kiran. Go cook some dinner. Eat well. Take care of your health."

"I will. You too. Don't forget—"

"To take my medicine. I *know*."

"Well, if you know, then you should do it, no?"

"You were always too smart for your own good," Baba grumbled. "Come home soon, beta. The house comes alive when you're here."

Kiran's memory jogged back to her younger years, as a child with little silver anklets tinkling when she walked and her father coming home to her and her sister.

My glory and my light, he called them, referring to the meaning of their names.

"I wish I could bring the light, Baba," Kiran said softly.

"You do well in America, and do your duty, beta. Your light will shine all the way to Delhi."

Kiran hung up, missing both her parents and their quirks so much that it ached inside her.

Chapter Three

NASH

A new start.

After driving a moving van fourteen hours, putting his stuff in storage, living out of a suitcase for two weeks while sleeping on his best friend Brandon's couch, and finally finding an apartment, Nash had a home.

It was the size of a shoebox...but it was a home.

He closed the door and turned to survey the studio. He didn't have much stuff—he'd sold most of it before coming up north. The windows behind his couch overlooked Third Street. His bed was pushed up against the left corner of the apartment, a nook where the living space met the outer walls of the bathroom, creating a dedicated sleeping space. The renovated kitchen lined the right-side wall, conspicuously smaller than any kitchen Nash had ever seen, with a door at the end for a bathroom.

He remembered the nights when the electricity went out and Mom had shouting matches with the electric company about extending their payment period. Memories of his twin mattress against the carpet made him thankful for the fact that he could afford a box spring now. While the walls could have used a new coat of paint, as Brandon so kindly pointed out, the place had character.

The truth was that college, a master's program, and a doctorate were all icing on the cake at a party Nash never expected to be invited to anyway. He was glad to be here, alive and successful.

It took him less than three hours to organize his apartment, and his appointments for utilities had been set up. It was time to explore the neighborhood and see some of the sights. Having a relatively free Saturday would be a rare occurrence after today, and since Nash loved history, perhaps it was time to look some up.

One of the other grad students at Vanderbilt, a Broadway buff named Rhett, had played the *Hamilton* soundtrack until even Nash was rapping along with every word. Alexander Hamilton was brilliant and a misfit and had moved to New York to change his life.

He didn't have a family either.

There was something about the connection to a great man that Nash loved, and he saw online that the Hamilton-Holly House, a place Alexander's son had owned, was close by. Better yet, there was a bagel place two blocks from there that had opened up again postpandemic to the joy of the neighborhood, according to Yelp reviews.

Nash's belly agreed with this plan by giving a loud grumble.

He tossed his sweaty move-in clothes into the laundry basket by his bed, took a shower in record time, and was out the door in clean jeans and a tee minutes later.

The sunshine hit him in the face when he stepped out of the building. Brandon had once mentioned that staying indoors wasn't much of a New York thing until the recent pandemic. And now that it was over, people flooded the streets again—some with masks, but all filled with relief at being able to escape their shoebox-sized apartments.

"Our apartments are so small, we like to get outside," he'd said.

Nash could see the truth in this observation. Everywhere he looked, people pushed strollers, walked dogs, and carried large bags that probably contained their entire lives.

He loved it.

He loved to watch people, to imagine what their stories could be. He was the example, after all, of not knowing what someone had been through to get where they were, and he often imagined the same of others. Perhaps the homeless person on a bench had been a war hero. Maybe the woman working at Starbucks had once been a corporate honcho who lost her job in a recession and needed to feed her kids.

He strolled up Avenue A and swung by the Hamilton-Holly House a few blocks away for a glimpse. He'd read that a store used to exist on the main floor but had recently been cleared for apartments, so he walked by instead, observing the old brick and the colonial-style roofline.

His belly gave a giant growl once more.

Time for the bagel place.

It was across from a park, where Nash could have sworn every bench was occupied with old friends chatting over coffee or letting their dogs roam in the vicinity.

He entered the shop, an unassuming narrow spot that deceived passersby by extending its wood floors deep into the building. A bakery bar was set up on the left with desserts and cream cheeses on display, with a kitchen behind it. The smell of bread wafted through the air, and Nash could see cooks mixing dough and placing giant trays of unbaked bagels into the industrial ovens. There weren't many seats, and a line wrapped around the store.

Nash's head spun with options. Birthday-cake icing with a cinnamon raisin bagel? Olive-pimento cream cheese?

"What can I get you?" The question came too soon.

"Uhh..."

Eventually, to the relief of the twelve people behind him whose impatient sighs turned audibly thankful when he settled on a sun-dried tomato bagel with jalapeño and cheddar cream cheese, he got his food at the end of the counter and satisfied his grumbling stomach while walking home.

Nash tilted his face up to the July sun. It was toasty but still cooler than it would have been in Tennessee where his skin browned with only a few minutes of being outside.

He tossed his bagel wrapper in a garbage receptacle out for trash day, took the steps two at a time, pulled the door to his building open, and reached into his pocket to unlock the second set of doors, which gave residents access to their apartments.

Nothing jingled.

Frowning, he fished into the other pocket on his left leg.

In the move, in the middle of the many times he and Brandon had shouted, "Toss me your keys so I can grab the box from the truck," and the unpacking, Nash—meticulous Nash—had left his keys on the foot of counter space next to the sink. And his landlord's number wasn't programmed into his phone yet.

He closed his eyes, clearly picturing the keys and cursing himself for handing them over to Brandon so often that he lost track of them.

Dropping his head, his hands on his waist, Nash tried to focus and come up with a solution. He could buzz every apartment in the building and ask someone to let him in. At least he'd be past one set of doors, though it wouldn't solve the issue of getting into his apartment.

He tried it. Not a single person answered his ring.

His lease was in his email! A rush of joy coursed through him. He'd be able to call someone to get him in.

Thank God for technology, Nash thought as he scrolled

through hundreds of messages in his inbox. Pulling up the number of his landlord from a scanned copy of the lease, he relished the surge of victory.

Until no one answered his landlord's phone.

"Goddamn! Do you hate me?" he exclaimed, looking up at the invisible being seated above, who he imagined laughing at his efforts.

"Should I give you a moment?" asked a voice from the door to the building.

Nash's head snapped to the door.

An Indian girl, with black hair to her waist, stood at the first set of doors, observing his conversation with...no one.

His blood rushed to his cheeks out of embarrassment, warming them.

"I'm sorry. I'm locked out."

"Are you new?" the girl asked, setting down two plastic bags of groceries that she'd been holding in one hand. "I don't think I've seen you around before."

"No... I mean, yes, I'm new, so no, you haven't seen me around before. I moved in today."

"Well, welcome. I can let you in if you'd like." She rummaged in her black tote and produced a set of keys... Was that a little elephant man hanging from the metal key ring?

Nash stared and she gazed at him expectantly.

"I just moved here from Nashville—and it's been a scatter-brained few weeks. You'd think I'd remember something like my keys, but nope. Here I am. Keyless. And the landlord won't answer his phone so I can't get him to let me in."

He was rambling and he knew it. Maybe it was the unexpected chaos that blew his typically calm demeanor to smithereens. Maybe it was the realization setting in that he had left his bubble, that he had no friends in the city besides Brandon, and that life was very different here than in the friendly confines of his former home, but it was like he couldn't get his mouth to stop spilling words.

It could also be that this girl was beautiful—and her expression hadn't become an ounce judgmental at his barrage of words.

Rather than look freaked out at the eruption of explanations, Nash noticed the girl's brown eyes had softened into sympathy. A smile crossed her face. Then she said something Nash didn't expect.

"Would you like a cup of chai?"

"Wait... What?"

"Well, the landlord only answers his phone after seven because he has a day job at the bodega, which he works most days of the week. You've got..." She checked her watch, one with an old-fashioned black leather strap and a simple face, and glanced up again. "A half hour to kill. And I've found that chai can fix almost anything."

"Like a chai tea latte?" Nash asked with a relieved laugh. "It seems like this city runs on coffee."

"Well...yes, on both counts. But you're also never allowed to say 'chai tea latte' in my presence again."

"Why's that?"

"Because chai *is* tea. Why do people call it a 'tea tea latte'? Just say 'chai.' And why add in the 'latte'? Chai is meant to be made with milk. It's such a redundancy. In a city that claims that time is money, you'd think they'd stop repeating their words, no?" She looked at him expectantly.

Her smile remained the entire time, and Nash got the distinct impression she wasn't criticizing him. Finally, her words caught up to him.

"Well, then..."

"Kiran," the girl supplied.

"Well, then, Kiran, I'm Nash Hawthorne," he said, extending a hand. "And I would love a cup of chai."

Chapter Four

KIRAN

He could be a serial killer, Kiran thought as Nash followed her up a flight of stairs to her apartment on the left-hand side. Oddly, the voice in her head sounded like Sonam's.

She'd never been the type to invite random strangers over for chai—her special treat, no less!—but the earnestness and overwhelmed look on Nash's face, and Kiran's own memory of being new to a place, had prompted her to extend the invitation.

Or maybe it was her bout of loneliness.

After an evening of chai with her friends and a chat with her parents while grocery shopping, Kiran sensed a piece of her was missing. It was always that way, wasn't it? People always fell into routines and, slowly but surely, emptied their tanks as they lived through redundancy. Time spent with loved ones always filled those tanks back up to the brim...and one always longed for that feeling to last longer than it ever did.

Kiran unlocked her door and held it open behind her for Nash.

He stepped inside, his eyes taking in his surroundings. "Well... your apartment is a lot nicer than mine."

"Why, thank you."

"My style is 'bachelor pad bare,' whereas yours is…"

"I think Americans describe it as 'hoarding,' no?" Kiran smiled and closed the door behind them.

"I think I'd describe it as colorful. This is a happy place to come home to."

"Thank you! I think colors can change people's moods so quickly."

"I'd have to agree. Waking up in this place must automatically give you some good energy."

Kiran's large studio was split into a living space and a sleeping space, with three windows looking over the street. Decorating each sill sat three little plants in small rounded pots, equally spaced apart and in the same colored order of metallic gold, yellow, and red. A bright-red love seat faced the brick wall, and a TV hung on the wall across from it. A fluffy blue armchair allowed a third person to be seated comfortably. A carpet with giant yellow sunflowers set against a blue background decorated the middle of the room. Blue saris with a gold design along the border, an impulse buy on her last visit to India, draped from an ornate gold rod hanging from wall to wall in the back of the rectangular space and created makeshift curtains to separate her sleeping space. Photos, all mounted in the same golden frame, took up much of the spare spaces on the walls and were lined up so cleanly that Kiran was sure her hours of effort with a ruler showed.

The entire space seemed to be blasted with color.

The kitchen was crammed full of pots, pans, and odds and ends—and a faint smell of spices lingered in the air.

Kiran slipped off her shoes at the entrance, neatly placing them on a shoe rack by the door.

Nash paused for a moment at the door. "Do you want me to take my shoes off?"

"Would you mind? It's kind of an Indian thing."

"Like, you don't want to ruin all the colors and pretty things in here?"

"Something like that."

He smiled and used the toe of one foot to pull the shoe on the other off. He carefully put them by the door and shuffled a few feet into the room, hesitating.

"Make yourself comfortable!" Kiran chirped as she placed her groceries on the counter and swiftly began to put them in their places. "I'll make the chai in a moment. Also, that blue chair is super comfortable."

Nash listened to her advice and sank into the armchair. "Have you lived in this place long?"

"About two years. I was in an apartment with my best friends when I first moved to the city."

"When was that?"

"Six years ago," Kiran remembered fondly. "I got a job in the city as a biomedical engineer right after graduation." She filled a small pot with milk and set it to boil on the stove.

"Ah, so you're a scientist."

"What do you do? Or, given you moved here five minutes ago, what will you be doing?"

"I'm going to be a child and adolescent psychologist at NewYork-Presbyterian."

"How exciting!"

Kiran chopped some ginger and sprinkled it into the milk and water, followed by cardamom, sugar, a drop of vanilla, cinnamon, nutmeg, black pepper, and anise.

The loose tea leaves were the last thing she added to the flavorful mix. As the concoction simmered, the aroma of spicy sweetness began to permeate the air, making the apartment a cozy, warm space that belonged in the middle of winter rather than the middle of July.

Kiran stirred as the milk turned frothy and then switched off the gas on the stove. She held a strainer and expertly filtered the liquid through it, filling each cup with steaming chai in no time.

She noticed Nash had turned his attention from a science magazine on a side table to the direction of the kitchen where the smell was the most intoxicating.

"You know, I'm simultaneously excited and nervous," Nash admitted as he watched her step carefully toward him with teacups in hand.

"About the tea?"

"About the job."

Something about the way his eyebrows rose as he said it made Kiran think he hadn't confessed this to anyone before.

"Why are you nervous?"

"You remember what it was like when you graduated from high school?"

"I knew I was moving to a different country. It was terrifying."

"Exactly. I've been in Nashville all of this time. Though it was a new phase of life, there was something familiar about the environment that didn't change. Now, it's all new."

She handed him a cup and sat on the love seat across from him, folding her feet beneath her.

"I don't have any doubt you'll thrive." Kiran smiled.

"This smells amazing, by the way. And once again, I will never call it 'chai tea.' Ever."

"The Indian in me thanks you profusely."

"Moment of truth…" Nash grinned, raising his cup to her.

He took a sip.

Kiran bounced her toes against the sofa as she waited, her own teacup steaming underneath her nose.

Nash stared inside his cup. "This might be the best drink I've ever had."

"Liar." But she was elated.

"For real. You've ruined coffee for me forever."

"We used to drink this every morning and every evening back in India."

"So that's where you learned how to make this nectar from heaven?"

"Indeed. Though my father's is better. It's the only thing he can make in the kitchen."

"Well, why learn anything else, right? If your sole expertise is this good. Can you cook too?"

"Are you hoping for dinner tonight?"

Nash shook his head, looking bashful. "You've been too kind. I would never ask."

"I was only kidding. But I can cook. I can also eat."

"Always a notable talent. Any favorites?"

"I am a world-class macaroni and cheese connoisseur."

"Wait, really? Mac 'n cheese?"

"Food of the gods."

"You live in the largest food capital in the world, and you're choosing toddler food."

"Yes. I stand by this choice."

"I am from the South, you know, so I make a mean mac," Nash said, taking a sip of his chai. "You'll want to stuff your face with it."

"That's what she said," she replied without missing a beat. Then burning heat rose into her cheeks.

Nash burst out laughing.

"I'm so sorry. My best friend, Payal, is a terrible influence, and sometimes I can't stop myself from saying things out loud that she would."

"You know, those jokes are a dime a dozen, but I sure as hell didn't expect it to come from you." He chuckled again.

"Is it that obvious that all my good jokes come from my best friends?"

"You just didn't strike me as a dirty joke kind of girl. I know that sounds weird... You seem innocent somehow."

"Ah, well, Mr. Hawthorne, I pride myself on being a woman of mystery."

"Unpredictability... I can roll with that."

"Actually, I am pretty predictable," Kiran confessed. "But it is way cooler to sound like an enigma."

Nash laughed. "Well, I think you're plenty cool, so don't you worry about that."

"Why, thank you."

They drank in silence for a moment.

"I never had it growing up," she said suddenly.

"What?"

"Macaroni and cheese. Cheese wasn't really a thing, outside of paneer. Or maybe it was but we couldn't afford it."

"Paneer?"

"It's like..." Kiran scrunched her nose as she tried to come up with the English equivalent for the buttery goodness that was well-made paneer. "It's like tightly packed ricotta."

"I'm not sure that sounds appetizing."

"Oh, but it *is*!" she cried out. "With tomatoes and onions, set up on a tandoor, spiced and sizzling."

The mental recollection of Ma's cooking was enough to make her mouth water.

"Okay, maybe that does sound great," he said. "And you miss it."

"How do you know?"

"I can tell. The way your voice changes. The way your face gets animated. Do you get to go back often?"

Her demeanor shifted like the breeze, a sudden gust before the calm. She inhaled, smelling the polluted and still, sweet air as if she'd stepped off a plane into the blast of boiling atmosphere.

"No," she murmured quietly. "I should. I've gone back once and invited my parents once."

"What did they think?"

Oddly, she appreciated the way he asked the question. There was no automatic assumption that her village-bred parents were in awe of the massive buildings and clean-kept parks.

"Like anyone, they were overwhelmed by all the different faces and languages. But in terms of chaos, New York is no change from India." She shrugged. "When you grow up around a billion people, you get used to having no personal space." *Not that we would have had it anyway in our home…and we like it that way.*

"Hey, if your parents came from a different country and enjoyed it, hats off to them. I've lived in the United States my entire life, and even I was scared shitless moving here."

His candor surprised her. His accent was the only indicator that he wasn't a native New Yorker…that, and his immediate warmth with strangers.

"That's surprising to me."

"Why's that?"

"You seem so sure of yourself." If she was honest, she was a little jealous. If Nash had a list, he'd probably have finished it by now…or so it seemed.

"I think you have to approach life with a little confidence. It works out in the end, and you have to stay in the moment and handle it as it comes."

"You mean like when you lock yourself out of your apartment and need to hang out with a neighbor you don't know?" It was her turn to tease him.

"Something like that, yeah!" He grinned and she smiled too. "So you said you brought your parents...no siblings?"

The abrupt pause in the conversation brought a twinge of awkwardness to what had become a comfortable afternoon tea for Kiran. Nash waited patiently, seemingly unaware that he had set off an internal bomb inside her. She chewed her cheek for an excessive amount of time, until she felt like the giant elephant in the room was shoving her.

"I have a sister."

"Are you guys close?"

This time, she was ready. "No, not really."

"Older? Younger?"

"She's older," Kiran said. "Fifteen years. She's in her forties now."

"Wow, big age gap."

What Nash didn't see was Kiran calculating whether Kirti would actually be forty-two or forty-three. Her birthday was on August 15, Indian Independence Day. It was only July now, so Kiran was a few months ahead on her estimation.

"Indeed. Any siblings for you?"

There was a strange impulse to poke at her own sore spots when finding out information. It was as if every time she asked friends about their brothers and sisters, she would push on her own throbbing bruise, hoping that with enough onslaughts, the ache would fade. Kiran wanted to find out about another sibling relationship and close the gap she felt every rare time she mentioned Kirti's name. She wanted her tough skin to become even more callused, to layer over all the years of protection she'd built over her heart in her sister's absence.

In the years following Kirti's departure from their family, Kiran had transformed into an only child. She learned not to mention her big sister's name and instead to focus on her own success so she never had to view her parents' disappointed faces. Even Kirti's face was fading.

But the ache never quite disappeared completely. And she couldn't place whether the hollowness in her heart was named after abandonment or sadness.

Chapter Five

NASH

Whatever the strange expression of expectation that Kiran had on her face was, Nash must have disappointed her with his answer.

"I'm an only child."

The way Kiran's face had fallen when she'd talked about siblings, as if she were bracing herself for a shock, disappeared as quickly as it came.

"What's your favorite memory of your sister?"

"Her wedding. It was nice to see all the family together."

"That sounds fun!"

"It was. I was only eight, but I danced at it, and it stands out in my mind as a good memory, you know?"

"I remember a trip to Disney World with my parents when I was three or four. Some memories don't fade with time. Do you still dance?"

"Mm-hmm. Mostly Bollywood classes around the city and a classical class here and there... There's a workout class called Doonya that I love going to because it's Bollywood dance-based, and the cardio burn is one you feel for days. But growing up, I was only ever classically trained."

"Wow, look at you. That's a big deal, right?"

"I suppose so. It's mostly a great release for me—tension fades away."

"I can see that. Even your face relaxes when you talk about it."

"As opposed to usual, when I'm uptight? You know, according to your vast amount of knowledge of me." Kiran raised an eyebrow.

"Exactly."

They both laughed.

"How about you? What's your favorite childhood memory?"

He lowered his eyes to the table next to them, then set his empty cup on a coaster, absentmindedly spinning it.

"Chasing fireflies with my mom when I was little. She was sick a lot when I was younger, and being able to spend that time with her is cherished now."

"I'm sorry she was ill." Kiran's eyes drooped in the corners, and her genuine reaction melted the cold of his memory. Not enough to eliminate it. But enough for him to notice.

"Thank you."

He didn't bring up the part about his parents both being gone. It wasn't that it lacked importance, but in this moment, he didn't want to weigh down the conversation. He didn't want the look of pity people gave him when he told them he had no family. Besides, saying he had no parents made it sound like he was alone in the world, and he wasn't. He had Aunt Kate, who supported him, and his friends.

"So you said you're from Nashville, right?"

"I am. I'm a southern boy."

"I went there once. My friend Payal is such a partyer, and she was determined to take trips to the biggest party capitals in the United States, so we wound up taking a trip to Vegas, followed by Nashville, followed by Austin."

"That sounds…exhausting," Nash said. "I'm not sure I would have survived that."

"We had barely graduated college, so it was much more bearable!" Kiran laughed at the memory. "It was like a celebratory trip. I think her liver is still recovering."

"And yours?"

Nash didn't mean to sound judgmental, but his tone came off that way anyway. He was always interested in the answers people gave to questions about drinking habits because he'd seen firsthand what those patterns could do.

"I don't drink that often, to be honest. I loved the environment, the energy, the music. Nashville has a little magic about it." Kiran's eyes lit up. "We were at this bar downtown—it was on top of a museum, overlooking the river—"

"The George Jones Museum?"

"Yes!" Kiran cried. "And we were sipping our drinks and it started getting dark outside. We're looking at the stadium and that pedestrian bridge, and we hear this man, around our dads' age, talk about Duke. So we mention we'd graduated a few weeks earlier from there, and he invites us over to chat with his family and then points out the moon rising. It's a beautiful, brilliant full moon. And he tells us that there are only twelve full moons in a year…and if a person lives sixty-five years, then there are only about eight hundred full moons to watch in a lifetime. Nashville makes me think of that memory, and it has so much magic about it—alcohol or not."

The way she seemed to burst at the seams, full of the very magic she was describing, made his stomach leap pleasantly, like her happiness was contagious.

Nash was also unexpectedly, inexplicably relieved about her party habits. "It does, I agree. I didn't really get to experience the beauty of it until college, but it's definitely a wonderful place to be."

"Why'd you leave it? What made you choose New York?"

"I grew up in Nashville. Went to college there. Graduate school. And then at some point, I realized that my bubble was tiny. There was an entire world to see, and I wanted to expand my own and let go of anything that held me back. It seemed like a great time to make a change. My best friend lives in the city, and he said it was amazing. I researched some psychology programs, and it turned out the hospital I'm at was hiring...so here I am."

"That's amazing! You must have worked so hard."

"Well, judging by the fact that you're from another country and getting here can be tough...I think you're pretty amazing too." Nash felt shy saying it out loud, nerves of unknown origin causing butterflies in his stomach. "Where were you before New York?"

"Well, I was in a village outside of Delhi for my early childhood, then got a scholarship to a boarding school in India, which was a giant leg up. Then went to Duke for undergrad and a master's degree in this combined five-year program. Then came here and started work."

"That's impressive." Nash had heard from his graduate school cohort members who had come from other countries that one had to be the cream of the crop to get admittance into an American university.

"I think everyone has a certain drive or goal that prompts them to success, you know? If you keep that goal in mind, then you work like hell until you achieve it."

"And what was your goal?" Nash asked.

"We didn't grow up with money. I wanted my parents to live a stress-free life."

"Are they?"

"I moved them into a place in Delhi so they have better access to things as they get older, like hospitals and doctors. They're elderly, and my dad had a heart attack a few years ago, so it's important to me to support them. What was your reason to become a psychologist?"

"Kids," Nash said simply.

Kiran's eyebrows shot up in surprise. "Kids? As in you have them?"

"As in I didn't have the greatest childhood, and I thought being a psychologist and allowing children to be themselves would be a great way to provide a safe space."

"That's noble, Nash. I'm glad that you ended up here." Her eyes dropped to her hands as she gave a soft smile.

His cheeks warmed before he spoke. "You know...since I'm new to the city, would you mind if I text you every once in a while to hang out?"

He felt like a child asking another to play, tentative and nervous for no reason other than wanting to be liked.

But the way joy spread across Kiran's face, like she was blessed that anyone would want to spend time with her, was so worth risking the appearance of idiocy. He'd never felt so proud of making someone's face light up.

"I'd love that."

Nash reluctantly looked at his watch, and it was a few minutes past seven. "Well, I should probably call the landlord."

"Sure. I'll give you a second."

He handed Kiran his cup, and their fingers brushed together. Nash had never been one to think sparks were real, but the tingle she left with her gentle touch was like a feather tracing circles along the back of his neck—and the sensation shot through his body, leaving goose bumps on his arms.

Her eyes widened for a split second before she hooked the handle of her own cup around a finger. She walked over to the sink as he dialed the number.

The phone rang six times before he reached voicemail. Feeling put out, he left a message and hung up.

"He didn't pick up," Nash said. "I'm really sorry. I can go to the Starbucks around the corner if you've got something to do."

"Give it a bit of time. Have you walked around the East Village much?"

"No, not as much as I'd like! I'm not an old-timer like you."

"Well, then why don't we take a walk?"

Who *was* this girl? Her kindness was unexpected—and certainly more than he ever thought possible in someone he barely knew. He couldn't think of a single person who would spend this much time with a total stranger.

"Are you sure I'm not imposing? You've already been so sweet." Nash hesitated.

Kiran smiled. "You're my guest, and I have a free night. Let's go."

She plucked her keys off the hook hanging by the door, slid on a pair of flip-flops, and held the door open for him, waiting.

He paused for a moment, then pulled his sneakers off the rack and slid his feet inside.

"Have you been to any food places yet?" Kiran asked as they stepped back outside.

"There's a bagel place on Avenue A close to Eleventh that I really liked today."

"Oh my gosh, Tompkins Square Bagels! The entire ten pounds I gained when I moved to New York came from that place. They should have named a bagel after me."

"I swear, their jalapeño cheddar cream cheese is laced with something. I'm already craving another one."

"I wouldn't be surprised if it was. I used to think a part of my day was missing if I didn't have breakfast there."

"So true love, then?" Nash joked, trying to ignore the curiosity piquing in his mind about what it would be like to be something she missed.

"The closest I've come to it!" Kiran giggled. "No surprise that it's with food."

"Well, you'll have to take me to all your favorite food places. I gotta learn your ways."

"You're in for a lot of nights, then, because I can't choose one or two!"

"I'm not going to complain."

"Okay, stop!" Kiran froze in her tracks.

"What? Are you okay?" Nash's training around erratic patients kicked into high gear, and he instantly prepared his mind for a number of outcomes.

"Turn around." Kiran touched his arm to guide him.

She left a soft imprint there. Even after he was facing the brick wall she had turned him toward, his elbow felt the pressure of her fingers, and he ran his hand over his arm to make it fade before he looked up.

Painted on the side of a building was a giant work of art with bright colors. Numerous faces and heads popped out from the image, tinted in hues of oranges, pinks, and greens. As he glanced downward, sculptures of metal dotted a green yard full of metalworks.

He had almost passed by without noticing.

"Surprise?"

Nash's mouth dropped open. "This is beautiful."

His eyes hungrily scanned over the curves of each face and the hardened lines on the features of the elderly.

"This is what I love about living in the East Village. You mind your own business and walk to run errands or get to work, but suddenly you look up, and there's art all around you."

"I guess you have to open your eyes to find the magic," he murmured, glancing around, trying to find more hidden gems.

Their eyes met. And in the sunlight, Nash could see every crystalline brown peak and crevice in the irises of her eyes.

Was that a twinkle?

His phone buzzed, and they both startled at the loud ring between them.

Hey, Nash, sorry I missed your call. I'll meet you in the building in ten minutes and will let you in.

"Well, the landlord says he can let me into my place."

"See? Your evening didn't turn out so badly, did it?"

"No. It was surprisingly wonderful. Thank you for hosting me and being so kind."

"Any time."

As they entered their building, Nash waved at Kiran.

She grinned at him, gave a wiggle of her fingers in response, and ascended the stairs to her second-floor apartment. As he watched her from the lobby, thankful for the kindness of strangers, he hoped this wouldn't be the last time he got to experience it.

Chapter Six

KIRAN

Sonam: He could have been a serial killer.

This is déjà vu, Kiran thought.

Kiran: Not a serial killer. A really nice guy.
Payal: Was he cute? Any prospects for us?
Kiran: I did mention American, right? So none for me.
Payal: Okay, then answer the first part. Cute?
Sonam: Always the first concern.
Akash: Why am I on this thread? I don't need to hear this.
Kiran: Remember that time Akash was into that magic show?
Akash: It was King Arthur! "That magic show." Listen to
yourself.
Kiran: He looks a little like the guy on it.
Sonam: He belongs on a magic show?
Akash: IT WAS A SHOW ABOUT KING ARTHUR.
Payal: Go play with your wand, Akash.
Sonam: Don't encourage him. He'll find someone to play with
his wand for him.

Akash: I hate you all.

Kiran tried not to giggle at the thread of text messages flowing between the group the day after she and Nash had hung out. At various points in the week, sometimes with a serious problem and sometimes with a funny story, the thread titled "CMC" on her phone would blow up with message after message between the four friends.

She had mentioned she was craving bagels that she and a new friend in her apartment building had discussed—but at the mention of the word *he*, this seemingly innocuous story suddenly had sparked a fire of intrigue in her best friends.

She tried to think about how Nash looked to accurately describe him.

His eyes were blue—the kind of teal-blue color that one saw in photos of the Caribbean but were never quite convinced actually existed. They were deeply and widely set, which hid the brilliance until Kiran had locked eyes with him last night.

His fine nose was somewhat dainty, but when he smiled, his strong jawline became more apparent, and suddenly, there was nothing forgettable about his face.

It was his smile, if anything, that she would eventually tell Payal about. He had the kind of smile that showed an entire row of perfect teeth, with full lips, the bottom one more prominent than his top.

His dirty blond hair didn't appear to cooperate much with what he was trying to get it to do, keep it off his forehead. It wasn't a clean cut, as though he'd let it grow out an inch longer than he should have and now the front flopped onto his forehead if he didn't run his fingers through it.

Yes. Nash was attractive. There was no question.

But she was only telling Payal because she asked.

Kiran found her mind drifting to that evening more often than she would have expected, flashing back to the ease with which Nash spoke to her and how it never felt like they were strangers, despite having met only moments before she invited him up to her place. Quietly, she hoped to see him around the building—perhaps on their way out to work or in after a long day—but days passed, and Nash was getting further away.

But lo and behold, sometimes when one wished, the universe gave.

Two weeks after that memorable evening, Kiran stretched out on her love seat, wanting to read, but the untouched book sat in her lap. She stared at her phone instead, mindlessly scrolling through Bollywood news stories. The latest actress to make it in Hollywood had recently married an American superstar, and Indian gossip rags were being surprisingly accepting about it.

A knock at the door prompted Kiran to jump, dropping her phone in the process.

Not recalling any appointments and thinking the CMC were all busy tonight with work or plans, she went to the door tentatively. She hoped it wasn't a solicitor. She was terrible at getting out of long, drawn-out sales pitches and squirmed through them instead.

The person on the other side of the door was far more welcome.

"Nash!" She tried not to sound too relieved, but it came out as a squeak.

He was wearing a red dress shirt and black dress pants held by a black leather belt. His sleeves were rolled up, and it added a certain carelessness to his otherwise formal outfit. His hair was as disheveled as it was the night they'd met.

"Hi! Do you want to go out tonight?"

"Like...?"

"Like dinner?"

No. No, no, no, this wasn't supposed to happen. She wanted a friend in the building. Had she given him signals that she was interested? Had she blown this friendship somehow? See, this was why she should never be nice. Wasn't there a rule about asking someone on a date the night of said date too? A three-day rule? She could have sworn Payal mentioned something.

She was *not* available. At least not for an American white guy who her parents would never be able to relate to.

She faltered, her grin disappearing in the race of thoughts. "I... Oh...well, Nash, I'm sorry... I don't date. I mean, I'm not dating right now. I mean, I can't—"

His eyes widened at her flustered response. Finally, when she'd sufficiently made a fool of herself, he laughed. "No, I didn't mean... It's my first day off in a while. I wanted to go out and do something. I wasn't asking you out."

"Oh."

Well, now she felt stupid.

"Not that you aren't worth asking out. I think you're wonderful, of course. But that wasn't my intention. I wanted food and thought company would be more fun."

"Sorry. I'm sorry," she said again. "I'm not high on myself... I just—"

"You aren't very good with being flustered, are you?"

She stared at him for a second. "No."

"I couldn't tell."

Despite his easy manner, she could sense the heat rising in her chest and cheeks, and she fidgeted in the doorway, wishing she could disappear. How could she have jumped to that conclusion?

"Kiran?"

Her eyes snapped up to him.

"Dinner? Would you like to go?" He gazed at her expectantly.
"When?"

"I'm going to change. Can we leave in ten minutes?"

She took a deep breath, collecting herself. "Absolutely."

The restaurant Nash wanted to go to was down the street. Kiran considered shooting Sonam a text to join them, since she worked nearby at Mount Sinai and Nash was looking for more friends anyway, but finally decided against it. Her instincts usually led her right, and for whatever reason, they shouted at her to go alone.

"How was your day?" Nash asked as he strolled up to her.

The red dress shirt and belted dress pants were now replaced by a pair of jeans and a black Henley. His sneakers and casual clothes seemed to fit his personality much better. Kiran's fingers were crossed that the restaurant wasn't too fancy, and she was pacified by Nash's casual appearance. She didn't feel out of place in her paisley-patterned blue-and-orange pencil skirt and blue tank top as they stepped inside the industrial chic establishment. Mason jars served as glasses at each place setting. The lights hung on coppery metal fixtures, reminiscent of a rusting water pipe. White wood paneling and exposed wooden floors added to the rustic vibe.

They were seated outside, on benches of yellow wood that blocked the sidewalk and allowed them to view both the hipster facade of the restaurant and the street with equal interest. Kiran's eyes drifted to the eclectic crowd walking by—an older woman dressed in neon leggings, walking her dog, and a couple in suits, holding hands.

Kiran loved summers in the city, especially now that it was alive again, and this night was no different.

"I've heard the bucket of bird is really good here if you like chicken." Nash broke the silence as he examined the menu.

"I'm vegetarian, actually!" She braced for the inevitable question.

"Oh, do you mind if I get something with meat, then?"

Okay, that wasn't it. "Oh. No. No, it's fine."

"Are you sure? You don't sound it."

She laughed at her transparency. "I'm sure. I was expecting another question."

"Whether it's religious or your choice?" He grinned, as if he knew exactly what she was thinking.

"Yup."

"Well?"

"Both. Started off one way and then became my way of life."

"Cool."

She felt a lurch of pleasant surprise at the way he simply accepted her answer without further questioning or, worse, a doubtful glance at a seemingly strange belief from an unfamiliar place. Whether it was her Indian accent or the color of her skin, she was so used to feeling outside the circle that Nash's acceptance was like a hug.

"I tried to choose a place that had mac and cheese." Nash smiled.

"Well, that's kind of thoughtful, thank you!" Kiran touched her heart.

"Don't count on it every time, though. I hear New York pizza is a thing, and if you put macaroni and cheese on that, I'm putting the kibosh on being friends."

"Pizza is a thing. There is nothing like it."

"I should probably make a list of things to check out, huh?"

An impulse simmered in her belly to tell him about her list—to confess that she wanted to be adventurous and bold—and maybe she wanted those things with him, because a new friend would be novel too.

"I— So my friends and I made these lists in college—and when we moved to the city, we had grand plans to do all the things on them. Payal found them the other day, and I didn't do very many of my things." It came out in one breath. *Smooth*.

"Like a list of adventures?"

"Exactly. I feel like I've been carrying it around as a reminder to be a little more conscious about getting out, especially now. We were cooped up for so long, and I took it all—being here—for granted." She pulled out the neatly folded piece of aged paper and held it in front of her.

"Well, let's hear it, then."

Her walls went up before she could stop them—and she ended up picking two of the most simple items. "I want to play at an American arcade. And I want to ride a horse."

"I don't know where you'll find a horse in the city..."

"Don't pee in my Cheerios!" It was Sonam's favorite phrase.

He glanced up with an amused expression. "Okay, no peeing in food items. What else?"

Kiran read the rest of the list she'd been pondering for the last two weeks but left out Ma and Baba and dancing under the stars. They were childish fancies. "Do you have any things you want to try?"

Nash opened his mouth.

"Wait! I have a notepad. Let's write them down!"

"You carry around a notepad? Do you have one of those bags like Mary Poppins?"

"I'm a nerd, what can I say?" She reached into her bag again, produced a small floral stationery pad with the words *To Do* printed on the top, and placed it gently on the table. She clicked a pen and pushed it toward him.

"Aptly labeled stationery," he commented.

"Indeed. Continue."

"I'd like to go to Top of the Rock at night. I've heard it's a great view. Of course, I'd love to check out the Brooklyn Bridge. I know—super basic and touristy. I also want to try a real New York pizza." He wrote them down as he recited them out loud.

Kiran observed his small block lettering. He was left-handed, and somehow that captivated her, like a poignant detail on a painting that changed the entire meaning.

"Do you have more that you want to add to your list?" Nash asked.

"A food festival in Brooklyn—I've done it once, but it was when I first came to New York. I told myself I'd do it every summer, but it's been a total fail. A quiet walk along the Upper East Side—which I've done plenty but is still one of my favorite things. The Bronx Zoo. I actually haven't done that."

Kiran noticed the tiny frown that wrinkled Nash's brow for a millisecond, but it was gone before it was really even there.

"What about non-New Yorker things?" he said.

"Are you going to write those down too?" she teased.

"I'm curious! Making this list is causing me to think."

"You'll laugh. Most of them are silly"

"Try me."

Her instinct was to change the subject—opening up about all the things she wanted to do to someone new was like exposing a nerve. Vulnerability with strangers wasn't her strong suit.

But then serendipitous optimism filled her. Maybe Nash would push her to look up and do the things she hadn't yet.

"Promise you won't tease me?"

"Cross my heart."

"All those little things you do on the spur of the moment that make you feel alive every time you think of them—a night of chatter under the stars, or dancing under them. Those are things I'd do. They aren't momentous or as cool as selling all your things and traveling the planet for a year, but they are the experiences I'd hold close. Adventures I'd want to have."

Nash smiled. It was the most peaceful, accepting smile Kiran had ever seen.

"There's nothing silly about those dreams, Kiran. Everyone has things they want to chase down because they fill something inside of them... Those are yours."

"Tell me about you. Do you have any dreams beyond New York City adventures?"

"I've only been out of the country once—can you believe it? I've always wanted to go to another continent. And I'd love to start a new tradition with someone that I keep up. My best friend and I used to write down the best thing that happened to us that year on New Year's Eve, and we put it in a jar."

"That's a really sweet tradition. You don't do it anymore?"

"We stopped during my freshman year of college. My mom over— She died," he said quickly. "And I guess college got to us too. We felt too old to continue doing it. But I'd love to have a new tradition to keep up."

"Well, it sounds like you will. And we have a great list of fun things to try now!"

"You should write some new ideas down too. It's only fair."

"Okay," she agreed.

As she finished writing, Akash's voice spoke in her head. *It's kind of nice to think about coming home to someone and knowing they're yours to share a life with.* After this dinner with Nash where she had laughed and a little sparkle had shown itself in her life, a pull at her heart made her write one more thing down on unexpected impulse. She also didn't want Nash to know this one.

Fall in love.

"Did you remember one more thing?" Nash asked, eyeing her with curiosity.

"Woman of mystery, remember?" Her eyes twinkled.

"I'm texting you now. If we're free, we go. Deal?" Nash asked.

"Deal." She grinned.

"All right, give me your number, and let's do this."

It was foreign reciting her number to an attractive guy outside of work or acquaintances of her friends—but perhaps it was time to shake life up and make some friends outside of the CMC.

Chapter Seven

NASH

After four years at different universities and an additional eight years apart while Brandon moved to Manhattan and Nash completed his postcollege education, it was a novelty to be able to pick up the phone and tell the other person to drop everything and meet him for dinner.

That was how Nash ended up sitting at 5 Napkin Burger on East Fourteenth Street across from his best buddy on a Saturday evening, a week after he'd asked Kiran to join him for dinner.

"What the hell was the point in you moving to the city if we weren't actually going to hang out all the time, dumbass?" Brandon asked, his mouth full of burger. "I haven't seen you in three weeks."

"Say it, don't spray it, dude." Nash made a disgusted expression.

"You work at a hospital. It's not like you haven't seen worse."

"Fair point."

"How's work been? Any cool cases?"

"The usual... Drug-addicted parents. Children with depression. Adolescents with eating disorders."

"Sounds depressing," Brandon said, blunt as ever.

"I don't know... I don't really think it is. I mean, it's sad, for sure, but sometimes you end up being this beacon of light during pretty dark times for these kids. It's rewarding in its own way. You have to be able to leave it at the door and come home and be normal."

"I have no idea how you do that, man. That's why I work with money. It's high stress but it's not like seeing people become their worst enemy or being the difference between a happy life and a sad one."

"You learn to, I guess. They train you well before you dive in."

"Given your history, sometimes I can't get over you doing what you do."

Nash picked up a couple of fries. "I guess that's why I *can* do what I do."

"My mom and dad say hi, by the way. Mom says she misses you."

"Tell them I miss them too. How's your dad been after the knee surgery?"

"Walks with a limp and talks like he's Usain Bolt...so, you know, the usual."

Nash chuckled. Brandon's sense of humor was inherited from his dad, a pediatrician in Nashville who got by in life on laughter and a prayer.

"You been seeing anyone lately?"

"This girl named Tasha. She's beautiful."

Nash gave Brandon a quizzical gaze. "Beautiful?"

"What?" Brandon asked. "I can't call a girl beautiful?"

"Of course you can. You usually go with a more mature 'sexy as hell,'" Nash said.

"Nah. I'm looking for the real deal now. She might be it."

"Really?"

"You look so surprised. I'd be offended if I had any shame."

Nash couldn't help but laugh. "I'm happy for you. It's a surprise coming from the guy I grew up with. I mean...I've known you since we were six years old. I've seen you in your head gear."

"We promised we weren't going to talk about that ever again."

"It's nice to see you settle down a bit, that's all." Nash sipped his soda.

"When are you going to? You can't be married to your job forever, you know."

"I need to get settled. Pay off my loans. There are a lot of shifting parts."

"There are always moving parts. I'll be honest with you... I love you. You're my best friend. But you gotta focus on you for a while. You can't use school or work or Kate or whatever else as an excuse for the rest of your life. This might be the time to focus on you and your life."

"I actually went to dinner with a girl last week."

"I think hell just froze over. You had a date?"

"It wasn't a date. It was a friendly dinner. She lives in my building."

"Well, it obviously stayed on your mind if you're mentioning it now."

Nash didn't say anything. Though he wasn't going to give his best friend the benefit of knowing he was right, he had been thinking about Kiran a little. Nothing huge...a passing thought when he saw a little boy eating macaroni and cheese and walking by an Indian restaurant in Midtown before wondering what paneer tasted like.

"You know how people completely fascinate you sometimes? Like...there's something about them that makes you want to know more because they've lived in a way you haven't."

"Yeah, sure. Their experiences have been so different than yours that when they talk about certain things, you feel like you're living through them."

"Exactly. That's how she felt."

"Well, friends or otherwise, that's never a bad thing. She might open your eyes to things you never knew."

"That's what I'm hoping."

"Are you hoping for more than that? Does she have potential?"

Nash shook his head. "I'm not even thinking about that."

"Why not?"

"From what I've read and all the stories you've told me, relationships in New York last a hot minute because people can find someone else in a snap. I am not looking to be left."

Brandon paused. "Not everyone leaves, Nash."

"Yeah...yeah. I know."

"It'll be good for you to break out of the psych ward and hang out with people who are outside of your work bubble anyway."

"That's the whole reason I moved here, right? I was ready for something I wasn't used to."

"On the subject of people you *are* used to... Have you spoken to Kate lately? How's she doing?"

Nash thought of his aunt in Nashville and realized he hadn't spoken to her in a few weeks. "I have to give her a call tonight. I haven't talked to her in a while."

"She and my mom are so close, you'd think I was her nephew now." Brandon rolled his eyes.

"I'd still be her favorite one," Nash said.

"You're everyone's favorite," Brandon grumbled. "I'm pretty sure my parents would have adopted you if they could."

"Don't sound so bitter."

"Please, if they adopted you, I would have had more time to

goof off while you were the perfect son. I'm not bitter. I'm mad it didn't happen!"

"*More* time to goof off? You brought a cow to school and let him loose on the track."

Brandon chuckled. "One of my best moments, to be honest."

"It was pretty good," Nash agreed. "Now...tell me about Tasha. You can't drop a bomb like 'I think she's the one' and then change the subject."

"I went to a networking dinner for Tennessee alums, and she was there, lighting up the room. She's a human resources specialist at a nonprofit, running the show behind the scenes. Loves football. Can drink like a horse. Goes hiking and rock climbing on the weekends."

"So the whole package?" Nash said. "What do your parents think?"

"They haven't met her yet, but you know them. Mom will love anyone who's willing to put up with me forever, and Dad's going to make fun of me until I want to crawl under a table and then tell me he likes her when she makes fun of me too."

"That sounds accurate."

"In all seriousness, she already makes me better. She calls me on my bullshit. She doesn't lose her patience with me when I'm irritating her." Brandon grew serious. "I was having fun until I met her, and now I can see a future that includes someone else."

"I can't wait to meet her, man. You look really happy. Why didn't you mention her before? How long have you guys been dating?"

"Exactly three weeks. We met the night you moved in, and you would have met her had you not been MIA since you moved into your place."

Nash nearly choked on his drink. "Three weeks?"

"When you know, you know. You just mentioned someone stuck with you after one dinner."

Nash couldn't argue there. "Well, I'm happy for you. For real."

Brandon had a reputation for having the biggest heart and the most enormous penchant for trouble. His teachers reprimanded him, then let him off the hook from any serious disciplinary action because he'd be the biggest fundraiser for all school charity drives. He had been the one to raise money for a classmate who was in a car accident, and he'd organized a date auction when a family from his church had their home burn down, serving as the pièce de résistance when he stepped out onto the auction runway in his boxers and with a six-pack painted on.

Nash couldn't think of a better person in life who deserved good things.

After they'd squared up their bill and wandered outside, Brandon gave Nash a big hug. "Don't be a stranger," he said.

"Don't get in too much trouble," Nash replied, patting his friend's back.

"See you soon, buddy."

Nash set off on the eleven blocks back to his apartment.

Brandon wasn't wrong—Kiran had stuck with him.

He wondered about her list too, what she wrote on the bottom of it before stowing it away again. A pang of desire bolted through his chest to be allowed into her thought process, to be allowed into a place she didn't seem to share with many. A woman of mystery, he recalled with a smile.

Everyone had their secrets. She was entitled to keep her deepest wants to herself. After all, he could relate. He'd been surrounded by friends but largely alone for most of his life.

What would be the secret thing he'd add to the bottom of his list? The one he wanted more than anything but couldn't admit to anyone out loud?

The look that swept across Brandon's face when he talked

about Tasha—the goofy grin, the eyes filled with happiness, and the smile that Nash had only seen on his best friend's face after he hit a home run. Maybe he wanted that too.

Maybe falling in love was the thing he wanted most, even if he was terrified of what it might cost him.

While he was walking, he decided to give Aunt Kate a call.

"Kate! How are you?" he exclaimed as he heard her soft greeting over the line.

"How are you, sweetie? I miss you!" Kate's excitement flooded through the speaker.

"I miss you too, and I'm doing well. I'm getting home after dinner."

"Did you have a date?" Kate practically squealed.

"Just Brandon. He's not exactly my type." Nash smiled at his aunt's excitement. "What are you up to? How's Stephen?"

"We're doing well…rebuilding the porch right now. Stephen's already hammered his thumb twice and broken the screwdriver."

"So it's going well, then?" Nash laughed.

"God help us…"

Nash could picture her sitting on the couch, cross-legged, as she talked to him on the phone. Her home was the coziest place he'd ever been, full of plush, flowered couches in a tiny living room filled with plants. The fireplace was a fixture from October to April because Kate couldn't stand the cold. And in the summer, she'd open up a small above-ground pool that she never swam in but always dangled her legs in while reading a book.

She'd married later in life, when Nash was in middle school—a quiet man named Stephen who probably couldn't get a word in edgewise because Kate never stopped talking.

Kate was his mother's sister and the only connection to family he had left.

"How's the new job been for you?" Kate asked.

"It's been good. I've been connecting with a few of the patients lately." He thought of one of his patients, a little boy whose mother had been arrested for drug use, and how he'd actually given him a hug the other day on his way out of the clinic.

"Are you taking care of yourself?"

"I am."

"I mean mentally. You deal with heavy things, Nash. Sometimes I don't know how you do it."

"That's easy. I think about who you were to me and try to be like you."

She sniffed on the other end of the line. "Thank you, Nashy."

"You are the only person who can make that nickname remotely appealing."

"I make everything appealing!" she argued.

"Have you tasted your baking?" Nash cringed, filled with memories of salty cookies and exploding chocolate Bundt cakes.

"Hey! You make it sound like they were a ten-alarm fire… It was only the smoke detectors and a couple of failed experiments."

"Yeah, well, they are burned into my memory…"

"Whatever, smarty-pants. I miss you. Take care, okay? And come home soon."

Nash felt a surge of fondness for his aunt. He knew she missed the weekly coffee dates they had while he was at Vanderbilt and vowed to try to make it home to see her soon.

"Love you."

"Love you too, Nashy."

He hung up and stowed his phone in his pocket, passing by a furniture store that had brightly colored curtains hanging in the window and a comfy-looking blue couch in the display.

Once again, Kiran popped into his mind, and he wondered what she was up to.

Chapter Eight

KIRAN

Unbeknownst to Nash, Kiran was having a reunion of her own with her friends…but it wasn't going quite as pleasantly as the one he'd just experienced.

"Stop moving!"

"I can't help it! You're taking a hundred years."

"I need these measurements to be correct."

"It's not heart surgery, and I'm hungry."

Kiran and Akash glanced at each other, half-amused and half-exasperated at the unending argument currently taking place between Sonam and Payal. They were both lying across Payal's couches at her apartment, waiting for Payal to snag Sonam's proportions for her latest clothing project.

"Okay, I hate to interrupt this love fest, but are we ordering these pizzas tonight, or am I going to go to the place down the street by myself?" Akash finally asked.

"Pizza…" Sonam groaned.

Payal glared at her before dangling the measuring tape around her neck and turning to them.

"See, this is why I need to have real models who let me get

the measurements I need without whining about how hungry they are."

"To be fair, most models are probably hungrier than we are..." Sonam muttered under her breath.

"Oh, stop bloody complaining," Payal snapped, her clipped British accent sharpening her words like blades.

"Okay, time out," Kiran commanded. "Payal, you can get your numbers when Sonam has eaten. Sonam, don't be mean. Akash, order the pizza. I'll cue up the movie."

It was like handling a million preschoolers rather than three adults. The four of them were best friends, but the sibling bickering never stopped. Tonight, Kiran was the mama bear watching over her three unruly cubs.

To celebrate her success giving a presentation at work on the reorganization of neural circuits and the nerve stimulation device her team was working on and to soothe Sonam after she'd had a particularly trying week at the hospital, the CMC had decided to have a movie night with their favorite Hindi movies while drowning their respective victories and sorrows in pizza.

Of course, the second they all got to Payal's place, the largest of all of their apartments, she wanted to finish up some sample sizes on her side project—a clothing design business she hoped to get off the ground in the next few years. In the meantime, Sonam snapped at everyone like she was a crocodile and they were fish, and Akash had complained of a headache from a tough work day, rummaging in Payal's cabinets for Tylenol the moment he entered.

"We're watching *Lagaan*," Kiran told them. It was her celebration, so she got to choose. A movie about a small village uprising resulting in a cricket match between the British colonists and untrained Indians was exactly the kind of story she was in the mood for.

"Do we have to?" Sonam whined. "Can't we watch something more recent like *Padmaavat*?"

"No," chorused Payal, Akash, and Kiran, in protest of the violent period drama about a Rajput princess who, along with the women and children in her city, self-immolated to prevent the rape and pillaging of their people after a wartime loss against the invading Islamic dynasties.

Sonam huffed and leaned against the cushions.

"Okay..." Kiran took a deep breath and turned to Sonam. "Before we watch this, you are going to tell us what's making you upset and unload whatever is burdening you. Once we help you, we are going to cheerfully watch this movie, and you are going to chill out. Deal?"

Payal and Akash exchanged grateful glances that someone had addressed the crankiness.

"I got in trouble at work today," Sonam mumbled.

"About?"

"This Indian woman came into the hospital today. She fell down the stairs. Her bruises were consistent with a fall. The attending still suspected abuse, and he went through all the protocol for reporting domestic battery."

"I'm sorry, but what's wrong with that? Maybe she fell, or he wanted to be thorough to cover his ass," Payal offered.

"She didn't speak English, Payal. I think she spoke Bengali. From the small amount I could understand, her husband was a cab driver who brought her in, and he was really concerned. He explained in Hindi that she'd tripped over the end of her sari at their apartment building and fallen down the flight of stairs. He tried to catch her, but he went down with her...and he had the bruises to show for it too, but he didn't want medical help because he said it didn't hurt much and he was worried about her."

Once the floodgates opened, Sonam began to speak faster, her voice increasing in volume and ferocity.

"I tried to tell the attending the story, but he filled out the protocol anyway. You know why? 'Because abuse happens often in *that part* of the world.' That's it. Because abuse happens in brown countries, obviously a woman *actually* falling down the stairs can't be believed."

The three others made grunts of anger but allowed her to continue.

"Anyway, I told him that he should believe what the patient says, and he told me I was too inexperienced to catch this kind of thing...and I told him I spoke Hindi and understood the culture. And the entire argument escalated until I told him his white savior racist ass didn't need to push his preconceived notions on an obviously terrified and injured wife."

Akash groaned. "Sonam, you didn't."

"Why not?" Sonam's eyes filled with angry tears. "It's not fair that someone else gets to tell women what they've experienced and not listen when we talk about what we've really gone through. It's not fair that this poor lady, who was aching and in pain and wanted her loving husband to be there with her, got separated from him and asked about whether he did this to her. No one even understood her properly anyway. Who knows if the translator did a good job?"

"Sonam—"

Kiran's warning glare stopped Akash from telling Sonam she should have been professional.

"You're right," Payal said softly. "It is unfair. Especially when we've all met women who have been abused. Her voice wasn't heard or taken into account before people made a rash assumption based on the color of her skin, her culture, and her situation."

"What if I'm not cut out to be a doctor? Maybe I should

have gone to law school like my dad told me to, or worked with a nonprofit where I get to make a difference. I failed her today. And I got written up for calling someone out." Sonam's shoulders hunched like she was trying to take up as little space as possible.

"Whoa." Kiran spoke now. "You didn't fail anyone. You are meant to be a doctor. You lost today's fight, but the fact that you fought at all is precisely why medicine needs you."

Sonam wiped her nose with her sleeve and sniffled.

"I'm sorry I took your measurements," Payal said suddenly, and the three others looked at her.

"*Really?* Right now, you had to say that?" Akash asked.

"I wanted her to stop feeling sad!"

Sonam laughed through her tears. "I'm sorry I was a bitch."

"You're always a bitch. It's okay," Payal said.

"I should have kept fighting for her."

"You believed her, and you did fight for her," Akash said firmly. "You did the right thing. She was heard. And when you get a chance to speak to your supervisors, you'll make sure they know their attending is an incompetent ass."

Sonam nodded.

Nash flashed through Kiran's mind then, talking about how he wanted to provide children a safe haven when they were experiencing difficult times, and it reminded her of Sonam's quest to give women justice.

She gazed at Sonam now, and exhaustion was overflowing along with her tears. Kiran had heard about residency being a marathon test of endurance and that residents had a high rate of suicides because of the pressure, the tiredness, and the skill required to save lives with no sleep or mental rest. She knew that Sonam would be an excellent doctor and that this was a bump in the road, but she also sympathized that it must feel like a mountain to her friend.

"You know, Sonam, I went to dinner with a psychologist the other day, and he may be able to help you or at least reassure you as you go through these next couple of years. I can connect you if you want."

Sonam opened her mouth to speak, but Payal beat her to it.

"A doctor? He? Who?"

"Calm down, Gossip Girl. It's my neighbor. His name is Nash. We had a harmless dinner the other night, and he's fun to hang out with."

"But you *never* hang out with guys!" Payal exclaimed.

"Apparently, everyone has forgotten I have a penis," Akash mused out loud.

"We choose to ignore it," Sonam replied to him before turning back to Kiran. "Connect me to him, please—"

"Wait, is this the same guy you texted us about?" Payal interrupted.

Kiran groaned inwardly at her gaffe. Two mentions would prompt plenty of curiosity.

"Yes. We went to dinner, as I said—"

"Are you guys dating?"

"Will you let her finish a sentence?" Akash exclaimed.

"No," Kiran answered. "On finishing a sentence and on dating."

"Would you?"

"What does that have to do with anything?"

But that was precisely the wrong question to ask. Kiran had tried to drive home that it was a stretch to associate dating and a friendly dinner, but her friends pounced like an animal on their prey as they erroneously assumed her question was, in fact, a denial of a love affair.

"You *would*!" Payal gasped.

"I—"

"Get out! You're dating a white guy!" Sonam exclaimed, her own woes forgotten.

"Okay, stop!" Kiran's loud voice silenced them all. "I *can't* date him. He's American. You guys know what happened with my sister. I wouldn't do that to my parents."

"Do you want to hang out with him again?" Payal asked.

"Of course. He's really sweet."

"And if this goes further than being friends...what are you going to do?"

Kiran groaned. "Could we focus on the movie now, please? I'm not thinking about the future."

"That's a first," Akash chimed in.

"Enough." The sharpness in Kiran's voice finally quieted their persistent questioning.

"Wait, wait, wait. First, did you guys bring your new lists?" Payal asked.

Surprisingly, they all nodded.

"I feel like we're all back at Duke and we just got asked if we completed our homework," Akash said.

"Well, when Payal assigns it..." Sonam shrugged.

Payal looked at them with fond pride. "Let's hear it."

Sonam spoke first, the Hermione Granger of their group. "I'd like to survive residency. Open a nonprofit. Write a book. Go to Europe. And fall in love."

"Good list," Akash said approvingly. "I want to serve on the board of an organization. Go to one of the national parks in the West—my parents took my sisters when we were at Duke, but I couldn't go. I'd like to kayak somewhere with clear water. And find a girl crazy enough to want to be with me."

Payal laughed. "Good luck."

"Shut up."

"Kiran? Did you add anything new to your list?" Payal waited, her eyes filled with anticipation.

She gave a soft smile, thinking of Nash and their dinner full of chatter, and read off her list: the arcade, horseback riding, food festivals, the Bronx Zoo, a night under the stars, moments of breathtaking beauty...and then she added, "I want to fall in love," before anticipating Payal would mention Nash and quickly qualifying, "with the right person."

"You will, Kiran, I know it. You know I'm going to start my fashion line at some point. I'd love to actually hear my parents tell me they love me. I'd love to have mind-blowing sex for the rest of my life. I'd like to go on a vacation with someone I love—besides you guys or my cousins. I guess that means I have to fall in love too. I'd also like to go to Disney World. I still haven't been."

Payal always wore her heart on her sleeve, and even her list showed it.

Kiran noticed the frown Akash was wearing.

"So, 'fall in love' was on all of our lists. And none of us have fallen in love yet." He looked puzzled.

"We've fallen in love. It just wasn't forever," Payal said.

"Fair point. Maybe there's something wrong with us," he said.

"Oh, stop. That patriarchal nonsense is so ridiculous," Sonam said. "There's nothing wrong with anyone for finding their partners after twenty-five, whether they're male, female, or non-binary. This timeline thing is illogical."

"I'm kidding. But given that we're doing all right in our lives, it's interesting that none of us have found what we're looking for in a partner."

Kiran gave a small sigh. "For all the bluster, we've never done the one thing that actually involves risk."

The room fell silent, Kiran's words sinking in.

"It happens when it happens," Payal said firmly. "We can joke about the pressure—and don't get me wrong, it's real—but we're not all going to find partners at the same time. Some of us may not at all. Maybe I was right in the first place that love doesn't even exist. Who the hell knows? But we'll take the risk when we find it worthwhile...and it's okay if we haven't or don't."

The pizza arrived then, and Kiran started the movie. The legendary Amitabh Bachchan's deep, signature voice began to narrate the prologue to the story, and Kiran's mind wandered.

She was an engineer and always thought through the process of her decisions the same way she approached her work. Analytical. Methodical. Meticulous.

But right now, her brain was frenetic.

And she didn't like it one bit.

Conversations about lists and risks and love swirled through her mind.

The truth was that she thought about Nash and felt drawn to him. The instant familiarity they displayed—"insta-besties," Payal would have called it since she had so much experience with the concept—was rare for Kiran, and it opened a window in her heart that hadn't been there before.

Then there was the electricity that sizzled in every inch of her body when he looked at her after viewing the art on the wall.

But that could be anything, couldn't it? It was so fleeting. Was it even worth thinking about?

Friendships had always served as an energizer for her, a burst of spirit to a worn-out soul. And quite frankly, she had begun to feel as though every day was following the same pattern, a little gray in a phase of life that she'd hoped would be full of color. Nash was a sudden firework on a slow, hot night in New York City, a break in the monotony.

As she watched the movie and concentrated on Gauri getting her palm read by the village lunatic, she wondered if she, like the fictional character in front of her, was setting her hopes on a romance...one that wouldn't fit the preplanned script of her life.

Her life wasn't a Bollywood movie full of lofty dreams and dance numbers around trees. She couldn't—wouldn't—entertain the thought of Nash as something more than a friend. No matter what, her family's past would always be her obstacle and a reminder of why she could never step over the line she'd drawn.

Chapter Nine

NASH

"I've never had a home that I can feel safe in," the boy said, his eyes falling to the hands tightly clasped in his lap.

Here it was. The root of his behavior.

"That must have been hard, Trent. Do you feel lonely sometimes?" Nash asked gently.

Trent shrugged. But underneath the pretending, the denial that he was lonely, Nash knew his patient felt utterly isolated in a world that had only handed him hardships. And his heart went out to the ten-year-old whose teachers had given up on him because of his defensive behavior.

He was the child of an absentee dad and a mother in and out of treatment for drug problems. She'd recently been arrested for the possession of two grams of cocaine and was spending six months in jail. She'd be returning to him after six months in a halfway house.

Trent had been bounced around from foster home to foster home, a ward of a system designed to defeat those whom it needed to lift.

"Sometimes I just wish my mom was back," Trent whispered.

"Was it better when she was around?"

"At least I had a mom... Sometimes she wasn't there or she was high, but she was mine."

Nash felt what the boy was saying in every cell of his body—the longing for something of his own, and missing a mother who never quite acted like one but was his all the same.

"Do you feel like you don't have anything that is yours?"

"All I have is myself. My mom's in jail now. I don't have a home or a family."

"You have people who care about you."

"They all ask if my foster home is treating me right. No one really cares."

"What if I told you I did?"

Trent gazed at him appraisingly. His hands tightened. "I don't believe you."

"Well, I hope that changes soon," Nash said easily. "Because I do. So what's your favorite sport?"

"Why?"

"I'm wondering. It's okay if you don't have one."

"I have one," Trent said quickly.

Nash raised his eyebrows.

"I like basketball."

"Well...lucky for you, I do too." Nash moved Trent's patient file from his lap to the table in front of him.

In the coat closet in his office, Nash had a shelf full of games. Some were puzzles. Others were brain-teasing trivia cards that simultaneously frustrated and encouraged children to use their minds. Still more, he had some tabletop basketball and foosball, in miniature so they were made for smaller hands.

Trent watched Nash closely as he put the tabletop basketball game down—two tiny metal hoops attached to both sides of a miniature backboard, with small catapults at either end of the baseboard, meant for aiming and shooting small orange beanbags.

"Want to play?" Nash offered.

The brief spark in Trent's eyes was unmistakable, but his mouth remained in a thin line. He pulled the board close and carefully positioned it in front of himself, kneeling on the floor in front of the coffee table so he could be at eye level with the hoop.

"Game until ten," Trent said.

"Okay," Nash agreed. "Ready, go!"

Trent was far more adept at getting the hang of the catapult. Nash often pushed too hard, having to scramble across the table to capture errant beanbags, while Trent continued to shoot and score.

"Yes! Ten!" Trent exclaimed triumphantly.

"Man, you're good." Nash laughed. "Honestly, I can never get the hang of this thing."

"You didn't let me win, did you?"

"No...I genuinely stink, Trent."

Trent cracked a smile. "My mom's old boyfriend taught me to play basketball. He was really good."

"I can tell. Even at tabletop basketball, you're talented."

"He used to take me to the park all the time. But I haven't seen him since my mom got arrested."

"That must have been hard. It sounds like you had a lot of fun."

"I got to feel good at something."

"You're still good at it," Nash said gently.

"My friends think so."

"Do you have a best friend?"

"Yeah. Sometimes I think he's the only person I have. But I'm jealous too."

"Why's that?"

"He has parents who love him. His dad takes him out to play football. He has a brother."

A pang of kinship struck Nash in the chest. Gazing at Trent's wishful eyes, he could see himself in them—a boy without parents, who loved his best friend for providing the home he didn't have and envied him for the very same things.

"I'm sure he wishes he had some of your talents too, Trent. You're doing great."

Trent nodded.

The alarm on Nash's phone rang, signaling the end of their session, the soft bells ringing the tune to "Hedwig's Theme" from Harry Potter.

"What's that song?" Trent asked as the alarm chimed.

"It's the theme song from Harry Potter. It's always been my favorite book series."

"I've never read it."

"Do you want to?"

"I guess… It's not like I have anything else to do." Trent's eyes flicked at the bookshelf, scanning it up and down in a flash.

Nash strode to his bookshelf, pulling out the blue book. "Well, here's the first one. Why don't you borrow it? I only ask that you please bring it back in good condition… Like I said, they're my favorites."

"Thanks, Dr. Hawthorne."

Trent took the book from Nash delicately, opening the cover slowly and running his hands over the page.

Nash wondered if he'd ever owned a book of his own.

As Trent stepped out of Nash's office and his foster mother stood in the hallway to take him home, Nash gave a smile and a wave. He watched them walk tentatively, a few feet apart, as though she didn't know what to do with him and he didn't care to allow her into his space or, as Nash knew, into his heart.

But before they exited the practice, she patted Trent's shoulder—a brief but poignant action that left Nash with a sliver of hope that perhaps this boy would find comfort and care in a world that hadn't given him much of those things.

Nash stood at the door to his office for a few minutes, reflecting on the session, until the administrative assistant, Bryony, broke his reverie.

"Are you okay, Dr. Hawthorne?"

Nash snapped to attention. "Yes, I'm thinking about my client. Sometimes you wonder if what you see will change down the road."

Bryony smiled from her desk. "I sure hope so. Isn't that why you do what you do?"

Nash returned her grin and nodded before entering his office again and taking a seat at his desk.

Isn't that why you do what you do?

Skimming again through Trent's file, a thick folder filled to the brim with stories of not completing homework, talking back to teachers, social isolation (with the exception of his single best friend), and a troubled home life, Nash thought about the boy with the big green eyes who had sat on the couch and who had appeared smaller than ever as social workers hovered around him on his first day in the office.

These don't sum up the kid at all. Even in the short month that Nash had been in New York, he could spot the human side of Trent, like the way his eyes widened with hope or the way he pursed his lips to fight a smile.

Isn't that why you do what you do?

Bryony was right. Whether it was Trent or any of his other clients, all Nash wanted was to be a source of light to a child who had only seen dark days and a person who only helped grow children into the giants they were meant to be.

Chapter Ten

KIRAN

Kiran stared at her phone and the text message Nash had sent her at their dinner to let her know his number.

Hi. That was all he'd sent, but even those two letters made her smile.

All she had to do now was say she was free today and see if he was up for a day at Chelsea Piers where her company was having a staff-wide family fun day.

Why did that make her so nervous?

Kiran: Hey. Chelsea Piers today? My company reserved the whole place, and I thought maybe you'd want to check it out. She typed and retyped that question in various forms until she thought she'd finally decided on the very first version anyway. She hit Send before she could contemplate it any further and drive herself crazy.

Nash: Yes, please.

She breathed a sigh of relief, as if she'd run a marathon but had to recover in two minutes.

For the thousandth time, she didn't know what it was about Nash that made her nervous. So far, he had been kind, sociable, funny, and a sweet friend to have in a circle that had shrunk to a handful of acquaintances, some friends at work, and the CMC.

"Get a grip, Kiran," she scolded herself. "This isn't like you."

Kiran: Let's go at noon. They have free food! Also, wear comfortable clothes.

His response was almost immediate: I shouldn't be surprised food was the selling point for you.

Watch yourself, she responded.

Promptly at noon, Kiran left her apartment with a surge of energy for the day ahead. She didn't carry anything on her except a small wristlet with her phone, cards, and keys inside. Her hair was in a ponytail, and her skinny jeans and plain white tee were paired with white Keds.

"Hi! You're here already!" she exclaimed as she descended the last few steps, pushing her diamond studs into place in her ears.

Nash stood at the bottom of the staircase, leaning against the banister and playing with his phone. His jeans and simple white polo, paired with white sneakers, offset his skin and browned him in comparison to his usual complexion, and his pale-blue eyes were sky against earth with his new hue.

"Only for a few minutes. I was looking at this place on my phone—good choice. You said the company reserved it? Look at you, with all that clout. Are you secretly the CEO?"

"It wasn't me, you goof. It's a family fun day or something, so they reserved it for anyone who wants to go and spend time there."

"You're taking me on a family fun day?" Nash raised an eyebrow.

"If you keep making fun of me, I will turn my ass around and go back upstairs and read a book."

"Well, that wouldn't be nice."

"Actually, I wouldn't stay here." Kiran grinned. "I'd tell you to take your butt home while I go play games all day."

Nash chuckled, and they began to walk in comfortable silence out of the apartment building toward the subway, but Kiran had a last-minute change of heart.

"Hey, let's grab an— Wait, did you realize we're basically wearing the same outfit?"

Nash looked down and then scanned Kiran from head to toe.

She blushed in response to his gaze, wondering if he saw curves and crevices or whether he didn't notice those things on her at all.

"Clearly, I've been a good influence on your fashion sense," he said finally.

"Hey!"

"I mean, you were cute before, but now you've elevated your game with the white tee and jeans."

"I hate you."

But somehow, the word *cute* replayed in her mind.

She summoned an Uber, miraculously already around the corner, and Nash opened the door for her, waiting until she got in before circling the car and climbing in on the other side.

They wound through the streets of the city, and Kiran marveled at all the things she took for granted every day. Each neighborhood had a vibe of its own. The East Village was a little hipster. The West Village was historic and reminded her of prim and proper aristocracy. She loved the meatpacking district, even with all its construction, for the brick-and-mortar industrial vibes and the quirky, cool stores she knew she'd find. She loved that in some neighborhoods, she couldn't see the tops of buildings as they reached for the clouds.

"I think people are going to recognize me someday by my chin and not my face." Nash broke the silence as he gazed out the window.

"What?"

He turned to her. "I'm not used to always looking up. And this city is all vertical. I mean, the beauty is in the brownstones, and the small stores, and the tiny little places you never thought you'd find...but I'm always drawn to these skyscrapers, and I feel like people are going to see my chin more than my face if I'm always craning my neck to see what's above me."

Kiran laughed. "Honestly, I still do the same thing. Every neighborhood has its own vibe."

"I'm beginning to get that."

They paused at a ticketing booth, and the cab pulled up to the curb of Pier 60 where they stepped onto the pavement and took a look around.

The three piers—59, 60, and 61—extended out from the side of Manhattan in the shape of a backwards *E* into the Hudson River. In between each pier was waterfront parking for tugboats and yachts to pull up for people to take a short cruise. Long buildings sat on two piers while the third had a driving range.

"Wow," Nash said softly. "This is an entertainment dream."

"Let's explore!"

They picked up the wristbands that would give them free access to the facilities from the friendly company representative manning a welcome table and walked into the building on Pier 59. Signs for bowling, rock climbing, golf, batting cages, gymnastics, and food popped up, leading to a hallway, pointing to a pathway down the parking garage, or directing people to sets of glass doors.

Nash was right. This place was an entertainment dream.

"What do you want to do first?"

"Oh my gosh, they have an arcade!" Kiran exclaimed.

Nash stopped in disbelief. "They gave you 475 activity options and you chose the arcade?"

"Nash! Can we play some games? Please, please, please?"

"If it makes you happy, yes. Just stop doing that puppy eye thing."

"I don't do a puppy eye thing."

"Trust me. You have puppy eyes. They're on your face. They're a thing."

She nearly skipped her way through the bowling alley to an area that couldn't quite be called a full arcade since there wasn't a wide variety of games but that filled her heart with happiness anyway.

"We're crossing the arcade off your list," Nash said as they walked in.

"Best day ever."

"What about these video games makes you so happy? You're practically flying."

"They remind me of high school."

"Do people *want* to be reminded of high school?"

Kiran slowed down, taking in the blue lights that shone around the walls, the children laughing with glee, and the ones who didn't put quarters into the machine but tried to drive the virtual cars anyway, turning the steering wheel this way and that.

"I think I told you before that I got a scholarship to my high school, right?"

"Right."

"Well, it was like a whole new world had opened up. Until then, I'd been in this village where the water came through pipes three days a week and we had to store it in giant plastic bins for the other four. Our electricity was spotty at best, especially during the summers when the heat would fry the grid. And boarding school...it wasn't even the freedom that got me but the mundane things all the wealthy kids got to do on a regular basis growing up that were novelties to me."

"Like video games?"

Kiran nodded. "Like video games. And giant shopping malls with air-conditioning and name brands. And Starbucks. And pizza."

Nash's eyes were on her as she continued, and she liked the way she seemed to captivate his attention.

"All of this takes me back to that. I'm still this Indian village girl at heart who finds these things amazing. I'm used to it now. I've lived in the United States for over a decade. But these tiny experiences are big reminders of what I didn't grow up having."

"I never really thought about it that way," Nash replied. "Though I can relate on being able to experience things now that I didn't when I was younger. A full fridge. A steady apartment... though if you've heard the way my floors creak, you'll question how steady it is."

She wanted to explore his mind, all the little nooks and crevices, and shine a light on the dusty corners he was unveiling when he threw in these tiny mentions of a past that didn't seem to match his disposition. But she didn't want to ruin the moment.

Instead, she stuck her tongue out. "I live on the floor below you. Trust me, I know."

"You find beauty in the small things," Nash said, and the tenderness in his eyes was unmistakable.

"Isn't that the only way to live? To find beauty in all moments?" Kiran asked.

And she couldn't help but find wonder in this one.

Chapter Eleven

NASH

These sparks of lightning between them, so quick and unpredictable, couldn't be in his head…could they?

Just as he'd feel awe at the brilliance and how they lit up his world, they would vanish. Nash couldn't gauge whether his mind was playing games or whether his heart was opening up to her—this girl, who had offered him nothing but kindness since they'd met, who loved video games and discovered epiphanies in the plainest of moments.

"What game do you want to play?" He had to change the subject so he wouldn't think about it anymore. He didn't want to ruin the day by pondering too much.

"Basketball, obviously."

Kiran's accent as she pronounced his favorite sport *bass-cut-bowl* was so endearing, he couldn't help but smile. He could have gotten tangled in the curves of her letters and the melody of her voice all day.

"You're, like…five-four. Do you even have basketball skills?"

"I'm competitive. That's all that matters."

"How do you figure?"

"A competitive person works to win. They're paying attention to how they play, and they practice until they score. I may not be the best right now, but I guarantee I'm more attentive to what I'm doing and whether it works than anyone else who takes things lightly."

"What if I'm competitive too?" All those years of trying to beat the odds had to count for something.

"Then we'll have a good game, won't we?"

"Is it a game if there's nothing to lose?"

"What are we betting?" She tilted her chin in defiance.

He thought about it for a second. This was the perfect opportunity to ask for a kiss or a date or be flirtatious...but a rope tightened around his heart, forcing him back, and his intuition warned him not to take advantage of this moment.

"Winner buys food for the rest of the day?"

Her face lit up. "Deal."

They loaded up on game credits and got ready.

"You know you're going to lose, right?" Kiran challenged.

"Did you just trash talk me?" Nash asked incredulously.

"I did."

"I don't even know what to say to you right now, but maybe when you're buying me my eighth bucket of french fries and you're down fifty bucks, you can think back to this moment."

They stared at each other, steel in their eyes and their hands on the buttons to release the basketballs from their prison at the top of the alley.

They pushed.

Of the eight basketballs in the cage, only six of Nash's came down the slide for him to shoot.

"Goddamn," he muttered to himself.

He snuck a glance at Kiran. All of her basketballs had come down, but rather than taking the time to aim and shoot, she was firing like a machine gun in the general direction of the basket, adjusting her force when the balls bounced off the backboard too hard or airballed.

"I think you have to aim," Nash said.

"I disagree," she shouted back, though they were standing next to each other.

"What's your logic?"

He shot three in a row, and only one made it in. The score was 8–4. How was she winning?

"Volume, not accuracy!"

He tried her technique, breaking habits from years of basketball practice in high school and pickup games in college to fire as quickly as possible without following through or waiting for the result.

He made two shots consecutively, and the score was 9–6.

The timer began to count down with ten seconds left on the clock. The basketballs they were now shooting stopped returning to them. Nash saw Kiran pick up speed in the corner of his eye with the balls she had left. A bead of sweat dripped from his forehead at his efforts to outshoot her, and his arms were heavy from his repetitions.

Beep!

11–9.

Kiran rubbed her arms like she was giving herself a hug and winced when she squeezed her shoulders.

"I'd say best out of three, but you might lose your arms," Nash teased.

"If you want to go again, we'll go," she said immediately, her face lighting up.

"You sure you can handle it?"

"Did you see the score? If you want to humiliate yourself again..."

As she made fun of him, her skin emitted a glow, like there were thousands of tiny fireflies casting a golden light on her.

Nash couldn't look away. Without a second thought, he stepped close and put his hands on hers, gently putting pressure on her shoulders over her own fingers.

Her eyes fluttered shut at his touch.

"You okay?" he murmured, simultaneously hoping she wasn't experiencing any achiness and wishing she would lean on him for a little longer.

She hummed in response, the way cats did when they purred in contentment.

The scent of musky roses, or incense, flooded him as he stood near her. For a fleeting second, he wondered what it'd be like to kiss her, to gently tug her ponytail back as he kissed her neck, and to pull her closer to him so there wasn't any room to separate them.

Her eyes opened suddenly, and she gasped—a strangled sound like she was shocked and couldn't breathe.

"I'm sorry," he stuttered, immediately withdrawing his hands and stepping back. "I didn't mean to make you feel uncomfortable."

"No... No, it's okay." She recovered. "We pushed a sore spot. I must be a lot more out of shape than I thought!"

Kiran's eyes had widened, but just as he registered her expression, it was gone. Nash wasn't sure how to respond, but his heart felt a longing to turn back time to ten seconds ago and freeze it to when he felt a peace he hadn't known he was missing.

Kiran, on the other hand, had bounced back and pasted an expression of contentment on her face.

"Are you sure you're okay?" He wasn't talking about the soreness.

"I'm fine, I promise." She touched his arm to reassure him, but when she let go, a void stayed between them.

He nodded, trying to smile and unable to speak.

"So," she said with a genuine smile on her face. "Bowling? With a side of french fries?"

Nash tried to recover the way she had. "Sounds great."

She brushed past him and began walking slowly to the bowling alley with her hands in the pockets of her jeans, wristlet dangling from her arm. Nash trailed behind, unsure what to say.

She turned on her heel, taking two steps backward slowly as she spoke. "So...about that basketball game."

"If you want me to say it out loud, fine... I lost. You won. I will feed you for the rest of the day and probably have to sell a kidney on the black market to afford it."

She laughed delightedly and shook her head.

"What?"

"I only made that bet with you because I wanted to win it—but you forgot the food was free today, didn't you?"

With that comment, all was back to forgotten.

Chapter Twelve

KIRAN

She shouldn't have recoiled when he touched her two weeks ago at the arcade. The truth was that she'd sunk into it, closed her eyes and imagined him holding her. She'd lost herself in the moment, being close to a man who oozed goodness, and had forgotten herself when she groaned.

But Ma had a habit of squeezing her shoulders after a hug, and something about that action had triggered Kiran's memory in a way that had her parents' faces slamming her out of her bliss.

She couldn't forget the look on Nash's face or the fact that she'd put it there. She didn't want to imagine how he'd react once she told him about her sister or that she couldn't date white guys, let alone fall in love with one.

Who knew if his heart beat a little faster when he saw her, the way hers had over the last week when she thought of seeing him again?

She had to pretend her growing attraction to him didn't exist. It simply wasn't there.

She didn't want to dwell on the way they were becoming routine parts of life to each other—their silly little texts and memes had become a seamless part of her day—because what would happen if it was taken away? But she also didn't want to find out what life would be like without his cheerful presence.

She knocked on Nash's door three times and waited.

Fake it until you make it, Kiran. If you don't think about it, it'll disappear.

A shuffle resounded on the other side, and footfalls creaked on the wooden floors as they came toward the door. Kiran wondered if her own footsteps were loud and if the person who lived underneath her could tell what she was up to if she was pacing her studio or skulking around her kitchen. She remembered the silly banter they'd had at Chelsea Piers about the sounds of their apartments.

She jumped as the door swung open, and Nash stood wearing a pair of jeans. He was shirtless.

"Oh…uh. Hey," Kiran stuttered. "Did I catch you at a bad time?"

"No, I was changing after work. Here, I'll grab a shirt."

Please don't. Kiran cleared her throat.

"Come on in. What's up?"

She stepped inside.

"I wanted to know if you wanted to take that Upper East Side walk with me."

As she spoke, she surveyed his place. It was smaller than hers. It hadn't been gutted and renovated, but the kitchen was new. And as colorful and full as Kiran's place was, Nash's was a diametrically opposite minimalistic space.

"I'd love to! I've been cooped up in the office all day. Let me use the bathroom and we can go."

His couch was black and had accent pillows—she guessed they came with the sofa—which were warm gray. His bedspread—*I wonder if it's comfortable to cuddle on*—was a black, gray, and white plaid print.

Photo frames were used sparingly—only two hung in the apartment, both in between the two windows. She stepped closer and looked at them—one of a woman who was middle-aged, curvy, and still held an aura of the beauty she must have worn in her prime, with her arm around Nash at his graduate school commencement, and another of a family and Nash dressed in matching baseball uniforms.

"That's my aunt Kate, and Brandon's family—the McGuires," Nash said, emerging from the small bathroom in the corner of the unit.

"Big baseball fans?"

"Nah, Dr. McGuire had a charity baseball game with his practice against another practice, and we all played. I wish I could say any of us were good, but Brandon wields a bat like a Flintstone, and the pitcher from the other team thought he was a major leaguer and kept trying to do us bodily injury with his pitches."

Kiran giggled. "I'm glad you survived the experience."

"It was close, but we made it."

Kiran turned her face to the photos again. "Your aunt looks kind."

"She's pretty great. Quirky. Fun. She called me last week talking about how she wants to take a road trip to see the world's largest things—world's largest sandwich, world's largest ketchup bottle, world's largest pizza."

"What was her reasoning?"

"That she was bored of the everyday, and she wanted to see life on a grand scale. I told her seeing life on a grand scale didn't apply to giant condiments and probably meant something like a trip to Vegas in a five-star hotel, but Kate likes to march to the beat of her own drum."

"I admire that," Kiran murmured. "So many people don't have the courage to really live life on their own terms. Think about our lists. We're young, capable, and energetic—and even we have so much we haven't done."

"Well, that's why we're changing that together, right?"

He slipped on his Converses and gestured at the door.

Kiran followed him out, wishing they could have spent more time in his apartment. She didn't know what it was—maybe being around the things familiar to him and being in his intimate space—but it made her feel special. It also prompted a longing in her to be able to get closer to him.

The pendulum swinging in her heart was on a wild ride, and she couldn't will it back to equilibrium or permanently stick it in the zone of friendship.

They walked to the Second Avenue subway station, making small talk about the restaurants in the area, and hopped on the train to Fifty-Ninth and Lexington.

"So I guess I should have asked this before. But why the Upper East Side?" Nash asked as he held onto the metal bar in the middle of the train car.

"You remember how we talked about different vibes in the city?"

"Yes."

"The Upper East Side vibe, at least along the river, makes me feel like I'm in Paris or something. I mean, I've never been to Paris, but what I imagine it'd be like. It's quieter. Sophisticated. My best friend, Payal, lives around here, and we've taken this walk a few different times, and every single time, I promise I'll come back and do it again."

"It must be pretty magical. I work up here, but I haven't taken the time to walk around much."

"I work over on Fifty-Seventh! I get it, though, the rigmarole of life...sometimes you don't get a chance to enjoy the things staring you in the face. I tell myself I'll come here on lunch all the time, but something always gets in the way."

"I'm glad we're doing this," Nash said earnestly.

"Me too." She gazed into his eyes, and the overwhelming surge of safety, of home, was too much.

She looked away quickly, pointing out that the next stop was theirs.

They walked in silence to the waterfront, winding their way along the pedestrian paths that crossed and uncrossed over FDR Drive.

It wasn't uncomfortable. But Kiran had the feeling Nash was in his head as much as she was in her own. Perhaps he needed the silence to sort out his thoughts.

It wasn't until they had crossed the bridge back to Eightieth Street that Nash finally spoke.

"If there was an Olympics for everyday activities, what would you win a gold medal in?"

She was so taken aback that she snorted. The grunting sound was so unexpected that Nash, who had apparently asked the question in total seriousness, let out a bellow of laughter.

Kiran couldn't help but join in, at first in embarrassed compensation for the awkwardness, and then in genuine mirth at the fact that Nash had slouched forward, his hands on his knees. The harder he laughed, the more genuine her laughter became.

"Where the hell do you come up with these things?" she asked, wiping tears off her cheeks.

Nash rested his hands on his waist, still chortling. "My guidance counselor in high school had these icebreaker cards. Now I use them in my practice. I have all sorts of things I do to get to know people. Icebreaker cards. Games. Trivia. Human knots."

"Yes, nothing like getting people to open up by ambushing

them with a question about their daily Olympics." She checked the back of her hand to make sure her mascara hadn't run.

"That's exactly the point! You catch them at a vulnerable spot, and then it prompts conversation."

"And I looked vulnerable?"

"No, but you looked like you were in your head."

It was like he read her thoughts.

Kiran let out a soft whistle. "Okay...then I'd win the gold medal in organization."

"You do have a lot of stuff in that apartment of yours. I imagine it wouldn't fit if it were disorganized."

"Oh, shut up. It is all about old habits. My dad was a neat freak. Now I am. Lists. Plans. Graphs. I like step-by-step actions and thoughts."

"I mean, seeing as we're literally on a walk because you created a list...I can understand that."

"Don't hate. What fad did you never really understand?" Kiran asked.

"Oh, you're playing my game now?"

"I figure you deserve a taste of your own medicine."

"Okay, then I never understood the full denim look. Or guys getting highlights or bleaching the tips of their hair. Or maybe the Backstreet Boys and NSYNC."

"If you say that again, I will wash your mouth out with soap."

"Please. They weren't any good!"

"So basically, you didn't understand the entire '90s?"

"Essentially, yes. Humanity hit a low point."

"We can agree to disagree."

The ruins of the old smallpox hospital from the early twentieth century rose eerily from Roosevelt Island. Kiran gave an imperceptible squirm at the idea of spirits who had died too early watching them as they walked with the sun setting on the west side of Manhattan.

"What's the cutest animal you can think of? And the ugliest?"

"The cutest is a baby tiger or a baby elephant. They look so innocent. Baby elephants, especially—did you know they throw temper tantrums? Oh, and the ugliest is a blobfish."

"I think you made that one up."

"I did not! Look it up on your phone!" She stopped and pointed at him.

He fished his phone out of his pocket and typed "blobfish" in Google.

"Oh, dear God! That's awful!" He stuck the phone out away from him and X'd the window.

"I told you it's real. Quite gross, right?"

"I'll have nightmares." He shuddered.

"How did you meet your best friend? Brandon, right?"

"Right. We went to the same school. We sat next to each other in kindergarten. That sums it up."

"You guys have been best friends your whole lives, and you summed it up with a single sentence?" Kiran smacked her forehead.

"I wish there was a—I don't know—romantic or bromantic story behind it, but I think I asked him for a crayon. It wasn't particularly monumental…though our friendship certainly is."

"Fair point."

"Before you make a call, do you rehearse what you're going to say?"

Kiran scratched her chin. "Yes. I'm not someone who likes to be unprepared or caught off guard. Obviously, it happens, but important conversations… I'm definitely someone who thinks about what to say beforehand."

"I have a little experience catching you off guard."

A little? Kiran thought to herself. *You've caught me off guard since the day we met, Nash Hawthorne.*

"I mean, I've flustered you before between asking you to dinner and...things like that."

In that moment, she knew they both were reflecting back to Chelsea Piers and that touch.

She cleared her throat. "Oh, I have a good one!"

"Fire away."

"What would be a great sport to watch if the athletes were drunk?"

Nash crinkled his nose. "And you ask me where I come up with this stuff?"

Kiran shrugged.

"Curling."

"What?"

"Brooms everywhere. Ice. Granite stones. It's kind of a recipe for disaster, but watching people hit each other with brooms while inebriated would be really funny."

Kiran giggled at the image of an Olympic team swinging brooms over their shoulders or tripping over them.

"If you could go anywhere and do anything, what would it be?"

"Wow, that's a good question."

"You didn't tell me everything added to your list before. And we know each other better now."

"This is true. But it wasn't on my list. Your question caught me off guard..."

"Well, let's hear it."

"I want to play with an elephant in Thailand. I know there's some ethical implications of that, but in my head, it's an ideal world and the baby elephants—because as I said, they are the cutest—need cuddles. I want to be a mom. I want to dance for all of Navratri, in Gujarat—"

"Sorry, what's that?"

"Nine holy nights in Hinduism. Good triumphed over evil. It's celebrated for different reasons in various parts of India, but Gujarat, this state in north India, has nightly dances with sticks called dandiya. They dance in concentric circles, and each circle does different steps. You can move between them, learn as you go, and dance for hours. It's colorful and bright and spirited. I would love to celebrate it authentically."

"That sounds beautiful."

"I imagine it is..." Her voice trailed off. "I want to see a cricket match live in Mumbai."

"People watch cricket?"

"You're such a hater, American."

"I'm not hating! I didn't know."

"Cricket is one of the world's most-played sports."

"That can't be." Nash scoffed.

"It is."

"Well, I guess you learn something new every day. What else?"

"I want to drive a Volkswagen Beetle across the country, like one of those pop stars from the nineties on a road trip. I'd like to see my sister again—" She stopped short.

Nash didn't miss that last one. He frowned at her. "What do you mean?"

What do I say? she shrieked internally. Her eyes widened, then darted to Roosevelt Island across the river—anything to avoid looking at his face.

For all her bluster about being prepared and about having rehearsed conversations, she hadn't expected to verbally vomit that she hadn't seen Kirti in years. And if she opened Pandora's box on this beautiful starry night, the monsters from her past would fly out and the light from the stars may never be seen with Nash again.

When Gandhi preached honesty and truth, Kiran, he didn't mean white lies, her conscience scolded her, but it didn't matter. She was speaking before she could ruminate on it for too long.

"I haven't seen her in a while."

"Why not?" came the inevitable question.

"Oh, you know. Family drama. I'm a woman of mystery, Nash, remember?"

Nash frowned slightly at her forced nonchalance but then smiled. "Indeed."

But it was a lie that humiliated her. Not only had she omitted the truth about Kirti's leaving the family, but she had thrown her family on the fire, making it sound like the most heartbreaking decision of her parents' lives was only a little drama. She hated that she burned the very thing she loved most to preserve a relationship...no, not even a relationship, a friendship that she had for a month and a half.

Then again...her family *was* torn apart in dramatic fashion, wasn't it? It wasn't a total lie. And someone in America, the land of the free, may not understand the complexities behind what happened.

"I'm really sorry," Nash said, his brows knit in a frown. "That must be hard."

"It is."

Kiran's mind went to her sister in India and wondered what she was up to, how she had chosen love over family, and what she'd say to her if they reunited.

Chapter Thirteen

NASH

Across from them, the tip of Roosevelt Island showed off its lighthouse. Beyond it, Astoria was on display, buffering the island and showing off parks of its own. Towers punctuated the landscape. The Robert F. Kennedy Bridge seemed to move with headlights of cars zooming across it.

Nash beckoned Kiran to a bench overlooking the breathtaking view. To their backs, a park still held remnants of action from visitors. Dogs played in the dog park, and the distant sound of basketballs bouncing against the court echoed among the buildings around them.

Nash exhaled deeply and shot a glance at Kiran.

Her hands were in her pockets, and she sat a couple of feet away from him. Her legs crossed at the knees, and she gazed out at the river. Her shoulders hunched.

"Penny for your thoughts?"

"You may ask for a refund." She offered a tight-lipped smile.

"Are you tired? We've walked around thirty blocks tonight."

"A little. Are you tired? Do you want to head back?"

No, Nash wanted to say, *I'd rather spend the night here with you.*

But he bobbed his head. "We have a rooftop deck, right?"

"Yes. I haven't been up there much, but it's nice!"

"Want to grab some beers and chill there for a bit?"

"Sure."

"Cab's on me. Let's get home."

A half hour later, she had procured beers from her fridge and brought them up for them.

"Akash left them at my place a while back. He's forgotten by now, I promise you."

The rooftop had wicker furniture grouped around tables in a surprisingly cozy atmosphere. No one else from the building was up there.

They settled into two chairs across from each other. Kiran slid her Toms off and crossed her legs, her bare feet tucked underneath her knees. Nash extended his legs out on the table in front of them.

There was intimacy here, the two of them in a smaller space, sharing a drink that decreased inhibition and heightened emotion. And when Kiran's hair moved in the breeze, he wondered, not for the first time, what it would be like to run his fingers in it and see the black run across his skin.

"So tell me about your family, since I've talked about mine," Kiran proposed. "No siblings for you, right?"

What. A. Buzzkill.

"Nope. It was just me and my mom growing up." That was a bit of a stretch, because Nash had largely grown up alone, but it seemed like the simplest explanation.

"You must be close."

"Oh." Now Nash squirmed. "Not so much."

Kiran waited. But Nash didn't elaborate.

For a summer night on a rooftop, the temperature around them had unexpectedly hit subzero and not for the first time that night.

A beat passed between them. Nash couldn't meet Kiran's eyes, and he could sense that she was looking anywhere but at his face.

"Well…it looks like it was my turn to make things awkward," Kiran said after a few moments, offering him a small smile. "I'm sorry if I hit a sore spot."

Nash shifted his weight. "It's not a sore spot. It's a…it's a void. She's gone."

"Tell me, Nash."

Maybe it was the alcohol. She said his name like a tender lullaby, and it disarmed him completely. He was unused to endearments and softness.

And her eyes—how had he not noticed the depth? Until he'd looked at Kiran's eyes, brown had always been a shade so dark that details didn't exist…but now, even in the muted lights of the city, he saw her irises cast light like whiskey bottles in sunlight or honey fresh from the comb. Clear. And deeper than he'd ever imagined.

"My mom," he said, his voice croaking on the words. It had been so long since he said them. "My dad… Sorry, I don't know where to start."

"The beginning," she said gently. She put her beer on the ground and leaned in a few inches.

Nash took a deep breath, willing himself to think back to twenty-five years ago, when his first memories came to the surface.

"My dad was amazing," he started. "I guess every kid thinks so, but he was a nice guy. My parents were young when they got married. Just out of high school, I think. My mom got pregnant immediately afterward. Maybe beforehand. She worked as a receptionist, and he was a mechanic who tinkered in shop class and got himself a job at a beat-up auto shop. They had me, and I like to think they were happy for a while.

"Then my mom lost her job…and she couldn't get another one because most people required college degrees—and who would want to hire a teenager with a baby and no degree when they could have someone educated, reliable, and single? My parents had bought a really small trailer to live in, and my dad was struggling to pay the bills, I guess, on one income.

"The story gets muddled here. I don't know what's fact and what's speculation."

He looked at Kiran, who was hanging on his words, and was mollified when she didn't look away. Her eyes were trained on his face, unmoving and fortifying him.

"My aunt Kate says my mom got bored being a stay-at-home mom and got back together with some of her high school friends, who were all in a partying phase. My dad, who already couldn't afford a house, a wife, and a kid, couldn't handle the partying. My mom said my dad fell out of love with her. All I remember is them fighting and the door slamming, and my mom leaning up against it and crying. I haven't seen him since."

"Nash," Kiran sighed sadly and imperceptibly shook her head.

"Eventually, we lost the trailer. We moved into a rough neighborhood. I…"

"You what?"

"I stole. I mean…I didn't think it was stealing at the time, but my mom had me ask neighbors for lunch money. She'd take my hand and hold onto my shoulders and mention to the neighbors that she'd be paid Friday from her gig at the gas station, but she needed to buy me a sandwich. And she'd collect all this money, and we'd still go hungry. I'm not sure what she did with it, but I know I wasn't getting any sandwiches with it. Maybe it went toward alcohol."

Kiran's hands made a sudden movement, as though they were about to fly to her mouth, but she forced them into place on her lap.

"It wasn't all bad. I had Brandon and his family…and my aunt Kate, my mom's sister, who tried to help her." At the mention of Kate's name, Nash couldn't help but grin. "She took care of me. Ice cream trips. School shopping. Doughnuts for every time I came home with good grades. I'd find ten dollars with Post-it notes in my backpack all the time. I think my mom knew about those, but she didn't touch them. They were my special gifts, and for all her flaws, she respected that.

"And my mom tried. Eventually, she sobered up for a while. She tried to come to some of my basketball games. She asked me if I wanted to go to college someday when she realized I was at the top of my class."

"Did she try and help you?" Kiran asked. "My dad didn't go to college, but he'd come home with information about schools, and I'm not sure where he even got it from."

Nash nodded, letting out a chuckle. "She actually spoke to one of my counselors, I think. He called me into his office in tenth grade, saying he'd gotten calls every day that he needed to meet with me and tell me what my options were, even though counselors were scheduled to do that during junior year anyway.

"Junior year rolls around. She's doing okay, my mom. She's got a job at a restaurant as a waitress. She works long hours, but she seems happier. Turns out, she's seeing this guy. She's excited about him, you know? Like her face glowed for the first time in my life and her skies were blue. She seemed more energetic, tried to cook more often, spent time at home talking to me. She got thinner, put on more makeup, and took care of how she looked. She had so much energy. We got closer."

Nash's words were coming faster now, as though he was watching a reel of his life spinning in front of his eyes. He was taken back to various ages in his life: five, ten, sixteen, seventeen, eighteen, like a train running out of control and heading toward a destination that he couldn't go back and change but that he didn't want to think about.

"I found the needles, spoon, and drugs in her drawer when I was looking for cash for milk. It was in this tin box...those cookie boxes you get for Christmas with those awful store-made short-bread cookies? It was green. I don't know why I remember that.

"I confronted her. Told her I didn't want to live with a junkie. That I didn't want to lose her. That we were finally on our feet and I was proud of us. She promised she'd get clean and that she'd break up with the boyfriend who had gotten her into it. And for a while, it seemed like she was on the up and up. I'd check the dresser sometimes and other places in her bedroom, and there was nothing to be found.

"I got into Vanderbilt. The funny thing is, I didn't tell her first. I told Brandon's family and Kate. They wanted to celebrate, but I really wanted to tell my mom. It felt like I'd finally done it...like I'd beaten the odds and maybe I could lift us out of this with a little more hard work. We could live in a nicer apartment. I could have a bed that wasn't pushed up against a wall in the living room. We'd be able to afford a car if I graduated with my degree.

"I came home with this giant envelope, and there she was at the table, with that goddamn cookie tin." His voice grew hard.

"Oh, Nash, I'm so sorry. What did you do?" Kiran whispered.

"I just silently slid the envelope across the table. I don't even remember what I said—*if* I said anything at all. I stared at her. She cried and told me she'd get help. I stayed with Brandon's family for a few months while she went to a rehab facility that his dad recommended.

"By the time she'd gotten back, I was into my senior year and working at Dr. McGuire's—Brandon's dad's—medical practice as an assistant. Basically, I ran and got him things, made coffee, cleaned up. I was saving up for college. She was clean. Graduation was approaching.

"I asked her to come to graduation sober and to be proud of what we'd done, because we hadn't let life's shit get to us and we'd made it this far. I remember how happy she looked. She smiled and told me she loved me and that it would be an honor to come to my high school graduation and she couldn't wait to see me walk across the stage at my college commencement either. We joked we'd go to Disney World when I did that, on our first family vacation with the two of us—like a redo of the time we went with my dad. A do-over."

Pain scratched lines into Nash's face as he spoke. "It was about a week before our ceremony. We'd finished finals and the rest of the school was taking theirs, so we had a few days off where all the seniors would goof off. We had picnics, parties, field trips... Brandon and I had gotten back from a friend's bash, and I needed my swim trunks for a trip to the pool.

"When Brandon pulled up to the housing complex, there were police cars at the apartment, and one of the cops was speaking to Kate. She was teary, trying to explain that my mom had called her and sounded out of it, apologizing for something and saying my name over and over.

"I don't even remember pushing past the police trying to get in the door, but I unlocked the apartment, and there she was."

Kiran's lips had parted, and her hands were clasped as though she were praying—but Nash knew prayers were too late now. They were too late even back then.

"She was on the kitchen floor. She'd been dead a couple of hours. An overdose."

Kiran's hands flew to her face, her skin pale in the night. "Nash…"

He shook his head. "It was a long time ago."

But he closed his hands into fists and crossed his arms, certain he could still feel his mother's cooling skin on his fingertips and the paramedic's hands on his shoulder as they pushed him away and tried to resuscitate her. The tiled roof around him transformed into cheap linoleum kitchen flooring, and he was no longer a thirty-year-old man but eighteen, a week before his graduation, with the echoes of Kate's cries howling in his ears. He stared into space, recalling how his mother's eyes had done the same thing—still, unmoving, and blank…and maybe even a little relieved.

Arms around him brought him back to the rooftop in Manhattan.

"I'm so sorry," Kiran whispered into his shoulder. "I'm so sorry."

He hugged her back, resting his hands on the curve of her waist.

"It was a long time ago," he whispered again.

"You're here now," she said as she pulled back and searched his face.

Despite the pinpricks behind his eyes, ones that he knew he wouldn't give in to—he never had—he wasn't broken. Kiran was right.

He was here.

He was alive. He'd made it through Vanderbilt. And while the loss of his mother wasn't one he spoke about often, as he felt Kiran's hands on the back of his neck as she hugged him again, he couldn't think of a single place he would have rather been.

Chapter Fourteen

KIRAN

Kiran opened one eye blearily, the other side of her face still smushed against her pillow, and glanced at the alarm clock on her bedside table.

She was old school—no cell phones until she'd woken up, brushed her teeth, showered, did her pooja, and sat with a cup of chai. She didn't need technology ruining her routine. A basic Harry Potter alarm clock would do the job.

But it was Saturday...so getting up later than "the ass crack of dawn," as Sonam would put it, was acceptable.

She sighed, half closing her eyes again. The temptation of another few minutes underneath her covers was drawing her in... And then the vague voice that speaks just as one drifts off reminded her what date it was.

Her eyes opened. The sleep, which had tugged at her eyelids and gently pulled them shut, vanished like smoky vapors in the night.

Sitting up in bed, her nightshirt slipping off her shoulders, she clasped her hands in her lap.

August 15.

"Happy birthday, Didi," she whispered.

She closed her eyes and willed her hushed message to go to India, to be heard in her sister's heart, wherever she was. Kiran hoped that DNA was stronger than a double helix—that it could serve as a connection that transcended continents and years. Maybe even lifetimes.

A memory came to her in that moment like a deafening roar of thunder.

"Didi, why are there fireworks today?"

The terrace of the house was hot on Kiran's small feet, even at night, but she didn't want to miss a moment of the sky lighting up in colored sparks.

"It's Indian Independence Day, Kiran. But, Chottu, do you want to know a secret?" her big sister asked, using Kiran's nickname—an endearment that meant she was the littlest.

She slid off her flip-flops and helped Kiran slide them on instead.

"Yes, yes! Tell me a secret!" Five-year-old Kiran hopped up and down.

"The fireworks are really because it's my birthday," Kirti whispered in her little sister's ear.

"Really?"

"And you want to know another secret? You'll do lots of big things, and Mama and Baba and I will celebrate you too. It'll be like we did tonight with sweets and balloons...maybe bigger!"

Kiran smiled softly to herself. It had been twenty-three years since that birthday, and she still thought of her sister as the reason fireworks went off on August 15.

Then another memory came to her.

She was older now. Ten, maybe.

"Baba, fireworks!" she shouted.

She raced upstairs to the terrace on top of their tiny house, where she had stood with her sister five years ago. Kirti's face was already fading over the years, but without fail, on her birthday, Kiran would remember the fireworks were for her.

She startled when she saw Baba standing next to her.

"Why don't you call Ma up too, Baba? Doesn't she want to see?"

"She gets sad on this day, beta. It's better to let her be."

As she observed her father's face, lighting up and plunging into darkness from the lights in the sky, she noticed a tear trickling down his cheek. She reached up on her tiptoes and touched his face.

He gazed down at her, a gentle smile playing at his lips. "Always taking care of us."

"Do you miss her too, Baba?"

"Every day, Kiran." He stared into the distance, his eyes empty and brimming at the same time. "But now my responsibility is to you."

He pulled her close to his side, and they watched the rest of the fireworks in silence.

Kiran had thought of Kirti more and more often lately.

What did she look like? Did she have any children? Was Kiran an aunt all these years but unable to celebrate birthdays, good grades, Diwali, and the start of summer with her nieces or nephews? Did her parents ever forgive their older daughter?

Nash had mentioned that his aunt had bought doughnuts every time he brought home good grades. Would Kiran have taken laddoos to their houses or gone to India more often to see them?

Even more than wondering about what life would have looked

like had they taken a different path, she often questioned how Kirti had come to her decision to marry the man she fell in love with. How she made the choice to leave the family for good. How she decided it was worth her parents' pain to chase her own happiness.

If she admitted it to herself, Kiran was mad too—mad at the fact that she lived life by the book because of her sister's mistake. Angry that her whole life had been planned based on making her parents happy because they'd already seen the worst and she never wanted them to experience it again. And ashamed when she thought of all her parents gave her, did for her, sacrificed for her, so that she could succeed.

But she wasn't so angry that she wouldn't check in on her parents.

"Hello, Kiran?"

"Ma, how are you?"

Kiran could hear firecrackers in the background, despite the pleas of politicians not to pollute the atmosphere further.

"Good...good," Ma said, subdued. "How are you?"

"I'm doing well. I was thinking of you and wanted to see how you and Baba were."

"Oh, Baba is fine. Here, you can talk to him if you'd like."

Kiran sighed, her heart aching for her mom and the silent pain she must have felt with every celebratory explosion outside.

"Kiran, Beta," Baba's voice came on the line. He was quiet, and Kiran had to press the phone to her ear. "How is the city? How is work?"

"Both are great. Is Ma okay?"

"She—" He hesitated. "You know how it is."

"Baba, have you ever thought about reaching out to her?" The question spilled out before she could stop it.

Baba remained quiet. If the fireworks hadn't gone off in the background, Kiran wouldn't have known he was on the other end of the line.

"Baba?"

"Let sleeping dogs lie, jaan."

"But if you just—"

"We let her go. She left. There is nothing we can do."

Baba's tone had turned curt, and Kiran knew not to push the typically levelheaded man any further.

"Okay. I'm thinking of you guys."

"We're always thinking of you too. The one consolation we have on this day is that you will always follow our rules."

Kiran closed her eyes. "Yes, Baba. Always."

"Go enjoy your day, Kiran. We'll talk to you soon."

The click sounded, and Kiran dropped the phone on the bed next to her.

"Argh!" she bellowed.

Silence resounded back. She whipped the covers off herself, letting a blast of cool air hit her.

Anyone up? She texted the CMC. I'm in my head and I need to get out.

Working, came Sonam's reply.

It's nine a.m. Go back to bed and sleep it off. Akash was a notorious late riser.

I'll meet you for coffee at the Starbucks by my place in an hour, Payal responded.

"So…what happened after?" Payal asked when they met up.

Kiran had recapped the night last week when she and Nash sat on the roof, telling her friend how he'd opened up about his mother but omitting the details—it wasn't her story to tell.

"We spent the rest of the night talking," Kiran said. "About how his friend Brandon's family is like his own. About how his aunt Kate got married later in life because she was so independent, and also because she always wanted to be around for him. We talked about how he loves brussels sprouts and how I hate the way cauliflower smells when it's boiled."

"Kiran, tell me something. Seriously. No filter. Do you want Nash? Do you like him?"

Putting it into the universe—saying it out loud—was more real than the very same question Kiran had been asking herself before bed, every time she was about to see Nash, and sometimes at random moments during her day.

She *couldn't* want Nash. Her sister was literally disowned for falling in love with the man of her choosing. How could she bear to make the same choice, knowing what consequences lay ahead—not only for her but for her aging parents who only had one child left to make their dreams come true?

Love was dangerous. And while some could argue that *like* wasn't quite the same or as risky and that perhaps she was due for some fun, Kiran knew better. She was nearly thirty, ready to settle down, and she didn't want to waste her time on *like*. If she wanted anything, it was to love deeply—and Nash couldn't be that person.

And Baba… His heart was already frail after facing the weight of giving up a child and years of trying to stay afloat. She owed it to her parents not to screw up, not to fall for someone different, and instead to do exactly what was expected of her. If she didn't, the results could quite literally break Baba's heart. He told her this morning that he trusted her to follow the rules, for God's sake.

But the idea of following the rules, of ending up with someone who didn't breathe life into her the way Nash had didn't settle with her.

Could Nash be that person?

Nash lit sparks inside her. There was an acceptance in him for all her traits that she hadn't experienced with anyone. Even the men she had gone on dates with didn't seem quite as interested in her, their eyes wandering as she spoke of home, ready to move on to the next American thing without being able to love where they'd come from. Nash didn't even have parents, yet he was thankful about the things he did have and approached new experiences as ones to learn from. Who wouldn't want that in their lives?

She was falling for him and she knew it. And while she thought he might feel the same growing sparks, she didn't know for certain. Certainty had always been something she needed.

Despite the stab of disappointment at the idea that perhaps he didn't feel anything for her, she couldn't ignore the hope it inspired too. It would make life so much easier. There would be no confusion.

"Kiran...you're in a different galaxy." Payal snapped her fingers in front of Kiran's face.

"Sorry." She blinked a couple of times.

"Tell me."

"You know, I shared with him that we had lists of things to do, and he's the one who encouraged me to add to mine."

"And?"

"He wrote one too. And we ended up expanding them and doing things together."

"And in that time, in those moments when you were ticking off things you'd always wanted to do but never had the courage or time or guts to do, did you look at him and think that he'd make a good person to keep trying new things with? Like...love?"

"There were other four-letter words involved."

Payal laughed. "I hope 'fuck' was one of them."

Now it was Kiran's turn to giggle. "Not quite in the context you're thinking. More like 'Fuck, what am I doing?'"

"And what are you going to do? And don't say 'What *can* I do?' because that's a cop-out. You do have options. You don't want to see them."

"Payal, if I tell him I like him, then I'm fucked. If I don't, my heart grows more burdened with keeping it to myself."

"Then unburden it...and don't worry so much about the future. You're worrying what happens if you fall in love and get married. You're thinking twelve steps ahead."

"That's what I do."

"I know. I'm reminding you to stay present."

"How?"

"See where it goes. Worry later. See how this plays out. Whether he feels the same... I wager he does, but guys are funny, so spend time with him. You might notice he's worth fighting for... and if he isn't, then he wasn't meant for you."

It seemed so simple wrapped up like that. And despite her gut telling her that she was a mess, Kiran tried to believe it was.

A week later, Kiran stretched out at her desk. She'd spent her Saturday morning at the office, tying up some loose ends from the week, and her stomach gave a rumble resembling a small earthquake.

"Yikes," she mumbled to herself.

Her favorite Indian restaurant was in Midtown, and she could stop there for a brunch special, but her taste buds were craving something different today. The weather was a balmy eighty degrees, and she didn't want to waste a minute of sunshine being inside for any longer than she had to.

Hit with an idea, she wondered if any of the CMC was free to meet but realized that Sonam was at the hospital, Payal was flying back to London to spend a long weekend with her grandmother, and Akash had his sister's Kathak dance recital to attend.

Nash.

His name came to mind like a flash of lightning. She *had* promised him good food. It'd been a week since they spent the night on their roof deck, and as much as she didn't want to admit it, she missed him.

> Kiran: On a scale of 1 to "I ate my arm three hours ago," how hungry are you?
> Nash: Hey, stranger! Long time, no talk…and my stomach is growling. Why?

Kiran's heart felt warm at his greeting.

> Kiran: Smorgasburg?
> Nash: Gesundheit?

Kiran didn't see that reaction coming, and she burst out laughing.

> Kiran: It's the food festival that happens every Saturday in Brooklyn. It's on my list. Want to go?
> Nash: Sold.
> Kiran: Meet you there in an hour?

Upon his agreement, Kiran packed up her bag and made a stop at the restroom to check her appearance. She hardly ever came to the office without dressing appropriately and having a dash of makeup on. The work environment automatically made her feel as though she needed to be professional at all times, even on the weekends.

She pulled a hairbrush from her bag and gently ran it through her hair, smoothing it out with a tiny bit of coconut oil from the bottle she carried. She glossed over her lips with a nude-tinted balm and tucked her white shirt into her flowing summer skirt crisply before heading toward the elevator.

Two subway rides later, she was waiting for Nash at their agreed-upon meeting spot in the middle of a giant crowd. It seemed like all of Manhattan had the same idea as she did.

"There are probably more people here than live in all of Nashville." She heard a chuckle from behind her.

"Nash!" Without thinking twice, she wrapped her arms around his neck and pulled him close for a hug.

"Hi! Thanks for inviting me. This was a great idea!"

"It looks like half the city is here. It's been ages since we've seen this happen."

Scents of food from various parts of the world wafted through the air, making her mouth water. Indian. Ethiopian. Colombian. Spanish. Persian. Every corner of the world was represented.

"So should I try Indian food here?" Nash asked.

Kiran considered it. "No...we'll save that for a special occasion. But let's try everything else!"

"Do I want a fried spaghetti doughnut?"

"Don't knock it until you try it. Those things are surprisingly good."

"Wow, you really are a foodie, aren't you?"

"Whatever. A girl should have a good appetite to do all she does."

"Okay, I can't disagree there." Nash put his hands up in surrender.

"I guess tasting all these different cuisines is my way of exploring the world and fulfilling childhood dreams."

"You didn't have a lot of variety in India?"

"Well, you have to remember I grew up in a rural area when I was young, and back then, there wasn't quite as much globalization. Indo-Chinese food wasn't unusual, but our family couldn't afford it, and everything else didn't become popular until the internet hit and the world got smaller."

"I never thought about that. I've always been used to having all these different things at my fingertips...though we couldn't really afford to eat out much, and I was a free-lunch kid."

"A free-lunch kid?" Kiran frowned.

"Yes, it means you fall below a certain income line and the school gives you free lunches and sometimes breakfasts."

"Wow. In India, if you couldn't afford certain things, you just didn't go to school. I was lucky we made ends meet, but there were plenty of children who never attended, especially in villages."

"It's sad that it's so different between countries and, at the same time, not different at all."

"Women and children are often the victims of societal failures, right?"

Nash nodded.

"Well, now that I've thoroughly succeeded in making this a depressing day...want to eat?" Kiran asked.

Nash threw his head back and laughed. "Trust me, you are the least depressing person. You're on."

Their world tour began with Ethiopia and ended with all-American ice cream. Nash even allowed Kiran to pay for half the stalls, placing orders at most of them based on her recommendation. She was sure he'd learned from the last time they'd gone to dinner.

"Here," he said, handing her a cookie-dough ice cream cone and holding his own chocolate brownie.

As she took it, her fingertips brushed against his hand. They closed around the cone, but Nash didn't move his hand. Their eyes locked, and the heat from his body felt like she'd sprung a fever, despite holding ice cream.

Her breath stuck in her throat. And when he released her hand, it sucked back into her lungs in one fell swoosh.

Kiran could feel the tingles he left there long after they found a picnic table.

"Ugh..." Kiran groaned. "I can't finish this."

She pulled the ice cream away from her lips and set her hand on the table, feeling nauseated. She had gotten through precisely half the ice cream before calling it quits.

"I'll finish it." Nash took the cone and licked it.

Kiran spotted his tongue and wondered what else it could do. Heat rose up her chest.

"How can you eat so much?" she asked, trying to distract her mind from the dirty thoughts it had.

"Seeing as you're a foot shorter than I am and probably half my weight, I feel like that question answers itself." Nash grinned, polishing off the last of the cone.

They stood, stretching to accommodate the giant meals they'd eaten.

"Hey! First off, not a foot shorter. I'm five four, and you are, at most, six feet tall. Secondly, you are nowhere near 250 pounds, so quit your sassy attitude."

"Should we prove that theory?"

"How—what? Nash!"

Before she knew it, Nash had scooped her over his shoulder and started walking toward an open space.

"Put me down!" She giggled. "Okay, you've proven your point!"

"Say it loud... I'm a monster!" Nash yelled in jest.

"You're a big, muscly monster!" She laughed, her belly against his shoulder.

He set her down and hunched over, his hands on his knees. "Okay, this big, muscly monster is not strong."

Kiran was hunched over too but in mirth. She'd seen Payal act this openly flirtatious with guys before, but she never thought she would be so carefree with someone, allowing them to grab her in public and play with her as if she were a toy that could be tossed around at will.

It was empowering.

But as she looked around, she caught the eye of an aunty wearing a sari, surrounded by her family. The disapproval on the elderly woman's face was enough to make Kiran feel shame in being so brazen. And she had to wonder, against her better judgment, whether she would feel as uncomfortable if Nash were Indian.

Chapter Fifteen

NASH

Kiran had stopped midlaugh, and Nash gazed at her, observing her serious face and wondering what she was thinking. She had a strong nose, sort of like those Roman statues that he'd seen in books. Her jawline was square underneath lips that were delicate against her other features, balancing them out. Her mouth fell into a pout when her smile faded, like the duck face girls sometimes posed with in photographs, except that she never put any effort into it.

Had he crossed a line? Again?

She had seemed comfortable, and his playful actions were something he'd never thought twice about before with other girl friends or girlfriends.

"You okay?"

She jumped. "I totally had a girl moment where I wondered if I turned off my curling iron!"

"You burned your apartment down, didn't you?" He knew Kiran was the type to triple-check whether she'd turned off her appliances.

"No big deal if I did." She shrugged. "I mean, it's only every single one of my possessions I've collected since I moved to the United States."

"Not a big deal at all. I'd offer you my place, but in this hypothetical situation, my apartment has burned down along with yours. Good work."

"Guess we're sharing a cardboard box together then." There it was again. That twinkle in her eye that made his heart skip a beat.

He had a vision in his mind of Kiran wearing a tee and shorts around his kitchen. The thought of her curvy legs with her brown skin exposed turned him on unexpectedly.

Kiran's eyes remained on his face, and Nash imagined currents flowing between them. He questioned whether he was losing his mind or whether she felt them too.

Then her mouth curved upward, and his gut lurched like it was taking a victory lap.

"Do you want to walk across the Brooklyn Bridge?" She gestured in the direction of the water with her head.

"Honestly, if it helps me stop feeling as if I've got a belly like a Teletubby...I'll do it." Nash tried to exhale but felt like his entire body was stuffed with spaghetti doughnuts.

"It's on your list. Also, what's a Teletubby?" Kiran asked as they started walking through Williamsburg.

Nash's mouth dropped open. "Please tell me you're kidding."

The blank expression on her face told him she wasn't.

"Oh my gosh! Kiran, I feel like you missed a giant part of childhood or something."

"Is it like *Sesame Street*?"

"Okay, now I feel a little better. Did you have a television growing up?"

"Nope."

"Now you're completely off the hook. The Teletubbies are

these cute, awkward alien creatures that make weird noises and talk to children."

Kiran stared at him. "That sounds so creepy. I don't actually ever want my children to watch a show like that."

Nash burst out laughing. "I can't blame you. It's more of a pop culture reference now than anything kids watch."

"If it makes you feel better, I learned about *Sesame Street* because I screamed after being accosted by Elmo in Times Square."

"That guy is creepy! Also, why does he charge five dollars for a photograph?"

"The fact that you know he charges five dollars for a photograph makes me question what I'm doing hanging out with you."

"Honestly, I was wondering why you hung out with me too."

Kiran finally broke their mile-a-minute banter by giggling. "Must be your good looks."

Warmth spread from Nash's heart to his extremities. Girls had told him he was good-looking before... He was somewhat tall, and he was blessed with good teeth. But none of those compliments had ever quite reached him the way an offhand remark from Kiran did.

What is going on with you, dude?

Brandon's voice from the other week rang through his mind: *I was having fun until I met her.*

Nash couldn't say for certain that life had completely transformed since he met Kiran. Love didn't work that quickly, as far as he knew. *Like* didn't even work that way. But a small seed had been planted inside him by Kiran's presence, one that prompted him to notice more beauty around him and feel a little happier. That was enough for him for now.

For now.

"I love this view," Kiran murmured as they stood in the middle of the pedestrian walk on the Brooklyn Bridge.

Here was the famed view on all the postcards of Manhattan. But Nash didn't think any of them did it justice. Beyond the brown brick, the crowds of people, the traffic flowing beneath them, and the cables crisscrossing in a hatch across the arches was the east skyline of the city.

The buildings on the south side of the island reminded Nash of an M. C. Escher painting, staggered and piled on top of one another. Rooflines appeared to collide, and various heights of skyscrapers contrasted against one another.

On the right of the bridge was the East Village and beyond. Nash could see Roosevelt Island, with its famed tramway. The river sparkled underneath them and on the left side, the Statue of Liberty raised her famous arm, welcoming anyone who wanted to seek solace here.

What a beautiful day to be alive.

"You're captivated," Kiran said at the observation of his open mouth and wide eyes.

Captivated was right. Kiran's hair blew wildly in the cross-winds, and her skin gleamed golden under the sun. She was half storm and half sanctuary, and Nash didn't know into which he wanted to sail.

Chapter Sixteen

KIRAN

"All I've wanted is Indian food for the last four days," Sonam said as the CMC lounged about her living room and went over the collection of takeout menus she kept in her odds-and-ends drawer.

"All you had to do was ask and I would have come over to make some," Kiran said.

"No, not like yours...bad-for-you Indian food. You make Indian food with lighter oil and no cream."

"I'm trying to be healthy!"

"Exactly. Sometimes what you need isn't what's good for you but what's absolutely terrible and makes you happy."

"Oh, hey, kind of like Nash," Payal pointed out.

Akash gazed at Kiran, who remained silent but glared in turn at Payal.

"Are we not going to address the hippo in the room?" he asked after a few seconds.

"It's an 'elephant,'" Kiran corrected.

"Wow, so it's an even bigger issue we're not talking about, huh?"

Smart-ass.

The three of them stared at Kiran, whose cheeks heated up and fists bunched under the scrutiny.

"What?" she said.

It was like each admission, each time she said Nash's name out loud, she was losing more control over the situation...over herself.

"Okay, I'm hangry, so you can blame the bluntness on that, but are we really going to dance around this? You're acting like it's not a big deal but, Kiran, you have barely hung out with friends outside of us. You go to happy hours sometimes with people from work, but we're the people you've allowed closest to you. And now, here comes this dude who you're hanging out with all the time. You can't argue that at the very least, something about him is different enough that you're letting him into your circle."

Kiran couldn't deny that. She frowned.

"I can't like him—"

"You already said you did," Sonam cut in.

"No, I didn't—"

"You told Payal. Don't deny it. She told us."

Kiran turned on Payal, throwing her hands up to ask, *What the fuck?*

"Hey, normally, friend code wins." Payal shrugged. "But you didn't have to say a single word. Your face says it all right now. So I say with all the love in the world, don't pin this on my traitorous behavior when you're looking for an out."

Kiran sighed. Her fists balled up in her lap. Her insides twisted as though they were being physically wrenched in two different directions.

"I do like him," she said. "That's not the question. It's just...I feel like I'm losing my mind sometimes. We're kind of flirtatious and we have a spark—and every time I get close to him, it's like this little light goes off in my head and sirens screech that he's supposed to be a friend and nothing more."

"Then do something about it," said Akash. "Tell him you like him."

"I think you're wasting your time," Sonam said.

They turned to her.

"Kiran, he does make you happy. Any fool can see that. But is it worth it? Your parents are *your parents*, and they've been through so much. You all have. Pouring gasoline on the fire is only going to burn you all."

Kiran's reactions zipped from understanding to irritation. Irrational anger filled her at the thought of giving up Nash and the mere suggestion that perhaps she should take the path of least resistance.

But then her mind flew toward understanding…because Sonam was right. Her family had been everything to her for twenty-eight years. She, Baba, and Ma had held themselves up as a unit, like legs on a stool, always preventing each other from tilting over and shattering.

"I think your eyes actually just crossed." Akash raised an eyebrow at her. "Don't hurt yourself."

"Shut up, Akash," Payal said. "Be more empathetic."

Akash rolled his eyes. "Kiran, you're smart. Literally one of the smartest people I've ever met. You're not going to make the wrong choice. But I don't think it's a choice right now. I think you can see if he feels the same way and figure it out one step at a time. I've got your back, whatever way you decide to go." He turned to Payal. "Better?"

Kiran smiled, though her heart still felt torn.

"We'll support you…but I think you need to think about it," Sonam amended. "Not because he's a bad guy or you're irresponsible. But because it's so easy to go down this road in bliss and not catch yourself until you've reached a tough situation."

It wasn't like Kiran hadn't thought about it herself—but one had a tendency to think too much when they were in a situation. She wanted validation from her best friends that she wasn't overthinking the entire thing, but it seemed like she wasn't thinking enough about it.

"Okay, so we keep framing Nash within the context of your family, but what about *you*, Kiran? What do you like about him? What makes him different?" Payal asked.

Kiran gnawed on her bottom lip, pensive, for a few seconds before she spoke. "When Nash and I met in the lobby that day, he seemed lost. Like the city was too big for him. Like he knew how immense the world was and he was too small for it. I know that sounds so crazy to sense in someone you met five seconds ago, but it was like I recognized it in myself too. And in the time that I've gotten to know him, it's like he's a corner of my life that I got to choose for myself. I didn't think about anybody else. Inviting him to chai and all the resultant hangouts after that have felt as though they were my choices. They were decisions made for me, not for anyone else. And I liked seeing that side of myself. I've never gotten to before, not on this level."

"There is a big sense of freedom when you finally stop apologizing for what you want," Payal said.

"But at what point does that become a detriment if it hurts everyone around you?" Sonam countered.

"I wish I had an answer." Kiran shrugged.

"Just be careful," Sonam said.

"If you'd like my advice, I'd say sooner rather than later, you'll have to either tell him how you feel or openly set your limits. You don't want to hurt him either," Akash said. "If he's hanging out with you this much, you probably mean something to him too, and you don't want signals to get crossed."

"I think you should go for it," Payal said. "You don't do these things often, and you have mentioned that this is empowering for you."

"You guys realize you just told me three different pieces of advice, right?" Kiran gave a small laugh.

"Obviously mine is the best," Akash said.

The other two rolled their eyes.

Kiran shook her head as Sonam finally picked out a takeout menu for a nearby Indian place and they all began choosing their orders.

If this conversation was meant to bring clarity, it had done the exact opposite. Sonam was right: her family was always first priority and would remain that way. But Payal wasn't wrong either; wasn't making a choice for yourself a sign of growing up?

And Akash had brought up Nash's feelings. Kiran was jabbed by the thought of hurting Nash if he did feel the same way she did.

Then again...she didn't know.

She groaned inwardly, vaguely listening to Sonam recapping a news article she'd read the other day. She'd have to stay the course. When the right moment came, she'd have to trust she and Nash would figure it out.

She only hoped it would be soon.

Chapter Seventeen

NASH

I have a new adventure in mind! Nash texted Kiran after work a couple of days after Smorgasburg.

> Kiran: Okay, let's have it!
> Nash: I want to see New York from above.
> Kiran: Did you grow wings?

Nash chuckled. He could hear her dubious voice in his mind, which only prompted him to continue texting.

> Nash: Wanna go to Top of the Rock?
> Kiran: I was about to say no if you asked to go to One World Observatory...too touristy after the day I've had. Though Top of the Rock is kind of touristy too, I guess...but it's on your list, so yes, let's go!
> Nash: I'm full of surprises. And quit complaining. I'll meet you in front of the building in an hour.

He took the subway from the hospital to Rockefeller Center, spotting Kiran in the crowd instantly.

She was wearing a pink cotton dress with a white shawl draped over her delicate shoulders. Her flats, the same color as her skin, made her legs look like they belonged on a runway, and Nash had to pry his eyes away from them.

"How do you always beat me to wherever we're meeting?"

"Superpowers," she answered. Then, "I work two blocks away, remember?"

"Superpowers definitely sounded cooler."

"Shut up!"

"You ready?"

"I always wanted to go ice-skating here," Kiran remarked as she gestured to the giant space where the ice-skating rink would be lit up over the holidays.

"Isn't that the most touristy thing ever, and didn't you say a little while ago that you're morally against that?"

"Okay, first off, way to take my words out of context. I'm not morally against tourism. I didn't feel like going to One World Observatory today, that's all. There's a difference."

"And how is skating at Rockefeller Center during Christmas any different?"

"Because I didn't grow up with it."

"So it's the equivalent of tourist macaroni and cheese?" He chuckled. "You didn't have it and therefore you must indulge in it?"

She laughed, seemingly delighted that he'd remembered her explanation for loving some things as much as she did. "Yes. Yes, it is!"

They stepped into the elevator up to Top of the Rock a few minutes later. Nash grew more and more excited with each *ding* of the elevator, hoping that tonight would be as magical as the last few outings had been.

The doors opened, and as he and Kiran stepped out onto the platform, she gasped.

"Wow. This is…"

"Everything." Nash couldn't find another word to describe what he was seeing.

A soft smile played at Kiran's lips as she walked to the barrier, and Nash followed. They stared at Midtown, glowing with shifting lights and skyscrapers. From up here, it seemed they could see the whole world. Even the Empire State Building looked attainable to the masses and less like the reigning symbol of the city.

The temperature was a few degrees cooler than it was at street level. Kiran shivered and the tremor in her arms pressed up against Nash's, prompting him to look down at her.

"Want my shirt?"

"While I'm sure the ladies here would be impressed with your six-pack, you should probably stay clothed," she replied dryly.

Nash gave her an exasperated eye roll. "I have a shirt on underneath. Here."

Deftly pulling the shirt over his head and tugging the tee underneath into place, he took her stubborn hands and put the Henley in them, raising an eyebrow to challenge her bubbling protest.

She gave up.

"Okay. Thank you."

"Thank *you* for not fighting it."

"I wasn't going to fight it!"

"And we're back, ladies and gentlemen."

Kiran giggled. "Maybe I just like fighting with you."

"Maybe I like that you do."

His gaze lingered on her face for a second longer than it ever had before. Her eyes remained locked on his too, before a visible shiver rippled through her body.

"Here. For real. You're cold. Put it on." He helped her pull it over her head, and as his hands lightly trailed over her shoulders, her body quivered again.

Kiran peeked up at him, and Nash's knees lost some of their stability. Her enormous eyes were filled with vulnerability, but when she peered up at him from underneath a blanket of eyelashes, there was a steely sultriness that Nash couldn't escape from.

She leaned in close, and her warm breath touched his skin, sending shivers down his spine.

He turned his head, achingly slow, toward her. Nash could smell her perfume, an intense mix of vanilla, patchouli, and jasmine, and it was intoxicating. He was drawn toward her like a moth to the flame.

"You have an audience," she murmured against his ear. "Don't look now."

He was so shocked by the turn in conversation and the way she made his body react that he glanced in the direction she was pointing immediately.

When his gaze fell upon them, a group of young girls widened their eyes and laughed. One flipped her hair. He smiled at them reflexively, and one blushed before he turned back to Kiran.

"Wow, I said, 'Don't look,' and you had to do it, didn't you?"

"They were, like, twelve. I much prefer women closer to my age." Nash took a deep breath to stabilize himself, but his lungs still felt like they'd been sapped of any oxygen.

"I'll be sure to let you know if there's a midtwenties woman worth your attention around."

"I'm looking at one."

She whipped her head to glance at him, her lips parted in a perfect O.

"Nash—"

He didn't know what she was going to say, but hearing his name on her lips was like she'd cast a spell over his entire life.

Chapter Eighteen

KIRAN

A beat flew by where she wanted to sprint into his arms and press her lips against his. But instead she stood there, staring at him.

"Check it out. The Empire State is different colors." He pointed.

The air around them sucked back into her lungs, and the people around them snapped into focus, making their presence known all of a sudden with their buzzing words and laughter.

"Oh... What... Yeah! It does that." She tried to recover quickly, but her heart simultaneously calmed and fell. It returned to a steady beat at the passing conversation but fell for reasons she couldn't explain. Like disappointment but deeper...and not quite reaching the level of heartbreak.

Instead, she watched the city lights beneath her. Her mind drifted, as it always did, to all the lives that could be changing within the glowing expanse. To her parents. To what the world was like "down there" versus up here, and how she felt removed.

"What're you thinking?" Nash whispered in her ear.

"Big things," she murmured.

Their shoulders brushed against each other. Nash leaned on

his elbows, set against the railing. Kiran kept her clasped hands against her chest as she pushed against the railing herself. Even leaning, Nash's height was a hair taller than Kiran's.

She grew aware of how close they were standing. Anyone who saw them would know they were together and that they were the only ones at the Rock that night in their party of two, a bubble of their own. She liked how she imagined they looked together, her dusky skin next to his white. She imagined someone would see comfort, friendship, and a home of sorts when they saw the two of them laughing together. The picture gave her an ache, a yearning to be the girl in a pair who could prompt anyone's gaze.

"Tell me."

"City lights make me happy."

"Why's that?"

"The enormity of it. It never fades. We're up here and watching these lights, and millions of people are out there. Someone could be having their heart broken right now. Someone could be having a baby—"

"Someone could be finding the love of their life," Nash interrupted quietly.

She smiled to herself. "Exactly."

"Do you believe in soul mates?"

He was looking out at the expanse in front of them, the lights reflecting in his eyes and adding a glint to his already existing mischief. Kiran gazed at his square forehead, disrupted by a small widow's peak. The outline of his face gradually dropped into his nose—straight, strong, and bigger from the side than anyone would notice from the front—and delicately led to a thinner upper lip and fuller bottom one. His jaw was square but delicately so, giving him a human edge to the marble statuesque vibe he exuded otherwise. His dimples and creases from his smile were visible even when he was serious. Whatever the opposite of a resting bitch face was, Nash was the unknowing owner of it.

She was poised to say no, she wasn't sure about soul mates, but she believed in destiny. Then he looked over at her and smiled.

"Yes. I do," she whispered back.

A nudge behind her heart told her she was staring at hers.

"Me too."

"I don't know that I believe in *one* though."

"Yeah? What do you mean? Like there's more than one person out there for you?"

"Like a soul mate doesn't have to be in the form of a lover. I would consider my best friends Akash, Sonam, and Payal to be my soul mates, but they aren't people I'd date. I think soul mates understand you in a transcendent way. They experience your worst with you rather than solely bearing witness to it. They fly with you when you soar rather than watching your wings."

"Hallmark card?" Nash teased.

"Archies," Kiran answered with a deadpan tone, naming the Indian equivalent.

"I have no idea what that is and now I feel really stupid."

"Now you understand what it's like to be me trying to keep up with everyone's references."

He laughed at their digression before turning serious again. "So multiple soul mates."

"I think so. How about you?"

"I believe something similar...that you connect with everyone you meet. But I think sometimes you fall in love with someone more deeply than you have before, and you can't explain why or how. They break through your defenses and create a home within you, and no one can ever occupy it again."

"That's a beautiful way of saying it."

"Really? Because I thought it was a little hokey."

"Never. There has to be a plan to it all, you know? Destiny. Fate. I find it depressing to think things weren't meant to be a certain way, because it means we've made choices and ended up there all on our own. That's a lonely thought."

"I agree. The dots connect eventually...at least that's what I'd like to think. I've never *really* been in love—first loves, crushes, things like that but never the kind of connection I hope exists out there."

She didn't want to ruin the moment and mention she was supposed to have a semi-arranged marriage. Bringing it up would only lead to more questions, and the wistfulness of this moment would be lost. Kiran wasn't ready for that. And explaining the practicality of an arranged marriage would tarnish the idea of soul mates and destiny. Kiran believed with all her heart that whoever she was to marry through an arranged match was also a product of destiny, but the intertwining of logic and destiny wasn't as romantic as believing that one person existed for her and that somehow, somewhere, he would find her.

"You've kind of grown on me, you know." Kiran bumped her shoulder against his.

"You mean you didn't love me at first sight?"

"I don't believe in love at first sight."

"Not surprising." Nash rolled his eyes.

"Why do you say that?"

"You're methodical. You're an engineer. Type A. Honestly, you believing in soul mates was a surprise."

"I believe in order and that you have to keep a level head. But sometimes...you have to believe in something greater than you. I'd like to think God has a plan for me, and even if that soul mate is someone I meet in an understated way, that they were meant for me. But love at first sight...it's lustful. It's just you falling for someone's looks. That's not destiny or fate; that's you thinking with parts of your body other than your head."

"Well...one of them, anyway."

"Nash!" Kiran tried to be uptight about his dirty implication, but she couldn't help the snort of laughter.

"It's true! Though I don't believe in love at first sight either."

"So...you've never been in love, huh?" She probed, wanting to know everything.

"A couple of times. But not a forever love. Does that make sense?"

"Yeah. It does."

Kiran tried to remember what she felt like with Vinay, her college sweetheart, but she couldn't sort out whether she'd felt love or obligation with him. It certainly felt like love at the time. But she didn't feel a fire with him. Did it still qualify?

"Have you?"

"I dated someone through most of college. He was my first," she admitted.

"Oh, so you do have a scandalous side, Kiran Mathur!" Nash laughed.

"Down, boy. I wasn't that wild!"

"Not love?"

"It was first love. Not forever."

They hadn't moved an inch as they talked of being meant for someone. Their tones were so hushed, they had to lean against each other to hear. The intimacy of being the only girl Nash was focusing on filled Kiran with a rush she couldn't describe. And while she had never experienced a true, forever love, as they chattered over the lights of the skyline that night, she suddenly felt as though maybe she deserved to.

· · · · · · · · · · ·

The funny thing about living in cities where there were famous sights was that natives never really went to them...or they were dragged there as children, got sick of them, and never visited again as adults unless they were taking guests.

Kiran had traveled up to the top of the Empire State Building. She'd made a visit to the Statue of Liberty to see the gateway to the nation she'd joined. She'd checked out Times Square more than she could handle. Central Park had received her footfalls plenty, with each visit showing her something new about nature in the middle of a concrete jungle.

But something had shifted. She found herself googling some of the other sights in the city.

Kiran thought back to the fact that Nash missed the South sometimes and that they both had experienced some type of loss. Sometimes, she wondered what he'd think of a restaurant she passed on the street or wanted to tell him about a joke she'd heard at work. Occasionally, they emailed journal articles back and forth about scientific breakthroughs made in diagnostics.

The involvement of Nash in her daily life was one of the most comfortable things she'd ever experienced. It was also one of the most terrifying.

No matter how much she wanted to run from the notion that she got butterflies when she thought of him or wanted to put some space between them, she couldn't. The draw to him overwhelmed any intent she had to separate herself.

And it was that very draw that had her texting him today.

Kiran: Zoo this weekend?

A minute passed.

Two.

Five.

Ten minutes later, Kiran was still waiting.

She figured Nash was busy at work. But she grew unsettled, uncomfortable, and worse, insecure at the strange gap in time.

Girlfriend...get a grip, she told herself and immersed herself in examining some of the results from the breast cancer study her team was working on. But she still found herself checking her phone more often than usual.

Four hours later, Nash finally responded.

Nash: Sure, sounds great. I'll meet you there around noon on Saturday?

On Saturday, Kiran's morning slugged toward noon, but she began polishing her cupboards out of desperation to make the seconds tick by faster, and before she knew, it was time to move.

For the first time since they'd begun hanging out, Nash had gotten to their destination before Kiran.

"Ah, looks like my superpowers rubbed off on you!" she exclaimed as she gave him a quick hug.

"Gotta be early when meeting a pretty lady!" He offered his arm.

She hesitated for a moment, as though his arm would wind around her heart and then she'd never let go of him, but then she thought better of it. She put her hand through his crooked elbow, and they paid for their tickets together before entering the zoo enclosure.

She noticed Nash take a deep breath.

"You okay?"

His jaw remained clenched as he nodded. "So...what animals do you want to see first? Baby sea lions?"

"Admit it, the baby sea lions excite you too."

"I don't think anyone can argue against baby animals unless you're heartless or a horrible human being all around."

Kiran stopped for a map to plot out their walk, but by the time she had formulated a plan and looked up, Nash was ten steps ahead, waiting at the opening to the sea lion tank.

"So I think I figured out the best way to do this..."

Nash rolled his eyes and took the map out of her hands. "We'll sort it out. Let's go."

As they walked toward the sea lion pool, Kiran swung her arms and nearly skipped at the sight of giant sea lions lounging in the shade from the sun.

They were like humans on a weekend, wanting to chill out and relax.

She and Nash paused at the tank, letting the scent of fish and salt water waft over them. The water glimmered underneath the sun, and children squealed with delight at every small movement each sea lion made, from a yawn to the twitch of a whisker.

In silence, when both of them had gotten their fill, they went over to the exhibit for penguins and other birds. There, they watched the antics of penguins diving in headfirst.

Kiran gave a shiver, unable to imagine living on ice for an entire lifetime. Though staring at a little creature that seemed to relish the attention by swimming near the glass and dancing against it with his wings, perhaps it wasn't so bad.

"Well, we know which penguin is the center of the show at home." Nash pointed and mimicked his swift wing batting.

"He seems happy."

"Why wouldn't he be?"

"I don't know. I love zoos and animals, don't get me wrong... but I can't imagine not being free. They spend their entire lives away from their natural habitat. These penguins are in a little tank in New York City."

Nash put his hands in his pockets, nodding his head as he considered it. "Well, it's all they know. Can you be unhappy if you don't know a different lifestyle exists?"

"I wonder if they've ever wanted more."

Her observation wasn't meant to be tied to her life. After all, she was gazing at little birds in a giant tank. But she couldn't help wondering if the notion did run parallel to her life.

"You never know. That one could want a life on Broadway."

"He definitely wouldn't be a chorus dancer, that's for sure."

"Did you know penguins mate for life?"

"No, they don't. Really?"

"Like eighty percent of the time, yeah. And for some breeds, the father penguin holds onto the egg and keeps it warm while the mama goes fishin'." The twang of the South slipped into his unguarded voice.

"I didn't know that either. Did you know that peacocks can give a little shimmy and change their vocal tone to attract females?"

Nash chuckled. "That can't be true."

"It is, I swear. They just"—Kiran shook her shoulders and her bottom like she was doing the chicken dance—"and their pitch changes."

"Can you do that dance again? I...uh, didn't catch it the first time."

She blushed, not even realizing she'd shaken it out in public, but like Nash's southern accent, it was an uninhibited rarity.

"That's such a random fact. How do you even know that about peacocks?"

"I'm from a tropical country and also from a village. I saw

them sometimes. How do you know that tidbit about penguins, Nash from Nashville?" She put a hand on her waist.

"I hoped to use that fact when I found my penguin." He smirked now.

"I should have known. You do seem like the guy who would learn random facts to impress girls."

"Kiran, I don't know why you choose to hurt me that way," he deadpanned.

"Whatever," she scoffed. "Like my opinion matters to you."

"Maybe it does. You matter to me. Therefore, your opinion matters to me."

Her jaw went slack, her breath escaping her in a *whoosh*. Could it be that she mattered to him as much as he mattered to her?

They spent the next hour wandering from exhibit to exhibit, making stops at various animals. Kiran had never been so close to a tiger before as one lying sleeping against the glass. As they circled through the park, Kiran laughed harder and harder at his jokes, drunk on hearing his voice. Nash's shoulders fell back as he eased up his guard, though Kiran never even anticipated he had one to begin with…but as he cracked more jokes and made fun of her, she could see that even he had a wall, paper thin but existent, that people had to rip through before understanding him.

And the significant nudge behind her heart told her she wanted to.

Chapter Nineteen

NASH

The more time they spent at the zoo, the more Nash thought about his mother.

When Kiran had originally mentioned the zoo, back when they had first gone to dinner, he hoped she'd forget it down the line.

Instead, she'd texted him about it, and he'd needed a few hours to reconcile his desire to spend time with her with his cherished memories that he held at bay. He hadn't anticipated such a visceral reaction, but then again, he hadn't been to a zoo since he went with Mom all those years ago.

To distract himself, he made Kiran laugh and willed himself to continue their banter, but he had to remind himself every few exhibits to shake off the weight. To stay present. To forget that there had at one point been hope for him and his mom to go on and have a solid family together.

As Kiran and Nash rounded a bend, an adorable animal, a funny little cross between a raccoon, fox, and bear, rested on a branch, chubby and content with an audience.

"Look at him! He's so cute and cuddly." Kiran's eyes went round.

"I'm pretty sure he's eyeing up the female one over there." Nash pointed to another little bear, hidden beneath some brush.

"Oh, shh."

"Excuse me, miss?" he asked the attendant who was coaxing a red panda toward her. "Do you breed them here?"

"We wanted to breed these two, but we decided they were too young. Plus, he kept showing interest in an older bear." She waited for Nash's follow-up question, which didn't come, and then turned back to the bears, clicking at them with her tongue.

As she turned away, Nash leaned toward Kiran. "Sounds like my kind of bear. Besides...when has being young ever stopped anyone?"

"Nash! You're shameless."

"I'm stating the facts."

"You want to know a fact?"

"What?"

"This is lovely." She'd blurted it out without any inhibition. His mouth twitched and happiness flooded him.

"Do you want to check out the giraffes and rhinos? I think they're around here somewhere, but *someone* took my map." Her pointed glare distracted him from the breath that caught in his throat.

"Yeah, let's go."

His legs were heavy as they took the wide path around the baboon reserve.

There the giraffes were, reaching their majestic necks toward some trees in the corner of the enclosure. He saw a black tongue poke out of a little giraffe's mouth. Nash rolled his fingers over his palm, remembering the scratchiness of the giraffe's tongue at the zoo when he was a child.

He saw an empty bench and wordlessly took a seat.

He could have been thirteen again, watching the giant beasts feed and play. He was hardly aware as Kiran sat next to him until she touched his arm, making him jump.

"Okay...what's wrong?" Her eyes bored into him.

He shook his head. "Nothing."

Her eyes narrowed.

Nash looked at his hands. He wanted to open up, but he was afraid that if he let the gates open now, years of holding back the flood would fail. He'd end up pouring his heart out. He wasn't sure he was ready for that. He didn't know if Kiran was either.

"Nash..." Kiran's tone was pleading. "Tell me what's on your mind. Do you want to leave?"

It was the idea of parting ways with Kiran early that finally made him turn his face toward hers and meet her eye. His cheeks heated under the scrutiny, and he forced himself to unlock his mental vault to open up.

"The last time I went to a zoo was with my mom. I didn't expect the memories of her to hit me hard, but coming here..."

"I'm sorry. Do you want to go?"

"No. I like being here with you." He lifted his chin. He wouldn't crack. Not now.

"You can tell me whenever you're ready. I'm right here, and I'm not going anywhere."

Seconds passed. Nash time-traveled mentally to seventeen years ago, on a summer day in Nashville.

"Giraffes were her favorite...and rhinos were mine." It seemed like such a lame explanation, but he couldn't start at the beginning and casually unload the weight on his shoulders. He had to lift the pieces off bit by bit, and Mom's face as she watched the giraffes was the first tiny bit he could let go of.

"Somehow, I don't find that surprising." Kiran grinned.

"The zoo was one of the few good memories I had of her." He

laughed unexpectedly. "I remember she kept mentioning that if I had a girlfriend—because I was thirteen and starting to get into girls—she'd have a heart attack."

"That must have been a fun conversation."

"From what I can recall, I wanted to be eaten by a lion."

Kiran giggled. "She'd be proud of you, you know."

"Yeah. I hope so."

Kiran took his face in her hands and rested her forehead on his. The touch of her skin was soothing, the way a warm compress calmed a headache. His heart settled into a regular rhythm rather than fighting to beat as though a weight were dragging it down. Even his breathing became effortless.

And the unusual display of affection from Kiran—when she always became defensive after any contact—replaced his sadness with surprise.

"I want you to listen to me," Kiran murmured against him. "You have overcome so many impossible things. An absentee father. A mother who had a problem. Not much money. And you're *here*, an educated, brilliant, funny, and sexy-as-hell man. You, Nash Hawthorne, aren't just someone who beat the odds. You are a superhero in every sense of the word."

He could have kissed her. If he closed the inches between their faces, it would have been easy to gently touch his lips to hers and convey all the explosive feelings Kiran created inside him.

But instead, he closed his eyes and allowed himself to breathe her in. Just like he had felt all those years ago, sitting on a bench in front of a herd of giraffes, he was safe.

Chapter Twenty

NASH

"So are you going to tell me what's on your mind, or do I have to wrestle it out of you like I did in the ninth grade when you had a crush on my girlfriend?"

"What're you talking about?" Nash couldn't disguise his smile.

He and Brandon were sitting at a Starbucks after work. Nash's mind drifted to Kiran often, despite his attempts to stay present. Judging by the expression on Brandon's face, his wandering thoughts were evident to anyone and everyone around him.

"It's the Indian girl, isn't it?"

"For being such a moron, how do you always figure me out?"

"Are you being serious right now? You remember I was around during your disastrous effort at hiding the fact that you liked my cousin, right?"

"Whatever, dude. We don't talk about that." He didn't need a reminder of how Brandon's cousin Marley had treated him like her own butler and how, in his besotted state, Nash had allowed her to.

"Okay, well, then let's talk about this girl. It sounds like things have escalated since your friendly dinner."

"I fell for her. We've hung out almost every weekend for the last three or four months."

"I knew it!"

Nash chuckled at Brandon's enthusiasm. "Actually, it was something you said about Tasha that made me realize Kiran might be more than a friend."

"What's that?"

"You mentioned that you felt like you'd been playing around until she showed up...and I sort of felt the same way about my life. Like I'd never let anyone in until her. I mean, besides you and Kate."

"Did you tell her about your parents?" Brandon gave Nash a knowing look.

Nash nodded. "We went to the zoo, actually—"

"That's big. You always skipped any class trips there."

"I guess I wanted to save any memory of spending time with my mom there before she died, and afterward, I couldn't bring myself to go."

"So you went to the zoo and..."

"It hit me a hell of a lot harder than I thought it would, man. I thought I'd dealt with all of it and come to terms with my history, because I figured everyone was at peace and it gave me the opportunity to focus on myself, but here I was, looking at a freaking giraffe and feeling like I was going to lose my mind."

"Did she calm you down?"

"She was amazing. I felt really chilled out by the way she handled it."

Brandon quietly watched Nash pour a packet of sugar in his coffee. After a few seconds of silence, he spoke with consideration and thought.

"You know, Nash, you've always kept women at an arm's

length. I won't go as far as to say you were terribly damaged—I think you came out more brilliantly than anyone in your situation could have. God knows my parents marvel about it all the time. A lot of that is a testament to your resilience...but I've always worried about you. When you dated Brooke in college and that girl in medical school—"

"Riley."

"Yeah. Her. You never even mentioned that your mom was an addict. Just that she had died. You hid parts of yourself. I don't know if it was because you were ashamed or because you didn't want to broach the pain. I don't even know if you're sure which one it was. But either way, this is huge for you. She has to be the real deal if you're willing to admit where you came from with honesty."

"How the heck did you get so smart? I'm the one with the psych degree."

"Dude, you've met my parents. My mom yelled, 'Make good choices,' every time she dropped me off anywhere—including at my fraternity in college. You think they'd let me get away with being a douchebag?"

"Fair point."

"Anyway...have you told her how you feel?"

Nash shook his head.

"Why not?"

Nash ran his fingers through his hair with more force than he intended to. "I know it's this massive milestone to have told her about my parents. But I worry about her getting too close... knowing the guilt I still feel, or the anger, or the abandonment. It's a giant can of worms. I don't know if she's willing to go in. And more than that, I don't know if it's selfish for me to ask her to."

"I think you're full of shit."

"How do you figure?"

"I think you're being a martyr by keeping it so close to you. It's probably not healthy. And the truth is, she's come this far and hasn't been scared away by your demons. You have to trust that she'll tell you if she is. I think it's more selfish for you to be a half-involved man than a flawed, fully invested one." Brandon shrugged, as if his conclusion was obvious. "But that's my two cents. I've only known you twenty-five years."

Nash chuckled. "Duly noted."

"Let her in. Tell her how you feel and hope for the best. I have a feeling she won't disappoint."

"She's also hard to read sometimes."

"Meaning?"

"We have these moments of connection where she... I mean, I can't think straight and she's the only person in the room to me. Then we'll touch or be flirtatious or whatever, and it's like watching a drawbridge go up. She closes her doors. Five minutes later, she's there but not there—close to me and completely unreachable."

"Is she fighting it too?"

"I don't know. She's...serious. I mean, she lets loose and is amazing to be around, but she takes life seriously. She came to the United States to set up her life, and you can tell she doesn't want to blow it. And I'm not sure I can be that guy who doesn't fuck up. Look at the stock I came from."

"You haven't fucked up. Ever."

"What if she isn't willing to give this a shot?"

"Did you ask her if she's holding back?"

"Of course not."

"You're a psychologist, idiot. You have to broach how she feels, don't you? Find out what she's thinking. Let her in too."

"I'm a little scared of that, if I'm honest. Getting attached to someone, letting them see my fears and hopes, and then having them leave." He gave a shudder.

Brandon paused. "It sure doesn't sound like she's someone who would throw something meaningful away."

Nash sighed and shook his head. "She's not. She's careful and meticulous. But that fear never really goes away, and if she's holding back, how do I know it won't backfire on me?"

"You won't know unless you try, Nash. Take a chance."

Perhaps his best friend was right. Maybe he had to let Kiran all the way in.

But first, he had to tell her how he felt.

Chapter Twenty-One

KIRAN

It was a Tuesday evening, and Kiran had been sluggish all day, uncharacteristically leaving off attachments on emails she sent colleagues, forgetting her lunch at home, and making mistakes on work assignments that she typically never would have.

She hadn't woken up on the wrong side of the bed; she was sure she'd proverbially fallen out of it.

And she couldn't get Nash out of her mind.

Kiran replayed their close contact on the bench at the zoo over and over again like a film reel on a loop. She could have kissed him. Maybe she should have. Maybe that would have cleared up how she felt. He would have pulled away and said, "Sorry, I don't feel the same way," or kissed her back, and she'd have a clear-cut answer on how he felt and what to do.

But instead, they'd sat close, with her cupping his face in her hands, and the warmth of his skin had gently cascaded through her palms, up her arms, and all the way to her heart.

To the outside world, perhaps they looked like lovers sharing an intimate moment. But to Kiran, it was a sweet aberration that had only muddled her heart further as she thought of Baba and Ma.

By the time she walked up to her apartment building at seven in the evening, she was mentally wading through quicksand.

"Kiran!"

Nash came from the opposite direction, clutching a plastic bag in his hand from the bodega around the corner.

"Hey, you." She tried to muster a smile, but the glumness in her voice was obvious.

They paused in front of the steps to the building.

"You look like you could use a drink," Nash commented. "You okay?"

"Just a very long day."

"Do you actually want a drink? We can go grab one if you want to vent."

Kiran sighed and closed her eyes for a second. She couldn't shake the irrational irritation with herself at the bumbling way she'd gotten through the day, and she was certain she would be terrible company.

But the hope in Nash's blue eyes turned the impending *no, thank you* to a *sure* before she could think twice.

"I'm giving you fair warning that I'm cranky today."

Nash smirked. "I can handle it."

Kiran gave him a small smile and gestured for him to lead the way.

They walked a few blocks in silence until they reached Avenue A and First Street. Boulton & Watt was a place Kiran had gone to multiple times before. Their brunch was a favorite of Sonam's after a long night shift.

Unassuming from the outside, the restaurant was on a corner, built with a gray brick facade and industrial windows. The inside was decorated with Christmas lights, planters hanging from the ceiling, and aluminum paneling above long, wooden tables with old-fashioned industrial bar benches underneath them.

Kiran and Nash took their seats at a table for two.

"Do you want to tell me what's on your mind?" Nash asked gently as they perused the menu.

But before Kiran could speak, a tall woman with beachy waves of blond hair and blue eyes touched Nash's shoulder.

"Dr. Hawthorne!" she chirped, her eyes flitting over Kiran for a millisecond before she devoted her attention to Nash.

"Oh, hi…" He stood. "It's nice to see you."

He placed his arm loosely around her waist when she reached in for a hug, his back stiffening.

Kiran waited to be acknowledged, plastering a small smile on her face in case someone turned to her. The woman didn't give her a second glance, speaking directly to Nash instead.

"What're you up to? Drinks?"

Nash's eyes darted to Kiran before gesturing to her. "Yes. Kiran, this is Doreen. We work in the same wing of the hospital. Doreen, this is my friend and neighbor, Kiran."

Friend.

Kiran barely had a second to ruminate on the word before Doreen turned to her.

"Karen?"

"No, it's *Kir-an*," Kiran enunciated slowly, the way she always did.

Doreen laughed. "I always have trouble with foreign names. Can I just call you Karen?"

"I–I'd really rather you didn't…" Kiran frowned.

"It's not that hard, Doreen," Nash said easily. "Kind of like that Irish name, *Kieran*—have you ever heard it? It's a really pretty name."

Kiran tried to force her face to cooperate and look pleasant at Nash's attempt, but she couldn't help but feel like she'd been slapped.

"That's true, it's not so tough. Just unusual." Doreen shrugged.

Sweat began to dot Kiran's forehead as the hair on the back of her neck stood up.

"Excuse me, I need to use the restroom," she said, and she loudly pushed her chair back, the metal legs grinding against the wooden floor and emitting a screech.

Once in the restroom, she hunched over the sink, closing her eyes and taking stabilizing breaths that did nothing for her racing heart and the heat rising in her chest.

Foreign. It was funny that a word could be weaponized so quickly.

Kiran thought to earlier in her workday, where a colleague had explained the mechanism for bioengineering a synthetic virus and that a key to it was making sure the human body didn't see it as a foreign body and attack. In that case, it was clear—*foreign* meant it didn't belong. It deserved to be attacked.

Kiran hated feeling like she didn't belong.

"People are stupid. You've had a bad day. Get it together," she mumbled to herself.

Sonam had warned her in college—when some frat guy had called her a "dot head" when she was walking back from a Hindu Students Association meeting. Kiran distinctly heard her voice now. *Kiran, I'm sorry...but you've got to grow tougher skin, because it's only going to get worse from here.* The onslaught of narrow-mindedness would be a constant assault, not an occasional fight.

Kiran ran some cool water on her hands and rested them on her cheeks, uncaring whether the wetness would ruin her makeup. She breathed in deeply again, picturing ocean waves, the sound of a rainstorm, and whatever else would calm her mind as she carefully dabbed a paper towel across her face.

Then she stared at her reflection in the mirror, nodded once, and chucked the paper towel and opened the door.

She could see Nash was alone at the table again, but she didn't have it in her to get a drink and act as though she felt normal.

Today, she felt anything but.

"Nash, would you mind if we go home?" She collected her bag off the seat and flung it over her shoulder.

"No drink?" Nash appeared surprised.

"No, but thank you. I'd just like to go home."

Once again, they walked in silence. Unlike on the way to the restaurant, Kiran didn't feel comfort at Nash's presence. He hadn't done anything wrong, but she couldn't help the anger at being marked as an outsider in front of him.

Kiran unlocked the doors to the building without a word, and Nash followed her through the lobby.

As she paused outside her door, trying to figure out what to say, Nash leaned against the frame.

"Are you okay?" he asked softly.

Kiran sighed and shook her head. "No. I'm not."

"Tell me what's on your mind."

She nodded. "Come inside."

She took off her shoes and he followed suit, reminding her of the first time they'd met. She tossed her bag on the table and sank into the couch.

Nash quietly took the blue armchair he favored.

"Do you want some chai?" Kiran remembered her manners—Nash was a guest after all.

"No, thank you. Just talk to me."

Kiran crossed her legs and tucked her hands under her thighs. "I had a rough day today at work. Nothing crazy. It was one of those days where things went wrong from the second I woke up. I spilled coffee on the first shirt I chose this morning, then ran ten minutes later than usual to work. It was basically a series of annoyances all day. And then I sent no less than three emails without the attachments on them and made a miscalculation of data that took me two hours to figure out, rectify, and inform my colleagues about."

"Bad days happen. I'm sure your colleagues understood."

Kiran shook her head. "Nash, it's much more than that. For me, a mistake is never a simple misstep. A mistake is one more tick mark against my very existence here."

His brow furrowed. "I don't understand."

"I see it on some of my colleagues' faces. The sympathetic glance when I ask someone to repeat their directions because they weren't clear. They not only go slower but enunciate, as though I didn't understand English the first time. When my coworkers forget an attachment on an email, it's an oversight. Today, I got asked by a person who has worked under me for two weeks if I knew how to use Outlook. I made a mistake on some data analysis that took me time to figure out. It was silly, yes, and not a big deal in the grand scheme of things. But people like me? Every day, we have to prove we earned the right to live here. Each mistake counts against that."

"That must be a burden to carry," Nash said softly.

"I don't break the rules—not because I don't want to but because of the massive assumptions that will be made about me and, by extension, immigrants from India if I do. Forget an attachment on an email? I must have grown up in a country that didn't offer technology. Cut someone off driving? Indians can't drive anyway. My God, I spelled 'color' with a 'u' in college once, and I had a professor suggest I take an ESL class—as if American English is the only English spoken anywhere in the world."

"It must feel like you're trying to outscore people keeping an invisible tally."

"Yes. I can't even say anything, because if I do, I look combative and not thankful to be here."

"You feel like you have to stay in your lane."

"Exactly. And Doreen tried to force that too. It was upsetting."

"I didn't think she meant anything by it." Nash frowned again, confused.

"She said my name was foreign and difficult. Did you not notice that I had to debate my own name? You had to stand up for me—and I appreciate you doing so, it was very thoughtful—but she didn't trust me on my own identity until you, a white man, told her my name was similar to an Irish one. But I am not *similar to an Irish person*. I am Indian. That is who I am. And it is not an argument."

He gazed at her, unmoving.

Kiran could see the cogs turning in his mind and his eyes slowly registering all that she was saying—and that her words didn't come from a place of anger at *him* but that this conversation was much bigger than the two of them sitting in this living room.

"I'm sorry. I shouldn't have made that comparison. I didn't realize it was reinforcing a problem."

"You have a lot of privilege, Nash," Kiran said softly. "It's not something you have to apologize for. But the word *foreign* doesn't mean I'm an exotic flower. It means I don't belong. And today was one reminder after another that I'm still on the outside, looking in, at a country I've called home for ten years." Kiran blinked back angry tears. "Sometimes, it's tiring."

Nash nodded. "Do you want a hug?"

She couldn't help the giggle that slipped out. "Yes."

He sat next to her and wrapped his arms around her. She tucked her head into the space underneath his chin and breathed him in, the scent of clean laundry and faint cologne wafting up to her. Her hands rested on his chest, and they sat, curled up on the couch, and after feeling like a stranger all day, she finally felt like she was home.

Chapter Twenty-Two

NASH

Kiran had opened her heart up about her vulnerabilities and experiences, and more than anything, Nash had been thankful to be in the room and allowed to see a side of her that he would never understand firsthand. Kiran's history as an immigrant and resulting life from that monumental move across the world was something Nash couldn't touch or begin to fathom.

But he wanted to. If anything, Kiran was proving he had a lot to learn about the world and about her, and he wanted to dive into her darkest corners, soaked in complexities, and shower himself in the light she brought to him.

Kate called as he stretched out on his couch after a long day.

"Nashy, tell me about your life! How's New York?"

"Kate, have you been drinking? You're awfully chipper."

"I'm happy to talk to you, that's all. Don't rain on my parade."

"It's nice talking to you too. I miss you."

"Now I'm wondering if *you've* been drinking. Are you okay? What's wrong, honey?"

Nash smiled against the phone, knowing his aunt couldn't see him. "Nothing. I'm doing well."

"Are you sure?"

"I feel like a kid telling you this, but I think I like someone."

"Oooh! Who?" Kate was like a child, whispering secrets on a playground.

"Kiran. She's my neighbor. We've been hanging out a lot, and it's been...eye-opening."

"What's her name again? Kee-ran?"

"Not *-ran*, but *-run*," Nash corrected, inwardly cringing at the recollection of the conversation the previous night.

"Kiran. I like that."

"Me too."

"Why do you sound so sad?"

"It's not sadness, just contemplation. I got my butt handed to me yesterday for making an idiotic move with her."

"Why?"

Nash tried to explain. "You know how we're white—"

"We're white?" Kate asked. "I'm so glad you noticed, honey. I always knew you were quick for your age."

"You are not funny." But Nash cracked a smile anyway.

"Sorry. Continue."

"It was stupid on my part." Nash gave her a quick rundown of the events of the night before, explaining how Kiran was firm but graceful in her explanation and how he felt as though he should have known. "I've spent so much time in school and learning about how people are different—and here I am, erasing her story, you know?"

"You didn't know better. You thought you were helping," Kate said kindly.

"I think that's the point. I erased her in the way I tried to help."

Nash couldn't find the words to explain why the intention behind his actions didn't matter here, that how he treated Kiran wasn't her responsibility to teach him. He had made her feel small—something he never wanted people to feel around him—and he'd made someone who already felt like an outsider on a daily basis feel like they didn't even belong in the room.

"Is that all that's bothering you?"

"No…I was thinking about Mom and Dad."

"What about them?"

"Kate, I like her. It's soon. I can't say whether this is forever. But I see something powerful potentially developing. And that is effing terrifying after seeing what my parents went through."

"What do you find terrifying?"

"That I could become like them. That I could walk away when times get hard. Or that occasional beer I have could trigger something in me that makes me lose control. Mostly, I worry I'll let her down."

"Nashy, you have never let any of us down. I don't think you would let her down either."

"It's not about me—but when I realized how little I knew about her reality, I felt so inadequate. Kind of like when I was little and I used to wonder why Dad left. And then I'd wonder if he didn't feel good enough to give Mom the life she wanted and maybe he left because it was too much for him, and if that's the case, and I keep missing pieces of Kiran's life too because I don't understand…what if I lose her? What if I screw up?" His words came faster and faster, loosely making connections but not capturing how scared he felt of falling for her, losing her, and screwing up, all at once.

"Nash, take a breath," Kate coached, like she did when he was little. "You're getting way ahead of yourself. That's not like you. Start with seeing where this goes. Then…?"

Her prompt slowed his racing thoughts. "Then I better tell her I like her."

"After that?"

"I'll do my best to be my best."

"That's all you can do. You know that. You carry a lot of burden from your past, Nash, but you can't let it anchor you in place. You've also overcome setbacks and taken life step by step. Do the same thing here…slow down. Handle each day as it comes."

Nash sighed. "You're right."

"I always am. I don't know why you doubt me," Kate teased.

"I don't either."

They talked about her dogs, about her husband and the new art class she'd signed up for, before winding up their call.

When they finally hung up an hour later, Nash felt at peace and more certain than ever that he wanted to do his best for Kiran and that she'd see nothing but his effort from now on.

Chapter Twenty-Three

KIRAN

"I think I might mix it up and get coffee today." Sonam fanned herself with a menu.

"Shut up and order your chai," Akash said.

"People can mix it up sometimes, nerd. I don't always have to operate the same way," Sonam defended.

"But you will," Akash said.

She scoffed, and Payal and Kiran rolled their eyes at the bickering.

"So...I'm thinking about quitting my job."

The three others all looked up at Payal's slow pronouncement.

"Bored with the public relations business?" Akash asked.

"I want to chase my passion, you know? I love designing clothes, and I love styling my friends. I'd love to take a year to venture out and see what I can do with it. Maybe this is the time to start the line."

"You would be amazing, Payal. Seriously," Kiran encouraged. "You have to do this."

"Thanks, K."

"You would be great at it," Sonam said. "You have a real eye for fashion, and you're always impeccably dressed. If that's where your heart is, do it. We're in our twenties, and we should take the risk now, before we're married and bound to obligation."

"Do it, Payal. I'm sure my sister Laila would love to cover you for her magazine if you needed PR resources. It's a great opportunity all around," Akash said.

"You've been talking about this for years, and we knew it was coming. Do it," Kiran said, voicing her approval once more for good measure. "You've been saving up to make a move."

The enthusiastic responses inflated Payal's chest, and she sat a little straighter. Her eyes lit up, and Kiran was thrilled to see Payal with more purpose and drive than she'd displayed working at her job at the PR firm.

"Hey, Payal," an insanely attractive Indian guy—tall, straight nose, thin face, straight teeth, facial hair that was neatly trimmed and soaked in pomade to an inch of its life—addressed her from his spot in line.

Payal simply nodded and gave him a wave—with a smile any of the CMC could tell was the kind you gave a person you hoped would never call when they said things like, "We should hang out sometime."

"Former hookup?" Sonam asked.

"No. We grew up in London together. Our families are close. His name is Ayaan."

"He's very cute," Kiran said.

"He's also about to suck face with the goddess that walked in…and trust me, he's not that attractive, the manwhore."

Kiran couldn't tell if Payal genuinely knew the beautiful, sharply dressed Indian girl who walked in with five-inch heels or if she was, in her own alpha female way, a little possessive of her territory as an It Girl.

But when the girl started kissing Ayaan in a way that was more than PG-13 for a public space, Kiran immediately sided with Payal, writing off Ayaan and the girl as mere distractions from a more important conversation.

The others seemed to agree as they all turned their attention back to one another.

"So…speaking of chasing passions…" Sonam started. "Kiran, did you and Nash hang out again?"

"We've actually gone out a lot and—"

"You boned him, didn't you?" Akash asked.

"What? No." Kiran cringed. "That's such a crass way of saying that, by the way."

"It doesn't change what's going to happen. This is inevitable. Be careful." Sonam pointed a biscotti at her.

"That's quite the advice coming from someone who generally tells the world to fuck off," Payal said. "And the girl who told me to go on a career adventure."

Sonam stuck out her tongue. "I'm saying…Kiran is usually the careful one."

"I don't know, guys. I'm not sure about that."

"Okay, well, since Akash interrupted and didn't actually let you finish…What happened?" Payal shushed the others with her finger and gestured for Kiran to continue.

Kiran shot her a grateful glance before continuing. "Something's shifted. I think about him all the time. Every time I spend time with him, I walk away wanting even more. And I tried to think of him as a friend, but when we're together…"

"So much for being just friends," Akash said.

"Are you considering dating him?" Sonam asked. "I mean, is this more than a fling? You've said you liked him and you're deciding. Have you decided to go forward?"

"It's…" Kiran struggled to explain the depths of what she felt for him. The boundaries drawn by her family all those years ago locked her vocal cords in place.

"You're more than friends. You can't deny that," Akash said. "It's already more than a fling."

"Okay, fair, but do you see a future?" Payal said.

"Does it matter?"

"Don't pretend you're stupid, Kiran. You're one of the smartest people we've met," Sonam stated bluntly before dunking the biscotti in her chai. "You know what your limitations are."

"I wish we could be exactly where we are forever. I wish we could be blissful and loving and in this bubble containing the two of us forever. Because he's so wonderful and he makes me so happy…but the more I think about it, the more worried I get. And the more I want him."

Payal watched her sympathetically, an understanding smile on her face. "That bubble sounds incredible. The world would be much happier if love were a place people could dwell in without any repercussions. But you're going to have to make a choice soon."

"I know. I can put it off for as long as I want, but it'll always be there, hanging over me."

"Have you told him about your sister? Have you shared your reservations with him?" Akash asked.

Kiran stayed silent.

"Kiran!" Sonam said.

"No…I said I don't see her often and there was a little family drama. Then we changed the subject."

"Wow, you sugarcoated that one…" Akash said.

"He'll run if I tell him the truth and what's expected of me."

"And if he doesn't?"

"Wouldn't you?"

"As a guy, I would want to know. Because if I really liked a girl, I'd want to know we're in it together and that we'd face the shit life has to offer...and if she's worth it, I'll do what it takes to be with her anyway."

"Romantic words from someone who has never been in that position," Sonam said.

"I'm telling you what I think from a neutral perspective, Sonam. Take it or leave it."

"Well, we won't tell you what to do, but we'll be here for you for whatever you need," Payal said.

Sonam raised an eyebrow. "'We won't tell you what to do'? Who are you right now? Of course we will. Kiran, the longer you put it off, the more it'll hurt. We won't tell you to date him or end it, but we will tell you that you have to do something. At the very least, you have to tell him the truth about your sister, or you guys start off on a lie."

Payal rolled her eyes. "Date him. Who the hell cares?"

"My parents will. They're scarred after Kirti."

"Ah, well, when it comes to parental relationships, I'm probably not the best girl to give you advice. The most time I've spent with my mother was when I was in her uterus."

Kiran offered her a reassuring pat on the hand to let her know she didn't judge. Payal had more contact with her family over email than phone calls, and most of their conversations revolved around the family import and export business near London. She understood cultural expectations and family ones but not the love behind those boundaries.

"Is it really that bad if you date someone?" Akash asked. "You've done so much for your family, putting them up in that place in Delhi, getting amazing grades and coming to the United States, and always thinking about them. They could give you a free pass."

"Girls have a different set of rules. Also, two minutes ago, you said you were neutral, and now you have an opinion," Sonam said.

"Hey, boys get the fortune, so we have our own set of rules to abide by. We always have to make the first move. We always have to think about what the girl is going to say to her family about us..."

"Did you really just use those as arguments? Really?" Sonam snapped.

Akash tried to hold back a laugh. "No. I have two sisters, plus you three idiots. I am aware I've got it good. My point is that Kiran has done the job of a loyal and obedient child. She's earned a choice of her own."

Kiran's head spun as she tried to line up the arguments in clean lines.

It was frustrating how many arbitrary guidelines there were for women. Women were supposed to be smart, strong, independent, forward, brave, fearless, and unique. But they weren't supposed to shine too bright, be too bold, too sharp. They were supposed to fit in, have friends, make people think they were sexually invigorated but not actually be sexy for themselves, and respect everyone so they would appear soft and feminine. This double-edged sword was encased in a cultural sheath. Every country had customs and traditions that were supposed to be valued and cherished, and India was no different.

Truth be told, Kiran had always felt more like an outsider than her friends because she hadn't been raised in the West. She was conscious of her accent sometimes—especially words like "water" or "vitamin," where her *w*'s and *v*'s swapped themselves at will. She hated that she sometimes googled pop culture references on the sly when Akash or Sonam threw them around casually, so she would have a clue about what they were discussing. She despised the occasional judgmental stare down she would get on a subway from an Indian American who had grown up here, who clearly thought to themselves, "Well, you came from India. You're more like my parent than my peer."

While these spotlights on her foreign status were another part of her day, today they felt like inadequacies. Being an outsider had become exhausting. Even the Indian Americans she was best friends with couldn't come up with a clear solution on what to do because she was so removed from their upbringings. She couldn't collect her footing anywhere or identify with any one perspective. Instead, they blurred together and made her mentally rip apart her cleanly organized list of pros and cons and crinkle it into a ball.

No matter how many thoughts were collected on paper in this imaginary trash, however, one colored and glittery heart stood out at the bottom. This talk of chasing passions for Payal and the idea that she was twenty-eight years old with the weight of her family on her shoulders... It prompted Kiran to feel as though for once, she should pursue what she wanted. She wanted Nash. She missed him when they weren't together. And a dim world wasn't one she could go back to now that she'd seen the light.

She had to tell him.

Chapter Twenty-Four

KIRAN

Did you know there's a Library Walk in Midtown? Nash texted.

Are you reading tourism books about New York and choosing things to do? Kiran couldn't help but smile, given her improved Googling habits for the very same reason.

Nash: Are you judging me?

Kiran: A little.

Nash: So I'll see you at six p.m. on the corner of Park and 41st then?

Kiran: …Yes.

Kiran's stomach did more loop-the-loops than the roller coasters at Coney Island while she waited on the corner near Grand Central Station. She shifted her weight from her right to left foot, grinding her jaw.

She'd made a stop at home, leaving work at five so she would have time to change. She had put thought into her outfit—too much thought in fact. She spent well over a half hour in front of her closet, debating between a sweater dress with a cream blazer or a pair of jeans with a white sweater and a scarf. It was silly, really. She and Nash were friends regardless how she dressed. But now she wanted to accentuate her legs, and the curve in her hips suddenly mattered to her. She knew she'd impressed him with her mind, but now her body cried out, *Look at me too!* She wanted to feel as sexy as she knew she could be—while being herself at the same time.

She finally combined the outfits in the end, wearing a blazer over a white tee with a long necklace, skinny jeans, and flats. She'd left her hair loose—clipping back the top with a slight bump and allowing her waves to cascade over her shoulders. A touch of mascara and lip gloss were all she wore.

Now, if only she could get her thoughts to be as coordinated as her outfit.

One second, she was certain she wanted to explore the possibility of a relationship with Nash. A few seconds later, she would backtrack and take it all back. What was she thinking? She reminded herself this wasn't a game. Nash had feelings too, and if he felt the same way, she had to be committed. She couldn't come and go as she pleased.

That meant she had to tell him about Kirti, about the weight of the expectations on her shoulders, how they might be doomed from the start, and how it would never be a relationship that started on a smooth road.

Then a tiny piece of hope would argue back that perhaps Nash would want her enough to be there, to fight for her. Akash's comments about wanting to fight for a woman he cared about could also apply to Nash, right?

As she paced back and forth on the corner, she didn't notice Nash come up behind her.

The hair on her arms stood on end.

He grabbed her by the waist.

Her elbow flew back reflexively and met his abs with the force of a truck.

"Sweet Jesus, Kiran! Houdini died like that!"

Nash was hunched, his back in a perfect arch as his face flushed.

"Oh my gosh, Nash, I'm so sorry! I didn't realize you were right there!"

Well...this is off to a great start.

Nash groaned as he stood straight. "Okay, well...at least I have some doctors on speed dial. I don't think you ruptured anything."

"To be fair, you snuck up on a girl."

"Probably not my best idea... Let's walk your elbow off, shall we?"

They walked toward the library. Every ten or twenty feet, a plaque stood out with a quote about reading and learning. Nash mouthed the words to himself as he scanned the words quickly, but Kiran read them out loud and allowed the words to sink in, the same way she memorized her textbooks in India. Lucille Clifton's words gave her the most pause—a poem about remembering one's own memories rather than the ones others had.

She fell into silence, holding her breath at the gravity of the words and how Clifton seemed to describe her. She must have stared longer than she had at the other plaques, because Nash turned around ten feet ahead and backtracked.

"You okay?"

"Just thinking."

"Want to share?"

"In a bit, maybe."

She crossed her arms, tucking her hands into the spaces in her elbows and finding warmth there.

"Sunshine disinfects." It was something Baba used to say when Kiran had left her freshly washed clothes in a bucket for too long and the mildew smell needed to be aired out. He said it when the truth came out about a scandal involving politicians. He always waved his hand cheerfully as he said it, as if the wave were a breath of air and the issues would waft away with it.

Nash was the sunshine now, but it wasn't as simple as bleaching a turmeric stain on a white shirt by laying it outside. On one hand, colors seemed brighter. Nights were more full of life than they'd ever seemed in Kiran's eyes. She laughed more. Words reached her more deeply, and so did observations about events around her—babies made her grin bigger, sadness was sharper, and now, words that she would have skimmed over and skipped caused her to pause.

Six months ago, those words would have been nothing. She may not have ever stopped. She probably wouldn't have even taken this Library Walk. But memories, hazy and small but memories nonetheless, came flooding back to her about Kirti—like the gap she had between her bottom front two teeth. How she always wore glass bangles until she'd accidentally cut Kiran when she was tossing her in the air and one cracked on her skin, and then she switched to metal, so her baby sister was never injured again. The way Kirti loved math the same way Kiran did, and using an abacus, Kirti had taught her basic arithmetic before Kiran had even entered school.

But the memories her parents cried about often overshadowed her own. The pain the panchayat had inflicted on the family and how it was Kirti's own fault it happened. Those were Ma and Baba's remaining memories because they were the most recent and the ones that shaped their lives the most. And Nash, like sunshine, had disinfected and cleansed Kiran's mind. No longer did she think about Kirti in the context of her parents' memories but in her own, which were resurfacing. The dust was being blown away, and clarity was appearing.

Nash was serving as a cure.

But with the antidote to Kiran's dimmed past came questions about Kirti's departure from the family. How was she, all these years later? Was she even alive? What was her life like now? Were there ever moments when she missed them?

And more than that came Kiran's epiphany that she wanted to build her own life and that doing so might not take her down a path that she was comfortable with. That was her word prior to Nash—*comfortable*. Now that Nash was around and these truths were coming to light in his brilliant presence, she wasn't sure how to move forward with the same concrete intention she had proceeded with before.

"So do you want to grab some chocolate?"

Nash's voice startled her, and she jumped. "Didn't you just get punched for that?"

"I'm sorry... I didn't mean to scare you. There's a chocolate place in the Grace Building. I figured maybe it would cheer you up to go."

"I didn't realize it was that obvious I was a little mopey."

"That's okay. It's my turn to be here for you."

She was amazed he could read her face, that her thoughts were racing, and that sweets were exactly what the doctor ordered. She grew acutely aware that her left hand had slipped out of her pocket and it was tantalizingly close to his. Her skin tingled with goose bumps as they brushed against each other, and she couldn't help but wonder if he felt the same way when he didn't move his hand or seem disturbed when it happened.

They walked in sync, breathed as one, and every hair on her body was set alight from the warmth of his body.

Chapter Twenty-Five

NASH

As they set foot in the small sweet shop, they were taken by the arrangements of handmade chocolates, each with exotic mixes of ingredients like herb and coconut (which didn't sound so appetizing) or almond hazelnut vanilla (which Nash could have eaten a box of).

"What do you want?" Kiran asked.

"Let's have the man behind the counter make up a box," he suggested.

"Do we trust his judgment? What if he chooses something we don't like?"

"Well, we can take it over to Bryant Park and try them out. It'll be like chocolate roulette."

Her eyes twinkled, and Nash beamed at the way he'd put the stars in her eyes.

"What can I get you, sir and madam?" the attendant behind the counter asked.

He was a tall man with browned skin. He was from the West Indies, perhaps, with golden skin and majestic stature. His accent was English, French, and Caribbean all at once—a combination that Nash had never heard but could spend all day listening to. For a moment, he wondered if the man was faking it to sound more illustrious and to match the jazzy tuxedo he was wearing.

"We'll take a combination of everything. Surprise us with a box of twelve."

Ordering for the two of them and being allowed that authority was a novelty. He wanted to take care of Kiran, to allow her to think and feel whatever she needed to while he held down the fort and supported her.

Without thinking, his hand moved around her. Nash rested his palm on Kiran's back.

For once, she didn't move away or react sharply.

Kiran slid gracefully into the curve of his arm, and he curled her in, loose enough to be comfortable, tight enough to say she was his.

His instinct was sure she was.

As the attendant collected various pieces of chocolate for their custom box, Kiran glanced up at Nash. He'd never seen that expression on her face before—like she fully trusted anything he'd do.

"I'll be happy to put one in on the house for you two tonight." This attendant was winning bonus points.

"Thank you!" Kiran's hands joined together at her chest.

"So much excitement for chocolate..." Nash laughed.

"What would you like, miss?" The attendant's white gloved hands gestured at the assortment in front of them, not smudged a bit by all the cocoa he was handling.

Kiran hungrily examined all the different types. "What do you suggest?"

"May I empower myself? I would recommend salted caramel peanut butter."

"Nash? Milk or dark?"

"It doesn't matter."

"It does too matter!" She stepped away in mock outrage.

"And why's that?"

"Because your choice determines whether I let you put your arm around me again!" she sassed back, a hand on her hip.

"If I were you, sir, I would pick," the man behind the counter chimed in and then mouthed, *Milk*. This fella was clearly Team Nash.

"All right then. Milk."

"Good choice," Kiran observed with a grin.

This time, he won the lottery. She rested her head on his shoulder, and his grip grew a little tighter.

"I don't mean to interrupt...but are you Indian?" the man asked.

"I am!" Kiran said. That warmth of reminiscence colored her tone, the way it always did when she spoke of home.

"You know, my mother was half-Indian," he began. "And growing up, she used to tell me of henna and order me sherwanis from the Indian store—which, of course, look the best with a tall figure like this." He flashed a pose with a head tilt and gestured at his lithe body.

"Indeed, they do." Kiran laughed.

"Clearly, your mother had style," Nash chimed in.

It was impossible not to feel cheerful around this man, in this setting, surrounded by sweets, and Nash's arm around a girl he cared for.

"Well, your culture is beautiful and so are you. Have a glorious night," the man remarked as he rang them out.

Nash opened the door and guided her out with his hand on the small of Kiran's back. His eyes darted up at the stars. But he couldn't make out the twinkles as clearly underneath the bright lights of the skyscrapers around them. The H&M building had a neon-red sign blaring. The Bank of America Tower projected colors into the sky with its bright antenna. Down the street, the Chrysler Building stood out as a landmark of the area they were in.

They crossed the intersection to the park, walking closer than they ever had before. Green metal chairs and tables scattered around the cement ground provided respite where groups of friends gathered. Laughter rang out around the square in the middle of the park.

Nash guided Kiran to a spot in front of the fountain where the sound of water could be heard and Times Square seen at a distance. A beautiful dichotomy existed between the lights of one of the most iconic landmarks in New York and the green expanse and library on the other side of them.

"Okay, well, the ninja attendant over there slipped in a guide so we know what we're eating if we have questions…but I say we go in blind and take bites and guess. We saw the labels anyway on each plate." Nash unwrapped the ribbon on the box and opened it, unveiling tightly packed chocolates in different shapes and sizes with patterns etched on some and ridges on others.

"Sounds like a plan. Ready?" Kiran pulled a milk chocolate one out and carefully bit half off.

"And…go!" Nash waited, staring at her in anticipation.

"Oh…" Kiran scrunched her nose, whipping her head around to find a trash can to gracefully spit out the bite she took, but she had no choice.

"Wow, that good, huh?" Nash doubled over in laughter.

"I don't get to suffer on my own!" Kiran managed and shoved the other half of the little piece into Nash's open mouth.

"Aww…gross…" His face mirrored hers, the corners of his mouth drooping down to try to taste as little as possible.

Kiran's giggles were endless at the disgusted expression on his face.

"It's like…jelly. With basil. And thyme. And coconut. With chocolate." Nash swallowed with great difficulty and shuddered at the aftertaste.

"Ugh, I can still taste it. It goes all the way to the back of my throat."

Nash's mischievous smile made Kiran do a double take.

"Why are you… Nash! Get your head out of the gutter!"

"Hey, you went there too if you caught on that fast." Nash chuckled.

She went to smack him, and he caught her hand midair.

Neither of them pulled away.

Instead, her fingers found the gaps in his, and their eyes locked as their hands entwined. The world stilled around them.

Nash's gaze hungrily took in Kiran's every feature. He lingered on her lips, her prominent cheekbones, her angular eyebrows. Her brown eyes on his blue were cemented in place, and nothing on the planet could have torn him from her. As Nash's fingers curled around hers, her fingertips sent electric shocks up his wrist and his arms, all the way to his heart. Heat crawled from his toes to his cheeks.

Kiran's sight dropped to his lips, and hers parted slightly as though she were kissing him midair. His parted too, and he was full of both longing and stubbornness. She inched a little closer, and Nash was drawn to her like a magnet.

"Excuse me, can we borrow this chair?"

An oblivious woman with a kind smile awaited an answer with her hands on the rung of the third chair at their table.

"Go ahead." Nash's sourness was unmistakable.

The woman dragged it away, the metal screeching against the pavement.

"Perfect timing, lady," Kiran muttered so quietly, he barely caught it.

Their hands remained bound despite their stolen moment. Nash hoped an opportunity would present itself when he could feel the same electricity again—it was a high he'd never experienced, having her so close—without her pulling away or making him feel silly for following his instincts.

"Okay...are we trying another?" He reached into the box.

"I'm afraid."

"Don't be. I'm going through it with you." He hadn't let go of her hand. "Here." He fed her half of a chocolate before eating the other half.

"Oh. I like this one!"

"Me too!"

They continued their pattern—bite into one and feed the other half. Nash loved the way she lightly kissed his fingers when she stole a bite from him and how she looked as she reached toward his lips. She felt like his. And tonight, he was hers.

"How are your parents?" He brushed a stray strand of hair out of her eyes.

"Good. Spoke to them this morning, and they're chugging away at life, as usual."

"And your sister? I know you said you haven't seen her, but I assume you guys speak."

There was something about her sister that made Kiran standoffish. Nash had noticed it multiple times—her eyes hardened, or other times, they darted away. It was exactly the same with physical touch until tonight. She'd welcome it, then change tack so quickly, he would be left in stunned silence.

The pause after his mention of her sister was no different than before. It seemed to ensue for hours rather than seconds.

"It's a long story," Kiran finally said.

"I've got time."

"Nash... I... This is new for me."

"What? Talking about her?" He searched her face for any sign of what was to come.

"Talking about her with someone who isn't Indian. It's a tough story to understand even for someone who is."

"Well...try me. I'll do my best not to be an ignorant ass." Nash rubbed her hand with his thumb.

The corner of her mouth twitched. "Thank you."

"So where would you like to start?"

"I haven't talked to her in twenty years."

The words hung in the air. Nash was sure he'd misheard her.

"I thought you said the coming and going stopped or something. You...what?"

"I haven't seen or spoken to my sister in over twenty years." The second time didn't lessen the strangled way Kiran said it. If anything, the pain etched on her face grew deeper.

Nash's instincts began to fire alarm bells, but he couldn't gauge why. He exhaled, remaining calm, and ignored the nagging prickle at the back of his neck.

"That must be so hard. What happened?"

"I'm afraid if I tell you, I'll lose you," she whispered.

Nash's stomach fell. He desperately hoped she wouldn't end whatever they were about to start...but he remembered what Brandon had said about finding out her story, understanding her, and letting her in. He had to keep trying.

"You won't lose me."

"I–I don't know all the details. I...we...grew up in a rural village a few hours outside Delhi. It's run by a panchayat—oh, what am I saying, you won't know a panchayat." She closed her eyes and breathed in. "A panchayat is like a village council. India is a democracy, but some small places still rely on justice through these councils. My uncle served as the sarpaanch, or leader of the panchayat. They solved disputes but also could rule on family issues sometimes.

"Kirti, my older sister, started going to college against the judgment of other elders in our family. My dad said she deserved a better life. The college was a small place about an hour away. She met someone there—an officer in the Indian Army. I guess he was a good guy, or so she told my parents, but they didn't approve. He was a different...lower...caste, and our family wasn't accepting of that difference.

"Eventually, my parents agreed to the marriage. Kirti was the most beautiful bride. I danced and danced at the reception and even put on a performance of classical dance that Kirti had taught me. My parents put all the money they had into sending her off after the ceremony in grand style. I don't know exactly what happened, but I've guessed. My uncle, the sarpaanch, whispered something to my dad, who got very emotional. They told my sister she wasn't allowed to come back. I don't remember much else, except that she cried and cried and held on to my mom until my dad had to separate them. At the time, I thought it was just the vidhaai, the moment the bride leaves her family home—it's symbolic and usually emotional. But this was different."

"I don't understand. Was she kicked out of the family?" Nash asked.

Kiran shook her head. "Because my uncle was the sarpaanch, what Kirti had done was embarrassing to our family...and it reflected on him, so our uncle told my dad that the only choice was to disown her. To tell her never to come back. And she never did."

"They never reconciled?"

Kiran shook her head. "My uncle died ten years ago. My dad had a heart attack, so I moved my parents to Delhi so they could be closer to some of the resources they needed. But Kirti never knew any of this...and despite the external situation being fixed, my parents were too prideful or heartbroken or *something* to find out where she was."

Tears welled up in Kiran's eyes, and Nash's heart went out to her.

"Falling in love is a big deal in our family. Parents usually choose who their children should be with. And when Kirti fell in love, it challenged everything. My parents never recovered."

The puzzle pieces began sliding into place, clicking together as one fact followed another.

"If you date me, you'll be doing the same thing," Nash said.

This wasn't how he'd wanted to bring up dating.

Kiran nodded, staring at their entwined hands. "I thought I'd gotten over losing her. I was only eight, so it's not like I can remember much anyway. But I've thought about her more and more lately. And it's because of you."

Nash's breaths came out quickly and unevenly as he took in her words. She was laying out her fears and trusting him to wade in them with her.

"Nash, you make me happy. Every day, I wake up and think about how much I want to talk to you. Our adventures together bring so much more joy than I ever thought I'd feel. I never thought I'd feel like this about anyone...but I like you."

In a million years, Nash never would have expected her confession to come like this. He was bitter, angry, thrilled, confused, empowered, uncertain, and swept away, all at once. Her story and her reasoning for holding back were like wounds in a war, each word serving as one more stab from a sword.

A flash of fury swept through him. She should have mentioned it, shouldn't she? Was it his right to know before she was ready? Neither of them had expected this.

But *she liked him*. It gave Nash life.

He brushed a solitary tear off her cheek and gazed into her eyes. "You make me really happy."

Her eyes sparkled through tears, and though her mouth had fallen through the course of her story, she didn't move away from him.

"What about my parents?" she whispered.

"Maybe time has healed them. Maybe they won't want to lose another daughter. Let's see where this goes, and if it comes to the point where we tell them, then we'll figure it out together. One thing at a time." *Thanks, Kate.*

She brightened and sighed with relief, letting tears fall freely as her head tilted forward and a burden had been lifted.

Nash lifted her chin with his finger and wiped her tears away with his other hand. He leaned close to her, his eyes never leaving hers. Her breath tickled his cheek as he came within inches of her lips, and the tingle it sent up his spine drew him in.

They moved together in symphony, as if they were being conducted to make up for lost time—for all the times Nash had thought he had it all and didn't need anything else. His hands traveled to Kiran's face, cupping it in his palms, his fingers winding through her wavy hair. Her fingertips stroked his stubble, an intimate gesture that left heightened tingles wherever she touched.

When they pulled apart and Kiran's enraptured gaze fell on him again, Nash knew his world had changed forever.

Chapter Twenty-Six

KIRAN

It's only Saturday, Kiran thought happily when she opened her eyes at nine in the morning.

She hated when a really wonderful Saturday night was followed by the realization that Sunday would be full of errands and prepping for the week ahead. But today, the day after she and Nash had decided to be together, she had an entire day ahead of her to simply be happy.

To ignore the jab in her stomach and simply bask in having a boyfriend.

"I have a boyfriend," she whispered to herself as she lay in bed and did a happy wiggle under the covers. Her phone already had an unread message from him.

Nash: Morning, beautiful.

She blushed. It was like high school. She was the nerd fawning over the jock.

Kiran: Hey, you. What are you up to?

Nash: I was hoping I could take you out today, actually.

Kiran: Two days in a row. I'm a lucky girl.

Nash: I'll grab the Zipcar and pick you up again around noon. Deal?

Kiran: Are you driving me into the woods to kill me?

Nash: One of those two things is correct.

Kiran laughed to herself. I'll be here.

Nash: Oh, and wear pants. And an old shirt. And maybe sneakers.

She frowned, unsure what he was getting at, but curiosity overtook her.

She bounded out of bed, full of energy and thrilled at the prospect of a few hours of being with Nash.

By eleven thirty, she'd showered, dressed in a pair of faded wash jeans and a teal-and-blue-plaid button-down shirt, rolled up to her elbows. She'd thrown her long black hair into a ponytail with some longer bangs framing her face and smoothed some sunscreen over her skin before putting on some eyeliner and mascara.

She pulled up her texts again, wanting to tell the CMC all about last night.

Kiran: Okay, are you ready? We're dating.

Payal, as usual, was the first to respond. Kiran knew she had her phone glued to her hand from the second she woke up.

Payal: YES I KNEW THIS WOULD HAPPEN GOOD JOB KIRAN!!!

For the typically grammar-obedient Payal, the excess punctuation was a big deal.

Sonam: Proud of you for making a choice that works for you. Can't wait to meet him!

Akash: Good job, K. Back to bed now.

Payal: Akash may go to bed but I want details. How did this happen?!

Kiran: We went to Bryant Park last night. Did a little chocolate roulette. Confessed how we felt. We even talked about my parents a little bit.

Payal: OMG! How do you feel?

Kiran: Today, I feel amazing. He is amazing.

Payal: Ahhh, this is so exciting! I'm thrilled for you. When are you going out on your first official couple date?

Kiran looked at the clock before texting back, Literally in ten minutes.

Sonam: So happy to hear that. Be careful and have fun!

Payal: Use protection!

Kiran rolled her eyes but couldn't help the goofy grin from stretching across her face as she stowed her phone in her bag—and the knock at the door made her jump.

Nash was dressed in a pair of jeans and a thin, black hoodie that had the Vanderbilt University logo in yellow lettering across the front. Despite being thirty, he could have passed for a college student in his casual gear and sneakers, like he'd just rolled out of bed and decided to go to the commons for breakfast.

The sight of him and knowing he was hers took Kiran's breath away.

"Hi," she whispered.

He grinned, flashing his big smile, and took a step toward her, his hands immediately traveling to her waist. His lips pressed against hers gently before he pulled away.

"Hi," he said, his face only inches from hers. "Ready to go?"

She slipped her Keds on and pulled the door shut behind her.

Nash took her hand before they reached the stairs. His strong fingers wove through hers, and Kiran couldn't remember the last time she'd done this with someone, relishing the safety and calmness it brought to her.

Nash had double-parked and left his blinkers on.

"I am ninety-two percent sure this is twenty kinds of illegal," Kiran commented.

"I thought my rebellious nature would impress you," Nash replied.

As they set off, their hands joined over the gear shift, and light music playing in the background—*was that Lewis Capaldi?*—served as a soundtrack.

Little butterflies cruised in Kiran's stomach, and they drove in comfortable silence up FDR Drive as she stared out the window at the skyline of Brooklyn, Roosevelt Island, and Queens as they passed her.

"So where are we going?" Kiran asked after a few minutes.

"We are crossing one more thing off your list."

"Oh, really? And what's that?" Kiran asked.

"You'll see."

"I don't remember putting anything on my list that involved a car."

"I told you… You'll see. Patience is a virtue."

"That's what people say when they want to keep secrets." Kiran pouted.

Nash laughed but didn't give in.

Buildings, tightly packed in the heart of Manhattan, began spacing out, and greenery appeared as they exited and merged on highways leading farther and farther north and away from home. Kiran stared, wide-eyed, at all the colors that had begun to appear on trees as a result of the September air.

"I need to get out here more often," Kiran murmured.

"It's beautiful," Nash agreed. "I guess we never know what's outside of the bubble. The city offers everything you could possibly need, and it's so easy to forget that this—nature—is the one thing it lacks."

An hour later, they had reached their destination. Nash pulled into a dirt parking area, and the smell of manure hit Kiran's nose, causing her to wrinkle it.

Nash put the car in park and turned it off.

Kiran climbed out of the car, stepping onto muddy grass and gently pushing the door shut behind her. She gazed around in surprise.

"A farm?"

"Horses," Nash replied, leaning against the driver's side door. He pointed behind her.

When Kiran turned around, a beautiful chestnut-colored horse strolled alongside a fence. When it lifted its head, Kiran swore it gave her a wink, though it probably blinked.

She gasped. "We're going horseback riding?"

"Two hours of trails." He stepped up next to her.

"Nash, oh my gosh…"

She threw her arms around his neck, nearly causing him to lose balance on the uneven grass.

"I figured we could do something new as a couple."

As a couple. The words brought a smile to Kiran's face, and her heart gave a flutter.

Kiran followed Nash into the main cabin where they met the man who owned the farm, signed some liability papers, and exited out of the back side of the ranch into a holding area between fenced fields.

The farmer, a man named John, had a handlebar mustache and a beard that Nash muttered, "impressive," in reaction to. He would serve as their guide, quietly following.

"Tug right on the reins to go right. Left to go left. If you pull back, the horse will stop. Gently knock your heels against their sides a few times to get them to go faster. And be nice. They are tamed and trained, but they are still animals. Respect them. Any questions?"

Nash and Kiran shook their heads.

"Well, you're about knee high to a grasshopper, so I'll give you Lightning," he said to Kiran, pointing at a black horse with a white marking on his muzzle.

"Oh, I get the Harry Potter of horses!" Kiran exclaimed.

"And you, since you're her sidekick, will get Thunder. He's a little wilder and a little bigger since you're taller."

"He gave him to me because I've got thunder down under," Nash leaned over and whispered to Kiran.

Kiran burst out laughing. "Behave."

But she had to wonder...

John brought the horses around, leading Kiran and Nash up to a step stool and directing them as they threw their legs over the sides of their horses.

"Now, I'll keep quiet and let you guys enjoy your ride. I'll follow the two of you, and your horses know where to go. But give me a shout if you need anything. That's what I'm here for," John said.

"So," Nash started once the horses took their first steps toward the trail. "Did I ever mention that I grew up terrified of horses?"

"What?" Kiran whipped around. "Why didn't you say anything?"

"You were excited, and I wanted to be there when you got to experience it."

"Why are you scared?"

"I'm not anymore," he said, but as his horse moved, he grabbed the reins.

"Liar. But for the sake of protecting your ego, I'll pretend I believe you. Why *were* you scared?"

"So when I was little, I went to a birthday party at a friend's. I must have been five or six. And they had pony rides. What kid isn't going to be excited, you know? But this little horse reared when I sat on it, and I fell right off, onto my ass, in front of the entire party."

"Well, I hope your ass feels comfortable on that horse now," Kiran responded, fighting a laugh.

Nash chuckled behind her.

The three set off, their horses gently leading them on a path of grass that had been run down and dried out, where countless other riders had trod before them. The path was enveloped by trees, occasionally opening up into fields of grass. The fall colors and the leaves on the ground made Kiran think she was surrounded by red, orange, and yellow confetti.

Occasionally, she turned around to check on Nash, who was sitting awfully straight and alert on the back of his horse for someone who claimed to be fine when Kiran asked.

But Kiran was at peace with the side-to-side sway as they roamed the countryside. Her horse was a gentle giant that seemed to know its way around, unbothered by who it was carrying on its back.

About halfway into their two-hour ride, they came to a clearing.

"I'll leave you two to your surprise," John said as he climbed off his horse.

Kiran gave Nash a questioning look.

He shrugged in response, with a smile.

John helped both of them off their horses and grabbed their reins, leading them to a nearby tree.

"What are we doing?" asked Kiran.

"I figured we could have some s'mores. I know it's a little less magical when it's not night outside, but I did my best."

Nash pointed at a firepit fifty feet away, with logs to serve as seats surrounding it.

"And," Nash added, "I asked for vegan marshmallows for you."

Kiran could have kissed him then and there. The thoughtfulness of this entire operation was staggering.

"Thank you," she managed. "Seriously. This is more than enough."

She hoped the look on her face could convey what her heart was screaming, that this man was amazing and that she adored him.

John lit a fire, adding kindling to it from a pile by the tree before going off to take care of the horses. They stuck their choice of marshmallows, vegan or nonvegan, on the ends of their roasting sticks and dangled them over the flame, watching the outside brown and crisp.

"This reminds me of fall back home," Nash said.

"Why's that?"

"I've told you I spent a lot of time at Brandon's house growing up. His family had a firepit in their backyard. We used to go to football games on Friday nights and then roast marshmallows and hang out with all our friends around a fire until midnight, or whenever we had curfew."

"Did you have a curfew?"

"Nah...my mom didn't lay down the law about that, but I think she knew I was always safe at the McGuires' anyway."

"My parents were really strict," Kiran remembered. "They were protective over Kirti, but it went to level-ten overprotection with me. But then they let me go to boarding school. I guess it was a balance of what they could control versus what they saw for me."

"Did you ever have a rebellious phase?"

Maybe now.

"No, not really," Kiran said instead, pushing the thought out of her mind. "Did you?"

"Nope. I mean...weed once or twice in high school. Typical stuff. But I'm pretty boring."

Kiran laughed. "I'd hardly call you boring."

Nash's cheeks tinged pink, and Kiran was endeared by his humility.

"Thank you, by the way."

"For what?" He peeled the marshmallow off the end of his stick.

"For being thrown off a pony and still giving me this experience."

"It was on your list...and I want to encourage you to keep crossing things off. You've done the same for me." He shrugged before murmuring, "And you mean a lot to me."

"You mean a lot to me too, Nash."

And his smile, it occurred to Kiran, burned brighter than any flame in front of them.

Chapter Twenty-Seven

NASH

Nash's runs were personal bests this week. He didn't know if it was from last Saturday and seeing the look of sheer joy on Kiran's face when she'd realized they were at a horse farm or from the simpler moments throughout the week, like Kiran knocking on his door and the two of them spending a few hours stealing kisses while binging on Netflix shows.

Either way, it was Kiran, the root of happiness for him. Add in a new city and exploring it in a fun way, a lot of laughter, Brandon nearby, and a job he loved... Well, Nash was pretty darn lucky.

Brandon: How goes it with Kiran?

Nash: She's awesome. How's Tasha?

Brandon: Also awesome. You doing anything today?

Nash: Yeah, I wanted to eat some good NY pizza. Kiran wanted to hang. Any suggestions?

Brandon: Di Fara in Brooklyn. Don't ask questions. Just go.

Kiran knocked on the door around noon.

When Nash opened it, he couldn't help but smile. She was wearing a pair of jeans with black flats and a pale-blue cardigan over a black tank top. Her hair, typically straightened and worn down, was up in a messy bun with tendrils framing her face.

"Hi," she said.

He grabbed her and pulled her inside in response, pressing his lips to hers and hungrily running his tongue over her bottom lip. Kiran responded with the same enthusiasm, wrapping her arms around his neck and pressing up against his chest.

"Hi," he said when they pulled apart.

"Well, now I can't remember what we were going to do all day, but we could do more of that." She smirked.

"You'll never hear me argue against it," he responded before kissing her again.

A few minutes passed, with Kiran leaning against the door and Nash's hands exploring the skin at her waist before her stomach gurgled.

"That was attractive," she mumbled.

"I didn't realize I was dating Godzilla!" Nash laughed.

"Watch yourself."

"Okay, well, let's fix that grumble."

"Let's get pizza. A proper New York pizza."

Nash thought of Brandon's text from the morning. "I have a place in mind."

It was a short walk from the subway stop in Brooklyn to Di Fara Pizza, a tiny place with a window where a worker was serving pizza to the line stretching down the block.

"Wow, Brandon wasn't lying," Nash said. "This place has to be good if there's a line, right?"

"Brooklyn's got some of the best pizza places in New York," Kiran said. "This will be worth it."

"Can your belly handle the wait?"

"We just spent an hour on a train to get this pizza. A few more minutes won't hurt." Kiran gave an exaggerated sigh. "The things I do for you."

Nash rolled his eyes and weaved his fingers through hers, leading her to the back of the line. It was silly how content he felt when Kiran's small hands fit into his, but that cliché about puzzle pieces was true—Kiran and Nash fit together.

"How are your parents doing?"

"They're good. My dad thinks he's young enough to do more than he should, and my mom is a mother hen who likes to tell everyone what to do." But the way Kiran softened when she spoke about them told Nash that her complaints were made with the utmost love.

"Have you thought about if you might want to tell them about us yet?"

"Oh. Um. Am I supposed to?" Her eyes darted away from him.

Nash felt a pang of something but couldn't place his finger on it. "No, you don't have to. We've only been dating a short while."

"I'll tell them," she promised. "But I want to enjoy you first."

Nash tried to ignore the unsettled feeling he had but reminded himself they'd been dating only a week and that while the intensity of what he felt was enormous, logic didn't dictate going all in after such a short time. She wouldn't leave—she just needed to do this on her time.

"Nash," Kiran said gently, pulling on his arm. "Come back to me."

He looked at her.

"I'll tell them. It's a promise."

The earnestness in her expression erased any doubt, and he nodded his head, pacified. "I don't want to force you. I know it sounds ridiculous mentioning it to them so soon. I know they're important to you, that's all."

"They are. You're right. And so are you." Kiran kissed his cheek.

He gave her a quick peck on the forehead, breathing in her scent of sandalwood and roses, the lingering fragrance from the incense he knew she kept in the corner by some Hindu figurines.

As they stepped up to the service window, Nash paid ten dollars for two slices of cheese pizza for the two of them.

Kiran took a bite before he did, and her cheeks filled up like a chipmunk's.

"Wow," Nash managed, staring at her. He took a bite of his own and groaned loudly, in awe of the fresh taste of olive oil drizzled onto the top of the slice and how it brought the flavors together.

Kiran's eyes widened; she blushed and looked away quickly.

"What? This pizza is like a slice of heaven."

"I just...had a dirty thought when you made that noise," Kiran mumbled.

Nash raised his eyebrows. "Look at your filthy mind, Kiran Mathur."

"Oh, shhh. If I made the same sound, you'd think it too."

"Hold on. I'm picturing that."

"Don't fantasize in public!"

"Too late."

Kiran smacked his arm playfully before taking another bite.

They leaned against a wall around the corner from the shop, eating in contented silence. Kiran finished in half the time it took Nash.

"Now I feel terrible about making you wait to eat. You scarfed that down. Do you want another slice?"

"No...I have a better idea."

"What?"

"Come with me."

She grabbed his hand and began pulling him toward the Avenue J train station. They scanned their subway tickets and listened to the loud screeches on the rails from other trains as they passed before finally boarding the one meant for them.

Finally, when Nash was beginning to think they'd looped around Brooklyn somehow, they arrived in Carroll Gardens.

"That took forever. Also, I always thought public transportation was supposed to shorten a journey."

"Well, Nashville, sometimes it doesn't. Stop whining. It's not like you have anywhere better to be."

"That's true. I'd rather be with you than anywhere else anyway."

Kiran lit up at his remark.

"Okay, so where are we going?"

"To one of my favorite streets in Brooklyn for a treat!"

Smith Street was like seeing multiple eras come crashing together in an eclectic explosion. The architecture contrasted between turn of the century, industrial, and modern, with boutiques, niche stores, and chains all at once. It was so unique in comparison to their East Village neighborhood that Nash spent most of their walk gazing at all the details.

"This neighborhood is so up your alley," Kiran commented.

"I agree. It's a little hipster. A little quirky. Lots of personality."

"Exactly. Just like you."

They stopped in front of a white building with projecting glass windows, seating placed on the inside so that visitors could watch those passing by on the street. Pink mehndi patterns decorated the windows, and a door in the same pink led inside.

"Ice cream?" Nash asked. "We couldn't go to a place nearby?"

"Not just any ice cream. It's all Indian-inspired," Kiran said, her voice bubbling with excitement.

"All right, I'm sold. Let's do this," Nash said.

The inside of the store was as minimal as the outside. The white stucco walls had a subtle, white mehndi pattern rising from them, a tiny detail that added culture into a minimal space. The hardwood gray floors added neutrality, while the pink back wall was the only major pop of color. The menu hung behind a white counter with pink designs on it, another splash of pink.

As Kiran and Nash neared the counter to place their order, his hand on her waist, he could sense Kiran's energy rise and a tiny bounce appeared in her step in excitement.

"What can I get you?" asked the girl behind the counter.

"Can I sample the masala chai?" Kiran answered before she'd even finished the question, her gigantic grin giving away how happy she was.

"You can take the girl out of the CMC but can't take the chai out of her, apparently," Nash said, remembering the nickname for her crew of best friends.

"This isn't for me, silly. Actually." She turned to the girl again. "Can I have two of those samples? Now he's making me want some too."

She turned back to Nash.

"It's for us. Chai is what bonded us when we met after all."

Nash gently rubbed her lower back in response, warmed to her sentimentality. "Then that sounds perfect."

The cool taste of cardamom, vanilla, sugar, cream, cloves, and ginger flooded his senses.

"Okay, I take back all the cynicism about coming this far for ice cream. This is amazing."

"I told you!"

They tried a few more samples of mango and cream, rose with cinnamon-roasted almonds, and sweet roti and ghee. Nash had never tasted so many rich flavors in desserts before, and he was eager to keep going, certain he'd try everything on the menu.

Eventually, he settled on a cup of carrot halwa, a flavor he had been dubious about because who puts carrots in ice cream? But he'd been so shocked at the pleasant sweetness of it that he'd found himself wanting a giant two-scoop cup of it.

Kiran ordered two scoops of rose with cinnamon-roasted almonds, in a cone made of jaggery.

"So what is jaggery, exactly?" Nash asked, staring at the cone Kiran was holding, when they sat at a gold table on pink chairs.

"It's a brown sugar. You can use it as a base in a lot of Indian sweets when you melt it with water or ghee."

"That sounds awesome." Nash took a lick of his ice cream, relishing it.

"It is. My mom used to make this sweet with jaggery for my birthday. She'd toast cashews in butter and mix them with a little cardamom, then mix rice with jaggery and put the nuts on top. She used to offer it at the temple first, as prashad, or an offering. I swear that only made it taste better," Kiran said fondly.

"Do you know how to make it yourself?"

"I do...but it's different when your mom makes it and it's infused with some sort of magic that you can never capture on your own."

Nash nodded, giving a small smile and feeling a small pang in his chest.

"Oh my gosh." Kiran paled. "I'm so sorry, Nash. I blanked. I didn't mean to be so insensitive."

"No, it's okay." Nash was honest. "I don't know what that feels like, but it doesn't mean I can't imagine it. And I imagine you must miss her when you don't get that sweet on your birthday now."

Kiran nodded. "That's something we'll have to learn, right? The sides of each other we don't immediately understand."

Nash gazed at her, earnestly looking back at him—with a giant blob of ice cream on her upper lip. He stifled a laugh.

"What?"

"You've got ice cream on your face... I'll get it."

And he leaned in and kissed it off her.

"That was such a Bollywood hokey move." She laughed.

"Would you rather I not kiss you?"

"Don't you dare. Get over here," she said before leaning in again.

A cool drip of ice cream hit Nash's hand, which rested on the table.

"You realize you're dripping everywhere, right?"

Kiran looked down. Lines of ice cream had begun to trail down her hand, and she frantically licked up her wrist, trying to prevent it from continuing to make a mess. Nash tried to ignore the sight of her tongue moving gently.

"I didn't catch that I was dating a toddler. Haven't you ever eaten an ice cream cone before?"

"Shut up! You distracted me!"

Nash got up and picked up some napkins from the counter. He wrapped his hands around her wrist, wiping down the stickiness, and when he touched her skin, Kiran locked eyes with him. He slowed for a second, allowing his insides to fill up with happiness.

And even when she pulled her hand away and playfully pushed her ice cream cone into his face, he was certain there was nowhere he'd rather be but in Brooklyn, at a tiny Indian ice cream shop, with a girl who made his world turn.

Chapter Twenty-Eight

KIRAN

"It's nice to see him make you so happy," Payal remarked as she and Kiran sat across from each other at a coffee shop on the Lower East Side.

"You know, in the last month, a switch has turned on. I feel fuller, like I'm carrying more happiness inside of me. I didn't know it was possible. It's not like I was incomplete before I met him. But the addition of him has made life...so much more." Kiran shrugged. She didn't have the words.

It had been over a month since the night in Bryant Park when she and Nash had decided to be together—and Kiran couldn't help but feel better for it, despite the nagging feeling that she was betraying her family.

"Have you told your parents yet?" Payal asked, as though she'd read the footnote at the end of Kiran's thoughts.

"Get out of my head."

"I can see it on your face," Payal said, pointing with a finger while she sipped her coffee.

"There are some palpable differences between us. He doesn't have a family. I can't live without mine. And being Indian is enough of a difference sometimes—explaining what it feels like to be an immigrant, or the world I grew up with, or even certain foods… translating meanings of words to convey a specific emotion. Some of those aspects are tiring, though I'm happy to do it because he's so special to me."

"I think that's the problem for anyone who straddles two cultures, Kiran. You're from India so that's a different experience. But for people like us, who grew up here, it's both similar and different. There are always two worlds at play, and they sometimes clash."

"Truth." Kiran nodded.

"You'll figure it out. You always do." Payal tossed her hair over her shoulder before speaking again. "Want to go shopping?"

"Isn't that what we did all afternoon?" Kiran said in disbelief. "We spent three hours walking around."

"Well, that was for me, but now I have to style someone, so I have to shop for them."

Kiran shook her head with a laugh. "I love you, but shopping for you is tiring enough."

"Fine, fine. Don't support my dreams."

"Don't even try and play that card, miss."

Payal stuck her tongue out.

"So what is styling people about anyway? I thought you designed clothes, not used other brands' clothing."

"Styling people lets people know what my tastes and aesthetic is. It builds up a good profile as I design and begin working on my own stuff."

"Are you nervous about this next step?" Kiran asked. "I would be terrified, if I'm honest."

"You know…yes and no. On one hand, telling my parents I don't want to take over the company they groomed me for will probably go terribly. But on the other hand, fashion makes me happy. I feel powerful. I don't know if I want to give that up either."

Kiran could relate.

"Then don't let go. Take the advice you gave me, and take it step by step. It'll work out."

"Thanks, Kiran," Payal said gratefully. "Are you meeting Nash soon?"

"Yes, he said he'd meet me around six."

"Okay, well, it's five now, and I know you wanted to pick up dinner, so I won't keep you from your romantic outing. Have fun. Use protection."

Kiran rolled her eyes but gave Payal a hug and left the coffee shop behind.

She strolled up Clinton Street to an Indian restaurant where she'd placed an order. She'd gotten Payal's help in selecting the best chicken dishes they had and ordered a few of her own favorites, resulting in a plastic bag filled with enough takeout to feed a small army.

She lugged it for twenty minutes, winding back down Clinton Street, all the way to FDR Drive. The November air was chilly, and the beads of sweat on her brow from her walk cooled as soon as they formed.

Nash shared his location with her just as she was arriving, and she found him sitting on a high bench chair, facing the water.

"Wow, you nailed it on the seats and the view," Kiran said.

"Hi, baby," Nash said as he slid off the seat and gave her a quick peck. "What'd you get?"

"I brought Indian food for dinner! I figured it was time."

"You're not wrong. Between this water, the view, and you... trying Indian food sounds like the perfect combination."

They settled into their chairs on the edge of a wooden platform that seemed to perch on top of the water as though they were floating in the middle of the waves.

The East River flowed quickly underneath the Brooklyn Bridge and the Manhattan Bridge in front of them. In the evening dimness, they appeared as twinkling designs of light against a darkening sky, with a backdrop of Brooklyn and all its glimmering activity. The sound of the water was soothing, like a hum or a whisper in the background, serving as a soundtrack to their night.

"Okay, what am I eating?" Nash asked, examining the spread Kiran had laid out in front of them.

"Samosas and aloo tikki to start. Chicken makhani, naan, and bhindi masala—which, fun fact, my mom used to say would make me smart when I was little—kheer for dessert and raita to cool off your belly at the end."

Nash stared at her. "Your appetite is simultaneously the sexiest and scariest thing about you."

"I'm going to take that as a compliment and start eating."

She pulled out the disposable plates she'd requested from the restaurant and doled out a little bit of everything onto the plate.

"Here, you take it," Nash offered.

"No, in India, guests are considered sacred. You get food first."

"But we're not at home...or in India."

"Well, we'll pretend since it's the food of my people."

Nash laughed. "Sounds good. But I'll wait until you've served yourself too."

"Okay, first bite of the samosa on three. One. Two. Three!"

Nash took a bite, and Kiran watched his face as she chewed on the fluffy breaded crust surrounding a spicy potato-and-pea mixture. Nash closed his eyes and smacked his lips together.

"Keep it coming. This is already an amazing meal."

Kiran couldn't wipe the smile off her face.

Something about Nash loving Indian food was as though he loved a part of her that the rest of the world didn't quite understand. It sounded silly, really, to think that way, but her roots were so embedded in the fiber of who she was that Nash loving that side of her was like he entwined himself in them too.

They devoured the fried goodness of the tikki next. Kiran showed Nash how to scoop bhindi masala into torn pieces of naan, feeding it to him and trying not to gasp as he licked the tips of her fingers when she fed him. She waited to observe how he responded to the chicken makhani and lost herself in the way he described it and inhaled the entire container full of it. They dug into the raita as Nash marveled over the slightly sour yogurt mixed with veggies. When they both dived into the kheer, the sweetness of the milk and rice was the perfect ending.

"I surrender," Nash said, putting his napkin down after they'd finished most of the kheer.

"Me. Too." Kiran shifted uncomfortably in her seat.

"That might have been the best meal I've had in this city. Thank you again for sharing it with me."

"I'll share everything with you," she said softly.

"Promise?"

"Promise."

They both stood, still moving heavily, as though their bellies had physically grown from eating so much.

Nash gestured toward the lighted pathway on the pier, heading farther into the middle of the river. A building on the left side had a white ceiling that swept upward above a wooden platform. The stairs leading up to the platform lit up in the night, and at the top, hanging from the perch of the white ceiling, were giant swings that remained unoccupied.

Kiran held Nash's hand, throwing away their bag of trash as

they made their way to the swings and sat next to each other, still gazing out at the lights and the water.

"Favorite playground equipment when you were a kid?" Nash asked.

"The jungle gym. What about you?"

"The swings. Brandon and I were swinging champions."

"Please don't try that here." Kiran giggled. "I don't know if these swings could handle it."

"I stopped being wild about it when we were eight," Nash confessed.

"Because you grew out of it?"

"Because Brandon tried to convince me he could fly, and he landed on his arm and broke it."

Kiran winced. "Yikes."

"I know. He ruined Superman for me for life."

"You know, you kind of are like Superman."

"How so?"

"A little bit of a loner...smart. Kind. Quietly saving people."

"Well, that might be the greatest compliment of all time."

"I mean it," she said, lightly tracing his fingers with her own. "Except I don't think you have kryptonite."

"I do."

"What is it?"

He remained thoughtful for a moment, his eyes drifting across the landscape before he finally spoke, his expression pained. "I'm afraid of being left."

When she frowned, he went on.

"Why else do you think I only have Brandon and Kate? It's not because I'm a mean guy—or at least I hope I'm not. But I tend not to form relationships unless I'm certain they'll last. I've been abandoned before. It also gives me less chance to screw up or hurt people."

Kiran put her head on his shoulder, taking his hand. "You wouldn't screw up."

"I don't want to take the chance."

"So...outside of the fact that we're dating, why did you tell me that?" Kiran searched his eyes.

"Because I connected with you. I'm in a relationship with you. And that means something to me and...I wanted you to know that. You. This. Us. It means so much to me."

A siren sounded in Kiran's chest, both warning her and indicating that she had lost control.

"You mean so much to me too," she whispered back before leaning in to brush his lips with hers.

They sat for minutes, maybe even hours, in contented silence—two people who began as strangers and ended up becoming so much more.

As Kiran climbed the stairs to her apartment after they'd taken an Uber for the short drive back to their apartment building, Nash followed close behind.

"Thank you for being vulnerable with me tonight," she murmured, leaning against her door. "I know it wasn't easy."

"I meant it. You're worth it...and I trust you."

She wanted to tell him he shouldn't. That the world was a scary place that had expectations of her that she wasn't sure she could measure up to. That she didn't want to try to meet them. That she wanted him and only him.

Instead, she kissed him. Slowly. Gently. And then harder.

And with each tiny gasp of hers and the quiet sighs he allowed to escape him, Kiran lost herself, and every thought about what would happen in the future evaporated in the space between them.

Her lips parted, and his tongue left tingles across her bottom lip as he trailed across it.

Nash kissed the corner of her mouth, his soft lips leaving pressure behind as he moved from her cheekbones, to her lips again, to her jawline, to her neck, and to her earlobe.

"Come inside," she gasped against his ear.

When he followed her in, she knew she'd never felt so alive.

Chapter Twenty-Nine

NASH

When Nash Hawthorne woke up the next morning, he felt like a giddy teenager.

His first thought on waking was Kiran, her back to him, her light breaths creating a steady cadence.

Having someone to care about was a novelty. It had been a few years since he was in a relationship, and this one was unlike anything he'd ever experienced before.

There was a difference between being alone and feeling lonely.

Nash had never wanted for company when he was growing up. His important moments always had loved ones present, even if it wasn't his parents who were showing up. Aunt Kate never let him down. Neither did the McGuires. He never felt lonely or depressed because no one cared.

But being alone was an entirely different concept. He had been alone. Aunt Kate, no matter her intention and support and efforts, wasn't his full-time mother. The McGuires might as well have been family; however, they weren't there every single night.

And waking up next to Kiran made Nash feel like he didn't want anyone but her next to him when he opened his eyes.

Kiran stirred. She rolled over and smiled at him, and his heart skipped a beat.

"What're you doing?" She rubbed her eyes.

"Thinking about a run...and watching you," he admitted, his cheeks warming.

"Cardio this early?" Kiran asked, making a face.

"Well, if it's like what we did last night, it could be fun..." Nash wrapped his arms around her waist and pulled her close.

"Good point," she murmured as she kissed him.

After a few blissful hours in bed, Kiran had to drop off some dry cleaning, and Nash finally dragged himself away to his apartment to change and go for a run.

As he pounded the pavement around a few blocks, he smiled at strangers, stopped to pet a dog, and even said hello to a homeless person to their puzzled bewilderment.

With his T-shirt soaked through and breathing heavily, he climbed the stairs to their apartment building.

Before he headed to the door of his place, he stopped by the mailbox.

He flipped through a few envelopes—electric bills from ConEdison, his cell phone bill, and a student-loan payment bill for the month.

The final letter caught his breath, and he stopped in the hall, unintentionally blocking another resident from exiting the building. He moved with an apology but didn't glance up as he stared at the handwritten addresses on the front.

The return address was from Philadelphia. And the recipient's name was one he never thought he'd see on any kind of correspondence again.

Kirk Hawthorne.

His father.

Nash flipped the envelope over curiously, and his fingers ran over the folded flap disguising whatever was inside. He couldn't help but imagine his dad sealing it with the intention of Nash reading its contents in a day or two.

Then an overpowering thought took over.

He didn't want to know.

How many times had he wondered while growing up what it would be like to have a father? He couldn't count the number of times he ran to the door when he was little and hoped his dad would finally come in after a workday. Why hadn't he even sent Nash a birthday card in all these years?

Nash's mother had told him that Kirk had even left the job at the auto shop when he fled home. He'd literally run away from his own family and his own life. He'd run away from Nash.

Would a letter change any of that?

Nash knew he couldn't get back the twenty-five years he'd waited for his father to show up. They were gone. He'd faced his mother's problem, his milestones like good grades, track awards, and graduations, and his mother's death all without Kirk. For all he cared, Kirk was a DNA donor and not deserving of the title of *father*.

Nash threw the letter on the counter where he left the rest of the mail and went to shower.

He had a beautiful girlfriend and a career he'd worked for his entire life.

A half-assed letter wouldn't change any of that, and Nash was going to move forward. The damage had already been done, and a letter was too little, too late to heal what Nash had faced alone.

Chapter Thirty

KIRAN

She didn't tell anyone of her plans—not even the CMC. Rather, she practiced in the mirror and envisioned how the conversation should go on the phone.

Ma. Baba. I love you. You are my world, and I have always respected all you've given up for me. I remember the nights when Baba worked all day and then came home to help me study. I remember the nights Ma made dinner and fed me by hand because I felt taking time to eat was a waste when I could be studying. Every move you have made has been to give me a better life. I hope that you trust I carry you with me every day. You must trust my judgment—that I would never do anything to hurt you. I know that when Kirti got married, it was devastating for our family. The panchayat changed our lives when they told us to disown her. But you live in Delhi now, and while I know that doesn't change mentality or the connections you hold to Ramnagar, I hope that it frees your burden. And I hope the move will let you accept me...because I've started seeing someone, and he's an American.

Ma and Baba would protest. They would ask how Kiran

would raise children with Indian culture if she was in America. In her mind, she formulated a response.

I know you're shocked and you're afraid. I'm a little scared too. But Nash is open to raising children any way I would like to raise them. And I have Payal, Sonam, and Akash as my best friends. Despite growing up in the West, they are aware of our traditions and our cultures. They can help me. I am confident that I can make you proud.

Kiran visualized the conversation more than ten times in front of the mirror, coming up with counterarguments for the inevitable arguments Baba and Ma would bring up. She thought through the entire problem like she would consider a project. What was the problem? What was the next step? What if that step failed? What was the backup?

But Kirti had dragged it out for nearly a year, sneaking out to see the man she loved and exchanging letters through friends when Baba and Ma had tried to confine her to their home. There was deceit and pain involved with the way Kirti had conducted herself.

Kiran didn't want to do the same thing.

When her heart had stopped pounding and she was confident in her canned responses, she slowly dialed the number for the apartment in Delhi.

"Hallo?" Ma's voice shouted a greeting.

"Ma?" Kiran said.

"Hanh, Kiran! Hello! Kaise ho?"

"I'm good," responded Kiran in Hindi. "I wanted to talk to you and Baba. Can you put him on speaker if he is there?"

"Hanh, yes!"

Kiran heard fumbling on the end of the line as Ma pushed the speaker button and moved around. She heard muffled shouts for Baba to come join her in the living room and that Kiran had called.

"Kiran! Beta, tell us. What do you want to talk about?"

Kiran took a stabilizing breath. Her entire prepared speech flashed before her eyes...and then fell to pieces as she blurted out, "I wanted to tell you that I've found someone. He's American."

Silence followed.

"Hello? Baba? Ma? Did the line cut?" Kiran glanced at her phone to see if the call had disconnected.

"That's funny, Kiran. You're a joker." Baba laughed, but there was no humor.

Kiran paused. Everyone knew she wasn't a mischievous person...and she certainly wouldn't play a prank with a subject that hit so close to home.

"Baba, I'm serious," she said softly.

"You *what*?"

Kiran recoiled as though her father had yelled at her in person. He hardly ever raised his voice. The last time she remembered him yelling was at a vendor who had cheated another shopkeeper in Ramnagar...when she was ten.

"Baba, I know this is scary. I'm afraid too. But Nash is a doctor. I hope you can trust my judgment—"

"We did not send you to America for this kind of betrayal!" Ma shouted.

Now both of her parents were worked up. Kiran winced at the turn of events she hadn't prepared herself for. She had fervently wished the conversation would go according to the script she'd imagined, and this was unfurling at a rapid-fire pace out of her control.

"Baba, I always did what we intended. I went to school, and I got a respectable job as an engineer."

"You think because you pay us money each month that you can do what you want? Is this an arrangement where you pay us so you can whore around?" Ma's words cut across Kiran's heart like glass across skin.

"I do *not* send you money so I can do what I want. Do you think you raised someone who would bribe you?" Kiran appealed to their reasoning, but the hurt she'd caused by admitting she hadn't stuck to the plan was too deep to repair. Ma was on a roll.

"My daughter thinks that because she went to the United States, she can do whatever she wants. You forget your roots, Kiran! You are a village girl."

"I never forget my roots!"

"Money has made you better than us," Baba said bitterly.

"Baba, I am still your daughter. Nothing has changed."

"I would rather have a poor daughter in Ramnagar than a rich one in the United States who does not value us."

Kiran felt as though she'd been beaten with a bamboo stick in a public place.

"You need to end this tamasha," Ma said, using the word for *joke*. Her tone was cajoling now, the way she spoke to Kiran when she was a child and had misbehaved.

"I don't want to. I adore him." Kiran sounded like a twelve-year-old, arguing for the boy who wrote her name on the corner of his paper.

"You don't know what love is! Love grows. Love comes from listening to your parents! Love comes from making others happy!"

"Do you know what would happen to you if you stayed here and had been disobedient with a good-for-nothing boy?" Baba roared.

"Baba, please calm down. You'll make your heart condition worse," Kiran pled now, fearing her racing mind's images of their next phone call being one where she was told his heart had quite literally shattered over her betrayal.

"I already wish I were dead. I wouldn't be able to see you

doing something like this, Kiran. If you were here..." His voice trailed off with deep implication.

"Would you do that to me, Baba?" Kiran murmured. "Would you threaten me?"

"*We* wouldn't. But can you imagine? Can you imagine what they'll say about us? They already said enough when Kirti ran away. Can you imagine what people will *do* when they find out you've done worse?" Baba's tone softened, but it was no solace.

The anger shifted to worry, and it would shift back again. Kiran was sure of it.

"This isn't about you, Kiran. This is not about obedience. It's about your safety. Can you imagine what people will say?" Baba asked again.

"I did imagine it. I know. I'm as surprised as you are. But maybe God wanted me to feel—"

"God would have wanted you to obey your parents, study hard, and marry well! He would not have wanted this for you!" Ma raised her voice.

"You're acting like I killed someone!"

"You did. You murdered the version of you we knew. Our daughter is dead to us."

With Baba's final words, the line went dead too.

Kiran stared at the phone in her hand, wondering if the unreliable line had the misfortune of disconnecting after such a dramatic and heartbreaking sentiment. But when she called back, there was no answer.

The phone rang and rang.

Finally, someone picked up.

Then, the line cut again.

Our daughter is dead to us.

· · · · · · · · · · ·

Like she'd looked forward to her chai dates with the gang, she counted down the days to the weekend—not only to relax but now with the added benefit of seeing Nash. The CMC was like a love affair she never got tired of with new stories to tell and new facts to learn about one another. But now, a real one was growing, and Kiran wasn't sure what to make of it.

She only knew she didn't want to lose it. Nash was built into her life now.

"I told my parents about us," she said softly a few days after the call from hell.

It had taken her that long to process the livid reactions her parents had. The words played so many times that they served as dull background noise on repeat as she got up in the morning, showered, worked, ate, and made the attempt to function as though her life hadn't been upended. As though her heart hadn't shattered and like it wasn't taking all of her willpower not to call them and beg for forgiveness.

They didn't mean it. They couldn't mean it.

"How did they take it?"

"They told me I was dead to them."

Silence followed her statement.

"I'm sure they didn't mean it." He echoed the hollow thoughts that repeated themselves in her mind and wrapped his arms around Kiran a little tighter on the couch.

"You didn't hear them, babe. They were so hurt. It had to bring back memories with my sister."

"Baby, your parents adore you. You guys are so close. They'll come around. Give them some time."

Kiran squeezed his arm, hoping he was right. For the last two days, she'd walked around with an anvil on her chest, wondering if she had destroyed her family forever. She hadn't spoken to anyone about it, hoping that the situation would resolve before she ever had to utter the words out loud that her parents had wished she was dead.

"I wish I could take you to India and prove to them how wonderful you are."

"I'd do it. I'd go with you."

"Really?" She would never ask him to, of course, but the thought of Nash going with her warmed her heart.

"Anything for you. I'll apply for a visa right now."

"No, you won't!"

"Try me," he challenged as he pulled his laptop across the coffee table with his free arm.

"I'll take you there someday." She pulled his arm close again and wrapped both of them around herself.

"Do you want to do something fun this weekend and take your mind off it? There's an Upright Citizens Brigade show I've been wanting to see."

"That'd be nice…but I'm going to a Bollywood night with the CMC on Saturday."

"Well, I'm sad I'll see it without you. But your night sounds like fun."

"Come with me," she said suddenly.

With Nash, meeting the CMC was a gut check. An insistent voice in the back of her mind grew louder by the second to include him in parts of her life that she'd cordoned off from other boys. The CMC held a sacred spot in her life—only the worthy crossed the gates to meet her friends. Perhaps it was silly and not a big deal at all to others, but to Kiran, meeting her best friends was like finding a room containing the Holy Grail—a coveted space that only the brave and pure could enter.

Maybe them loving him would make the sting of her parents hating him hurt less.

Maybe for one night, she could forget how much it was tearing her apart to have them so angry at her and have her other family accept him instead.

"Are you sure?"

"Yes. I want you to meet them."

"Let's do the show and then head over there for my inquisition."

"You mean introduction?"

Nash grinned. "Same thing."

On Saturday, she called Payal at ten in the morning.

"Kiran. Go back to bed," Payal's sleepy voice lazed over the phone.

"I've been up since seven!"

"I don't understand your obsession with being awake early."

"The day is wasted otherwise."

"Exactly. Let me waste my day. I was up late."

"Stop it, Grumpy. I need to know what to wear tonight."

"For India Night?"

"For Nash at a comedy show and then India Night."

"Wait, is he coming to India Night?" Payal shrieked.

She had gone from zero to sixty so fast, Kiran felt whiplash.

"Yes…" Kiran said cautiously. "Though I'm reconsidering that invitation if you're going to be screaming all over the place."

"No, I promise I'll be good. Maybe. Anyway, wear that dress I bought you from that designer in London."

"Isn't it a bit much?" Kiran glanced at the single-shouldered, flowy black dress embellished with beadwork, which hung untouched in her closet, still in the garment bag.

"We're Indian. Nothing is too much," came the duh-obviously response from Payal.

"Isn't it too sparkly?"

"It's Saturday night. In New York City. And you're going to a Bollywood event. You can wear a disco ball and you'll still fit in. Trust me."

The irony in Payal, who had never been to India, telling Kiran about Indian clothes wasn't lost on either of them, and they both laughed.

"Oh, and wear the simple black heels."

"And hair and makeup?"

"I'll come over and do those for you."

She knocked on Kiran's door at precisely 6:00 p.m.

"You know I know how to do my makeup, right?"

"Yes, but it's so much more fun when someone else does it for you!" Payal sang.

Kiran couldn't argue. Soothing tingles ran up her spine as Payal told her to look up, look down, turn, and suck in her cheeks. The bristles of the makeup brushes Kiran used made her wonder if Nash had shaved the fuzz that had grown on his jawline when they'd seen a movie the weekend previous. Her toes curled underneath her chair as she imagined the scruff running against her skin, prickling it in all the right ways. Payal's deft fingers smudged her eyeliner and smoothed out any blemishes in her makeup.

"You're smiling," Payal noted.

"Random thoughts," Kiran lied.

"If you say so," Payal replied with an all-knowing gaze of her own. "I'm straightening your hair."

Over the years, Kiran had come to embrace the way her hair fell in waves, reining it in with smoothing oil and allowing it to remain natural unless it was a special occasion. Payal, however, had deemed tonight worthy of a blowout that belonged at the Oscars. Using a giant round brush, she pulled Kiran's hair into a pouf on the top of her head with the rest of her hair cascading down her back in a fountain of jet black. It was longer straight, and Kiran marveled at how glamorous she looked with this tiny change in her routine, though it took too long for her to care to do it every day.

"Now. Go put on that dress. Shoes too. Let's see how all of this looks together."

Kiran slipped the georgette fabric over her head, pulling it over her nude lace strapless bra and underwear. Brightly colored rhinestones, beads, and sequins curled their spiraling design along the border of the black dress, down the one shoulder, across Kiran's breasts and around her back. Kiran was reminded of the head of a peacock near her shoulder with a sparkly plume wrapping around her opposite side. The high heels added two inches to her frame and elongated her legs, giving them a soft shape she loved when she glanced in the mirror.

"Wow," Payal gasped as Kiran stepped out from behind her room divider.

"Too much?"

"Just right."

Payal had done a marvelous job of accentuating Kiran's eyes with enough black eyeliner to tar a highway—giving their gradual curve a dramatic overhaul as the liner swept up at the outer corners of her eyes and created a perfect teardrop-shaped gaze. Mascara turned her gently lifting eyelashes into ski jumps that granted Kiran a sultriness that she wore effortlessly. Her lips wore a mauve stain that contrasted with the gold in her skin and dusted onto her eyelids. The black dress hugged her curves in all the spots that Kiran felt most confident about—her B-cup breasts, her flat but wide hips, and her exposed arms that emphasized the long muscles dancing had contributed to.

There was no doubt about it: Kiran was, and felt, sexy. Her fears about feeling uncomfortable in a dress that showed more skin than usual evaporated. She was empowered. She was a force. She felt like a goddess.

"Are you meeting Nash downstairs?"

"No, he had some errands to run and had to stop by work for a while, so he said he'd meet me there."

"Off you go. Also, take a cab so you don't sweat off my masterpiece on the subway, you hear?"

Kiran complied. An attractive Indian man gave her a second glance as she hailed a cab, giving her cheeks a pink tinge of happiness.

The cab drove to Hell's Kitchen from the East Village. She spotted Nash from a block away, his height and messy hair giving him away.

Dressed in a fitted forest-green dress shirt and black dress pants, he could only be described as elegant. His hands were tucked into his pockets, a glint from his watch gleaming in the evening light. His skin, which Kiran always admired for its smoothness, was tinted bronze in the green of his shirt. His hair was gelled in the front, in a style Sonam used to call *the frat-boy look* but that Kiran secretly loved as the perfect balance of boyish and put together.

Nash's eyes followed the cab as it pulled to a stop. Kiran swiped her credit card, tipping the driver her typical 20 percent before shifting her weight to the edge of the seat and keeping her legs together so passersby didn't get a glimpse of her girlie bits.

When she extended her leg out of the cab door and pulled herself gracefully to a stand, Nash's mouth dropped open.

Kiran burned from the sear of his wide-eyed gaze as she walked across the crosswalk toward him. His hands had pulled from his pockets and frozen at his sides as though he were trying to capture her in them. She grew conscious of the subtle sway her hips had taken on in these heels and loved the way his eyes grew as she approached him.

He parted his lips to speak, but his voice cracked. He cleared his throat and opened his mouth again.

"You're beautiful," he whispered.

Kiran bit her lip shyly, but unable to hold back, she smiled so big that her cheeks nearly ached.

Nash seemed unable to gather his thoughts, and the wave of happiness in knowing that she could cause any semblance of speechlessness in him was overpowering.

"Um, do you want to go inside? You're beautiful. Sorry. I had to say it again."

She brushed her hair onto one shoulder. "Thank you. The green is flattering on you."

"This old thing?"

"You wear it well."

They took their seats, overdressed for this particular theater but content in their togetherness. Nash murmured that the cast of UCB often got chosen for SNL skits and that many famous comedians of the last ten years had gotten their start performing improv at these very theaters. As the lights dimmed and the actors came out to perform their improvisation routines, she could see why.

The actors ran with the most mundane of topics—often asking the audience to choose a word and then formulating an entire skit around it. Kiran marveled at the improvisation talents they had, amazed that they could roll with an unexpected change in direction or create a joke with such fluidity. It was inspiring in a way. For someone who did well with routine and order, she was dazed by their ability to put together magic out of nothing, with no blueprint to follow.

She loved the way her and Nash's eyes met when they laughed too hard, sharing in the moment as though the show was solely for their benefit. While the rest of the audience wore jeans and Saturday night outfits for club-hopping and going to a bar, Kiran felt like royalty with a prince by her side.

The magic of laughter making their sides ache caused a flood of happiness in Kiran. The final rounds of applause for the cast were raucous, and she fervently wished the night wouldn't end.

And it was only beginning.

"That was awesome!" Nash declared as they stepped into the night air again.

"It really was. I don't know how they can come up with things like that on the fly."

"Serious skill…"

They chattered for a bit about various acts, with Nash being partial to one about a powerboat and Kiran asking questions about slap bracelets, a concept she couldn't grasp.

"They're bracelets that are flexible. You slap it against your wrist, and it wraps around like a bracelet."

"You slap yourself to get a bracelet on?"

Nash burst out laughing. "You don't slap yourself. Well, sort of." He demonstrated by sticking his arm out and mimicking a whipping action. "You have this plastic stick, and it bends into a circle when you whip it against your wrist."

"Your childhood was weird."

"Well, what did you play with?" Nash grew comically defensive.

"Cricket!"

"And you say I'm weird." He rolled his eyes.

"Hey! It's a common sport, thank you very much."

"A common sport played by no one?"

"A ton of people play cricket!"

"I'm sure the three people in other countries who play it appreciate your defense."

"Okay, we've argued about this before. It is played by 125 countries, including a country with a billion people, good sir. Get some culture, why don't you?"

"I plan on learning, seeing as I'm coming to an India Night with you."

"You're uninvited now."

"It's too late. I dressed up for this." He threw his hands out. "You're stuck with me."

"Ugh," she groaned.

"I'm going to ignore that. So...how do you know everyone? You've mentioned chai and calling yourselves the CMC."

"We met in college," Kiran said with a grin as her memory took her back and she began recounting the beginnings of the CMC.

She'd arrived from India the week before, armed only with a suitcase full of clothes and a carry-on full of textbooks from her two years at an international boarding school where she'd completed her junior and senior years. While she'd offered tentative smiles at the girls who looked like her, she was overwhelmed with the whiteness and how different she seemed compared to the other brown girls.

She'd never experienced that before.

Eighteen-year-old Kiran wasn't nearly as confident in her ability to fit in. Like all freshmen, she was enthralled at the freedom this newfound country offered—and was determined not to take advantage of it. She'd already been without her parents. She was here to make their lives better. But it didn't change that she was in a new country with no family nearby and too many quick American accents to keep up with when her English still contained remnants of Ramnagar and Delhi.

As the freshmen introduced themselves, all eyes fell on Kiran as the introductions turned to her.

"Uh. Hello. My name is Kiran Mathur. I am from India. I will be majoring in engineering and—"

She caught two girls meeting each other's gaze and stifling laughter at her accent. The mockery immediately made her stop.

Another girl, Indian perhaps, with flared jeans and a tight black T-shirt, gave them a death glare. "Do you mind? Everyone listened to you go on about how you wanted to be a teacher, Carly, so you should probably quit being a jerk and pay attention."

The girl turned bright red under the unexpected scrutiny and immediately stopped laughing.

"Sorry. I'm Sonam. Continue, Kiran."

Her boldness had empowered Kiran to continue about her goals of working for a bioengineering group. For the rest of the meeting, Kiran snuck glances at her savior. Sonam's hair was the kind of curly Kirti would have loved—a little wild and a little careless. Her neighbors in Ramnagar would have condescendingly called her "healthy." Kiran called her beautiful. With big, watchful eyes and a sharp tongue, she consistently kept the group giggling at her smart-ass remarks and intelligent commentary.

At the end of the meeting, all the girls on the floor began to pair off, heading to whatever social plans they had the night before classes. Kiran hoped to look welcoming so someone would talk to her, but she was a fly on the wall.

"Hey, Kiran," Sonam said, approaching her like a storm.

"Hi!" Kiran said with too much enthusiasm. "Sonam! Thank you for—"

"Don't even mention thanks. Friends shouldn't do that. Besides...they were being bitchy. Do you want to come to a meeting with me?"

Kiran had been taken aback at the language and the warmth Sonam extended. She got the impression no one said no to Sonam. "Um, what meeting?"

"It's for Freshmen Feminists. It's called the Freminists. Weird, I know, but we should check it out."

"Oh...I wanted to start studying."

"Classes haven't even started yet. Come on. I promise you one night without studying won't fail you. Let's go. Payal's coming too."

"Who is Payal?" Kiran asked, embarrassed that in her nerves about meeting so many people, she'd already forgotten a floor-mate's name.

"Her."

She pointed at a supermodel. Well, perhaps not a real super-model, but she might as well have been. With long, straight hair, heavy eyeshadow, shimmery lips, and exactly the amount of makeup to counter Sonam and Kiran's bare faces, Payal Mehra was breathtaking. Kiran could see that even without any makeup and even if she was wearing a burlap sack rather than the Portofino shirt, jean shorts, and sandals she was currently making a runway statement in, she would still capture the attention of anyone in a room. Payal laughed at someone's comment, and her perfectly straight teeth gleamed in the light as she threw her head back without any inhibition.

"Wow," Kiran managed.

"'Wow' is right. Money is on her getting more action than anyone else on the floor. Who could resist those legs? Anyway, let's introduce you guys and we can go."

They took steps toward Payal, with Kiran trailing Sonam like a shadow.

"Kiran, right? I loved what you said about bringing design to life and serving practicality and purpose. You pretty much summed up our company's mission statement." Payal extended a hand and flashed a megawatt grin even more captivating than Kiran had noted a few seconds before.

She had a British accent too. Kiran wasn't sure why she found that remarkable. She'd always laughed when her boarding school classmates in Shimla had discussed British guys becoming infinitely hotter because of their classy lilt, but Kiran wondered if that applied to the entire population now.

That wasn't the kicker, however. For Kiran, who had grown up in a village where most people spoke Hindi and who had learned English from a tutor, TV programs, and reading books, a most fascinating fact was that these girls looked like her. The same brown skin with a golden hue. The same big brown eyes. The same black hair, though Payal's had streaks of brown in it from a summer somewhere tropical (or perhaps a great colorist). But they sounded so different. With one word, any stranger on the street would be able to gauge their background, the country they grew up in, and despite all of them being described as "the Indian girl," each of them had a history unlike the other two and created in a different country. Kiran marveled at this concept. Until now, most of the Indians she had met were like her: homegrown. Here was an entire world of people who had been raised within one culture, encased within another.

"You have a company?" Kiran asked Payal as they stepped into the hallway and made their way outside.

"Well, my family does. We import and export technology in England. But I'm an only child, and I've been marked to head it up next, so it might as well be mine!"

Kiran hesitated to say her father owned a business. It wasn't a corporation. But what the hell—they already knew she was from India. She shouldn't be afraid of speaking out. "My baba owns a small business," she said quietly. "It is like a small shop for all the essentials our village needs."

She half expected a compulsory comment of appreciation, but Payal's eyes lit up. "That's fantastic! Small businesses in rural India are necessary. I read a whole article about it and..." She continued on and on as Kiran glowed with the feeling of being accepted.

This was where the elite went, she thought as they strolled through Duke's campus. Academia oozed from the pores of each arched window she passed. Kiran's sense of accomplishment grew in tandem with her gratitude toward her family for allowing a village girl like her to pursue her intelligence in greener pastures. She never wanted to let them down.

"Sonam, what are you majoring in?" Kiran asked.

"Premed. You know, like every other Indian in this place." Sonam rolled her eyes. "I come from generations of doctors. You know how it is. Khandaan and family pride stuff."

"So...you'll get to play doctor with all the cute boys then." Payal grinned mischievously. She opened a door to the Brodhead Center and waited as the other girls passed through.

"Please...I am so not interested in guys." Sonam waved her hand dismissively.

"Well...I can think of one I'd play doctor with."

Payal had found her next target—a sole boy standing in the corner of the meeting room, holding a cup of juice. His free hand played a game on his phone, and his head remained ducked, avoiding any attention.

He was handsome, Kiran had to agree.

He was tall and a little bit skinny, with hair spiked in the front. His cheeks still held a touch of pudge, making him look even more baby-faced than his cleanly shaven jaw. He had big eyes with a fringe of dark lashes so thick, Kiran wondered if he smudged kohl on them the way the village aunties did on babies.

"He looks enthusiastic," Sonam noted dryly.

"I hope he is tonight." Payal waggled her eyebrows and then beelined for him, leaving the other girls to watch.

Her walk transformed in the short distance between them and the boy from casual to confident. She strode—Kiran might have used the word *strutted*—up to the boy and snatched his phone from him.

"What, too good to talk to the girls here?" Payal teased, and she flipped her hair over her shoulder.

"You clearly don't think so," his deep voice returned. He made no move to retrieve his stolen phone.

"I mean...we are at a feminist meeting, right? Aren't we arguing equal footing for everyone?"

Kiran watched her like an artist inspired by a muse. She had never seen such a calculated charm offensive—Payal's warmth radiated from her naturally with a few deliberately added embellishments, like the way she touched the boy's arm or wound her long fingers through her locks. She was effortless.

In the years following, this encounter would turn into a CMC joke—about how Payal had erroneously thought this boy would be a one-night fling and not a forever.

"Oh, girls, this is Akash." She waved Kiran and Sonam over. "These are my girls, Kiran and Sonam. We live on the same floor."

"So...flag-waving feminist. It's impressive, you're the only guy here."

Akash laughed. "Maybe a surrender flag. I'm a feminist but

I'm the guy dragged here by my older sister. She's the president of the Femme Fatales, the club throwing this thing."

As if she'd heard him, a girl with the same dark eyelashes rose at the front of the room and called for everyone's attention. The group hushed and found seats together near the front of the room. A welcome by Akash's sister, Laila, was followed by another round of icebreakers. Kiran was more comfortable this time, as though she'd found her niche in the last half hour and was heartened by the warm welcome and lack of stares at being an outsider.

It was ten in the evening by the time the meeting ended.

"You know what I'm in the mood for?" Sonam had said the second the meeting had been called to a close.

"What?" Payal and Kiran asked together.

"Chai. Mom-style. Akash, want to come?"

"I have some ingredients for chai masala in my room," Kiran volunteered.

And thus, the CMC was born.

Chapter Thirty-One

NASH

Now, ten years later, as Kiran recounted the memories of their meeting to Nash, she was astounded at how far they'd all come and how they'd still remained the same. So much security existed in the CMC bubble to be who they were—without ever changing their roots.

"So you guys have been friends since that night?"

"Yup. Since the night Payal wanted to hit on Akash." Kiran laughed.

"Did they ever get together?"

Kiran shook her head. "It's always been platonic between all of us…though Payal's man-eating attempt has been the butt of our jokes for the last ten years, and Akash likes to let it go to his head sometimes."

"I'm excited to meet them. I don't have friends like that from college. I mean, Brandon and I have been friends since we were kids, but I floated a lot through college and grad school."

"So you were a social butterfly and I was a snail, is that what you're saying?"

"That's exactly it. But being a snail sounds like it worked out really nicely for you." Nash chuckled.

"I wouldn't give them up for anything. They've become my family in the United States."

Our daughter is dead to us, she heard in her mind.

But I'm not to the CMC, she thought defiantly. *Nothing is going to ruin tonight.*

They had a few minutes to kill so he gestured to walk around a couple of blocks. They continued to walk down Houston Street instead of crossing it, quietly taking in the life the streets had to offer. Couples strolled by, hand in hand, and groups of friends gathered outside bars, filled with buzzing chatter. Nash loved the distant view of the Williamsburg Bridge as they traveled down Allen Street and turned on Delancey Street, exposing the structure in the opening between buildings and seeing the headlights of cars reflect back.

They approached the bar on Essex. Kiran texted the others to see if they'd arrived.

Nash was pleasantly surprised to see a number of Indian people mixed with others of different ethnicities. Even from the street, they could smell the appetizers being made inside—samosas, aloo tikka, chaat, bhelpuri, and a plethora of other dishes mixed with spices like cumin, mustard, turmeric, chili pepper, and cardamom.

"Something smells amazing," Nash commented and looked around.

"Why, thank you, sir." Payal appeared from nowhere and met Nash's eye. "I did wear my favorite perfume."

Payal was stunning. Kiran had Nash's eye, but he could see exactly where her descriptions of Payal came from—black skintight dress, long, straight hair, makeup that looked profession-ally done and sultry, and overt confidence that entered a room even before she did.

Kiran laughed at Payal's entrance and gave her a quick kiss on the cheek. "Nash, this is Payal."

"I've heard a lot about you. Something about Akash, I believe."

"You didn't tell him that story!" Payal mock-glared at Kiran. "You're blacklisted tonight."

"What story? Oh, you mean the one where you tried to get in my pants?" Akash came up from behind them.

"You guys are all like ninjas tonight," Kiran said.

"Well, if you and Nash would look away from each other, you may notice the rest of us," Payal mumbled out of the corner of her mouth, but Nash caught it anyway.

Kiran hip-checked her in response.

"Sonam's running late. Patients."

"From the sounds of it, she'll be drinking tonight," Akash said.

"Hey...I remember hospital misery, though I was on the psychology, not psychiatry side. I'll buy her a round for her ordeal," Nash said.

The foursome found a booth and ordered some appetizers as Payal described each one in painstakingly creative detail.

"Samosas are fried dough pockets of goodness stuffed with spicy peas and potato stuffing." Payal smacked her lips together.

"Hey, I've had those! Kiran got me some recently."

"I can't believe you hadn't eaten Indian food until Kiran, man," Akash said.

"I feel like Indian food is one of those things you need an experienced person for, you know? Kiran's luckily the most experienced person I could ask for, so now that we've started, I can't imagine stopping."

"Sonam!" Payal cried as though she hadn't seen her in years.

"Is she two or three drinks in?" Sonam asked. She gave Akash, who sat at the end of the booth, a quick hug.

"Two, but a third's on the way."

"I'm joining in… Know-it-all patients," Sonam said.

"I'm buying. I was telling the others you deserve a round on the house after all you've dealt with in med school and post."

"I like you already," Sonam said with a high five. "Thank you! Also, I'm Sonam."

"Nash." He extended a hand, but Sonam went in for a hug anyway.

Nash was struck by the warmth and welcome of this group. They hadn't batted an eyelash yet that he was new to New York and new to their culture.

"Your outfit looks amazing, by the way." Payal gave Sonam the once-over. "Did you choose that yourself?"

"Why do you sound so surprised?" Sonam grumbled.

"Because you're usually in scrubs or in really comfortable swingy clothes. This is uncharacteristically stylish."

"Gee, thanks!"

"You didn't choose it yourself, did you?" Akash held back laughter.

"No. Now shut up." Sonam didn't meet their eyes.

Nash suspected there was more to the story than Sonam was letting on, and a quick glance at Kiran affirmed his suspicion as she narrowed her eyes and frowned a little as though she was reading Sonam's actions.

The appetizers arrived, and they dove in.

"I am famished," cried Sonam, groaning as she took a bite of samosa.

"We can't tell," Kiran said.

"Oh my God." Nash's eyes rolled into the back of his head. "How did I miss this for so long?"

The starch of the potatoes also had a tangy spice to it, countered by the sweet peas. The crust of the samosa tasted like a pie crust and dissolved into flaky, buttery goodness in his mouth.

"Welcome to the club," Akash said.

"So you're British Indian, Payal," Nash started a few minutes later, after listening to Payal talk about different combinations of sauces and appetizers.

"Is there a question hidden in there, or are you commenting on my accent?"

Nash chuckled. "Well, if you identify as British Indian, Sonam identifies as Indian American, correct? And you too, Akash."

"Yup." Sonam swigged her beer.

"And Kiran is Indian Indian…but if I ask any of you how you identify, you'll answer—"

"Indian," they all said, then met one another's eyes and laughed.

"As long as you're not asking the question 'What are you?' I think we'll be just fine. That's the most annoying one," Sonam said.

"Oh, and if our parents own a gas station or a hotel." Payal shook her head. "My parents own a corporation, Sonam's are doctors, Akash's parents teach at Columbia, and Kiran's father has a shop in India."

"We have twenty-nine states, seven territories, twenty-three official languages, four major castes, and hundreds of subcastes, at least nine major religions…. We aren't the same," Sonam said.

"I had no idea. That's a lot of combinations." Nash blinked a couple of times, trying to wrap his head around the diversity.

"Have we confused you yet?" Kiran teased.

"I can handle it."

"Okay, are we dancing yet? I'm buzzed." Payal's accent came on a little stronger now.

"I don't know what to do," murmured Nash into Kiran's ear as they slid out of the booth.

"No worries, mate," Payal said, overhearing him. "There's three moves you need to learn. Right now. Are you watching?"

"Like a hawk."

The latest Bollywood tunes mashed with R & B tracks pounded through the speakers, encouraging all those on the outskirts of the dance floor to find their way in. Payal's extended arms began turning as she pretended to screw a light bulb in what she promised was a basic bhangra move. Kiran swayed side to side and moved her arms slightly, letting her friends take the spotlight and the teaching credit as she watched. Nash couldn't take his eyes off Kiran as she began to unwind and merge with her culture. The side he never got to see before, her authentic origins, was on full display, and he was utterly enamored.

"Look at her go!" Payal cheered as Kiran took over the middle of their circle.

Kiran shimmied her shoulders as the bass thumped through their chests. She gracefully hopped back and forth, even in her heels, like a goddess in classic bhangra style. Nash's eyes followed her across the circle. Sweat poured from their bodies as they danced to music from a world away.

It wasn't just Kiran feeling the beat—Nash let it move through him too. It was different from anything he was used to, but it was becoming more and more important by the second because it was so crucial to who Kiran was...and he was enjoying himself.

This culture was colorful and loud and boisterous, but the friendliness and camaraderie were unmistakable and so unique.

The club closed at two, and every minute was spent laughing, making jokes at the others' expense, and dancing. Between the food, the company, and the night, Nash and Kiran stepped into the night air in a bubble of bliss.

"Well, guys, thank you for an incredible night." Nash sighed. "I am gonna hurt like hell tomorrow, but it'll be worth every second." His shoulders ached from throwing his arms up so much and shrugging to the beat.

"It was so nice meeting you!" Sonam said genuinely. "We'd heard so many nice things, and finally getting a chance to get to know you was amazing."

"I'm going to go with Payal, Nash. She's a little worse for the wear," Kiran said to him.

"Do you want me to come?"

"No, I've got it. I'll come back to the apartment later or maybe spend the night at Payal's."

"I'll call you tomorrow?"

"Yeah," she said, locking eyes with him. "Can't wait."

"Sonam, call me anytime you're stressed...and, Akash and Payal, I'll see you guys again soon, I hope."

As Nash headed off in the direction of the East Village, he couldn't help but feel thrilled that his circle was expanding into one giant family.

Chapter Thirty-Two

NASH

When he woke up the next day, Nash thought he'd been spared the pain of a tough workout—one he didn't expect to get through dancing to Bollywood tunes.

Then he sat up.

Aches coursed through his abs like he'd done multiple circuits of crunches and push-ups. He put his bare feet on the floor of his bedroom, and his calves screamed in agony from all the moves he'd been taught that required bouncing on toes.

Kiran's culture was hard-core.

As he stretched out, he laughed a little to himself at the introduction he had to Kiran's life and then winced as the knots in his back unwound themselves.

After he used the bathroom and let warm water soothe his muscles in the shower, he entered his kitchen for a smoothie.

Kirk's letter sat on the counter, unopened, and Nash stared at it for the millionth time, wondering if he should read it.

Between work and Kiran, he hadn't been home often. He had wanted to be there for Kiran while she was stressed about her family. Her anxious eyes gnawed at him when they were together, as if she was asking him whether this was worth it, and he was full of determination to prove they were.

Since Kirk hadn't been a part of Nash's life in ages, ignoring the letter and moving forward was second nature. Forgetting about it had been surprisingly easy. Kiran's relationship with her parents, however, was a part of her day, and the silent treatment her parents were giving her affected her more and changed the way she operated.

To tell the truth, he didn't get it. The entire situation was foreign to him. He didn't understand having concerned parents, though he could recall plenty of times when Aunt Kate reprimanded him for not listening to her or for being stubborn. Having an authority figure in the family wasn't a strange concept.

But the ultimatums and the threats of disowning Kiran were what confused Nash. While he hadn't left Nashville often when he was younger, he had certainly read enough to understand that in some parts of the world, a child's job was to take care of their parents after a certain age. He didn't, however, understand why marrying someone different could impact a family so deeply.

Kiran had tried to explain to him the concept of caste. It seemed like discrimination to Nash, though he didn't say so. She attempted to break down the idea that families from her area weren't as contemporary and that they worried about what would happen to their families because they already fought to survive on a daily basis. But he couldn't imagine his parents having a say over who he dated when they had nothing to lose. He didn't understand the concept of village justice and the panchayat either, especially because India was a democracy. How could a small council run a village, and how could a giant government allow that to happen?

All he could do was be there for her and promise her that he wouldn't leave because things were difficult. She was too important to him for that.

He also couldn't help but hope she wouldn't leave either.

He had a few hours before he had to head back to the office to finish some paperwork, and the letter was beginning to eat at him.

Instead, he picked up the phone.

"Nashy!" Kate exclaimed into the phone.

"Hey, Kate."

"What's wrong?"

"How do you know something's wrong?" He didn't think he had any tells.

"I have a feeling."

"You freak me out when you do that."

"Well, I know you, baby boy. Also, you sound like you got hit by a bus."

"I got a letter from Kirk."

Silence filled the line. Nash couldn't gauge whether Kate's temper was about to explode or whether she was in shock.

"Wait, your dad?"

"Don't call him that, Kate. He hasn't been around since I was little."

"I'm sorry," she said in a hushed tone. "What did he want?"

"I don't know. I didn't open it."

"Why not?"

"Because...I don't know if I want to know what it says."

"Why wouldn't you want to know?"

"He's been gone twenty-five years."

"What's the harm in opening it?"

Jesus Christ.

"Kate, if you keep answering me with questions, I might actually lose my mind."

Finally, Kate laughed. "Sorry, buddy. Do you want my advice, or do you want me to listen?"

"What would you do?" Nash finally asked.

A thoughtful pause ensued. "I would open it."

"Really?"

"Now who's asking the questions?"

"I'm surprised. You hated him for leaving Mom and me behind… I'm taken aback that you'd want to know what he said. For years, you said he had no excuse."

"I'm thinking on your behalf, Nashy, not as your aunt. As a person, I think what Kirk did was despicable, cowardly, and fearful. But for you…given that you've lost your mom, you have a chance to have a parent again."

"I don't know if I want one. I'm thirty years old now. The years of needing a father around are long gone, you know?"

"Sure. That's true. But there are still lessons you can learn from another adult in your life. Even if he left for the years where you needed a dad, there's no reason he can't grow to be a friend now."

"Do I want a friend who would abandon his wife and leave his kid?"

"That's for you to decide, honey. You have to navigate whether you want a relationship with him—if there's something to salvage."

"He abandoned us."

"Then maybe this is your chance for closure, to stitch up old wounds, and not be so alone."

"I'm not alone!" Nash protested more vehemently than he intended.

"You're not alone. We're all with you. But, sweetheart, you know that these things can have long-term effects. Please consider your own mental health and then make a decision."

Nash hung up soon after, ruminating on what Kate had to say. His thoughts went back and forth, so he picked up the phone again and called Brandon to ask his advice.

"You know what I remember about us being kids?" Brandon asked.

"I bet you're about to tell me."

"The look on your face when I'd mention my dad. It got to the point where I felt bad mentioning him—and that's not a guilt trip—just that I would watch your face fall and then be excited for me because I got to do something cool with my dad. But there was still that split second where I knew you felt sorry."

"And you think now is the time to change that?"

"I think now is the time to see if you can repair the damage that's been done...and if not, then you did beautifully without him, and you'll keep on doing awesome things anyway."

"Thanks, B."

"Also, if it makes you feel better, he's still a dick for what he did."

That prompted a laugh.

Nash hung up for the second time and held the letter in his hands. Perhaps he'd get an answer for why he wasn't wanted. Or maybe his dad died and someone else wrote it. Whatever the reason for this note, he might as well find out.

Dear Nash,

It's been a long time and I'm sure you have questions. To be honest, I'm not sure I have all the answers, but I'd love the chance to speak with you or, even better, meet in person. I know I've been absent over the years. There isn't much I can say to fix that now. I know it's my fault we didn't have those years together. But if you're willing to give me a chance, then perhaps we can make up for lost time.

Love,

Dad

Nash skimmed the back of the paper to see if anything else was written on it, but it was blank. Frustrated, he crumpled it up and threw it in the trash before sitting on his couch with his head in his hands.

I'd love the chance to speak with you or, even better, meet in person.

Nash had just hurdled over the first bump in the road, and now he was hitting a brick wall with the idea of meeting Kirk in person. Kate's and Brandon's words about mending old fences played in his mind like a broken record, but Nash wondered whether the damage could ever truly be fixed.

Chapter Thirty-Three

KIRAN

Kiran spent the night and most of the next day at Payal's apartment, where her best friend had woken with a hangover of legendary proportions. Kiran had used the night to ensure Payal wasn't throwing up and most of the day handing glasses of seltzer and painkillers to her. Exhausted from the night—and making comments every hour about how they couldn't handle partying the way they did at twenty—they'd lounged around the sofas and ordered takeout.

By the time night fell and she'd texted Nash to check in, she was ready for her own bed and fell into it.

At 2:00 a.m., the phone rang and jolted Kiran awake. Her heart raced.

A middle-of-the-night call was never good.

"Ma," she answered.

"Kaise ho?"

"Is everything okay? It's two in the morning here. Are you okay?"

"I forgot about the time difference."

Relief flooded through her, and Kiran dropped her head back into her pillow. The fear turned to elation. *They wanted to talk to me!*

"How are you and Baba?"

"We're good. I wanted to see how you are doing."

"I'm fine."

"Are you eating?"

"Yes."

"Are you sure? You sound angry. Are you angry? Are you sure you ate? Eat some daal—it will make you feel better—"

"Hai Bhagwan, Ma, I told you I'm fine!" She laughed.

"Okay, beta, if you're going to say you're fine, then you're fine." Kiran rolled her eyes. "What are you doing?"

"Being yelled at by my daughter for caring about her welfare."

"I'm not yelling. Tell me what's going on."

"Your baba doesn't want to talk to you."

"Oh…" Kiran's heart fell. *Leave it to Ma to tell it like it is.*

"He thinks you've betrayed us."

"Ma, please don't tell me this."

"We expected that you'd listen to us."

"I *have* listened to you."

"You're so far away, and we miss you. You can't blame us for taking care of you or trying to monitor how you are. You're our daughter. Beta, you saw how terribly our family treated us when… well, when this happened before. You're the only person who we can look out for who watches us too."

You would have had two if it weren't for this entire load of garbage we've all gone through.

Kiran wasn't a rage machine. She bowed her head when Baba shouted and did her best not to raise her voice back at her mother, even though she knew most Indian moms and daughters had the type of relationship where all could be forgiven after a tiff.

But fury coursed through her. They hadn't spoken to her. They'd said she was dead to them. And Kirti hadn't been spoken to in years... Was it so easy to cut daughters off and bring them back into the fold? Was their love contingent upon her obeying them for the rest of her life? Did Ma or Baba have the right to complain about having only one person to take care of them when they had forced their own hand and made that choice?

"Whose fault is that?" Kiran fired back. "Whose fault is it that I'm the only one to take care of you?"

Forget digging her heels in and remaining calm. Her mouth decided to take a running start to a free fall off the ledge. A beast had awoken within her, roaring at anyone who came near her wounded heart, whether they were friend or foe.

"Yeh kya bakwaas hai, Kiran?"

What kind of craziness is this? The kind of lunacy that resulted from losing a sister because of archaic rules and pressures that tore apart a family. How could any of this possibly make sense?

"Ma, I am in love with Nash!" she snapped.

It was true that sometimes the truth slipped out in unexpected moments.

She was in love with Nash. And the realization knocked the wind out of her as her mother gasped on the line.

"Love? You don't know love if you can't love your family and honor it."

Kiran tried to compose herself, to speak from a place of logic and reason.

"You and Baba don't understand. Every time I see him—"

"You saw that boy again? We told you that you were forbidden from seeing him."

"You're focusing on the fact that I didn't obey you, not what this is going to do to me or us!"

"This is why we can't trust you anymore. You deliberately choose to disobey us."

"When have I ever disobeyed you? You have to trust me!"

"We did trust you." Ma changed tack, trying to be gentle again. "Kiran, this isn't about freedom or control. We happily sent you to boarding school. We didn't want to marry you off too early because we knew you deserved better and wanted more. We sent you to America to study and make a successful life for yourself. You can't tell us you want to be a member of this family, after all we've gone through together, and then go see him—"

"I love him!"

"You have to make a choice at some point."

"You made Kirti choose too, and she chose him! Why are you making this so difficult?"

"Fine, then choose him!" Ma snapped back.

"I don't want to choose anyone! I want us to be happy."

"If you are with him, we will never be happy. That should make you upset."

"Ma, you already lost a daughter, and now you're making the other one pay for it!" Kiran snapped.

"You never argued like this until he came along! Until you went to America and got these fancy ideas in your head about what a girl should do, instead of understanding our fears and soothing them. Are you sleeping around now? Are you being a whore?"

The insult was as if Ma had hit her with an open palm, leaving a reddened sting on her cheeks in front of a gawking crowd. This was the second time Ma had come at her with the lowest of insults, the one that all women were called for having ownership over their lives.

"I am *not* a whore. How dare you!" Kiran's fists clenched, her heart racing.

"How dare *you*. Log kya kahenga? They will all say we raised two daughters who couldn't keep their lust in check. Two! I don't know what we did to fail as parents, but every day, I ask God the same question."

Kiran ignored the stab of guilt she felt. She could picture Ma at the mandir, head bowed, hands together in humility in front of the priests who would ring bells, circumvent fire around an idol as a representation of God, and handle all the masses who would come to ask for a million different things.

The old Kiran, untainted by love and unbroken, would have caved immediately. The mere image of Ma and Baba's sacrifices would have been enough to whip her back into line, outmarching everyone else in the ranks. But she was so off-kilter, so shaky, she couldn't find her center to handle Ma's guilt trips with any grace or amusement.

But lust and love weren't cause and effect. Lust wasn't the reason Kirti and Kiran turned to people around them. It was just love. There was no mark on their character.

Mustering up what little dignity she could feel within herself, she braced and answered Ma. "I'm sorry you got hurt. I never intended for that. I love you and I'm doing my best. I don't know what else you can ask for."

"I can ask you to *listen* to us! You haven't seen your baba. Since you dropped this news on us, he's been depressed and down. He yells. He's damaged, and it's because of your decisions. Whether you're with this boy or not, you've broken us, Kiran. You broke us."

"Then I don't even know why I'm talking to you."

This time, Kiran was the one who hung up without another word.

Chapter Thirty-Four

KIRAN

When Kiran was a teenager and the United States was a dream away, an article had come out in the paper about a girl from a nearby village. The newspaper dubbed her *Roshni*. Her name, the equivalent of the word *glow*, was meant to disguise her now-darkened life...one she would never get back. Aunties whispered in somber tones about Roshni's fate, and fathers insisted their daughters be escorted anywhere they went as terror and sadness spread through the small locale.

Roshni had been accused of being in a relationship with a boy from a rival caste. Kiran had no idea whether it was true. In fact, she wasn't sure anyone did. But the power of the societal hierarchy put the blame on her, a high-caste girl, for falling for a lower-caste boy. They "dated," according to one newspaper. They had an "affair," according to another. Words like *clandestine*, *forbidden*, and *steamy* were thrown around as though the two people involved with the story weren't people at all—just zoo animals meant to serve a morbid interest.

The tale itself wasn't about the relationship. It was the insinuation that they had sex or participated in something that no parent would want their child to undergo. And dating became the face of a tragedy that superseded the violence itself.

On her way home from school, Roshni had been attacked with acid by a same-caste member of her village for bringing shame on her family and the caste itself. The perpetrator wasn't even related to her. He had only heard of the gossip and decided she should pay. Her face, burned away by a simmering bottle of poison, was scarred forever. No one wanted her after that. She would be mocked incessantly as a mutant. In an accompanying photo of her story, she wore a scarf over her face, one eye drooping farther than the other from the damage caused by the incident. She had lost her vision, her looks, and the life she had seen for herself.

Kiran was never sure what had prompted an acid attack on one girl and disowning another. Kirti's punishment, in relative terms, seemed less severe. Perhaps she had even escaped a terrible fate by being banished.

"Ma...could someone do that to me?" Kiran had asked her mother.

"We would never, beta, but you should always follow the rules, so no one has reason to do something like this to you." The reply served as a warning from an equally shaken Ma.

"What are the rules?"

"Listen to your parents and Bhagwan. You will never go wrong. Let's go to the mandir."

Listen to your parents because she didn't—and Roshni deserved it. No matter how well meaning Ma had tried to be, the sympathy came with a dire consequence and an equally strong warning: Breakers of rules would be punished. Follow the path laid out, and you would be safe.

In the years following, Kiran often wondered what Ma prayed for in the mandir that day. Ma stood in her red salwar kurta, her dupatta dutifully pulled over her head as married women did, and her eyes were closed in feverish concentration. Even her breathing slowed, the twinkle in her necklace no longer catching the sun from movement. Kiran wondered if she asked for peace. If she asked for dutiful daughters. If she asked for solace for Roshni and her family, who would never find peace again.

Perhaps she asked God not to allow her daughters to fall from grace and earn that punishment.

Kiran never asked. Maybe she was too scared to.

But a stab of righteous indignation and cowardly fear still blew over her every time she thought of the article and what could happen to a young woman for doing anything that could impugn her family's reputation...how an action—whatever that may be, like having feelings for someone, dating someone, sleeping with someone, or having her own mind—could lead to catastrophic consequences for the rest of her life from strangers with a sense of ownership over her choices. Maybe her family would have accepted it down the road, but their choice for their daughter, and her hopes and dreams, were taken away by a society so bent on keeping collective control over their image that they took the situation into their own hands.

Her family would always be branded as the parents whose daughter fell in love out of caste.

Kiran: My mom said I broke them. She also said I was a whore.

Payal: WHAT?

Akash: Are you okay?

Sonam: Why is that always the first attack...ffs. I love your mom but the foodgasm she gives me isn't enough to keep me from calling out how wrong she is here.

Payal: Sonam, they don't know much better than to attack.

Kiran: You think people will hold it against my parents if their second daughter does what the first did?

Sonam: If they do...are you able to cope with that?

Kiran: Honestly? I don't know. I feel responsibility toward the place I grew up in. Geography doesn't change history. And ours is full of pain.

Akash: Whatever you decide, we're here for you.

Baba had lovingly caressed her forehead with damp washcloths when Kiran had gone down with typhoid during her seventh-grade final exams—tests that the government didn't allow students to make up without repeating a year, and the state had forced her to take them anyway. Ma had sold a set of her gold wedding bangles to pay for Kiran's schoolbooks.

Nash had been around for months...and in comparison, while his emotional weight held strong on the scale Kiran measured him on, the time she had with Ma and Baba always weighed in their favor. The things they had given Kirti and Kiran—educations despite the small towns they'd grown in, textbooks despite their income limitations, love despite being girls in a society that valued boys— those counted for more than few months of butterflies, right?

Her body squirmed underneath the sheets that night, suddenly hot and cold at the same time. Her body reacted to the decision she made with violent chills. The creaking floorboards from the apartment above her screeched in the quiet.

That night, her dreams were full of smoking flesh and screams of agony.

I'm coming over. She texted Nash in the evening, after she had spent hours trying to talk herself out of what she was about to do.

She buzzed up to his apartment, feeling a rock settle in her belly.

"Hey, I was hoping to see you. I wanted to talk to you about something," Nash said as she entered the living room.

The apartment was clean, as though Nash had spent the entire night scrubbing everything in his sight. An open letter was the only thing askance on the coffee table. But right now, Kiran had to speak.

"Can I go first?"

Nash's face wasn't helping. He was so hopeful and delighted that she'd come over, and she couldn't stand the way his blue eyes widened like a child's.

"Nash, my parents are really upset. They aren't supportive of this at all. My mom called me a whore." Her voice cracked. "I don't know about this anymore. It doesn't feel like it's going to settle down."

"We can face this together," he said. "Anger always comes first, but it has to fade at some point and leave room for conversation, right?"

He leaned down to kiss her, but she turned her head, resulting in a misplaced peck on the cheek.

"No...I don't think we can face this at all."

"Kiran, I know it's weighing you, and I'm sorry for that. But we can make it. I promise you we'll survive. You just have to keep working at it with them."

"For how long? My sister fought it for months. They were forced to let her go for that decision. And they never forgave her for it either."

"This isn't like that."

"How? It's exactly like that. Potentially worse. Because you're—"

"Because I'm what? White?"

Nash's words were true—and Kiran's blood boiled at it. She wouldn't give him the benefit of answering that accusation, knowing how bad it made her and her family sound to someone who didn't understand the nuance of a foreign culture...and also because it made her question it too.

He glowered at her now, his characteristic patience and understanding evaporating in front of her eyes.

"I don't get it. You stay with me, and they'll eventually come around. That's the only way they'll get used to the idea, isn't it?"

"Can you please stop assuming you know how to fix it? It's not going to work."

"You keep acting like I'm the one who's been holding this over your head and telling you that it's me or them."

"Aren't conversations like this exactly that?" Kiran snapped. She couldn't handle that he was right, that she was doing this to herself.

"Of course not. You brought up why you were upset, and I was offering a suggestion. You're writing me out of this narrative completely. I have zero say. You've decided. You want to go."

"It's not like that…" She struggled to explain. "I can't choose you over my family! After all they've gone through, I can't do that to them."

"I never asked you to!"

"Don't you get it? The mere idea of us—you and me together—is already making me choose."

"My God, Kiran, all I've wanted for my entire life is a solid home. A place where I can rest my head and know that in the morning, there will be stability, love, and a reason to look forward to every day. I thought I found that with you, yes, but I wouldn't ask you to give up your family—the same people who have given you that very thing—just to fulfill my wish. Who the hell do you think I am?"

"Then what do you want?"

"Anything but this!"

The words hung between them, like dangling stalactites in a cave, threatening those who dared to walk underneath.

"Then why don't you look for *anything but this*?" Kiran hissed.

Her last baiting idea was to toss the idea of a more suitable partner, an American woman, at him and hope he'd get fed up with her. How else would she get him to see that it would be easier with someone else? It would be so much easier if he saw that he was worth more than this and if he called her on her shit and left.

"Don't you dare do that. Don't you put words in my mouth and try to twist this so I'm the bad guy, when you've had the power all along. I don't want *this*, this ridiculous in-between where you want to play both sides but don't want to move forward in any direction."

"You don't get it! And you won't try to."

"I *don't* get it. I'm trying, but you won't let me in to see how I can make it better for you. You've already given up, and I'm the only one here fighting."

His attempt at convincing her to stay only broke her heart into more pieces. She wanted to take back her words and go back to the blissful nights they'd spent cuddling on the couch.

Our daughter is dead to us.

"We need to break up," she said. The monotony in her voice frightened her—a robotic tone that lacked any vitality or conviction.

Nash's face reddened. He exhaled and turned away from her, his hands on his head. Then he whipped around.

"I expected better of you. I thought you'd fight to make this work."

"Well, clearly that wasn't the case, was it?" Kiran snapped. "And how could you think that, Nash? My family disowned my sister for doing the same thing. It's always been a choice—you or them. If I choose you, I lose them because how could they forgive a child who has done this to them after seeing what they already went through. I would actively hurt them—I would make a choice to hurt my parents. And if I choose them, I lose you, because that's the only way they stick around."

"But I don't understand how you could make a choice like this so easily."

"How dare you!" she shouted back. "Do you really think this was easy?"

"Oh, stop it, Kiran. You're in America. You have options and freedom—"

"*You* stop it, you arrogant jerk," she hissed. "The world isn't America."

"You have the freedom to choose here."

Kiran scoffed, and he frowned at her accompanying dubious laugh. Freedom. No one was free. Every action had a consequence.

"What, you think *your country*—"

"Stop. Stop it now, Nash." Kiran put her hand up and leveled her voice, though the deadliness in it could kill the most indomitable enemy. "You're about to insult a place you haven't been and a culture you don't understand. Not only is that beneath you, but I will not stand here and let you insult my family, my village, my education, and all we collectively worked for because you're on your high horse."

His face crumpled at being called out on the worst of him. "I didn't mean—"

"You did. Don't pretend."

"*I don't understand.* I get that you have commitments. I respect that. I respect what your parents been through. But I don't understand why it's a choice. Why is this an us or them? Why can't it be all of us? Or how can a single decision negate all that you mentioned—your family, your village, your education, and all you worked for? Those things should hold steady regardless who you fall in love with. That's literally the biggest decision you'll make."

"Nash…I love you for being so idealistic, but the world doesn't work that way," Kiran said sadly. "And it was always a choice. We're toxic to each other. Look at what we've already done to our relationships."

Her relationships.

Incredulity bled across his face. His fingers tightened into fists, as though he was catching his rebuttal in his knuckles instead of allowing the painful words he was fighting to tumble out of his mouth.

"That's really how you feel?"

No, of course not, you idiot.

But anger from his impending bigotry and frustration at being unable to speak to her parents flowed through her veins like blood, feeding every cell in her body to end it now and go back to when life was simpler.

"Yes. Yes, I do."

"We never stood a chance, did we…" It wasn't a question. The bitterness seeped from his every pore as he muttered the words with disgust. "I never stood a chance. It was never about me at all."

"Nash…" Kiran's eyes filled with tears.

How could she explain that years of watching her parents wipe their eyes on Kirti's birthday and pretending as though Baba's long hours hadn't been to pay for her schooling were just a denial of the truth: that love was never in her future on her terms and that her family had sacrificed all they had to get her where she was.

"I can't make you understand. I'm so sorry."

"No…you can't. You'll never understand that it didn't have to be this way."

"It was always a choice, whether you wanted it to be or not," she tried to explain. "They already went through this once! How can I ask them to do it again?"

"Well, now I guess you don't have to. You should leave."

Kiran recoiled. "Nash…"

"Go."

But she stood in place, frozen in shock at the vitriol in his voice.

"Fine. *I'll* go," Nash muttered.

He slid his feet into the running shoes by the door and slammed the door on the way out, leaving Kiran shell-shocked and forced to calm herself down alone.

Chapter Thirty-Five

NASH

Walking out was the most childish thing he could have done. It was his dad's style, not his.

But his dad was precisely why he was so agitated, and Kiran's unilateral decision that they couldn't be together only exacerbated the loss of control Nash was experiencing.

He needed to go for a run or something to clear his head and separate all the issues crowding his mind. They were encroaching on each other's space, and he hated how his dad was influencing how he dealt with Kiran and Kiran was impacting how he handled his dad's letter (or didn't handle it at all). He wanted to pry them apart so he could think about it all one thing at a time.

He had to change before he headed out again, so he walked back to his apartment, dropping a dollar bill into a homeless man's cup as he approached his building. The thudding beats with which his heart pounded were like punches he was landing on a boxing bag of issues.

He unlocked his apartment and let himself in. Quietly, he hoped that Kiran was still there—that perhaps his walkout would be forgiven and that she'd take back the breakup. Maybe they could talk like adults and navigate this unknown territory together.

But she was gone.

He stood in the living room for a breath, letting her absence wash over him before throwing his keys on the counter and going directly to his closet. He rummaged for his sneakers and some gym clothes before changing and grabbing his keys again. His headphones were in his ears before he had even shut his front door.

The cement sidewalk against the soles of his feet was the kind of therapy no psychiatrist could provide. The anger, confusion, and aggression his body needed to express fueled the way his legs pumped, and with each block he added to his run, his tension fell away, allowing him to think clearly.

Deep down, he knew he was in love with Kiran.

He adored her laugh. He loved the strength of her jawline and how it added a little defiance to her face, especially because she was someone who had such a sense of duty. He thought of her hair and how silky it felt to the touch when his fingers ran through it. And her mind was the most beautiful thing of all… He never got tired of exploring its crevices and discovering new paths in it.

Being in love with Kiran was like an adventure every day, and he was addicted to the pursuit of discovering her. And having her was having a home.

Resentment bubbled inside him against her parents—people he'd never even met who were living their lives on the other side of the world, unaware how they were impacting his. He didn't understand why he was undergoing punishment for falling in love. Variety was supposed to be the spice of life, right? He couldn't imagine loving or marrying someone within such a strict set of guidelines. God, how many people did that leave once all the criteria were met anyway? Did they really expect their daughter to marry one of the three people who fit every quality on their list from caste to ambition?

The point he struggled with most, the one he didn't even want to admit to himself, was that he wasn't good enough for her family. He had spent his entire life proving that his circumstances were no indicator of the type of man he was...and here he was, educated and in love with Kiran, and unable to do anything about it. His background as a white man, his parental history of abandonment and drug abuse, and the mere fact that he was born into a family different from her own was being held against him. It was out of his control. He couldn't help a single thing that was being used as an argument against him.

Just like he couldn't help the fury that raged inside him when he thought of his father reaching out.

While he was able to say that his mother was dead and that his father had abandoned them when he was a child, his past was a certainty. Even though it was being held against him with Kiran, he still knew exactly who he was and where he stood in relation to his parents—he simply didn't have any.

But now, Kirk had complicated everything. He wanted a relationship.

What would make up for twenty-five years of absentia? What was left to say? Nash had come to terms with not having a father, and it was a foreign concept to introduce one to his life now.

The unsettled, anxious, wobbly wave of emotion he was facing kept him from finding a pace on his run that suited him. Winded and annoyed, he headed back to his place where he picked up the phone, dialing Brandon.

"You got a minute?" Nash plopped onto his sofa, exhausted and too flared up to rest all at once.

"What's up?"

"She broke up with me."

"No way." Brandon's incredulous tone made Nash feel worse. "Why?"

"Her parents, I guess. Cultural differences."

"Did you do something offensive?" Brandon sounded confused.

"I don't think so. Maybe existing."

"I don't know what that means."

"I don't know either," Nash snapped. "It's like…one second, I'm in love with her and we're so happy. The next, she's in my apartment telling me she doesn't think we'll make it because her family disapproves of her decision to date me and I don't fit into their plan for her to marry someone they choose."

"That's not ideal. But maybe it's expected?"

"What? Does it make sense to you?"

Nash hadn't known Brandon to solve many problems before he did.

"It's not like I *get* it," Brandon said, and Nash could imagine him shrugging. "But based on what you've told me, she worked hard to get here with the support of her family, and it sounds like they've all been through a lot. It must be hard to let that go and shift your path. Maybe they expected her to respect that journey."

"It's not exactly respectful to me."

"Hey, I'm not arguing with that. I am on your side. Like I said, I don't pretend to understand where she's coming from. It sucks. But try and empathize. Maybe that will give you a solution that makes sense. It's what you do."

"There's literally nothing I can do."

Brandon stayed quiet, confirming Nash's thoughts. A couple of seconds passed.

"You said you loved her."

"I do."

"That's big."

"It's huge. And don't say 'That's what she said,' because even I can't handle a sex joke from you right now."

Brandon chuckled. "I thought it'd break the ice! But for the sake of your grumpy ass…sleep on it. You're too pissed and upset to talk to her right now. But eventually, you may have to."

"Thanks," Nash grumbled.

"If you need me, I've got you. I'm a call away."

"I appreciate it," Nash said.

They hung up.

"Ughhhhh!" he groaned in frustration as he rubbed his hands on his face.

He wanted a solution from the universe—a way to fix this so that Kiran could keep her family's love but he didn't lose her. Darkness fell, and only silence echoed back.

Chapter Thirty-Six

KIRAN

"You look like hell," Akash noted before his bottom hit the chair.

"Thanks," mumbled Kiran, five minutes early to their chai date, even when she was miserable.

"Have you been eating?" Sonam's eyes were full of concern as she studied Kiran's pale skin, thinning wrists, and blank stare.

"A little."

Payal watched them, her arms crossed with one hand under her chin. "Have you spoken with Aunty or Uncle?" she asked.

"I tried." Kiran's voice cracked. "I called them this morning. My mom answered—then my dad shouted not to talk to me. He said he didn't have a daughter. Then she hung up."

Kiran had jumped at the bellow her father had let out at her mother, even from across the planet. Ma had been curt—not the kind of stern one used at an incessant telemarketer but the kind of coldness one used with someone they deeply loathed. Kiran had only heard that tone once—when their aunt had greeted her after Kirti's wedding as if nothing had happened and asked how Ma was doing.

All of them jolted like they'd been hit. Kiran couldn't imagine them having blowouts with their families—Sonam, so close to her parents and her brother. Akash, with his baby boy status. Payal, with two parents who were distant emotionally but never ceased to give her what she needed.

"We have each other." Baba kissed her forehead. *"We're richer than most. And I have my ray of sunshine in you."*

We had *each other,* Kiran thought angrily at the memory of her and Baba visiting the mandir and discussing all they had together.

But an equally powerful memory slapped her in the face.

Tenth standard—in America, they called them grades—exams were rapidly approaching. Eight days were left when Kiran's skin began to flush. The fever set rapidly after that. If she didn't take the examinations, she would be considered a failure—not by her family's standards but by the school and government's strict no-exceptions rules.

Typhoid or not, she had to sit for the tests.

Baba had sat quietly by her bed, as she drifted in and out of her delirious state, with a cold compress on her forehead. He stroked her hairline through her worst phases of the illness until she had finally opened her eyes and slowly begun to swallow water. Then plain yogurt and rice. Then mango. He fed her carefully, not even allowing Ma to come near the bed, relegating her to standing by the doorway instead.

When she'd finally grown strong enough, after five days, to sit up straight and read the newspaper, Baba had told her that he'd tried everything to get the school to postpone her exam but that in three short days, she would have to sit anyway.

"I will help you," he promised a tearful Kiran. "You won't give up. I won't let you."

For three days, if Kiran wasn't sleeping, she and Baba were reciting historical facts, mathematical equations, and physics principles to each other.

She'd finished second that year—the only time she'd ever dropped from first. But she wore that badge of honor proudly, because she and Baba had earned it together despite him not having more than a high school education and she being fever-ridden.

"We are a good team," he said and laughed. "Maybe I should have had you to get me through my exams too."

Now, they weren't even speaking. The man who had nursed her back to health wished she never made it.

"They told me I was dead to them," Kiran repeated for what felt like the millionth time in the last few weeks. No matter how many times she said it, the unforgivable, painful accusations of betrayal and impropriety burned her. "Maybe they meant it."

"It was a violent reaction but they didn't mean it," Sonam said with certainty. "They're upset. Parents speak out of turn as much as we do when they're angry."

"My dad asked if I knew what would have happened to me if I lived there." Her eyes welled again.

"What do you mean?" Payal's brows furrowed.

"An honor killing?" Sonam's voice rose an octave, her outrage evident now. "They wouldn't."

Kiran shook her head. "They wouldn't. I know that. But that they could even threaten me with something so extreme...even *mention* something like that." She shuddered.

"Kiran, I want you to know something. Whatever happens with Nash going forward, we'll be with you, and we will support you." Sonam put her hand on hers.

Kiran attempted a smile at the solidarity.

"But I'm not sure being with Nash is the right move for you at the moment. I think you did the smart thing."

The way her voice became soothing but firm, her eye contact unbreakable, and her typically forceful demeanor transformed into an unnaturally negotiating one... Suddenly, Kiran had become a patient to Dr. Sonam Joshi.

"I love you. We all do. But your family has given up so much for you. I was thinking about what your mom said—we may not get where they're coming from. But honor killings and acid attacks? They gave up their daughter and were willing to cut her out, to prevent any chance of that kind of harm coming to her. The sacrifice, in their minds, is that they proved their honor and followed their elders' word by cutting Kirti out...which may have saved her from all the things they feared. People forgot she existed rather than seeing her do what they thought was dishonorable, and maybe your parents saw that as the better option. They're terrified of feeling their circles of loved ones put pressure on them again, afraid of the consequences that come with defiance, and worried about having to give you up the same way. Maybe there's nuance we don't understand or even agree with. I'm not saying you had to sacrifice your love in order to pay them back, but the risk may not be worth the damage it'll do to them, especially with Uncle's health. You've always talked about providing them the opportunity to relax and enjoy their lives. I don't want to see you lose sight of that, even if it hurts."

Kiran nodded.

The entire world seemed to be telling her she was doing the right thing...but why was it so damn hard?

Chapter Thirty-Seven

NASH

Everyone had days when they didn't want to go to work. Even Nash had them, despite loving his job and being able to talk to the children under his care.

But today, he wasn't having any of it.

The children weren't the issue; surprisingly, Nash found them to be full of clarity and realism. It was their parents who were the problem.

"What do you mean my daughter has an eating disorder? She's just lost a little weight! And it's about time, given that she's always been a little chubby," one mother protested.

"Antidepressants? He's thirteen. He sleeps all day and ignores his schoolwork for attention and because he's being lazy, not because he's depressed. What does he even have to be depressed about?"

"How come Dr. Brigham isn't taking care of this case? Why would he pass it on to a new doctor?"

It was only noon, and Nash had a headache that seared through his entire brain, throbbing and pulsing behind his eyes. He rubbed his eyes with the palm of his hand, trying to relieve the pressure somehow, but it didn't help. Even pain relievers weren't kicking in.

And he had to keep it together for his session with Dr. Brigham.

David Brigham was like a dad to all the psychologists at the hospital—a little older, a little wiser, a little more full of corny jokes during the rare, off-the-cuff moments one caught him, like grabbing a drink of water or in line for snacks at the cafeteria.

He was the type of mentor Nash had hoped for when he moved to New York, a blessing he hadn't counted on that life had seen fit to give him.

He and Dr. Brigham were seeing Trent Dagmar's mother today. She had been released from rehab recently, and Dr. Brigham wanted to check in with her to see how the transition was going, if Trent needed anything, and how the family was doing overall. While Nash worked with Trent, Dr. Brigham dealt with the psychology of adults, so they wanted to tag team this case.

Nash silently followed Dr. Brigham into the room, sitting in a seat in the corner of the room to observe rather than participate in the session.

"How are you doing today, Rhonda?" Dr. Brigham asked, looking at her chart before setting it down.

"I'm fine. Got released a week ago."

"And how do you feel?"

"Honestly, like I really need a hit."

Nash was used to answers he didn't expect. He never knew what could come out of a patient's mouth. But this time, his objectivity was clouded, and he frowned at her response.

"Have you spoken to your sponsor? Have you been using your coping techniques to help you get over the tough moments?" Dr. Brigham asked.

"I've been trying. But I miss the high. It's easier to deal with the high and the feeling of invincibility than it is to be a mom or handle the lows. I've been tempted more than once to call my dealer."

Dr. Brigham patiently noted something down, likely about her cravings.

"And how does Trent feel?"

"He's been acting out more often at his foster home. He has a good situation over there; I'm not really sure why he's been so pissed at me. Sometimes I think it's better that I'm gone from his life anyway—like he's getting a better upbringing without me."

"Do you think you'll feel like a better mother once you've been sober for longer?"

"I don't know if I will be sober for that long, Doc. I mean, it's like they said in rehab. 'Once an addict, always an addict.' Right now, I'd probably trade Trent for a hit." Rhonda laughed.

If Dr. Brigham was shocked at Rhonda's confession and joking tone, he didn't show it.

But something snapped inside Nash.

It wasn't funny. This wasn't a joke. Whether it was a coping mechanism, a bad sense of humor, or an urge, Nash saw red at the woman's dismissiveness about her addiction and the damage it had caused.

"Rhonda, you do know that all Trent wants is for you to be sober and come home to him, right? He still believes you can overcome this disease, like the hundreds of people who have come through here and sat in that very chair that your uncaring ass is sitting in and who *have* fought through hell to come back and make a life for themselves. And here you are, joking about how you'd trade in a son for more drugs—maybe he should give up hope. God knows I would."

"Nash!" Dr. Brigham said sternly.

Rhonda's face reddened, like she'd been punched.

"Dr. Hawthorne. Outside. Now," Dr. Brigham commanded.

Nash knew at that moment he'd crossed a line and he owed everyone an apology. There was no excuse. Hell, even he hadn't given up on Rhonda. How many times had Mom tried to stay sober? And how many times had others been successful? He wasn't a crystal ball that could predict what the Dagmar family's future looked like.

With a level head, Nash knew that Rhonda was doing what addicts did—going through various cycles of healing, utilizing different methods of coping with the effects the addiction had on their lives, and trying to navigate a new life where they'd be labeled an addict forever.

He'd never had an outburst in his life, always more focused on the positive results of these sessions on children rather than how damaged all the involved parties could become.

But life had finally pushed him over the edge, to the point where he could feel himself free-falling through an abyss. No one could catch him now, and he was beyond being able to reach out and grab a hand.

"What was that, son?" Dr. Brigham asked with a surprising amount of patience.

"I am an ass," Nash said. "I'm so sorry. I owe her an apology. And you. I snapped in there at how carelessly she talked about Trent, who has literally spent the last few months telling me how much he wants his mom to come home and how tired he is of taking care of himself."

Dr. Brigham sighed heavily and nodded, considering the options. "You've done enough today. I'll talk to her for you and tell her you weren't feeling well. But I suggest you take a few days and go home. Nash, you are one of the most brilliant psychologists I have ever seen. You've made breakthroughs with patients that even I'd given up on. But if you're taking it home with you, for your own sake, I suggest you take a look at yourself and why you're doing this."

"No, sir, I can work. I apologize. I—"

"That wasn't a request. You need to take a week. I'll have another psychologist cover you, and you can swap your weeks. But you need to take time. Go home."

"I'm sorry." Nash bowed his head. "I don't know what got into me."

"It happens to the best of us, son, but that's why you need to take care of yourself."

With the suggestion in his mentor's voice, Nash knew he was being dismissed.

· · · · · · · · · · ·

Nash berated himself the entire train ride home, using a colorful set of four-letter words in his mind to describe the disaster of a career move he'd just made.

What. A. Clusterfuck.

As he moved toward the door to the apartment, he saw a flash of a familiar set of Keds step out the door, followed by legs that had wrapped themselves around him. Kiran's face was pointed in the opposite direction, but as she turned and came down the stairs, she saw Nash and froze. Her eyes widened, and her mouth dropped open.

They faced off in the middle of the sidewalk.

Nash couldn't help but notice the hollowness in her eyes and the pale shade her skin had taken on, the telltale sign that she hadn't slept. She probably saw the same exhaustion in him.

"How are you?" She broke the silence.

Nash tried to say "Good," but he couldn't lie. He shrugged instead.

"Me too," she whispered. "I miss you. I haven't been able to sleep—"

"Kiran, has a single thing changed about your situation?" Nash asked, refusing to let her make him feel pity.

"What? No...I mean, I haven't talked with my parents about it—"

"Then I'm not sure what sympathy you're trying to gain, but it's misplaced to think it'll come from me."

Her mouth fell open, and the hurt in her eyes broke him further inside, but he didn't give in.

Kiran gave a quick nod, as though she was telling him she got the message, and pulled the bag in her hands to her shoulder as fast as she could, jostling its contents. A couple of receipts floated to the ground, and some spare coins jingled against the cement.

She didn't even notice as she increased her pace and brushed past him.

He closed his eyes, a whiff of her perfume making him long to be with her, and his eyes followed her past him.

As he turned back, he saw a folded piece of paper on the sidewalk among the clutter that had fallen out of her bag.

He leaned to pick it up, wanting to call out and give it back to her, knowing it was probably one of the million lists she used to keep her life organized. But he couldn't bring himself to do it, holding it in his hand like it was a piece of her that he could cling to.

When he went inside, desolate and defeated, he wished it were her he was holding instead.

Chapter Thirty-Eight

KIRAN

That night, Kiran sat in a daze on her couch. She had gone through her workdays over the last week in a quiet hypnotic state, unaware of any conversations or projects going on outside of her own.

Nash's face replayed in her mind, and she couldn't shake the chills that came from how empty his tone had been when he'd spoken with her.

She didn't know what she'd expected—certainly not kindness. But disinterest hurt more than she ever thought it would.

Her phone rang, and she ignored it. When it rang a second time, she finally looked over and saw Ma's name across the screen. She scrambled to answer.

"Hello?"

"Kiran." A statement, not a greeting.

"How are you, Ma?"

"Did you break up with him yet?"

Kiran hung her head and whispered, "Yes. I broke up with him."

"Good," Ma said with more energy this time. "How is work?"

"They promoted me."

Earlier that day, she had received a yearly bonus and a

promotion to senior associate. She had mustered a thank-you and sent the compulsory emails to her bosses about her excitement, but inside, she'd felt nothing. A light inside her had switched off.

"Very good work. That's what we sent you to the United States for. We're proud of you."

"Thank you," Kiran said softly. "I'm glad I make you proud."

Every day when she was little, she'd hoped to hear those words from Ma—words that had been doled out to Kirti on a daily basis and that Kiran felt she had to measure up to.

"You do when you listen to us, beta. I know it doesn't sound like it now, but we know what's best for you."

"I'm sure you do. I'm going to go now, Ma. Payal is coming over."

"We'll talk soon."

It was simple how quickly she'd fallen back into her parents' good graces with a promotion and obedience. But conditional love wasn't enough anymore. Their relationship had irrevocably changed.

Kiran turned her phone off and settled in on the couch again. She didn't want to be bothered for a little while.

The teacup Payal placed on the table an hour later was a gong in her ears. "How are you, honey?"

"Okay."

"Talk to me. You shouldn't keep that type of ache inside."

"Have you ever felt misplaced? As though you're not quite doing anything truly inspiring and you're going through the motions?"

"Yes. I think everyone has." Payal crossed her legs on her section of the couch and settled in with a pillow on her lap.

"That's how I feel. I was inspired with him. And now, the world is dimmer."

"You have us. You have your family. You have your educa-tion. The world is bright. Your future is brilliant."

"But the colors don't seem as bright as they were."

"You sound like poetry."

Kiran smiled sadly to herself. "You know...I think love does that. Life becomes poetic, and words you never thought you'd use to describe something become the only ones you can use."

"Preaching to the choir, aren't you?"

"You can probably understand since you've been in love more than any of us."

"All twelve times were brighter than the one before it." Payal giggled.

Kiran laughed, and the effort it took sounded like a cough.

"Do you know I have a wedding box?"

"A what?"

"A wedding box. I found jewelry once in New Jersey that I fell in love with and wanted to wear at my wedding. It's in there. There are magazine cutouts from over the years. Color swatches. Pictures of celebrities in lehengas. Bollywood CDs from my teenage years of songs I wanted to play at my reception. I have an entire box dedicated to how I envisioned my future husband and what my life would be." Payal's cheeks tinged pink, but she smiled unashamedly at her confession.

"I didn't know," Kiran replied, surprised that her best friend held sentimental value in relationships. "I always thought you were a free bird."

"I am. I love being a free spirit. I love doing what I want... but I've always wanted the love story. I always wanted a man who would transform the way I saw the world. Not because I need to be changed or because the world needs to be brought to life... It's magical already, you know? But because going through it with someone at your side is so much less lonely. It's less scary to think someone could see you at your depths of misery and your heights of success and love you all the same. That kind of bond...that unbreakable vibe, I've always wanted that. I can't judge you one bit for missing Nash or wanting him by your side when you think you've found someone that monumental."

Kiran's eyes filled with tears at Payal's empathy and at the accuracy of her soliloquy. At the end of the day, she missed the feeling of having something of her own that had permanency to it.

"Now who's the poet?"

"Ahh, well...like I said, love brings it out of you, I guess. But can I tell you something else, Kiran?"

"Of course."

"There are family photographs in that box. They aren't even my own! They're ideas and pictures of weddings I've been to and the families in them." She looked down at her hands. "For the longest time, I was jealous of you, Sonam, and Akash for having amazing relationships with your families. Sometimes I still am. I spent more time lying on Akash's and Sonam's families' couches over holidays than I did my own and had a better relationship with my house mother at boarding school than with my birth mom. I could light myself on fire and my parents wouldn't notice, other than to wonder who would take over the company.

"But you gave up your own happiness for your family, and your parents were forced to give up their daughter when mine would have given me away for free. I can't tell you what it all means, but I can tell you I'd give anything to have parents who loved me the way yours did. I don't deny how much pain you feel breaking up with Nash...but in a twisted way, this girl thinks you're lucky to have family you'd be willing to put first."

Kiran's eyes widened. Her hand went protectively to Payal's

on the table, and Payal gave it a squeeze. And they sat in understanding silence.

Kiran had always seen Payal as the antithesis of how she grew up—wealthy enough to take island vacations and buy Louboutins, free enough to leave a trail of broken hearts in her wake because she didn't want to be tied down, and educated at schools Kiran could only dream of, full of libraries and books. She'd seen glimpses of Payal's vulnerabilities over the years—after all, being best friends had that effect. But she'd never recognized the depths of Payal's wish for a family who loved her or a love that would choose her. She'd always seen her friend as a girl who was blessed in other regards, never as the girl with a hidden wedding box. For a split second, Kiran felt lucky that she'd had both kinds of love instead of being the little rich girl with none.

The perspective didn't give her clarity, but it gave her respect. The burn in her chest was quelled as she took to heart the soothing tone Payal used and that while this choice was never ideal, at least she had experienced enough love from her family and from Nash that she could say she'd fallen in love and been loved growing up, even it had resulted in a heartbreaking battle between the two.

"I'm sorry you didn't have a family who adored you, Payal," Kiran whispered.

"I'm sorry you had to choose between yours," Payal murmured back. "But we have each other."

"Always."

That night, Kiran twisted and turned in her sheets until she was tangled up so tightly, she couldn't break free. Appropriate. She fought against them, breathless, before finally navigating through the fabric binding her limbs together as patiently as she could. By the time she'd set herself free, she sat in her pajama shorts, wide awake, raking her fingers through her hair.

She'd never have a peaceful rest again. Every time she began to doze off or focus, a reminder of Nash would throw her senses into overdrive again. From the extremes of peace or concentration, she would wobble off-kilter until she was sure she'd fall and never be able to get back up.

Kiran readjusted her sheets in the dark and tried to fix her disheveled tank top before giving up and hunching over her folded legs. She pulled her knees to her chest and stared into the night.

Outside of her window, the wail of sirens served as a disturbing lullaby. She could hear the drunken shouts of those who had stayed out until the bars closed and the laughter of friends who were having a fun night in the city. She wondered if anyone was at the Top of the Rock tonight, staring down at her building...if they were sending hopes out to anyone who felt alone tonight.

Chapter Thirty-Nine

NASH

"Have you showered in the last three days?" Brandon asked, glancing around Nash's pigsty of an apartment.

"Yeah. Once."

"You reek, man. You need to take another."

Nash bobbed his head, unsmiling, and Brandon's joke fell flat on its face.

"Talk to me. What's going on?"

"Well, you know, my deadbeat dad's letter brought back all the trauma I thought I dealt with, I got my ass dumped, and then I got suspended from work for yelling at a mother who is a recovering addict."

Brandon's eyes widened at the latest addition.

Nash was convinced they'd roll right out of his head.

"Um…well, I didn't see the suspension coming."

Nash gave a half-hearted chuckle. "Yup. Me either."

"What does Kate have to say?"

"Nothing. She's called a few times and asked me to call back, but I haven't been in the mood."

Brandon flopped on Nash's couch, pulling a pair of jeans out from underneath him. "This is gross. Clean up."

"You drank your own pee at band camp in seventh grade."

"Yeah. Seventh grade. On a dare. We're thirty. This is real life. Get a grip and tell me where your head is at."

Nash sighed and began his tale. He mentioned how Kirk's letter had remained on his mind since they'd last spoken, poisoning everything and making the world feel less bright—or maybe that was just the breakup with Kiran making Nash think he'd never feel hope again. He recounted the horrible way he blew up on Trent's mom and how Dr. Brigham had been more understanding than he should have. He told Brandon he felt like he'd failed.

"To be fair, having your girlfriend dump you and your deadbeat dad show up after years of abandonment...you were kind of a pressure cooker waiting to explode."

"Well, I exploded. I've never lost my temper on a patient in my life. I've had psychiatric patients attack me and still remained calm...and this mother who happens to be an addict tells me, to no surprise, that she wants a hit, and I lose my mind. You'd think I was a rookie person off the street who didn't know she is fighting a battle and happens to be struggling. I was an ass."

"You were an ass," Brandon agreed. "But as your best friend, I'm qualified to tell you that while your reaction wasn't justified, your feelings were."

"I don't even know what to do." Nash stared at his hands.

Brandon popped his legs up on Nash's coffee table. "You meet your dad."

"I'm sorry... What?"

"Right now, that's the event that had the longest impact on you. Close the chapter. Whether that means shutting down your resentment or never speaking to him again, handle that first."

It was surprisingly sound advice.

"And what about Kiran?"

"I've been giving this a lot of thought since we last spoke. I didn't know what to say at first. It made no sense to me, if I'm honest, but I was playing devil's advocate. It also sounds more complicated than we'll ever understand. It's fucked up that she has to choose. It's a mentality we won't understand, because we grew up in a different country. We could go there a million times, and we still wouldn't know firsthand. But if she's worth it to you, then you need to fight for her and deal with the fact that her parents will probably hate your sorry, white, suspended ass until you prove yourself somehow. And even then, they may not like you."

"That's...not comforting at all," Nash groaned.

"Nash, buddy, I'm trying to tell it like it is. You love her? Do what it takes to support her. I know it's hard, but imagine what it's like for her. If I had to choose between Tasha and my parents, I don't know what I'd do, and it would be a crummy place to be. Kiran's probably as confused as you are, so don't make any hasty decisions. See what you can work out."

"And what about work?" Nash threw his hands up.

"You're suspended for a week to ten days, right?"

"Yeah. Until I can come back in without my head firmly up my ass."

"Ten-day vacation then." Brandon shrugged. "Like your mentor said...you reevaluate. In the meantime, fix your sitch with your dad and Kiran. I think that's probably the root of all evil anyway."

"He wrote his email address on the bottom of the letter. Phone number too."

"Then shoot him a text. Tell him to meet you for coffee. Figure your shit out. Then tackle the rest of your life accordingly. Do it now, before you change your mind."

Nash stared at his best friend. Then he got up, fished through the trash for the letter, and pulled it out.

"You really couldn't have written the number down before drowning yourself in garbage?" Brandon asked sarcastically.

"Screw off, dude."

Hi, Kirk. It's Nash. Can you meet me for coffee tomorrow at 2 p.m.? There should be a few trains from Philadelphia in the morning. Gregorys near Sixty-Ninth and First.

"How'd you get so wise anyway? I'm usually the one telling you what to do."

Brandon shrugged again and then offered Nash a grin. "I learned from the best."

The phone buzzed.

Kirk: Good to hear from you, Son. I'll see you tomorrow.

Chapter Forty

KIRAN

As she approached her office door after an early-morning meeting, the receptionist for the floor—"Farrah with the fab hair," Kiran used to remember her by—called out to her.

"Kiran, your cell phone has been on your desk, and I can hear it from here! It's been buzzing nonstop."

"I'm sorry, Farrah," Kiran answered, puzzled. "I'll check that now."

She took quick steps to her desk and didn't bother sitting down. Reaching over a neatly stacked pile of books and her laptop, she grabbed the buzzing cell.

Twelve missed calls from Ma.

Three from Sonam.

Two from Payal.

Five from Akash.

Twelve voicemails.

She didn't want to hear whatever bad news was coming from a voicemail, and she ignored them as she called Ma back. The phone rang once, that awkward ring that only international calls made, before Ma's hysterical voice cried through the line in Hindi so fast, even Kiran couldn't keep up.

"Kiran, tumhari baba…Baba. Baba."

Kiran's stomach dropped every story in the building each time her mother repeated Baba's name.

"Ma." Her voice cracked. "What happened to Baba?"

She tried to steel herself for the worst news she could. Her knuckles turned white, gripping the desk with her eyes clenched shut against the blow. She stopped breathing, as though her heart wouldn't beat or react if that vital component of life was missing.

"Baba had a heart attack. He is in… He's… ICU." Ma's tears spilled through the speaker.

"Tell him to hang on. I'll be on the next flight."

While all other threads seemed frayed at the moment, this was a promise she intended to keep.

The following hours were a blur.

She vaguely remembered telling her superiors that she had to go back to India for her father's hospitalization. They had agreed wholeheartedly and offered their best wishes. She'd only taken a sick day when she had pneumonia. In her peripheral conscience, she registered their sad and reassuring smiles. She'd thanked them, flat-toned…thanked them for best wishes that her father wouldn't die, as though she were acknowledging something as mundane as the fact that it was a Tuesday or that the sky was blue. It was so strange how crises propelled calm, that the eye of a hurricane could even exist amid a storm.

Then she'd called Sonam, Akash, and Payal, who had received hysterical phone calls of their own from Ma, as they were the closest people to Kiran that Ma knew and had contact information for.

"Do you need me to come with you?" Sonam had asked.

"You're a doctor, Sonam. You and I both well know you don't get time off." Kiran stared at her closet. All the dress shirts, dresses, blazers, and T-shirts overwhelmed her. *Who even needs this many clothes?* she thought to herself in passing as she selected some cotton T-shirts that would allow her to beat the heat. *You grew up with four outfits.*

"I'll find a way. I can take time off for a family emergency or figure out a way—"

"I love you, but we both know it's not going to happen," Kiran responded, loosely hanging on to a tunic in her hands. "And I need to do this on my own."

Payal's sentiments were similar.

"Are you sure you don't need me to come with you?"

"Payal, you wouldn't survive, and you'd have no idea what to do. You haven't been to India in your life. But the thought is so appreciated, and I love you for it."

Akash's too.

"You're like my sister. I can come. I insist."

"Akash, it'll be okay. I have to see them on my own. You don't want to be a part of the mushroom cloud that is about to explode. Please."

"Okay," he said soothingly. "But text me once you land."

Kiran smiled—one of her only expressions in the last few hours. She tossed the final pairs of underwear and bras in her suitcase.

She hardly remembered the drive to JFK airport. She wasn't sure if she thanked the Uber driver as she hauled her carry-on out of the trunk and beelined for the ticket counter. Even her check-in and security were forgettable, unusual since she was brown and foreign, a source of stress for her when she flew.

It wasn't until she was gripping the armrests of her seat as the plane taxied down the runway that she recognized what she was doing. Suddenly, the bag at her feet felt like it was growing—the passport with the emblazoned gold Lion Capital of Ashoka pushed against her calf, burning hotter against her skin as if to remind her where she was going and where she came from.

The plane rose above the clouds, flying north to Canada before making its sweep across the Atlantic. Kiran hated flying, but she loved this part when she got to look down below. She was lucky she had a window seat.

Lucky.

How could she even use that word right now? She was on her way home after finding out her father had almost died. He was so close to the brink of death that she didn't know what news would greet her when she landed...whether she still had a father or whether she would have to watch a male cousin perform his final rites.

No, she told herself. *Don't think like that. You're not lucky, but you're going to count the good things.*

And so, she began the fourteen-hour flight, counting all the good things that had happened that day.

She had managed to get on a flight. She got a window seat. The security line wasn't terrible. The TSA agent was friendly. Every member of the CMC offered to come to India with her.

But she didn't have Nash.

Though she had the support of her office mates. She was allowed to leave immediately. They wished her the best.

She managed to get an Uber with a two-minute wait time. The driver played music from an app that had no commercials. She didn't smell the sewage on the tiny strip near the airport that always reeked of waste.

Every time the solitary little voice shouted in the back of her mind that it was a crisis situation, that Baba could die, or that she had no one, she grasped on to a thin string of hope and the seemingly stupidest optimistic piece of her day she could find. When she ran out of positive things for today, she went back to yesterday.

As the cabin grew dim and her positivity exercise exhausted her mind, she fell into a shaky sleep.

When she woke, she didn't know where she was. The hum of the flight and the snoring of the passenger next to her disoriented her. Planes always smelled a particular way to her, the same way hospitals did.

Hospitals.

It was that word that caused her stomach to lurch and forced up, like bile, the reason she was on a plane.

She bent forward, resting her hands on the seat in front of her and steadying her breathing.

Baba could die. And his last words to you were that you were dead to him.

Kiran choked back a dry sob. *Think about something happy*, she pleaded with herself, but the one thing that planes didn't carry was the ability to stop thinking—and nighttime was always the worst for that, despite where she was. Even when she was thirty thousand feet above the ground, it didn't matter. Darkness surrounded the plane and pervaded her thoughts like smoke.

Baba had fought tooth and nail to provide a home to his family. She could remember the way his reputation for honesty preceded him the second she mentioned her name to anyone in town.

Despite the rumors and gossip that had spread through the village upon Kirti's wedding, Baba was somehow spared the criticism. Ma had borne the brunt of it. Probably because she was female and home with the children, Kiran realized now, but she couldn't help but think Baba's character was a talisman. They viewed him with pity rather than judgment.

And now, if he died with two dishonorable daughters, his entire legacy wouldn't matter. His goodness wouldn't matter. *He wouldn't matter* because he would have seen himself as a failure.

The sting of tears threatened her eyes, but she wasn't going to cry. She had to face this bravely. As far as she knew, he hadn't left the earth yet, and until that moment came, she would fight like hell to bring her family back together. She wouldn't be the one to destroy it.

Instead, Kiran joined her hands in prayer and rested her forehead on her thumbs, silently begging the gods that she was flying nearer to now. Perhaps the geography would make them hear her louder.

If you let Baba survive, I will bring our family together again. Please. Don't take him away from us.

She inhaled, fervently holding her wish inside before blowing it out. Going back to the beginning of the year and ticking off all the good things that happened to her, she glanced at her watch. She had five hours left.

Chapter Forty-One

NASH

Nash tapped his foot underneath the table.

He was many things, but indecisive wasn't one of them. Yet his mind swung back and forth like a pendulum as he sat in the café.

One second, he wanted to stay, meet his dad, and know what he was missing...and the next second, he berated himself for thinking one coffee could make up for twenty-five years of being gone and wondered why he even bothered.

Morbid curiosity filled him. Did he look more like his father or his mother or act more like one of them? Mom said he was quiet sometimes like Kirk. But what about everything else?

Humans had a fight-or-flight response when threats approached. He could run now, or he could stay and fight.

But the truth was, he didn't know if he wanted to do either one. Running would continue a trend where he shut out his past and continued to move forward with his career, never really dealing with it—like the damage that could be done to tendons and never fully heal until it caused pain and hurt years later.

But if he stayed and fought, he'd open himself up to more

injury. His old wounds would be torn open and left to bleed when Kirk inevitably left again, and in his weakened state without Kiran and under the pressures of dealing with psych patients, he wasn't in the position to repair the damage.

Nash gave his head a little shake to clear the deafening thoughts.

Brandon had been right. This had thrown him off balance completely.

Nash glanced at the door and froze.

A man, no older than his late forties, stepped into the café. He was wearing a pair of jeans, worn but not tattered, and a green-and-black-plaid shirt rolled up at the cuffs. He had hair exactly the same shade of Nash's—dirty blond sprinkled with brighter strands. He had hazel eyes under a bush of eyebrows that reminded Nash of the caterpillar-like bushes on his own face. They had the same cheekbones, and Kirk's smile lines were in the same place as Nash's, with added wrinkles around his forehead. He could tell they were the same height, even from his seated place in the corner.

Kirk's gaze fell on Nash almost immediately, and he stopped in the middle of the café.

As the two men locked eyes for the first time in twenty-five years, Nash finally knew where he'd gotten some of his features.

Kirk slowly walked toward him, and Nash got up, unsure what else to do.

They came to a stop three feet from each other and paused, both uncertain about whether to hug.

It was Kirk who put a hand forward first. "Hello, Son."

Nash glanced down at the peace offering. "Hi...Kirk."

"Do you come to this place often?" Kirk's eyes rested on the industrial decor, a far cry from the secondhand coffee maker they'd had when Nash was growing up.

"Every morning on my way to work," Nash said. "But the coffee stand down the street is better, to be honest."

"Mmm," Kirk hummed like an acknowledgment. "You look good, Son."

Son. He'd said it twice now. But Nash didn't feel anything attached to the word. There was no long-lost feeling of fondness or belonging that suddenly came upon him in a revelatory wave. Instead, he stared at his father for a few seconds in silence.

"Well, now I know where I got my hair from."

"Your mother was blond too," Kirk said with a smile.

"I remember."

They stood in line in silence. Nash could feel Kirk's eyes on him, scanning his face, maybe even holding out hope that they'd leave this coffee shop as pals.

Nash shoved his hands in his pockets.

"What can I get you, sir?" the man behind the counter asked both men.

"A black coffee," Kirk answered.

The server and Kirk looked at Nash.

"Oh, uh…a chai," Nash said.

He pulled out his wallet, but Kirk beat him to it.

"I got it, Son."

Nash gave a terse nod.

"So, chai, huh? What happened to good old-fashioned coffee?" Kirk asked.

Between Kirk's gaze and his smile, Nash couldn't tell if he was being teased or if it was a genuine question. "I have a…friend. She's Indian. She got me into it."

"Indian, huh? Does she wear saris and go on about cows being sacred?"

Judging by his nervous laugh, Kirk may have been trying

to fill the air with something other than the frostiness Nash left behind...but Nash bristled, anger and annoyance surging in him.

"Don't do that. You're only going to look like a fool when you talk about things you clearly don't know a thing about."

Kirk's face fell. "Just trying to make a joke, Son."

"Her culture isn't a punch line."

They stood in silence, waiting until their drinks were delivered to the end of the bar.

"Do you...do you want to sit down?" Kirk asked.

Not really, Nash wanted to say, but instead, he replied, "Sure."

They sat across from each other. Kirk hunched over the table, his elbows resting on the wood. Nash's hands found their way to his pockets again, where he played with his keys.

Awkwardness filled the air. Nash had no idea if Kirk knew Mom was dead. He didn't know anything, in fact, and suddenly, meeting felt like a mistake.

"Why did you—"

"So, listen, Son—"

They spoke at the same time, and Nash looked away, embarrassed. Kirk gestured for Nash to go ahead.

"Let's just cut to it. Why did you write?"

"I was diagnosed with cancer last year," Kirk started. "And chemo was hell. I lost my hair, right down to my eyebrows. And when you're watchin' your life flash by and you're convinced you're gonna die hooked up to machines, you begin to think about what you've done in your lifetime."

Nash watched his dad. His father's voice was as deep as the flashes of memory Nash had from his childhood.

"Anyway, I was sittin' with my chemo drip, two divorces

under my belt, not even fifty yet... I began to think about my biggest regrets. And I kept thinkin' about how I left you and your mama behind."

"So this is you atoning for it because you didn't die?" Nash's words were edged with glass.

"No. This is me wantin' to say I'm sorry I left. I wish I could take it back."

"You can't," Nash said roughly. "You've been gone twenty-five years, and I'm supposed to say it's okay now because you've magically seen the light and want to make amends?"

"You don't have to say it's okay, Son. God knows I'll never forgive myself. I wanted to see your face, I guess, and tell you like a man that I'm truly, from the bottom of my heart, sorry that I didn't see you grow up."

Nash wanted to fire back that the manly thing would have been to stick around and raise his child. But as he gazed at his dad, older and apologetic, he found himself asking another question with less animosity.

"How did you find me?"

"Well, Facebook and the internet are helpful sometimes." Kirk shrugged with a chuckle. "And then I tracked down your aunt Kate."

"You spoke to Kate?" Nash asked in surprise.

"Only last week, after I hadn't heard from you. She's still a spitfire, that one. Gave me an earful before she told me she'd listen to whatever I had to say. I was thankful for that."

Kate's missed phone calls and requests to call her suddenly made sense to Nash. "Yeah, that sounds like Aunt Kate all right."

"I'm sorry you had to face your mom's passin' and her addiction by yourself."

"Yeah, well, it's not like you were around. I didn't have a

choice." Nash tried not to sound bitter, but long-buried emotions were digging out of their graves and rising to the surface.

"You shouldn't have had to go through it without a father."

"Why did you leave? I mean, even if you were unhappy, didn't you ever think about a divorce or any other option other than leaving your five-year-old son behind with an alcoholic? Do you know how many things you missed?" Nash hissed.

Kirk's eyes drooped, and he looked at the table, shamefaced. "I wish I had a reason other than being young and stupid, but that's all it was. I was hotheaded. I grabbed my stuff and left and started driving. I didn't realize until I'd reached Ohio what I'd done, and by then, I thought the damage was done. Your mama and I were fightin', and I didn't want to face that. Eventually when she signed the divorce papers without a fight, I figured she never wanted me back anyway and she was glad to see my backside."

"I would never do what you did," Nash stated furiously.

"You're a better man than I am, Nash. By all accounts... A psychologist. A man who didn't go down the same paths as your mama and I did. I can't ever picture you doing to your kids what I did to you."

At the mention of *kids*, Nash thought of Kiran and how he had imagined their children running around a large backyard.

"You look like I slapped you with a sausage, Son. Spit it out." Kirk waited expectantly for Nash's outburst.

Nash shook his head. "It's nothing. A lot on my mind."

"Kate told me you were datin' a new girl. How's that been going?"

The disbelief washed over Nash. Was he really about to talk to his dad about girl problems? The same dad who he was meeting for the first time since he was a child?

Nash shrugged. "We broke up."

"Did you love her?" Kirk asked, and the earnestness in his eyes struck Nash.

"It doesn't matter," he muttered.

"I really did love your mom, but I gave up on her too fast... And maybe if I hadn't, if I'd hung in there and insisted we work it out, we would have gotten to be a family."

"But we didn't, Kirk," Nash snapped at the word *family*. "Do you know who my family was? Aunt Kate. Brandon. And lately, Kiran. It never included you. Hell, it just barely involved Mom. I've had to fend for myself all these years, and now you're back, on your own time, like it's not going to fuck me up all over again. So don't talk to me about what a family is supposed to be like and all we could have been, because anything I learned about that concept sure as hell didn't come from the two of you."

The words were out there. Nash grunted slightly at the effort it took to unleash the anger he'd kept deep inside, locked away in his heart, for the better part of his life. He swallowed hard, a lump forming in his throat, and thought he'd choke on the Herculean task it became.

He rubbed his eyes furiously, as if he were trying to wipe away the stinging in them.

Kirk's eyes too were red-rimmed as he took in the magnitude of hurt he'd caused his son.

"I wish I could show you how sorry I am," he whispered.

"You can't," Nash said simply.

All he wanted was to get out of there. Suddenly, every piece of him, all the way down to his soul, was exhausted. He stood.

"I should go, Kirk."

As he stepped toward the door, Kirk grabbed Nash's wrist gently. Nash grew aware how soft his grasp was, nothing like the strong mechanic that Mom had described.

"Thank you for comin' today, Son. I know I haven't been there for you…but I hope I can be when you're ready. I love you, and there hasn't been a day I didn't think about you."

Those were words that Nash had wanted more than anything when he'd been waiting by the door for his dad to come home. But now…now, he wasn't sure if they meant anything at all.

Chapter Forty-Two

KIRAN

When she landed in Delhi, it was as though the ten years of living abroad had never happened. She threw elbows like she was a WWE wrestler in line at a temple with thousands shoving for a pilgrimage and made it to the front of the plane with her handbag on her shoulder before most of the other coach passengers.

The doors opened to the jet bridge, and a wall of smells hit her. Kiran compared the scent to a combination of weed, dust, and incense, a comparison that Nash had laughed at but that Kiran still found to be true. It was home.

She moved through the Delhi airport, renovated since the last time she'd come back to India with marble floors and a more sophisticated touch than the developing country the news depicted India as. She knew to queue up quickly for customs so she could beat the rush, and she was successful in reaching a counter.

"Name?"

"Kiran Mathur."

"Purpose of your visit?"

My father had a heart attack. The words got stuck in her throat. "Family emergency," she croaked out.

"Who are you staying with?"

"Family. My parents." She didn't know if she'd even be welcome at home, but she took a wild guess and hoped it was the case.

She texted the CMC to let them know she'd landed and would call them when she found out the full story. Once she was through the doors, she scanned the crowd gathered at the metal barriers outside. Her *mama*, Ma's younger brother, waited in a simple white kurta and jeans. Kiran waved and walked toward him with bated breath.

White was the color of mourning.

It was also the color Rakesh Mama wore all the time.

"Kiran, beta, welcome home." He patted her shoulder.

"Is Baba… Did he… Is he…" Kiran couldn't bear to utter the word *dead* and *Baba* in the same sentence.

"No," he said reassuringly. "He is still in ICU, and there has been no change."

Kiran breathed a relieved sigh, and her head dropped.

Rakesh Mama pulled her in for a hug and kissed her forehead. "Let's go. We have a little drive. Is this all you packed?"

"I don't need much to survive."

"My darling, your mind always got you where you needed to go." He kissed her forehead again.

It took them an hour and a half to drive from the airport to the hospital, during which time Kiran tried to describe New York City, her friends, and her work to Rakesh Mama, who was a farmer. He'd only come to Delhi when he heard about Baba. He asked questions about the efficiency of machines he wanted to buy, how to improve upon the old rusted tractor he piloted around his fields back in Ramnagar, and whether there was a way to economically change their irrigation system—questions that Kiran suspected he knew the answers to, but as her uncle, he wanted to distract her from the heavy atmosphere that would otherwise occupy the seats of the old Maruti 500 he drove.

Kiran wondered if Rakesh Mama knew all that had transpired between her and her parents before this visit. She wished she could ask about whether the extended family knew about the turmoil with Kirti before Ma and Baba had agreed to her wedding or whether it was a surprise to her uncles, aunts, and cousins that Kirti was suddenly getting married. Rumors always spread between families as easily as they did through the community—but Ma and Baba could be tight-lipped when they wanted to be. After all, it was not like Kiran knew the specific details about the events leading up to Kirti's wedding even now, and they were sisters.

"How is Ma, Rakesh Mama?" Kiran toyed with the hemline on her shirt, trying too hard to be nonchalant.

"Your ma is...handling your baba as well as she can. They have been married a long time. He is her support here. But they'll make it. Have faith in God that your baba will be okay and your ma will be fine too."

While the answer was sweet and thoughtful, it wasn't indicative of the environment she would be walking into...but Kiran didn't want to focus on Nash at a time like this either. Baba's health was priority. Reuniting her family was of utmost importance. Ma's well-being was critical. Nothing else mattered.

"Would you like to go home before you go to the hospital? Have some chai. Wash your face."

"Why, do you think I'm smelly?"

"If you are, you'll fit right into India, New York girl!"

"Let's go to the hospital. I need to see my parents."

Kiran had visited hospitals in the United States before. She'd gone for routine blood tests and spent a night next to Payal during their junior year when she drank too much on her twenty-first birthday. She'd cared for Akash when his appendix ruptured during their first year in New York City.

But nothing ever compared to a hospital where your parent was a patient.

When Akash's appendix had ruptured, Kiran had wholly trusted the doctors and nurses who wandered in at all hours to draw his blood, ask how he was doing, and check on his incision. She believed in his ability to get better because he ran every day, this was the first time he'd had a health issue in all the time she'd known him, and he was at one of the best hospitals in the city. She watched in admiration as nurses washed their hands before they touched him and doctors took copious notes as they spoke to him, putting everything he said on the record and writing their thoughts there too.

But hospitals in India were another world entirely. Dr. Ram Manohar Lohia Hospital was filled with those seeking care. The disparity between the poor and those who could afford surgeries, X-rays, and blood tests was a stark reminder of why Kiran had paid for her parents to move to Delhi from Ramnagar. While the wealthy had rooms with beds that were, at minimum, taken care of, many of the walk-ins were literally off the street. They waited to be seen, with dirty cloths covering their cough-filled mouths and an unwashed stench filling the halls. Kiran discreetly tried to cover her face to protect herself from the sick smell but selfishly to shield herself from whatever diseases were being carried. Her heart broke at the lives she knew some of these human beings lived in huts and sewage-filled slums, but even in the hour or two she'd been back in the motherland, she felt her "survival of the fittest" mentality rolling back.

All she wanted to do was see Baba and make sure he had a

good bed and quality care. After all, what was the point if she was unable to provide for them after being apart? Unlike Akash, Baba wasn't young and vital anymore. He didn't take care of his health with as many yearly checkups, and he didn't get bloodwork often enough. He wouldn't know if his heart had a block from a stress test. Instead, his version of feeling well entailed remaining somewhat active, giving up eating his daily paan because Ma hated the way the betel nuts stained the sidewalk outside their home when he spit them out, and not smoking.

Rakesh Mama led Kiran down a hallway with cement floors. Yellow plaster decked the walls. Nurses walked by in white dresses with white hats, reminding Kiran of movies like *Pearl Harbor*. He guided her to a room with seven beds, all split with enough space between them to accommodate the many family members accompanying each patient, but a crowded room on a busy day nonetheless. Kiran's eyes frantically jumped from bed to bed for Baba's face, but they passed through the room and down another hallway.

A set of doors opened to the ICU, where each patient shared a room with just one another person—not a huge change from the life she'd grown accustomed to in the West.

She froze at the doorway as Rakesh Mama stepped into the room, bracing herself.

Baba was on the bed on the opposing side of the room, judging by where Rakesh Mama went, curtains drawn around both beds. She smelled iodine, bleach, the salty tang of blood, and sourness. Steeling her will and cementing her insides so they wouldn't react with fear, she followed.

Ma was sitting in vigil next to Baba, her hand on his.

Kiran barely recognized Baba. The man who had tossed her into the air as a child and caught her with glee and only bought the freshest of flowers for the mandir was lying prone on his back, his eyes closed. He was weaker than she remembered as more skin hung off his forearms and his face cast a sallow tinge. His head leaned back against a pillow, wires ran to numerous monitors, and tubes pumped God knew what into his body.

Ma wiped a tear on her pallu and rose stiffly. She hunched a little bit when she walked now, Kiran noted. She tried to smile at the unfortunate circumstances they were meeting under, trying not to wonder why it took her so long to visit again.

"Kiran," Ma managed as tears streamed down her face. "I am glad you're here."

Kiran pulled her mom into a hug. She couldn't believe as Ma came close that she had betrayed their relationship with Nash— these were her *parents*.

"It'll be okay, Ma. I'm here."

Ma pulled away, more suddenly than Kiran hoped she would, and cleared her throat. "The doctors say he needs a procedure, but they wanted to wait. I don't know why. Something about seeing where he is in twenty-four hours from the heart attack. They put in some...lines... I don't know."

The English to Hindi hadn't translated. Even the Hindi hadn't properly conveyed what was needed for Baba's life. Ma had no idea what was going on, whether her husband would make it or not, because she couldn't even understand the doctors who attempted to explain all of it. The lack of understanding unleashed both fury and heartbreak in Kiran's heart.

"I'm going to talk to the doctors."

She stepped outside the room, keen to find a hospital worker to ream out.

The logic behind the personnel's decision to keep Baba in a room with other patients blew her mind.

"If he's under intensive care, why is he sharing a room? What happened to privacy?"

"Ma'am, your father had a massive heart attack, and we needed to stabilize him," the customer service rep said, not meeting her eye. "However, if you would like—"

"How much will it cost?" Kiran got directly to the point.

"I can print a receipt for you."

Kiran glanced at the figure—far beyond what Baba made but within reason for her to cover.

"Get him an individual room. No expense spared on his treatment. All decisions are run by me. Do you understand?" she said with so much force, a boardroom would have quaked.

The worker looked as though he would pee himself. "Yes, ma'am."

"Now...about that single room..." She pulled out her wallet.

An hour later, Baba, with all of his tubes and monitors, was set up in a single room. He woke up once, briefly, and he didn't appear to be there at all. His gaze traveled around the room, barely resting on Ma or Kiran, before he closed his eyes again and slept.

Ma didn't move from the chair next to him. In silence, she and Kiran sat on either side of his bed. Occasionally, Kiran could feel Ma's eyes on her, but for the most part, they were silent. The lack of catching up amplified the beeps on Baba's machines and the sound of his breathing. Kiran began counting his breaths to occupy her time.

Two hundred breaths later, she was beginning to believe her father was channeling Darth Vader.

"Ma, how are you holding up?"

"What are you supposed to do when you can't do anything? It's all in God's hands, but I don't think a trip to the mandir can fix this."

"It will be okay, Didi," said Rakesh Mama.

"Raku, you should go home," Ma directed. "Kiran is here. We will call you if anything changes."

"I can stay," Rakesh Mama insisted.

"No, no, go to your sister-in-law's home and take some rest," Ma said again.

Rakesh Mama finally acquiesced, giving Kiran a kiss on the forehead before heading out.

It took over three hours before a doctor finally appeared to discuss Baba's case. Those hours were filled with silence and glares between Kiran and Ma.

"Ma'am," the doctor said. "Who is in charge of Mr. Mathur's medical decisions?"

"Me," Kiran answered. "What's going on? Why did this take so long?"

"Miss Mathur, your father needs a triple bypass surgery. Traffic had been very bad when he arrived, and he was delayed in arriving, which eliminated the window to perform a catheterization. Because he is diabetic, the dyes used in an angiogram are harmful to his kidneys, and due to the medications we gave him while he was under observation, we must wait three days before performing a triple bypass."

"What are the risks of a bypass? It's an open-heart surgery, correct?" Kiran tried not to convey the sheer terror she felt at the idea of opening up Baba's chest cavity and stopping his heart to operate on it.

"It is an open-heart surgery. I cannot lie to you. Any major surgery such as this comes with risks. Bleeding, heart arrhythmias, infections, memory loss, kidney issues because of his diabetes, stroke, or another heart attack. In the worst case, death..."

Death.

"Are there any alternatives?" Kiran asked quietly. "There has to be something you can do other than opening him up and manually fixing this, right?"

"I'm afraid not."

Kiran nodded. In a daze, she signed the papers required to allow Baba to have the surgery he needed.

Now she had to tell Ma.

Kiran tried to explain what was about to happen. The concept of cutting into someone, exposing their heart, stopping it, and starting it wasn't easy to comprehend in English, let alone another language.

But Ma only had one question.

"Risk kya hai?" Ma asked.

Kiran was at a loss for words. She couldn't possibly tell her mother that the bypass was invasive and dangerous. The concept of stopping a heart and restarting it hours later was daunting even for an educated mind grappling with the patient being her father. For Ma, it would be impossible to handle.

She had also lied enough to her parents in the last months, and one more lie in a crisis of this magnitude could finally prompt destiny to push them all over the edge. That was the last thing Kiran wanted.

"Ma, the risk is high. But this is our only option. His heart attack was massive, and this is the only way he'll survive. This is his best chance."

Ma's eyes widened, then filled with tears. Her shoulders hunched, and she sat back, her face in her hands. She shook a little as she wrestled with the implications of what Kiran had just said. While Kiran may have spoken of Baba's best chance, Ma, as his wife, could only hear the loss, and Kiran couldn't blame her mother one bit for that.

Ma's reddened eyes glared at Kiran as she lifted her head. Her voice was shaky. She was maddened with grief and heartbreak, but when she spoke, there was undeniable conviction in her voice.

"This is your fault. Your baba might be taken away, and if he is, it'll be your fault."

Kiran was gut punched, and her lungs hurt. It took every ounce of strength in her legs to hold herself up against the door and keep from crumbling in half.

"I'll go home and get you some food," Kiran said soothingly. "You must be hungry."

In a daze, she collected her bag and suitcase, blindly dragging it behind her as she headed toward the exit. There, she hailed an auto rickshaw. The driver subtly nodded when Kiran directed him and didn't speak again as he drove her from the hospital to the apartment she had rented for her parents in Lajpat Nagar. She suspected he had heard a touch of American accent in her voice and seemed determined to take her through a scenic route to their apartment in Lajpat Nagar. They passed the president of India's home, Rashtrapati Bhavan, and the Nehru Planetarium on their route. Embassies lined the street, waving their flags in patriotic pride. India Gate, a giant arch memorializing the forgotten colonized soldiers from 1914–1921, rose into the sky on Kiran's right as they rounded a giant hexagon. Even the high court was visible.

Each landmark was a jab at her.

Look at where you're from.

You live in America, but you are not American.

Act like an Indian. This is your heritage.

As they pulled into the block where houses packed next to one another with hardly enough space to roam in between, Kiran shoved a handful of rupee notes into the driver's hand.

"Please, ma'am," he implored, gesturing for more.

Kiran blankly gave him another hundred rupees, careless about whether she was being ripped off or not. She glanced upward at the cement building in front of her. Six stories with faded and peeling yellow stucco decorating the front, the apartment building was foreign compared to the home Kiran had grown up in Ramnagar. She had recruited Rakesh Mama to find this place within her budget for Ma and Baba to move into.

She found the thick ring with the giant skeleton key hanging from it, which Rakesh Mama had left in her bag. She unlatched the room.

The first smell that hit her was of incense—the same incense Baba always lit when she was growing up.

As she closed the door behind her, she sank to the floor against it and finally cried.

She didn't know how long she spent on the floor, sobbing until her eyes were red, raw, and burning. Her nose stung, and her head hurt, a combination of exhaustion and aches from the labor of traveling across the world.

She'd always thought of India as home, but now she wondered how home could feel so empty when her heart was thousands of miles away.

Nash didn't know.

Her dad was in the hospital, her family was fractured, and all she wanted was comfort from Nash, who had no idea she was struggling and had no idea how sorry she was.

Whether he wanted to talk to her, whether he *would*, whether there was any hope at all, she didn't care. Without thinking, she fished for her phone in the bag she'd dropped on the floor next to her. Sniffling, she dialed, fighting back another wave of tears.

"Hello?" Nash's voice was hesitant.

"Nash?" Kiran said, her eyes overflowing again at the sound of his voice.

"Kiran? Are you okay?" He sounded concerned.

Or maybe that was what she hoped, that he'd forget her idiocy.

"I'm in India. My baba—my dad—had a heart attack."

"Is he okay?" he asked quietly. "Do you want me to... Do you need me?"

"I've always needed you," she said, letting out a small sob. "I just don't know how to...what we can do about all this. This is my fault."

Kiran could hear Nash breathing in and out slowly on the other end of the line, and his quiet presence calmed her.

"What can I do?" His voice was so low, so quiet, that Kiran strained to hear.

"I miss you." The words were out before she could stop them or think them through.

Silence.

Kiran pulled the phone away, frowning at the screen to see if the call had cut, before she heard Nash clearing his throat on the other end. She slammed it back to her ear.

"I miss you too," he said.

Relief coursed through her. She wasn't the only miserable one. He missed her too.

"But, Kiran, you broke up with me," he reminded her.

"I'm sorry. I'm so sorry."

"'Sorry' doesn't make the ache go away. I know you're sorry. But it doesn't change anything."

"Nash—" Kiran struggled to explain anything.

Exhaustion hit her in waves.

But he was right.

"I just need you to understand," she whispered. "You are...

everything. You're smart and funny. You saw me in a way I'd never been seen before. But I'm in India... My dad is having a triple bypass soon to save his life.

"When they gave up Kirti, every holiday was muted. People talked about them in gatherings and at religious events. It hurt them, but they never let it show. But if I fall in love, and they go through it again... Kirti couldn't say no, and I get why. I know how much that would have hurt her." Her voice cracked. "But if I don't, then I put my parents—the two people who stayed up with me each night to study, sold their possessions to support me, and did everything in their power to let me succeed—in a position again where they've bet and lost."

"Kiran, you're in America now. Okay, maybe not literally now. But they have to understand that times have changed and that you've made it so far that they have to trust your choices."

"You still don't get it, Nash! Just like you didn't understand the big deal about my name. You have a set of privileges and some values that are different from mine."

"They aren't worse—" he protested gently.

"Just different," she finished for him. "You grew up without much family around. And I'm so sorry for that. Freedom didn't come to you without loss, and it didn't come to you easily...but you've been able to live your life without a binding tie."

"That freedom is a human value, though."

"No, Nash, it's an American one," Kiran pressed. "I'm not saying it's a bad one. It's beautiful in its own way and has benefits, but not every culture works that way, and it's not fair of you to expect me to follow the American way just because I live there. And it's not fair for me to hold you to this expectation either. I can't do that to the family who got me to America in the first place."

"I don't understand why it has to be me or them."

"I don't know any other way," Kiran confessed. "Because the pain it'll cause them, the social stigma they fear, the fact that they already lost one child, and I can't bear to make them feel like they lost another one... I don't see another way. I don't *want* this. I want you. But I can't have you."

"Don't you have a right to fall in love with the person you spend your life with?" Frustration and pain bled into his voice.

"A right, yes. But that right comes with sacrifices sometimes too."

"It's hard to let you go," he said quietly after a moment's pause that felt like an eternity.

"Honestly? Nash, I don't want you to. This isn't what I want. It's what has to happen." Kiran welled up again, not believing what she was telling him to do.

"If I proved myself, or...I don't know, if things were different, would you be with me?"

"In a heartbeat."

"I don't know if that feels better or worse," he whispered.

Kiran wasn't sure if the click she heard was from him hanging up or if it was her heart cracking in half as she started to cry in earnest all over again.

Chapter Forty-Three

NASH

Nash was drained.

He held on to the phone, his grip refusing to loosen in case she called back and changed her mind, as he lay on the couch, limp and unwilling to move.

Minutes, then hours, passed while he stared at the ceiling. His heart thumped steadily, but he had no idea how it was still going when his life had been sucked out of him.

And the phone didn't ring again.

His father's words played through his mind over and over about loving Mom, not fighting for her, and the life of regret he'd lived by wishing he hadn't given up so easily.

Nash didn't want to experience the same wishful, retrospective thinking that his dad had. He wanted to do it right the first time around and live a happy life. After all, hadn't everyone told him that he had beaten the odds by succeeding? He didn't want to go down his parents' path of regret and missing out on the things and people they loved.

He got up to get a glass of water—pausing to contemplate a

beer before deciding against it because he couldn't bring himself to drink in the morning—and a folded piece of paper on his counter caught his eye.

He frowned, wondering what he'd left there, before he remembered picking it up outside. The same paper that Kiran had dropped when he'd last seen her.

Curious, missing her, and figuring he couldn't lose anything more, he unfolded it.

Her curly handwriting spiraled through alternating lines on the paper, and Nash imagined her in front of him now, writing out her list of things to do. His heart felt crushed, thinking about how he'd wanted to know the girl in front of him back then and how he couldn't let her go now.

Each item was crossed off. Nash paused on each one, remembering her look of glee at seeing horses, the way she curled into herself in the night air on the roof.

His eyes trailed to the bottom of the list, where smaller writing spelled out a short sentence. Three words.

Fall in love.

They were crossed out.

Nash's heart stopped.

He read it over and over, saying the words to himself and seeing the neat line across the words she'd jotted down in secret, hiding them from him.

She'd fallen in love.

She'd fallen in love *with him.*

But she left you anyway, a voice in his mind said loudly.

If I'd hung in there and insisted we work it out, we would have gotten to be a family, his dad's voice said in his head now.

Maybe he needed to fight harder and convince her to hang in there.

His phone buzzed, making him jump.

He sprinted to the phone resting on the sofa cushion and picked up so fast, hoping it was Kiran, that he hit himself hard on the side of the head.

"Hello?" he answered breathlessly, wincing at the ache before realizing he hadn't even looked at the number that had called.

"Nash?" a female voice asked on the other end.

It wasn't Kiran. His stomach plummeted. But he also had no idea who the hell it actually was either.

"Yeah?"

"Oh, hello." The British accent grew familiar. "I hope you remember me. It's Kiran's friend, Payal."

"Of course I remember you. Hi. Why... What can I do for you?"

"I wanted to let you know that Kiran went to India. Her father had a heart attack, and she left yesterday."

He sighed. "Thank you for letting me know. But I did find out a couple of hours ago. She gave me a call."

"Did she?" Payal sounded taken aback.

"She did."

"Ah. I take it it didn't go well, did it...?"

"I wouldn't say it was a great conversation, no."

"How are you, Nash?"

He was touched and surprised at the softness in her voice—the genuine care for a person she'd only met once but likely heard plenty of great (and not great) things about.

She mistook his silence for questioning and spoke again. "I'm not trying to be nosy. I wanted to check—"

"No, no," he said quickly. "It's nothing like that. I know you were looking in on me, and I appreciate it. I guess I don't know where to start. I don't understand... I mean, I do on a peripheral level, but it's hard to catch up emotionally."

"If it makes you feel better, she's a mess."

He gave a small smile and a shake of his head that she couldn't see. "It doesn't make me feel better."

"Would you like to talk about it?"

"I found her list, Payal."

"Her list?"

"The ones you all made...your adventures, or plans, or dreams, or whatever. She added 'fall in love' to the bottom. And she crossed it off."

Weighty silence filled the air.

"Wow," breathed Payal.

"Yeah," echoed Nash in the same, awed tone.

"So what are you going to do?"

"I need to go to India."

It was nearly comical how obvious it seemed to Nash. He'd hardly been out of the country—save for a trip to Mexico with Brandon's family after college graduation—let alone across the world, and here he was now, talking about setting off on a journey for a girl.

But it wasn't just *a* girl. It was *the* girl. Kiran needed him. And he would be there.

Silence hung between them for a split second, when Nash was certain Payal would try to talk him out of it.

"I think you need to go to India too." Payal made the statement with a tinge of mischief that didn't escape him.

"I don't even know where I'm going."

"Well, Dr. Hawthorne..." Payal schemed. "In that case, I happen to have her address."

"You are a goddess, Payal."

"Just a mere mortal, but I do try to be divine sometimes." She laughed.

"Also, Payal? How did you get my phone number?"

"I called your office and asked for it."

"And they gave it to you? Maybe I need to fire the admin…"

"I mean, would *you* turn me down? Can't blame her, can you?"

Nash chuckled at her spunk, and it was as though he hadn't laughed in years. He'd found an ally.

Despite the rush to look after Kiran and save the day, Nash had to be rational and patient. He booked a red-eye for the next day, allowing him and Payal time to coordinate a trip and find out details about Kiran's stay. He called into work, requested an additional few days off in case his trip had to be longer than he anticipated, and packed a suitcase—after referencing weather reports because he had no idea what to expect. He let Brandon know he'd be away, eliciting a whoop of joy and promising to text when he landed.

Maybe he was crazy, crossing the world for a girl who had broken up with him.

While it was impulsive and whimsical at the time, he'd never been so thankful he had thought ahead to the inevitability that he would end up on a flight. He wished it wasn't under these circumstances.

Though his meeting with his dad had reopened old wounds and Nash wasn't sure how to heal them, he knew deep down there was wisdom behind Kirk's words. The big gesture was real. And determined as he was not to live out his parents' lives, Nash would do what it took to ensure he never had the same worries.

Chapter Forty-Four

KIRAN

The next day in India, unaware of Nash's efforts and after a night filled with an additional trip to bring her mom food—and to try and convince her to swap shifts, to no avail—Kiran awoke in her old bed. The sun had barely come up, and the sky was turning the indigo hue before dawn. But the birds always woke earlier than that. They cooed loudly to one another from outside in the trees, and while Kiran had never figured out which species was loud enough to wake the neighborhood, they always made their presence known. This was the coolest time of day, when the pollution of Delhi's traffic hadn't hit the air yet and the earth's damp mustiness reminded her of rain. Bharat ka darti. India's dirt. The words in English would never capture the essence of what the smell reminded her of when she awoke to it.

Disoriented and blank, she rolled over on her soft, cotton-stuffed mattress only supported by a wood frame built far before she was born.

There was an old quote she'd read somewhere that she wanted to believe she'd found in a book but had likely seen on Pinterest. It talked about when someone wanted to know where their heart was, they should look to where their mind went when it wandered. Another clichéd old verse had spoken of the first thought that crossed someone's mind in the morning being their reason for waking up.

She imagined Kirti waking up with her husband's name on her mind. Akash would think his oldest sister's moniker because she was his favorite. Sonam would use her brother's image to propel her day forward. Payal would probably think of herself, because she was unattached, free, and happy.

For the last month, Kiran had woken up with the same name on her mind the moment she opened her eyes.

Now, in India, she woke to a different tune.

Baba. Then her stomach sank, hearing the last words they'd said to each other and picturing the hospital where he still lay.

Ma. She'd be hit with another punch, which would knock the wind out of her. Even if Ma was fine physically, Kiran could sense her growing further away with Baba's surgery only two days away. Ma's proclamation that this was Kiran's fault carved a hole in her, and she wrapped her arms around herself as if the grip would hold her broken insides together.

Then...*Nash.* Kiran curled into a ball on her side, willing herself to breathe and to brace for the ache slowly seeping into the void the thoughts of Ma and Baba left. She heaved once, though nothing was there to wrench out of her body. Not even tears.

Get up, Kiran. Come on. Baba needs you. Ma can't do this alone. You have to find Kirti.

Sitting up took Herculean effort. With every centimeter her limbs shifted, she talked herself into another task. *Wash your face. Brush your teeth—your toiletries are in your suitcase. Fill a bucket. Put the immersion heater in the water. Wait five minutes. Pour it over yourself to shower. Pack a bag for the hospital. Turn on the gas stove with a lighter. Ma keeps the flour in a pink bin—where is it? Find it. Make chapatis.*

Step by step, direction by direction, Kiran found herself at the hospital again.

"You can cook."

The monotone made it difficult for Kiran to tell whether Ma was impressed or stating the obvious as she took a bite of the homemade curry and chapatis.

"I learned from the best," Kiran murmured as she adjusted the blanket over Baba so he wouldn't be cold.

"Cooking wasn't what we would hope you would learn." There it was. Ma's dig was in the same bland voice, as if she didn't have the energy to pick a fight.

Kiran kept herself from taking the bait—or perhaps it wasn't bait at all, just the truth. Either way, she said nothing.

The sound of Baba's breathing got louder again.

"Ma, do you want me to take you home? You can shower and sleep."

"I vowed to stay next to him."

"It's been days."

"I brushed my teeth, and Rakesh brought me clothes. I am fine."

Kiran gave up the fight.

A few hours later, Rakesh Mama came to relieve her of her vigil by Baba's bedside.

"I don't want to go. It's okay." Kiran tried to argue, but Rakesh Mama shook his head.

"Take a break. Go ahead. Come back for a night shift if you'd like. I'm too old to be doing those."

She giggled, knowing he would stay for three days and three nights without complaining if they asked. "I'll be back in a few hours."

When she stepped into the setting sun, she flinched at the way the light hit her eyes. The hospital was dank and darker than she would have liked, and she stood outside, breathing in the air for a moment.

Baba had been sleeping an awful lot. At times, he would open his eyes into a lucid gaze around the room before falling asleep again. Kiran wondered if it was his meds or whether his body had decided to take a break.

The surgery was in two more days. Kiran wondered if anyone kept in touch with Kirti—whether she knew their father was suffering.

Kiran pulled out her phone. She searched for the nearest detective and directed an auto driver to take her there.

If she had two days before Baba went into his operation, she would find her sister and reunite the family before it was too late.

Twenty-four hours later, she was standing in an unfamiliar area a couple of hours outside Delhi, with her balled-up fists trying to loosen up and failing.

105 Gandhi Road, near the rail tracks crossroads.

The torn piece of paper shook in Kiran's hands. Ahead of her, two rusted tracks ran across a street that formed an X. Litter and broken plastic were scattered on both sides of the road. A sign on the house on her right read 103 in hand-painted blue numbers, looping to form numbers in dripping script. Two houses farther was 105.

The home was as nondescript as they came in an Indian village. Tan in color, with a front that appeared to be made of stucco but Kiran knew to be cement. Two stories. Windows with scrolling metal screens on them. Stairs on the outside of the house, uneven in their spacing and familiar in height only to those who walked them every day. A walled-in terrace on the roof with a hanging clothesline, draped with colorful saris and, to Kiran's surprise, a pair of jeans in a size close to hers.

But this home wasn't nondescript otherwise.

Kirti lived here. She and Jijaji, whose features Kiran could only remember with fuzziness, and their children. Maybe his parents. She had no idea.

The detective, a Mr. Bhatt, had found Kirti within hours. When Kiran had posed her question, he had sat like a policeman in an old Bollywood movie behind a desk, with inquisitive eyes studying her from the other side of black-rimmed glasses. He was unremarkable in his speech, promising to find her as soon as possible and kindly showing Kiran out after he'd gathered the information he needed. She had trusted in his disciplined notes, his thoughtful questions, and his deliberate consideration as he jotted down additional information she provided.

She had received a phone call at 3:00 p.m. the next day. Kirti's husband, Gautam, was an army colonel, and the family lived at the Delhi Cantonment during the school year. When the kids were off from school—Kiran had no details on whether these children were boys or girls or what ages they were—Kirti stayed at the ancestral home that Gautam's family had left them on the outskirts of Delhi...a mere hour's cab ride away. It was religious festival time in India now...and Kiran was taking a wild guess that the family had retreated to their family home.

That was where Kiran stood now, debating whether she should make a move toward her past or stay rooted in the present.

Baba's surgery was tomorrow.

It was now or never.

How had twenty years passed without contact? Kiran touched her belly, where someday, she hoped a child would grow. She couldn't imagine being separated for that long from her child—and hers hadn't even been conceived yet. How had Ma and Baba allowed Kirti to disappear? How had Kirti listened?

So many questions whirled through her mind, and the tornado of emotions swept Kiran away. She turned around suddenly, earning a jingle from a swerving bicycle rider's bell and a curse word she hadn't heard in ten years. *What was she even doing here?*

"Are you lost?" a young voice asked in Hindi.

"Ummm," Kiran stuttered as she stared at the piece of paper like it held answers. "No. Yes. I'm looking for Kirti Lal's house, but it's okay—"

"Oh. I can take you." The puzzlement in the girl's voice prompted Kiran to look up.

A younger version of herself gazed back at her, brows furrowed. Long wavy hair, thinner and well-oiled, was plaited down to the girl's waist. She had long legs and, surprisingly to Kiran, who hadn't grown up wearing Western clothes at home, was wearing jeans and a stylish white cotton tunic on top. Big, lined eyes peeked out from underneath angular eyebrows, and her square jawline, strong but gentle at the same time, balanced her soft features. She was lean but soft. She couldn't have been more than seventeen.

"Come. Follow me."

"Didi!" a voice called out from the door of a house that had a car sitting in a car port—*we never had a car when I was young*—and a child around the age of ten bounced out in a bright yellow cotton dress.

"Hi, Chottu, did you have a good day at tuition?" the teenager asked as the child wrapped her arms around her waist.

Kiran sucked in her breath at the nickname.

"Aye, Anjali, wait! That girl—always running off... You're in the middle of your tuition homework—"

Kiran stood frozen on the cement path. The address was clutched in her palm, her fingers wrapped so tightly her nails cut into her palms.

After twenty years, her sister—now, clearly a mother—rushed out of the home clad in a blue sari. Her hair had thinned slightly over the years but still held the wave that she had so longed to preserve when she flipped it over her shoulder as a college student. She had grown softer, as age often allowed, and was still as womanly and beautiful as ever.

"Anjali—" Kirti's eyes darted behind her daughter at the statue Kiran had turned into.

Then she stopped. Her eyebrows flew into her forehead as her mouth dropped open. The universe stopped moving. No one existed but the two sisters, staring at each other after twenty years of separation and so many missed milestones. Kirti's entire pregnancy or, Kiran suspected, *two* pregnancies judging by how much the older girl looked like her. Kiran's first period. Her first crush. Her relationship with Nash. Kirti's move into this home. Countless birthdays, anniversaries, family celebrations, and tragedies. Baba's heart.

Kiran parted her lips, but no sound came out, not even a squeak.

Kirti's eyes, the size of full moons, stayed focused on Kiran's. Then slowly they traveled to her hair, which curled at the ends in the Indian humidity, hanging off her chest. Kirti's gaze went to her waist, to Kiran's long legs and the shoes she was wearing—sandals with a bit of a heel—and lingered on her clean, painted nails, her neatly groomed eyebrows, her soft skin. In a flash, she would be able to gauge that Kiran hadn't seen the same hard labor that their family had toiled at. She had none of Ma's cracked heels, coarse but loving hands, or sun-soaked skin that Baba wore.

Kiran was unsure and unmoving. The hungry stare Kirti was

giving her was one she understood. She was giving her big sister the same savoring gaze, taking in every detail—the burn on her forearm, likely from a hot tava, the strands of gray that struck through the jet black Kiran remembered, and a ring she wore on her right hand—Ma's old ring—that Kiran could recall Ma lovingly handing Kirti on her wedding day.

"Chottu." It was a whisper.

At the sweet lullaby of her childhood nickname, Kiran's eyes filled with tears, and she grinned despite the wetness threatening to run down her cheeks.

"Didi," she murmured back. The word was so foreign but so natural rolling off her tongue.

Kirti and Kiran bolted toward each other.

Kiran's arms wrapped around her sister's shoulders, feeling a warmth on her forearms that she hadn't felt since she was a child. Her sister's coconut-oil hair still smelled the same, and Kiran inhaled until her lungs were about to burst.

"I missed you so much," Kirti said, tears running down her cheeks too.

"Didi," Kiran choked out again.

She repeated the word so many times, over and over and over again, until it sounded like one long sentence of two syllables that ran together like a hum.

"You've grown up." Kirti sniffled and laughed through her tears. "Twenty-eight years old. How did that happen?"

"Slowly," Kiran joked.

"Kiran masi?" the younger child, now without a doubt Kiran's niece, tentatively asked. The question was directed at Kirti more than Kiran.

"Yes, jaan," Kirti responded, wiping at her face with the end of her sari's pallu. "This is your Kiran masi."

"We've heard so many things about your childhood." The older girl studied Kiran.

"Kiran, this is my older daughter, Radha, and my younger, Anjali."

"Ma was right. I look like you," Radha murmured.

Kiran could tell their personalities were probably similar at that age too—that Radha was responsible and quiet.

"Kiran masi!" Anjali cried out as she threw her arms around Kiran's waist. "Do you like to play carom?"

Kiran startled at the burst of energy and affection from her little niece. "I used to. I'm not very good."

"Come, let's teach you!" She pulled Kiran's hand toward the house.

Kiran was hesitant to barge into their lives, although she'd already entered with a bang. Was she welcome? She tugged gently at her hand, enveloped in Anjali's, but Kirti was right behind her with a hand on her back to guide her way.

"You're old enough for chai now. Or do you like coffee? Come. Radha, go get some snacks from the shop. Samosas, paneer tikka, and anything else you like." Kirti's enthusiasm propelled Kiran to follow all of them into the home.

"I drink coffee or chai. Anything." Kiran's English use of the word *anything* caused Kirti to glance at her.

"Listen to that accent! Where did you go to school?"

It was that question that washed away the dam and caused Kiran's tears to fall freely. *Where did you go to school?* If only Kirti knew how far she'd come since their days in Ramnagar. Her sister didn't even know she'd moved to the United States. She had no idea about Baba and his current vigil at death's door.

"Chottu," Kirti hummed with the soothing tone of a mother. "Anjali, go finish your schoolwork—"

"But, Ma!"

"Chal hat!" Kirti mockingly raised a hand to smack her daughter, and Anjali ran away, giggling, unaware that the dismissal was a code for adults-only conversation.

"Kiran...talk to me. Come sit down."

Kiran followed Kirti to a sofa in the living room and glanced around as she tried to compose herself. A simple mandir sat in the corner of the living room, built into the wall with cement and a pagoda. Off the living room was a small hallway with a kitchen on the left and two bedrooms on the right. A bathroom at the end of the hall. It was a medium-sized home, much grander than they ever could have dreamed when they'd shared the same one. But, as Kiran noted, it had a touch of Kirti to it, with warmth that carried through the years and transcended financial status. A splash of color here. Religious idols there. A photo or two of the girls when they were younger and a picture of Jijaji, still appearing young though his features were different than Kiran remembered as a child.

"We have a lot to catch up on," Kirti said softly. "Tell me everything."

"I don't even know where to start."

"Anywhere."

"I went to school in Shimla after tenth class. Then to Duke University in America. I'm an engineer. I live in New York City. My best friends' names are Akash, Sonam, and Payal. We met during college and stayed best friends even now. I'm not married."

It seemed an odd summary. A SparkNotes version of her entire life summarized in a few sentences.

Kirti's eyes were red as she gave a small clap. "I knew you were smart. America. Look at you."

"It's something," Kiran said with a small laugh. "It's different from what I—we—grew up in."

The elephant in the room went from the size of a Chernobyl mutant to becoming bright pink as well. The quiet that followed filled itself like a balloon with the implication that they'd grown up together but not side by side. The emphasized absence of Ma and Baba in the conversation was suddenly so apparent, it pressed against both of them like an expanding brick wall.

If Kiran talked about why she'd pursued college in the United States, the conversation would turn to her having a better life... which would result in Ma and Baba's sacrifices.

If she spoke of Nash, it would come back to Ma and Baba not approving and their fear of being ostracized.

If they discussed why Kirti hadn't been in touch over the years, it would turn to how Ma and Baba had to cut ties.

This was too much. Maybe she shouldn't have come. Why had she disrupted everyone's lives by being so impulsive?

Kirti's eyes rested on Kiran, but she couldn't meet her big sister's intent gaze. Instead, she allowed her eyes to wander around the living room again.

There. It was so small she'd missed it the first time. A tiny photograph from years ago of Kiran and Kirti taken before the wedding when they were still a family rested next to the mandir. In a black, simple frame, it was dusted and clean—and Kiran wondered if Kirti thought of her every time she wiped off the photo frame. While some of the idols had collected a sprinkling of dust over the years, this photo looked as though it was diligently kept pure.

Kirti followed her eyes to the photograph.

"It was the only one I had of us," Kirti said softly. "I didn't want to take anything else from home...but you were my baby sister, and I had to have that photograph at the very least, so I smuggled it into my trunk of belongings I took with me after"— Kirti cleared her throat—"after the wedding."

Kiran looked at her sister in shock, half expecting to have no signs that she ever existed in Kirti's life and blown away to find that there had been one every day right in front of her...right next to her shrine for God. A million trails of thought sprang from the realization that Kirti had had a reminder of Kiran in front of her every single day, and it ambushed her senses, causing reactions that crashed against one another in a tangle. Her fists clenched as her heart slowed. Her heartbeat raced, and she fought back tears again. The wetness dried immediately as her cheeks grew warm. She half smiled before her brows furrowed themselves again. Making heads or tails of her emotions was impossible.

Instead, the first coherent thought she had escaped her mouth in a tumble.

"Why didn't you call?" Kiran tried remaining neutral, to keep the tone of accusation out of her voice, but the bitterness rang out like a gunshot.

"Kiran, it wasn't that simple—"

"What wasn't simple?" Kiran challenged. Her empathy cried to give her sister a chance to speak, but she'd been faced with silence for over twenty years, and she wanted answers. "You left. And Ma and Baba *let you*."

Years of pent-up frustration and anger began cascading down Kiran's cheeks as she shouted. "How could you leave me like that? I was eight years old! I needed my big sister. You weren't there for any of it—my first A or when I ranked in class. You weren't there when I gold medaled. Baba dropped me off in Shimla for boarding school alone. Every time Ma made aloo di pyaaz and stopped talking when she'd serve it because she knew it was your favorite. The silent reminders of you on your birthday and wedding anniversary when Ma and Baba would cry in their room. You weren't there for my graduation from Duke or my first love. I didn't get to talk to you when I fell in love and had to give him up because of all this! And now..."

Kiran tried to swallow, but she choked as she sobbed out her anger. Her arms closed themselves around her chest as she tried to hold in the heaves, but they forced themselves out of her body anyway, in raspy gulps that could only indicate that she had finally lost all control. Twenty years of being diligent and careful went to pieces. She forced her fists closed as tight as she could, as if the grip would close around her emotions, but her nails dug into her skin, sending pain up her hands that she hardly noticed. She did it again just to try to feel something when Kirti stood, crossed the space between them, and sat next to her.

In silence, Kirti's arms wrapped around her shoulders and brought Kiran's face to her bosom like a mother would...like a sister would, who had been there all these years without missing a beat. Kiran grasped her hands as she felt wetness from Kirti's cheeks fall into her own.

The familiarity Kirti's scent brought and the warmth she was showing toward a young woman who, essentially, was a stranger finally dammed Kiran's river of tears. She hiccupped and gasped at the air finally filling her lungs.

"I thought of you every single day," Kirti whispered. "You were my baby before my children. Every time I looked at Radha, I swore I saw your face looking back at me."

"You never bothered to come back. Twenty years..." Kiran's voice trailed off in disbelief. "How do you stay away from family for twenty years?"

"I was told not to contact Ma and Baba again. I thought if I followed through, it would be easier. Even the teachers at your school were talking about it, and I was afraid you would take the brunt of it."

"I did," Kiran said simply. "But not the way you thought."

"I'm sorry for that."

Kiran sighed, sitting up and wiping her face with her dupatta. "Don't apologize. I can't imagine it was any easier to have your younger sister show up on your doorstep after twenty years."

"It wasn't expected." Kirti gave a small laugh. Then she brushed the hair out of Kiran's face. "But I wouldn't have wanted anything else. You've given me years of my life back by visiting."

Would Baba feel the same way? Would Ma? This brush with death...would it make them reconsider their lives? Kiran desperately wanted to believe it would. Her entire heart yearned to have her sister back in their good graces and to have her family again. To feel like a home existed in the world.

Kiran's face betrayed her thoughts.

"What's on your mind?"

"Everyone suffered from this. The panchayat may have changed in Ramnagar, but the decisions from then are still affecting our family...and everyone is lesser because of it."

"Did Baba and Ma send you here?"

Kiran wished she was able to lie better—just to appease the hopeful look in her sister's eyes. There was nothing like granting someone's wish and telling them the greatest news of their lives, and Kirti's fervent hope that she was requested back would go unfulfilled today. Kiran hated it.

This dialogue reminded her eerily of a Bollywood movie she'd seen—the younger brother had lied. The older brother had called him out.

And Kiran was tired of all the lying.

"They didn't send me, Didi. But..."

Kirti recoiled at the blow that her parents didn't send for her but attempted to recover quickly. "What?"

"Baba's in the hospital."

Kirti said nothing, only blanching at the news.

"He might not make it," continued Kiran, sounding removed from her own body. "He had a small heart attack four years ago. He had a major one a few days back, and they kept him under observation. They had to wait three days before doing an angiogram, and now they've decided to do a bypass."

"When?" Kirti managed to speak smoothly, but her sari bunched in her fist.

"Tomorrow. It's risky." Kiran's shoulders fell as she explained the situation.

"You should go back to the hospital, Chottu. Ma and Baba need you," Kirti said softly after a few moments had passed.

"Come with me."

Kiran wasn't sure if she was going to ask Kirti to come back today or whether she would wait until a more opportune moment and stay in touch during her week or two in India. But as she explained her father's condition aloud and saw her sister in person, the fleeting length of life was upon her. She didn't want her family to face any more tribulations apart. She wanted Baba to hear Kirti's voice and forgive both his daughters before he entered surgery. He deserved the peace. They all did.

"Kiran," Kirti said gently before shaking her head. "I can't come back."

"Why not? Didi, Baba might die. He might die! How can you not come back?"

"They wouldn't want to see me. At the end of the wedding, Baba told me I was dead to him."

The breath caught in Kiran's chest. She knew all too well what those words could do to someone. Kirti had carried them around for twenty years. Kiran hadn't even carried them for twenty days.

Her heart softened at the burden her sister bore as she replayed those hurtful words every day, anytime she thought of making contact again.

"I got that too, Didi. Those were his last words to me on the phone...and I'm still here. Please."

"Why? Didn't I tell you to take care of our parents?" Kirti asked indignantly.

"I was eight when you asked. I didn't realize we'd grow up and things would get complicated!"

It would have been funny. This bickering, the back-and-forth of siblings trying to escape the blame of their shortcomings and pin responsibility on the other, should have been a daily occurrence as they grew older. Now, the future wanted to redeem itself. And the past was in no mood for redemption.

Kiran sighed. "I fell in love. He's American. White. I never meant for it to happen, but it did. I told Ma and Baba, and they told me never to speak to them again. Baba said I was dead to him. The last conversation I had with Ma at the hospital was her blaming me for Baba's heart attack."

"It wasn't your fault. You didn't cause it."

Kiran paused for a beat. "I feel guilty. Like maybe I did cause it. Then I get angry that I'm taking the blame. Then I feel guilty that I'm angry when Baba could die. It's an endless cycle, and I can't escape."

"Our lives have become an endless cycle. History is bound to repeat itself," Kirti whispered almost to herself.

"I don't even know the history..."

"Baba and Ma never told you?"

"No," Kiran murmured. "I pieced it together, but whether the equation adds up accurately or whether I'm filling in gaps blindly, I don't know."

"Your jijaji, Gautam, and I met through friends. His sister was my friend when we were taking classes, and he was training to be in the Indian Army. We began as friends. I saw him occasionally at their house when I went to study, but it wasn't anything serious. Eventually, we started to feel something more. But he was a lower caste than us—and it wasn't appropriate for people as traditional as the ones in our village. Eventually, some of the girls in my class started gossiping, and the news got back to the panchayat. Even then, we denied it. In the meantime, Gautam's parents went to Baba and Ma about it to see if they were willing to arrange a wedding. Baba and Ma weren't happy. But they didn't say no right away. I was sure they'd come around. I told his sister, but the sarpaanch's daughter, our cousin, heard me and told her father. He told Baba and Ma that it would be inauspicious, and it would dishonor our village if I married a boy from a low caste."

Kiran could see herself in Kirti's shoes, and all of a sudden, the anger that had pervaded her for so long evaporated as she began to understand.

"But you said you would anyway."

"I was hotheaded then," Kirti admitted. "In hindsight, I wouldn't have acted so rashly. Perhaps I should have waited. Maybe we could have persuaded Ma and Baba to leave the village. Anything but holding an ultimatum over their head or forcing all of us into these decisions.

"Baba and Ma seriously considered uprooting our lives and leaving the village, but the wedding drained their savings. They didn't have much money to begin with. But in order to stay and be accepted, to allow you to go to school, and to keep their shop running, the sarpaanch demanded they cut ties with us. I didn't think they would do it. I kept telling them I would run away to be with Gautam or that we didn't need to be married to start a family—imagine the shock that caused!" Kirti laughed a humorless laugh before continuing.

"Ma and Baba gave in. They saw that in the end, I wanted to be with Gautam. They held the wedding. But at the end, Tauji told Baba he must act. Baba told me at my vidhaai that I was never to come back. I was not to contact anyone. I was to leave the village forever, and I was dead to them."

"All this time, I thought you forgot us," Kiran said quietly. "How else could I have explained that you willingly followed that rule? You *listened* when they said they didn't want you to call."

"You never forget your blood, Kiran. You carry the happy memories and the pain. I cried often—when we bought this house, I thought of the one we grew up in. The first time we hired help to mop the floors and do the laundry, I missed Ma and the fact that if she lived with us, she'd never have to do hard labor again. When we got a car, I thought about how easy it would have been to take Baba anywhere he wanted to go. You carry happy memories," she said again. "But you never forget the pain."

"Didi, you have to come back... Please. You have to fix this. We have to mend fences. This might be our last chance."

"Perhaps...but they didn't send you to get me, Chottu. They probably don't want me back."

"You don't know that!"

"And you don't either. From what I gather, you're not reading their minds particularly well at the moment, are you?" She raised an eyebrow.

"I know that doing the same thing over and over and expecting a different result lends itself to stupid choices!" Kiran protested. "And this is a ridiculous decision. Why are we so insistent on being miserable?"

"I love you. I am so happy you came here. But I cannot come back. My decision is final."

Kiran glared at her sister, furious at her pigheadedness. But Radha walked in the front door loaded with enough food to feed an army, and Kiran had to pretend no verbal altercation had taken place, that she hadn't been shot down from reuniting her family.

Anjali peeked out from the other room. "Are you done yelling, Ma?"

"We weren't yelling, Chottu."

"Yeah, we were," Kiran answered in unison with Anjali.

The oddball similarity between generations prompted a laugh from Kirti. Anjali brought the carom board out, and Kiran indulged her in a game or two but couldn't meet Kirti's eyes again.

After an hour's time, Kiran suggested she go.

"I have an early morning tomorrow," she said by way of explanation to Anjali, who asked her to stay the night.

"Send my love... Take it quietly," Kirti murmured to her sister as she hugged her goodbye. "I am so happy you visited, Chottu. I missed you so much."

"Please come back," Kiran implored one last time.

Kirti shook her head. "I can't. But I trust you'll take care of them."

Kiran nodded and waved as she left the property and walked toward the taxi stand. Despite her elation at the reunion with her sister, she couldn't help but feel she had failed at her mission.

Chapter Forty-Five

NASH

"Welcome aboard Flight 102 to New Delhi, India. Please turn your attention to your flight attendants as they demonstrate the safety procedures…"

Nash listened as the attendants described what to do in an emergency landing, paying attention to the lilt of the Hindi translation and remembering how Kiran sounded when she spoke it.

And after the longest flight he'd ever been on, over 48 hours after speaking with Kiran and realizing she loved him too, he landed in her motherland.

He had hardly slept, with an older gentleman snoring next to him through the entire flight. Nash had stayed alert, watching movies on the screen in front of him and reading journal articles he'd saved to his laptop.

As they descended on India, Nash could only see an expanse of twinkling lights reaching the horizon. He'd followed the journey on the tracking map on the screen, and from the moment they had crossed the border into India, the lights had become visible below.

Kiran had always mentioned that India was packed to the brim, but Nash never completely understood what that meant until he saw veined patterns of highways and villages and towns from above. No land had been spared from human touch.

The flight culminated in the longest taxi of his life before they finally pulled up to the gate. Then he stepped off the plane into the strongest combination of smells he had ever witnessed.

Weed, dust, and incense, Kiran had once mentioned to him, and he had chuckled at the odd description. But now, he understood.

The heat was stifling, even at night. Humidity turned the air into a thick wall of moist air, and Nash could swear he was wading through it as he wheeled his carry-on through the airport.

The customs line took an outrageous amount of time. Only a few booths were open, odd considering the sheer number of people who had descended from their aircraft into the marble lobby.

One by one, each person was called forward, interrogated about their intentions, and sent through to the duty-free stores on the other side. Nash noticed the stares of some of the people around him and felt conscious of his white skin. While others were mostly shades of gold and oil, he stuck out like a sore thumb.

Was this how Kiran and her friends felt every day?

The customs officer glared at him with some suspicion as he passed through the line, but when Nash pulled himself up to full height, the officer let him through without much fuss.

Immediately upon exiting the building, he was ambushed by taxi drivers.

"Sir! Sir! Taxi? Follow me!" A number of drivers accosted him, attempting to buy out his business in their luxury cars.

Taxi stands every hundred feet were swarmed with more people who were trying to rent official cabs. Judging by the yellow upper half and black lower half, Nash guessed these were the equivalent of the Yellow Cabs in New York.

Payal had put a hotel room on her credit card for Nash, using her Marriott points. While Nash had tried to fight her on it, she said it was for love and that she expected a thank-you at their wedding someday, arguing until Nash gave in. She'd also told him to look out for a cab driver with his name on a card.

Payal had thought of everything.

As Nash got swept away in the crowd of people pouring out of the terminal and into the waiting crowd, he spotted a sign held by a neatly dressed man.

N. HAWTHORNE.

"How was your flight, sir?" asked the driver.

"It was good," Nash said. "It's definitely different here."

The driver, named Mohammad, gave him a polite smile and nodded.

Small talk wasn't much of a thing here, apparently.

Mohammad led him to a neat Honda and drove him a short distance away from the airport to the JW Marriott hotel. When Nash entered, the enormous lobby reminded him of the places he'd stayed in the United States, and immediately he felt less like a stranger and more like a vacationer.

Maybe that was what Kiran meant...that he'd centered himself as an American in his view of the world and associated it with good things, rather than recognizing the beauty in other traditions.

It was already 11:00 p.m., and Nash couldn't wait to hit the bed before he found Kiran in the morning.

Chapter Forty-Six

KIRAN

Kiran was at the hospital by five in the morning though the surgery wasn't scheduled until eight. She had tossed and turned with dreams of Kirti whimpering that she couldn't join them and Ma's shouting of broken promises. She needed a moment of silence from her own thoughts, and she entered the hospital room. Ma snoozed, snoring quietly, on a cot next to the bed.

Kiran sat in the other chair and stared at her parents. Ma's loyalty was admirable. She wanted a love like that—one where she could go to all lengths of discomfort to ensure that her partner was safe. She wondered if she and Nash could have had that but brushed the thought away as she glanced at her parents again. Even in their sleep, Baba and Ma breathed the same. Their light snores whistled in symphony.

At six on the dot, Ma stirred. She looked around and spotted Kiran, who closed her Kindle cover on her lap.

"When did you get here?"

"Just a little while ago."

"What have you been doing?"

"I was reading."

Ma nodded. "That used to be your answer anytime I asked you what you were doing when you were a child."

Kiran smiled. "You should go freshen up and wash your face, Ma. It'll be a long day. You'll want to have some energy. I'll stay with Baba in the meantime."

Ma said nothing but rose, pulling a bag with her to the washroom. When she left, Kiran stood and sat on the space next to her father's hips.

"Baba, it's me," she whispered into his ear in Hindi. "I'm here. You've been sleeping for most of the last few days. I don't know if you've seen me. If you've known I'm here. But I am. I flew back because I didn't want my last words from you to be telling me that I'm dead to you. I didn't want my last memories of my parents together to be fighting with them and hanging up from across an ocean. I want you to go into this surgery and fight hard.

"You know, when I was little and I got a bad grade, I always took it hard when I didn't do well on an exam. And you used to tell me I was a Mathur. I asked you what that meant. You told me Mathur meant we were learned warriors. Baba, I wouldn't have become educated if it wasn't for all you gave up. But now I need you to be the warrior... I promise if you pull through, we'll get through everything together. Because I found Kirti. And she needs to see her baba too and hear him speak to her again. You have granddaughters who want to see you. Our family has been apart for too long. And you need to come back to us for that to happen. You can't yell at me if you don't wake up." Kiran giggled and choked back a sob. "Come back to us, Baba. Fight hard."

She kissed his forehead. Ma arrived then, clutching a small Ganesh statue—a twin statue of the one Kiran housed at her apartment in the States. She didn't let go of it as the doctors wheeled Baba's bed out of the room to prep him for surgery, silently following the group while murmuring prayers for her husband. Kiran held onto Baba's hand until the last possible second.

Just as she was about to let go, she swore she felt him squeeze her fingers.

Then, they were gone.

The double doors closed behind them with a final *thud*.

Tick. Tock. Tick. Tock. Tick. Tock.

The second hand on the waiting room clock amplified the longer Kiran listened to it. Silence couldn't continue any longer, or she'd lose her mind.

Over the last two hours, she'd paced, performed her positive thought ritual, tried to convince herself that Baba's hand squeeze was a divine sign that it would be okay, told herself she should quit her job and move back to India, and had mentally written her resignation letter twelve different times.

It didn't make the hours go by any quicker.

Finally, pushed beyond the brink of mental exhaustion, she plopped herself back into a waiting-room chair with her hands over her eyes to keep out the irritating white fluorescence from the lights.

Tick. Tock.

"Where did you go yesterday?" Ma asked after another half hour of silence.

"I–I went and saw a...friend—"

"Your father is in the hospital, and you chose to see a friend?" Ma's voice rose an octave and a decibel.

"She came to see me." A third voice rang out in the room.

Kirti stood at the waiting-room doors in a pale-blue sari. Her hair was pulled into a neat plait, and she held a straw bag in her hands, filled with canisters of food and, from what Kiran could tell, a few extra saris.

Ma's jaw dropped. Her eyes reddened, and she blinked rapidly, staring at Kirti as though she had seen a ghost. Even her skin paled.

"Ma," Kirti whispered.

Elation swept through Kiran, who wanted to prance into Kirti's arms, cry tears of impatience and joy, and thank her for coming. But the look on her face and on Ma's forced Kiran to remain a third party on the outskirts. She chose to stay hidden from the line of fire. This was something Kirti needed to do on her own.

Ma looked like a woman about to be thrown on a pyre. She stood. She jerked as if she was going to step toward Kirti and hug her but then thought better of it and stood back, grasping the backrest of the seat so tight her knuckles turned white.

"What are you doing here?" Ma asked quietly.

"Kiran told me Baba was having surgery. I wanted to be here."

"You haven't been here for twenty years."

"Whose fault is that?" Kiran chimed in.

"Kiran," Kirti reprimanded and shook her head, as if to say, *Peace, child, don't lose your temper*. Then to Ma, "I'm here now. And I'm not going anywhere."

Ma's reddened eyes darted between her daughters and toward the door. For a moment, Kiran wondered if she was contemplating leaving herself. But then she sat.

Kirti sat across from her.

"Kiran, why don't you get some chai for us?" she requested kindly.

As Kiran shot a glance behind her, the two ladies in her life had locked eyes for the first time in two decades.

She wanted to give them time to discuss anything they wanted to get off their chests. As she tried to find the canteen to buy some chai, Kiran trailed down an endless maze of hallways, conference rooms, and corridors leading to outdoor gardens. Eventually, her wandering became less deliberate, and she found herself in the main lobby again, looking up at the vast expanse of light casting down.

She wondered why the rooms themselves were so dimly lit when the lobby resembled the surface of the sun, but she was too tired to contemplate it further.

A murmur grew in the crowd, and Kiran noticed a few people pointing in awe. Most of them were poorer, dressed in shabbier saris and torn pants marred by years of dirt and grime. She followed their extended fingers, and the level of exhaustion she had hit finally peaked.

Standing in the middle of the waiting room, all eyes on the gora who stood a head taller than most of the people surrounding him, was Nash.

Kiran blinked twice. She needed to sleep if her hallucinations were this vivid. It had been well over five days since she'd gotten more than two hours of rest, and the hospital chairs weren't doing her any favors. She closed her eyes, willing her mind to stop with the overactive games and to power through a few more hours before she could go home. She only needed to make it until she knew Baba was safely out of surgery.

"Kiran."

Her eyes flew open.

He was really here. Disbelief filled her chest as her mouth dropped open. Her vision was hazy, but he'd started taking steps toward her. Kiran glanced at the others around her to see if they noticed the white boy moving through the lobby, and sure enough, many stared at him, in awe of his pale skin.

"Nash," she managed before taking a running start.

She leapt into his arms, throwing her own around his neck. He pulled her right off her feet, and one of her legs bent to shift her weight as she sank into his chest.

"Are you okay? Is your dad okay?" he asked, putting her back on the floor and searching her face.

"He's having a triple bypass right now," she croaked out, wrung out with relief at seeing him.

"You look exhausted. Have you slept?"

She shook her head. The effort was like lifting a weight using her neck. "I've mostly been at the hospital. I go back to the apartment to shower...but Ma needs me. I wanted to be here."

He brushed her greasy hair off her face. "How's your mom?"

"A mess. We haven't talked much. It's just..."

Boring into her were the eyeballs of the room, and she gestured toward a less populated hallway. He followed her as she found an empty waiting room.

Closing the door behind them, she stood near him. They didn't touch. Only inches apart, Kiran merely wanted to feel him, to know that he was breathing the same air and that he had her back on all the chaos blowing her off course. He was her lighthouse in a hurricane moving too quickly to keep up. She tried to focus on his glow and anchor herself to him instead of blowing away.

"Kiran, look at me." He tilted her head with his fingers, and tears burned her eyes.

"What are you doing here?" The question tumbled out.

"I love you." He said it like it was an explanation, the most obvious of reasons in the world. He said it like he was telling someone it was Tuesday or to grab an umbrella because it was raining outside. Obvious. Nonchalant. Simply the way it was.

"But what are you *doing here*? You live half a world away. You have a job."

"I love you. And your father had a heart attack. You needed me. And I'm here."

"But your clients—"

"Are taken care of. Kiran, there is nowhere I would rather be."

She looked into his face, a face she loved more than anyone else's in the world, and the earnestness in his expression was too much to take. Tears welled up in her already heavy eyes. She gulped to contain herself, to force the emotions back inside, but it was too late. She reined back a sob and whimpered as it made its way from her body anyway.

"Shh, baby." Nash wrapped his arms around her waist and pulled her close.

Kiran breathed him in. His cologne was fresh. She gripped his shirt and buried her face in his chest, wishing she could find a home in his heart and stay there, protected.

Tears kept flowing out of Kiran, unleashing a deluge she'd kept bottled up. Nash's hand stroked the top of her head, and his fingers ran up and down her back to quell the heaving sobs. He rested his head on hers, kissing her forehead every now and then and allowing her the space to feel something.

After a time, the cries didn't come so violently, and she was able to step back, still grasping his shirt so he wouldn't float too far away. She closed her eyes, a dull ache behind them and inside her head from the tears and the stress and now the relief of having someone on her side.

"Do you want to go back to the waiting room your mom is in?"

"Kirti is there too."

Nash's eyes widened. "You found her?"

"I couldn't do it anymore, Nash. I didn't want my family to be held back by the past and continue to suffer. Baba's last words to me were that I was dead to him. No one deserves to…" She couldn't say the word *die*. She was afraid the Tatastu devas—the gods Ma told her about when she was growing up and warned her were always listening to her words in order to grant them—would hear her and make them come true.

"No one deserves to go into a life-changing situation without their children by their side. No child deserves to face the prospect of a crisis without their parents knowing their love."

"You amaze me," he murmured. "I don't know where you get your strength, Kiran, or your conviction about the way the world should be…but I'm so proud of you for finding her. You're right. The patients I've seen at the hospital are always regretting words that were unsaid and bonds that were broken. Your father—no father—deserves that."

His expression changed as he said those words, like he was having an epiphany of his own. She brought him close again. He held her up.

"How's your mom taking all of this? God, your family's dealing with a lot of moving parts right now."

"They've shouted. Been in silence. Scratched more wounds into each other. But I hope they find their way. I hope we all do."

"Maybe I should wait to make an appearance. This isn't a good time."

Kiran wanted to argue, to tell him she needed him and that his presence would be helpful…but a quiet voice in her soul told her to agree. This wasn't the time to ambush Ma. Kirti was enough of a shock. Baba was still in surgery. This day was already too much.

She nodded. "Where are you staying?"

"I got a hotel room at the Marriott near the airport. Actually, Payal got it for me."

"Payal?" Kiran looked at him quizzically.

"Apparently your friends are fans of the setup."

Kiran giggled through her teary eyes. "Go rest... I'll call the hotel if anything changes."

"I'll come by the second you need me."

Kiran trusted his word.

"Nash."

"What?"

She wanted to express her gratitude, tell him that she loved him and that he was everything—that this trip meant everything—but she couldn't find the words to accurately convey the wave of thankfulness she had.

Instead, she kissed him. His free hand rested at the small of her back, just under the hem of her shirt. Her tongue explored his mouth, and her fingers toyed with the hair on the back of his head as she brought his head closer to hers, moving together.

When they pulled apart, they both were breathless. Nash's lips remained millimeters from Kiran's, and she could still taste him on hers. His hot breath tickled her face, and she didn't move her hands from his chest and the back of his head, tempted instead to pull him close again and make up for lost time. He rested his forehead against hers and closed his eyes.

"If you do that again, I'll never leave," he whispered to her.

"Don't leave," Kiran whispered back.

"Okay. I'll stay."

"Go get some rest."

He kissed her forehead. "I'll be back."

"I'll be waiting."

As they left the room and turned in opposite directions, Kiran's heart, though still heavy, was unburdened of one weight. Being less alone in the world and knowing someone was behind her to catch her if she fell served as an antidote to every stress. She stopped at the canteen on her way back to the waiting room where Ma and Kirti sat, picking up two chais.

When she entered the room, Ma and Kirti were sitting in chairs opposite each other. Neither was looking at the other. Ma's arms were crossed. Kirti stared at the floor as though she hoped it would open up—but a trace of determination crossed her face as Kiran walked in. Ma, on the other hand, was unimpressed.

"Where did you go to get those chais—Hyderabad?" Ma snapped as Kiran walked in.

Kiran silently handed her a chai and offered the other to Kirti.

"Thanks, Chottu." Kirti held onto Kiran's hand in gratitude.

Ma looked up at Kiran's nickname, and her sight drifted to her daughters' joined hands. Her expression remained neutral, but Kiran wondered if she'd imagined the softened corners of Ma's eyes.

"How are the girls?" Kiran asked.

"They understand that I need to be here. Gautam—"

Ma grimaced.

"—took leave so that he can spend time with them."

Kiran sat next to her, crossing her legs and resting her chin in her hands. "I'm sure Anjali asked questions."

"She wanted to know why she couldn't come, but she understood when I said it was something I had to take care of first."

"If you're going to talk, you might as well do it out loud. Secrets are unnecessary. We are numb to your deceptions now."

"You have two granddaughters. I was telling Kiran they are at home."

Ma took a sharp breath.

Kirti reached in her bag but hesitated. Kiran nudged her, gesturing at it with her chin to encourage her. Kirti pulled an envelope out.

"I have photographs if you want to see, Ma."

Ma considered it. But her decision was a split second too short for it to come off as nonchalant. She reached out her hand without meeting her daughters' eyes, instead glancing at the clock on the wall.

"The older one is Radha." Kirti's voice shook. "She is eighteen years old. The younger is Anjali. She's nine."

Ma held the photographs gently in front of her, pulling them closer to her face to see the detail. Kiran watched her lips part as she lingered on Anjali's face and then Radha's. Ma ran her nail-bitten fingers over the photo.

"She looks like Kiran." Ma noted the resemblance so quietly that both girls had to lean in to hear her.

"She does. Every time I looked at her, from the day she was born, I noticed the same face." Kirti paused. "In a way, seeing her grow up has given me peace, because it's been like watching Kiran instead."

Kiran turned to her sister, surprised. "I didn't know that."

"What is she like?" Ma asked. "And...Anjali." Saying their names was an effort. Ma swallowed and forced her face into an expression of neutrality.

"Radha is serious. Very studious. Sometimes I think that in my attempt to understand all her problems and be supportive, she caught on that I was trying to make up for the lies I told...the understanding I didn't have. She's a smart child. Anjali still has her innocence. She has a lot of energy."

"She's a firecracker." Kiran laughed. "Let's not mince words."

"So were you. And look how you turned out. I have high hopes for both of them."

Ma listened in stony silence. The trip down memory lane about Kiran's childhood ought to have brought Ma's proud moments to the forefront, but instead, she receded into her shell. Kiran noted that even after only a few days, she had aged, and it had nothing to do with the lack of sleep or the stress. Her hair was thinner now—only a fraction of the thick mane she sported as Kirti and Kiran grew up. Her red sari bore faint turmeric stains from her long days in the kitchen. Her skin had freckles from the time she spent in the sun when she worked in the garden in Ramnagar but had grown a translucence that could only be associated with remaining indoors in Delhi. Her heels were cracked from barefoot days on cement floors, and her feet, with their unpainted toenails, were swollen now from sitting and waiting for hours.

Perhaps Kirti had hoped for a warmer response to the mention of Ma's granddaughters. After all, children mended the most damaged fences. So many marriages had begun with animosity, only to be smoothed over once parents became grandparents and noticed their own children experiencing motherhood and father-hood for the first time. Children were the bearers of innocence and hope—and they brought those to even the darkest of places.

Kiran noticed her sister's shoulders fall an inch and a quiet sigh escape her. For the first time this morning, Kirti was dejected. Ma and Kirti had resumed their game of observing two halves of the room and acting as though the other wasn't occupying the same space. Anytime they appeared to let their gaze fall on the same imaginary line between them at the same time, their heads snapped back to facing opposite directions.

Another hour passed in quiet.

"Excuse me, Mrs. Mathur?" A nurse came in.

The three of them rose and met her at the door.

"My daughter." Ma gestured at Kiran. Then she saw Kirti. "Daughters," she corrected herself. She smacked her lips together as though she were tasting how it sounded.

Kirti and Kiran tried not to smile.

"We had a complication—" The nurse's words snapped their focus into place.

"What complication?" Kiran interrupted.

"We are still in surgery with your father. It may take a few more hours. The doctor will speak with you afterward."

Kiran's heart fell. "Can you give me some details?"

"No, miss. Unfortunately I cannot tell you any information as the surgery is still going on. We wanted to give you the courtesy for the sake of time."

Kiran nodded. Kirti returned to her chair, dejected, and Ma stood in the same spot long after the nurse had disappeared.

"Ma, please, sit down," Kiran soothed. "We have to wait. Keep hope."

In silence, Ma sat on the chair next to her, farther from the two of them and isolated.

How much longer would this go?

Kiran pulled her phone from the pocket. The nurse said there was a complication and it'll take a few hours. I don't know what happened.

Nash texted back immediately, I'll be there in a bit.

Kiran bent her head, finally resigning herself to clasping her hands together and resting her forehead on them. Her elbows sat on her knees, and she tried to pray for strength, for Baba's recovery, for anyone and anything to hear what her family had to ask for. Kirti glanced over and rubbed her back soothingly, her own chin in her other hand.

When Ma spoke after a half hour of quiet, both girls startled.

"For years, I had hoped I would someday see the two of you holding hands and being sisters," Ma said quietly, not lifting her eyes. "No one deserves to lose their daughter. Sisters should always be close."

"Ma?" Kiran wasn't sure she had heard her mother correctly.

"When I first gave birth to Kirti, the entire village filled up with her cries," Ma recalled. The expression on her face was a million miles away. "She had such a set of lungs. She was only a few hours old when the jyotish was brought to cast her horoscope. He said, 'This child will be your fame, your kirti. She will bring your name far and wide with her kindness. And there will be two of your children, both destined to change lives.'

"We waited and waited for Kiran's birth, but it took much longer than expected. When we finally found out we were expecting another, Kirti was already fifteen years old. At that point, your baba's parents had passed away, and I only had my father left and he was unhealthy. We desperately wanted a boy. Every jyotish was dragged to our home. Any swamiji or rishi who passed through Ramnagar was asked to make a stop at our house. Each and every one of them told us we would be blessed with a boy to carry on our name and to bring light. Imagine our surprise when, at the crack of dawn, we had another baby girl. A calm child who hardly cried and gazed at us with eyes that saw into our souls.

"Like we'd done with Kirti, a jyotish cast the horoscope. He said this child would be our ray of light. That's why you were named 'Kiran.' He said you were born at the most auspicious moment as the sun came up and that like Suryadev, you would be brilliant at all you touched. Your father was quiet. I don't know if he was disappointed that we had a girl or worried about our future. He said nothing. He escorted the astrologer out of the house, and he was gone for a few minutes.

"When he returned, he told me, 'It doesn't matter that we don't have a son. We don't have to try again. We have our glory and our light, and this is enough. We were told they would bring us both these things, and that's all we need. Let's trust God. This child will have the freedom in life to pursue anything she chooses, just like a boy would have.' It scared me. How could we let our girls have so many things when we couldn't afford anything ourselves? But I trusted your baba and what he was saying. I trusted God. That was why Kirti was allowed to go to classes and why, Kiran, you were granted the permission to study outside Ramnagar and Delhi. It was your baba who decided that you should not be held back.

"And Kirti's kindness was all the glory we needed as Kiran grew up. Every day, another aunty would tell me a story of how she needed help choosing vegetables or bringing them home, and Kirti would be the first to assist. By the time you were nineteen or twenty, Kirti, I never had to lift a finger before you'd already done the tasks at the house for me and twelve others for the neighbors. I remember once I went to pick up jeera from the spice vendor, and when I returned, you had washed and hung all the laundry, finished a lesson with Kiran, cut vegetables for Chaudry Aunty next door when her arthritis hurt, and done the evening sweep of the floor. And when I entered the house, you asked if I wanted chai because *I'd* had a long day. You were my right hand. And then you were gone."

"You let her go, Ma... How could you let her go?"

"We worried about your future too, Kiran. We couldn't move away. We knew Gautam would take care of Kirti—our responsibilities as her parents were finished with her when we got her married. It's our culture. She is a member of Gautam's house. And we tried to protect both of you from the brunt of people's opinions by letting her live her life, separately but safely. But we still had responsibilities toward you. You were so little."

Kiran was torn between sympathy for her mother's plight and residual anger. Kirti hadn't spoken, soaking in her mother's words.

"You were wrong," she said quietly. "Ma, I was wrong too.

I never should have threatened to run away. You were right that Gautam would give me a good life. But it was a lonely one. We had no one to support our decisions. His parents got ill and died soon after our wedding. My daughters grew up without grandparents and without their masi."

"Losing Kiran to her American ways was like losing my left hand. Suddenly she left all the things we taught her behind and decided to put herself first," Ma said softly. "I am helpless. Now, if your baba… I am alone."

Kiran wiped her face with the back of her hand as Kirti did the same with her pallu. "Ma, you aren't alone. We're right here. We have a chance to rewrite everything! We don't live in Ramnagar anymore. We can move forward."

"How do you catch up on two decades?"

"By not looking back. We've lost enough time," Kirti said.

Ma gazed at her daughters, considering the weight of what they'd said. They were together at last. Her dreams had come true. She had to act now and put the past behind them. But Kiran knew that history could weigh even the lightest of people down, and she was afraid Ma would give in to damage and call it irreversible.

Before Ma had a chance to respond, however, a doctor arrived.

"Can I speak to the person in charge of Mr. Mathur's medical decisions?"

"That's me," Kiran said.

"Ma'am, can I speak to you in private?" The man, evidently a student, looked at Kirti and Ma in their saris and fidgeted uncomfortably. "Perhaps we can step into a hallway and discuss your father's condition."

Kiran nodded and then looked at her sister and mother. "I'll be right back. He wants to talk about the surgery. Let me find out what's going on, and I'll be back to let you know."

They both nodded, worried looks on their faces as they let her go. Kiran followed the doctor down the hallway, catching an entering Nash's eye as she passed the main lobby. Nash immediately followed. The doctor knocked on a number of doors to conference rooms, but all were occupied. Instead, he led her to a quiet part of the hallway where only an orderly stood, folding bedsheets.

"Is this man..." The resident faltered.

"He's with our family. Please speak," Kiran ordered.

"Ma'am...he flatlined..."

Chapter Forty-Seven

NASH

Nash hadn't understood what Brandon meant about doctors being brazen until the moment the cardiologist in India told them Kiran's father had passed away. Nash knew from firsthand experience that hospital staff distanced themselves from crises so they wouldn't take the tragedies home...but what about the families themselves? They had to go to empty homes.

Nash could read Kiran's devastation in her eyes. How would her mother go home without her father?

But the doctor continued speaking, and it took concentration to recognize his misguided attempts at explaining what the end game was.

"Ma'am, there was an unexpected complication... He flatlined—"

"Is he alive?" Nash asked.

"Yes, sir. He gave us a scare, but he is in recovery. We will see for the next three days how he does and then continue to monitor him."

"My dad is alive?" Kiran's voice emitted a cry, laugh, and sigh of relief all at once.

"Yes, ma'am," the doctor said, relief flooding his voice that his message had been heard. "A nurse will alert you when he wakes."

The doctor left the room.

Kiran glanced up at Nash, exhaustion in her eyes and joy on her face. Nash kissed her again.

"He made it, baby. He made it."

Kiran leaned against the door of the tiny waiting room and slid down it, rubbing her sleep-deprived eyes with her palms. Her shoulders dropped in relief, like a tsunami wave.

Nash bolted to her side. "Kiran, come here," he said softly as his arms found their way around her shoulders. "It's okay."

Kiran cried into his shoulder for another five minutes. Nash let her pour out the tension she'd been feeling—for her sister, for her mother, for her entire family and the years they'd lost. This was far more than a physical victory for her father. Nash knew it was a victory for all of them.

"He made it. He's a Mathur, baby. What did you expect?" Nash murmured.

Kiran looked up at him suddenly as her eyes widened. "What did you just say?"

"I said 'He's a Mathur.'"

To Nash's slight bewilderment, Kiran laughed and threw her arms around his neck, pulling him straight to the floor next to her.

"I love you," she said to him.

Nash felt his mouth fall open, caught off guard by the emotional weight of the moment, but she spoke again.

"You said you loved me when you got here...and I love you too, Nash, so much."

Nash leaned down and kissed her softly, gently sucking on her bottom lip. She gasped and pulled at him hungrily. Her sounds of wanting him turned him on, and he had to force himself to get up.

"Let's go, baby. You have to tell your mom and sister that your dad's coming home. I'll be at the hotel... Meet me there when you're able to."

Kiran wiped her eyes, giving him one more hug.

She left to meet her family, and Nash walked through the lobby to find Mohammad again. He wanted to get back to the hotel—he had an email to write.

Chapter Forty-Eight

KIRAN

When she broke the news to Ma, Ma collapsed in a chair, weeping over her Ganesh statue. Kirti joined in, sinking to the floor near Ma's feet. Slowly, Ma's hands found their way to Kirti's head, stroking her hair as she cried into her lap. While it wasn't a verbal acknowledgment that the past was in the past, the sight of Ma's motherly action and Kirti becoming a child again was too much for Kiran to bear. Tears streamed down her cheeks.

"Let's go see Baba," she offered.

Ma went in first, spending ten minutes inside the room alone with Baba before coming out again and signaling for Kiran to take her place.

"He's groggy," Ma warned.

Kiran approached the bed tentatively, stepping lightly on her tiptoes so she wouldn't disturb him and wake him prematurely.

Within a minute or two, Baba's eyelashes fluttered, and he looked around the room. His pupils focused on Kiran's face, and his eyebrows lifted as he recognized her for the first time in three days.

"Kiran."

She had never been so happy to hear her moniker. Taking Baba's hand, she kissed it gently, repeating his name until he was able to speak.

"Maine tumhari baathon ko sunliya," Baba croaked out.

Kiran's heart leapt. *I heard you speak.* She wanted to ask questions, but Baba's lips parted, and she silenced herself, willing to stay quiet forever if it meant she got to hear her father speak again.

"I have granddaughters."

Chills ran up and down Kiran's arms, as though someone trailed a feather on her skin. She held on to his hands, his clasp a weak but determined one. How had he known?

"You brought Kirti," he mumbled.

"Yes." Kiran half laughed, half sobbed. "Kirti is here. Ma is here. We're all here. We're so happy you fought through, Baba. I promise you can yell at me all you want, and I'll hang on every word." She kissed his hand again.

Baba took his hand and patted Kiran's head as she rested her own next to his shoulder and cried. He let her weep with relief for a few moments. When he spoke, Kiran was convinced the universe had heard her, listened to her, arranged the world to carry her, and insisted on bringing her family together.

"We had prayed for a boy. I needed someone to run the shop. Your ma and I thought it would bring balance to our family to have a girl and a boy. We performed poojas, and your aunties in Ramnagar were convinced based on where Ma's belly sat that she would have a strong and healthy male child."

Kiran drew in a sharp intake of breath. It was as though he knew all that he had missed while he was floating between life and death.

Baba paused for a few moments, breathing in and out steadily.

"But when you were born, I swore you knew we were disappointed and you stayed so calm. You held my fingers so tightly, as if to show me that you too had strength. As I walked the astrologer to the door, he told me you would bring the brilliance of ten sons...that you would see the world and light ours. He gave me a warning that fame was not always positive but that it was God's plan to turn it into a lesson. And he told me not to fear any obstacles. You would be the one to unite our family. In times of darkness, Kiran, you would be our light. You, beta, are one of two of my greatest joys. And I am sorry that I spoke in anger. I am sorry I did not have faith in you or in your sister." Baba's eyes were red.

Kiran shook her head, dismissing his fears. "I didn't want to make you upset. I shouldn't have been so careless with my words."

"Parents are wrong sometimes. You shine your light on our mistakes." He patted her hand.

"You're my light too, Baba," she whispered, and for what felt like the thirtieth time today, she cried tears of joy.

Epilogue

Nash sat with his laptop on his legs, stretched out on the bed in his hotel room.

Hi, Kirk. Delete.

Dad. Delete.

Finally, he bit the bullet and decided to speak from the heart. This was his big gesture to his dad.

Dear Kirk,

I wanted to call you Dad, but I'm still struggling with that. I imagine I will for a while…but I did want to thank you for your advice. You told me that you hadn't fought hard enough for Mom. She never knew how much you loved her. And because of your regrets, you'd missed out on a life you wished you had.

I decided to demonstrate a big gesture to Kiran and flew to India to be with her when her father had a heart attack a few days ago. She's mine again. I guess I have you to thank for that.

All my life, I didn't want to be like you and Mom because I was afraid of what that meant. But people are complicated, and as I watch my girlfriend reunite with her family, I realize how many layers people have to the actions they choose. Even this psychologist never appreciated it until now.

When Kiran was upset about her father, she mentioned that no parent deserved to face a crisis without knowing how much their child loved them. I had responded that no father deserved to regret bonds that were broken or words that were unsaid. And I realize that if I don't give you that chance, I will be a hypocrite. I'll be denying you your big gesture to me, writing to me at all and being willing to meet up.

I can't promise you a close relationship right now. I can't vouch for anything, other than giving this a fair chance...giving you a fair chance. And if you want forgiveness, then you have it.

Nash

As he hit the Send button, he was filled with a peace he hadn't experienced before.

It was strange how life linked together. The lessons he and Kiran were learning were being taught simultaneously, across cultures, across countries, across the globe. Their parents had taught them far more than they gave them credit for.

Nash had never thought he'd be able to credit family for the experiences he'd had in the last few months.

Picking up the phone, he called Aunt Kate.

"Nashy! You're in *India*?" Kate cried out when he greeted her and told her not to worry.

"Yeah, in New Delhi, believe it or not."

"What prompted that?" Curiosity filled her tone.

"Kirk Hawthorne coming to town and somehow influencing me to fight for what I love."

"Really?" Aunt Kate's voice had a tinge of knowing wisdom to it.

"Of the many things he wasn't there for, at least he gave me the idea to come be with Kiran."

"How is she doing?"

"Really good. Her father had a heart attack and had to go to surgery. But he's survived. She found her sister. Her family is together. It's really good," Nash said again.

"And how are you, after all you've been through? Nice work on getting suspended by the way. It was lovely to find that out from Brandon."

Nash laughed sheepishly. "Sorry...I wasn't in a good place."

"I can't blame you. It was a little bit of a circus."

There was Kate...never hiding what she thought. "You're right. But it's better now. I'm going to give Kirk a chance. We missed enough time...and none of us deserves to have regrets. And Kiran and I are together again."

"I'm so happy to hear that, Nashy. It sounds like there's been a lot of reuniting in the last few days."

Nash grinned into the phone, struck by the accuracy of her words. "There has been. There've been a lot of beginnings, and I'm looking forward to seeing how they play out."

· · · · · · · · · · ·

"And they invited Gautam Jijaji and the girls to the house for the first time when Baba gets released."

"That's great, Kiran. I couldn't be happier for you." Nash squeezed her hand as she sat across from him.

"I couldn't have done this without you. Knowing you were there…knowing I had you. Nash, I will never be able to repay you for all you've done for me."

"I didn't do anything. You did it yourself."

"You were here. You flew across the world for me."

"It was on my list."

"I knew it!" Kiran laughed.

"Kiran, I am in love with you. I know that being here probably brings the situation even closer to you now…and I know that when we go back, maybe you'll decide not to be with me. So much has happened in the last few weeks with both of our lives, and now that it's calmed down, maybe you feel differently. But God, I am so in love with you, and I will be here for you forever. I don't care what that means—friendship. Boyfriend. Husband. Neighbor. Whatever. I'm here for all of it."

In that moment, a flashing revelation occurred to her that all of this was wrong—not just the type of feeling you get when something doesn't sit right in your gut but fundamentally against the way the world is supposed to turn.

She wasn't supposed to be away from him.

How exactly was she supposed to convince her heart that Nash wasn't meant for her? Any of the million reasons she had not to be with him—he was American, his upbringing was so different from hers, her parents wouldn't feel comfortable, her father's heart was already weak—all sounded like her brain reciting the laws of thermodynamics. Monotone. Memorized. Dutiful.

And for once, the laws didn't have to make sense for her to know what was right.

On the weighted scale of life, the support for him didn't exist. Kiran's culture, family, and all else would take the balance to the ground in a millisecond. His side would hang in the air, no weight to it at all. But her heart, when placed upon the scale, would break it to pieces with the resolution it carried today.

There was no going back. She was setting herself free from the past.

"No, Nash. I am yours. And I will fight for you if that's what it takes."

Nash's face lit up, like someone had ignited a fire in the pitch black. He stared at her in wonder, and before she knew it, he had pinned her down on the bed.

"You're mine, huh?"

Kiran laughed, her eyes drooping in sleepiness. "I'm yours. I'm so sorry that I ever doubted it."

"Well, then…before you sleep until next week, why don't we prove that?"

The sight of his tousled hair called for her fingertips to run through it, and his lips so tantalizingly close were the only triggers she needed to pull him close and bring her lips to his.

Kiran's arms rested on the back of Nash's neck as he molded his lips to hers. The tip of his tongue slid gently across the middle of her bottom lip and sent flutters deep into her belly.

Her fingertips traced his back, sliding underneath his shirt and leaving a trail up his spine. Nash groaned, and she felt the goose bumps rise on his skin.

For once, Kiran wasn't fearful. Instead, she got lost in the oceanic depths of his eyes and let herself feel unanchored from the world.

"So…you said you were sorry." Nash's voice grew deeper.

"I am. You were right about us."

"How sorry?" He raised an eyebrow.

In a flash, they were wrapped up in each other. His strong arms lifted her weight as her hungry lips devoured his. She wrapped her legs around him, her fingers stroking the stubble on his cheeks and cupping his face as she kissed him over and over.

Kiran ran her fingers through his hair, feeling the soft texture between her knuckles and thanking her lucky stars in wonder that Nash had been sent to her and that they could be together.

Nothing could touch them now, and nothing ever would.

· · · · · · · · · · ·

His faint heartbeat thumped against her head resting on his bare chest. Kiran's hair fanned out behind her, draping over Nash's shoulder. The white comforter tucked underneath her arms, cocooning their body heat and creating a sparkling sheen of sweat on their skin to add to the salty taste it had acquired from their exertions earlier that evening.

"Tell me a secret," she murmured. She traced a circle under his nipple, across his ribs.

"Like what?" His voice was rougher, fighting the urge to groan at her touch.

"Anything." She propped her chin onto the back of her hand and stared up at him.

He gazed at her, a twinkle in his eye, and searched for an answer. "I love you."

Amused, she gazed into his eyes with a soft smile at her lips. "I love you too."

Those three words would never get old.

"This feels surreal," Nash murmured as he traced circles on Kiran's bare back.

"We're in India," Kiran said in disbelief.

"Our families are together again."

Nash had filled her in on meeting Kirk, and Kiran had gasped.

"Way to bury the lede! I had no idea you got a letter!"

"Well, you broke up with me when I was dealing with it..." Nash shrugged.

"I'm sorry." Kiran's mouth fell.

"We're together now." Nash kissed her so the pout would disappear.

"You know, I never realized how much our families influence how we love..."

"What do you mean?"

"I was always afraid to love wholeheartedly because Didi had fallen in love, and then there was so much pain all around. My parents had to cut their ties with her. But now we're together again. And hopefully, our story won't be a repeat of twenty years ago."

"I guess you're right," Nash said thoughtfully. "I had always feared becoming my mother. I knew addiction was a disease. I knew she tried to win against it. But admitting that my mom had essentially chosen drugs over me and that I didn't catch her habits... There was so much guilt there, and heartbreak and the feeling of never being chosen. Especially because my dad left too."

"Now he's back," Kiran said, resting her head on his chest.

"He is. I was so angry. He said that when he had cancer, his biggest regret was leaving me and never making the big gesture with my mom, who he loved."

"How did you feel about that?"

"It's hard, you know? I'm angry. Like most of my life, I didn't want to be him. But I think by coming here, by admitting I still wanted you, by fighting for us...I'm already different."

"By flying here for me?" Kiran smiled.

"Exactly. And I think your dad probably realized that too

while he was in the hospital. He was on the brink of death… He wasn't thinking about all the great things he did in life. He missed you and your sister."

"So you're saying we've tried not to repeat their mistakes, and they've realized that they love us despite them?"

"Yeah, I guess so," Nash said.

"I find that comforting," whispered Kiran. She wrapped her arm around him.

He pulled her close, resting his head on the top of hers and breathing in her sweet, musky smell.

"You know…I do too."

"So…what really made you decide to come here? Was it because you didn't want to be like your dad?"

Nash smiled. "No."

He tossed the covers off himself and went to his backpack, unzipping a pocket and pulling out the now crumpled, travel-worn list.

"It was so I could give you back this." He handed her the note.

Recognition dawned in her eyes as she stared at the list in her hands.

"How did you—?"

"And also, so I could give you this."

He handed her his own piece of stationery.

Nash felt a gentle sting behind his eyes as Kiran studied his list, her lips parting as her eyes rested on the final item.

~~FALL IN LOVE~~.

She grinned and leapt into his arms, kissing him hard and wrapping her legs around him. Nash had never been so happy. It was thanks to this girl, this ball of energy resting in his arms, that he had been able to cross that item off.

· · · · · · · · · · ·

While Nash slipped into the shower, Kiran turned on his computer and logged into Skype. Hoping the connection would hold, she pressed the button to call Payal.

"Kiran! Kiran, Jesus, is everything okay? Are you okay? Wait. I need to get the others on a conference."

Two minutes later, it was as though Sonam, Akash, Payal, and Kiran were together at a coffee shop, though it was midnight in India and two in the afternoon in New York City. Sonam was even sipping coffee, to bring the imagery to life.

"So? What happened?" Akash asked, frowning. "Tell us about your dad."

Kiran did. She spared no detail, recounting her mother's parting words as she returned home, the shock of finding out Baba had to receive a triple bypass surgery—"What do you mean they don't have protocols in place for those without money?" demanded Sonam—and coming to the decision to find Kirti.

"What's she like?" Payal asked with curiosity.

Kiran noted her wide eyes hungry for details about a long-lost sister, reunions a long time coming, and love shared between a family. "Just like I remembered her...but magnified because now it's not a memory. She's real. She's kind. She's a mom. I have two nieces. One of them looks like me."

Payal gasped, and Sonam and Akash grinned at the goofy smile on Kiran's face.

"We're proud of you, you know," Sonam said. "It takes balls to challenge what you were raised with. And you did it with grace and dignity, like we knew you would but probably even more than we ever dreamed."

"You're a fucking badass," Akash said. "How is your family handling it now?"

"I'm not sure," Kiran admitted. "There's been a lot of arguing and a lot of crying. But to see my mother filled with any kind of life is a transformation from what I grew up with. And truthfully, I'd rather have my family shouting with my sister there than have a void where we know she should be."

"I can't imagine what that must feel like," Payal said. "To be separated and then coming back together. It's beautiful."

"It's something." Kiran laughed. "Now to handle Nash..."

"So tell me something. The white boy shows up *in India* when you wouldn't let us come. He literally flew across the world to be with you and support you during your time of need, and you're still talking about 'handling' him?" Payal asked incredulously.

"Payal, you said I should have walked away!"

"Until he knocked it out of the park and proved that you'll never find that kind of loyalty ever again!" Sonam interrupted. "Your choice was understandable at first. But he played a move so spectacular, you're checkmated for life. If you walk away now, Kiran, I don't know if we can support that."

"Fight for him, Kiran." With Akash's input, the vote was unanimous.

"You guys?"

"What?" they all answered in unison.

"I was never going to walk away. I was just trying to figure out when I should introduce him—now or later. I'm his. No question."

And to that, they all cheered.

· · · · · · · · · · ·

"I'm a little nervous," Nash confessed in the car on the way to the hospital.

"Me too," Kiran replied.

"That's not comforting! You're supposed to be sure of yourself."

"I am sure of myself. I'm sure I want to be with you. I'm not sure how they'll react to that."

Nash rolled his eyes, and Kiran gave his hand a playful squeeze.

Nash's suspension would end in two days, and he was flying back late tonight. Kiran would follow once her father was settled back in at home. But one thing remained to be done: Nash was going to meet Kiran's family.

"Are you sure this is a good idea?" Nash asked again.

"I'm sure," Kiran said confidently. "It's because of you that he's gotten the care he needs."

Nash had come to the hospital and remained in the lobby, helping to navigate Kiran's father's care with her to the best of his abilities, making calls to colleagues in the United States and friends who practiced medicine for second and third opinions.

"I wouldn't go that far," Nash smiled.

"Your support was everything." Kiran squeezed his hand again.

Kirti met them in the lobby first, flanked by Gautam and the girls.

"Didi, what're you doing here?"

"If we're going in to talk to our parents about a love match, you'd think I was the expert, wouldn't you?" Kirti asked her little sister. Her English was fluent, though heavily accented in comparison to Kiran's.

Kiran giggled. "You're the older sister. I guess I'll follow your lead."

Nash gazed at Kiran, awed at the way she took direction from her sister and the way she immediately fell into the role of a younger sibling. After witnessing her take charge, watching her be babied was a new experience for him and one he loved to see.

"Nash. It's so nice to meet the man who insisted my father receive better care." Kirti shook his hand, and Gautam followed.

"Can I touch your hair?" asked Anjali, who had never seen a white person with straight hair in her life.

Nash bellowed laughter at her question and leaned over, chuckling as she ran her small hands over his head.

"Oh. It only looks gold." Anjali's face fell.

"Tragically, it is only hair, not gold," Nash said. "Yours, however, is far more impressive."

Anjali's two long plaits were looped around and tied with ribbons in a unique hairdo Nash had never seen before, but Kiran's eyes registered a familiarity, like recognizing an old friend.

Nash was led by the small caravan of Mathur family members into Mr. Mathur's hospital room.

"Ma, Baba..." Kiran started in Hindi.

Nash caught his name and put his hands together at his chest in a namaste. Kiran's mother reciprocated the gesture while letting her eyes fall over every inch of him.

She was a shorter woman with strong features, much like Kiran's. Her gaze was piercing, and if it could be translated into an attitude, then Nash knew exactly where Kiran got hers.

While Kiran's father was still in a hospital bed, he reached out his hand. Kiran gestured for Nash to go and take it.

"Tu mere Kiran ko ghar laaye."

Kiran's father expressed an emotion that Nash didn't need to be translated to understand. He was thankful.

Kiran wiped at her eyes. "He says you brought me home."

"Want to tell him something for me?" Nash asked.

"Sure."

"Tell him wherever you are is home to me."

Kiran translated the comment, gazing at Nash's face the entire time. Her father watched the two of them, his face contemplative, as he nodded. Nash wasn't sure whether he was being accepted, but he had a feeling that he was at least being considered. For now, that was all he could ask for.

Her mother remained quiet for the entire visit, seemingly assessing Nash the whole time.

Kiran's family hardly spoke to Nash, but he got the distinct feeling that he wasn't being ignored. So much had happened in the last few days. There were shifts happening between relationships every minute—Kiran and her parents, Kirti and her parents, Kiran and Kirti, the kids and each adult… Gautam was as new to this as Nash, and he stood in the corner, chiming in sometimes in Hindi but still on the outskirts of this family circle.

As they stood to leave an hour later and Nash gently shook Mr. Mathur's hand again, Kiran's mom met his eye.

Slowly, she raised her hands in a namaste, and a distinctly different feeling came across Nash. This wasn't a hello or a goodbye. Her expression, serious and unyielding, was one of deepest gratitude. And above all, her face was filled with respect.

Nash responded with the single formal Hindi word he had studied on the plane.

"Shukriya."

Thank you.

. . . .

As the jet taxied down the runway and increased its speed, Kiran felt no need to clutch the armrest and pray she'd get to see her family again.

She had no worries that they'd be alone.

And she knew exactly what she was heading back to as the plane gently floated over continents on its way back to the United States.

Peace was a word that she had never completely understood

until now. The concept that one could have no worries, live in the moment, trust in their relationships, and best of all, know their future was assured was completely foreign to her. There hadn't been a day in her life when she'd experienced those things simultaneously.

But now she was able to rest her head against the window and watch the land pass below without an anxious thought about Ma and Baba's welfare and whether someone would be there to look after them. Kirti was a part of their lives again. Kiran had no concerns about whether her own life would be full of love and togetherness. She had the CMC and Nash for that. And the magic in the small things, like knowing someone would be waiting at the airport when she arrived home, cast a glow on her skin that the sun had nothing to do with.

She was heading home.

And for the first time, home felt like a state of mind and not a destination.

. . . .

The phrase "Blood is thicker than water" had always been a load of malarkey to Nash.

His loved ones had been those who weren't tied to him by genetics but who had chosen him every day. But now, he was recognizing the value in owning the roots he came from.

For over ten years, his heart had been a Pandora's box of confusion, resentment, and anger over the fact that his own blood had seen him as a disposable or avoidable part of life.

But now, a window into his heart had been discovered where his friends, his family, and Kiran could reach in and clean out the cobwebs and clutter when it got too messy in there. Sunshine poured in, and everything about his heart and soul felt lighter since the flood of fresh air had come through.

As he stood waiting at the arrivals terminal at JFK, Nash gazed at the reunions of those around him. People who were meeting for the first time. People who had only left temporarily. And those who hadn't seen each other for years, their stories taking them in different directions before bringing them back to the same road.

And no matter how bumpy his road had been, he finally embraced the fact that it was his to own. People had come, gone, and joined him for the ride for short bits of time, but he had been exactly where he was meant to be.

The girl who emerged from the gate, with her toasted butter skin, was who he was meant to travel with for the rest of his life.

Kiran caught his eye in the crowd and pulled her suitcase toward him, increasing her speed until she was nearly running. Then she stopped and burst out laughing, a tinkling sound that he knew he would never get sick of.

He was wearing a Team India cricket shirt.

When Nash leapt over the barrier, too impatient to wait as Kiran walked around it, and buried his face in her neck, he knew exactly what the words meant as he said them.

"Welcome home."

Kiran's
Bucket List

- ☐ 1. Visit the Empire State Building.
- ☐ 2. Take a boat ride on the Hudson River.
- ☐ 3. See a Broadway play.
- ☐ 4. Ride a horse.
- ☐ 5. Dance under the stars.
- ☐ 6. Do a macaroni and cheese tour.
- ☐ 7. Go to Smorgasburg every summer.
- ☐ 8. Play in an arcade.
- ☐ 9. Reunite with a loved one.
- ☐ 10. Take a quiet walk along the Upper East Side.
- ☐ 11. Visit the Bronx Zoo.
- ☐ 12. Spend all night in sparkling conversation.
- ☐ 13. Fall in love.

Acknowledgments

Whoa. I didn't just write one book. This is my SECOND BOOK. How cool is this?! I wouldn't have made the long leap from *The Rearranged Life* to this series without pep talks, guidance, love, some kicks in the butt, and grounding from amazing people who are in my life for reasons I was beyond lucky to have and never quite understood. After all, how did I, a bumbling girl in Pennsylvania, end up with a pride of lions and lionesses strong enough to hold me up when I fell and keep me at the top of the world when I flew?

My parents—the Indian city kids who turned into immigrants who turned into the best friends I could ask for. I don't know what I did to deserve you, but I thank my lucky stars every day... and then you gave me a brother! How many more amazing things could you have done? Sri, you are the best friend, roommate, hero (because secretly, even I'll admit I'm the sidekick on our adventures), and all-around dude. Just don't forget you loved me most in the world when we were little.

Sanjeev...man, am I glad you texted me again after I bailed on our first date. I wouldn't have imagined all that came afterward in our story. You are the best part of every day.

Every woman needs a circle of other powerful game changers

around her. Mine is no different. Mamata Venkat, you are not only a YouTube TedX star but a shooting star who hasn't even peaked in its glow yet—patient, empathetic, and kind, you are my very favorite gift New York City gave me. Melissa Torres, I don't think I understood what soul mates were until I met you. And in typical fashion, the emotions expressed to each other are deeper than what we say to boys. To the mother of my favorite little girl but, equally as importantly, my best friend since I was thirteen years old, Liz McCallips. Every adventure is better when we get to go through it together. Some friends are better in twos—Sunita and Dr. Sarita Kambhampati, you are family but friends too and so fabulous that God had to make two of you to handle it. To Dr. Trusha Patel...whose medical expertise and patience are not only the foundation of half my writing, they talk me out of chaos every time I think I have caught a contagious deadly illness. Thank you for being the kind of woman I want to be. Kamna Gupta, your moral support, cheer, and insta-friend status put you miles ahead of everyone else. You have the biggest heart. Nehal Tenany, you are an exceptional friend and business partner. To Bhargavi, the in-law who is now a sister. You are a burst of sunshine to my day and I am so happy you're in the family...it's not a Pisuparty without you. And to the Sridhara, Pisupati, and Reddy families for all the love and laughter throughout my life.

While I should thank Twitter, Facebook, and Instagram for the copious amounts of knowledge about what I should and shouldn't do regarding writing, the people behind those accounts became the best online allies and eventual real-life friends ever. Amanda Heger, your kissy face emojis are little rays of sunshine to my day. You are a listening ear, a fabulously talented writer who talks me through big decisions, and a friend who I cannot imagine life without. Meredith Tate, your strength through adversity and your determination to remain the happiest eighty-seven-book-bearing plane passenger ever makes you one of my favorite people. To the South Asian writers who share cups of chai and daily gupshup: Nisha Sharma, Namrata Patel, Sonali Dev, Farah Heron, Suleikha Snyder, Mona Shroff, Kishan Paul, Sona Charaipotra, Falguni Kothari, and Sophia Singh Sasson.

Writing may be a business, but it has given me an incredible friendship—especially in you, Stacey Donaghy, my dear friend and agent extraordinaire. You fight my battles, serve as armor, and are always willing to steer the ship when I am in the back, having a meltdown. Thank you. Cat Clyne, thank you for bringing me on board with an idea. And Christa Désir and Mary Altman, thank you for bringing that idea to life, smoothing out wrinkles, laughing through editorial calls, and shining your light on this story. To the entire team at Sourcebooks—it takes a village to raise a child and a company of superstars to publish a book—thank you for working on mine.

The last thank you might be the most important—the one I delay on because I am speechless when I think of you. It is you, lovely reader, who has chosen to spend minutes of your precious and beautiful life reading words I wrote. Despite the three hundred pages of my words you are reading, I cannot come up with adequate ones to express my gratitude for the love you have shown me. By buying my book. By following me on social media. By sending me a message about how much you love my writing. Whatever you have done and whatever you will do, my best wishes are with you—shine bright.

About the Author

Born in Delhi and raised in central Pennsylvania, Annika Sharma followed her Penn State–loving heart to college in Happy Valley. There, she graduated with two bachelor's degrees in biobehavioral health and neuropsychology. She also holds two master's degrees from Penn State and George Washington University, respectively, in early childhood special education and public health.

She is a co-founder and co-host of The Woke Desi podcast, one of the largest independently run South Asian podcasts in the world. She currently lives in New York City and works as a health communications manager by day, while juggling her writing and podcasting careers by night. She is a lover of endless conversations, college football, social justice, traveling, books, all things related to England, dancing, superhero movies, and coffee.